Kingdom of Shadows

A.G. BOOTH

Kingdom of Shadows

Copyright © 2024 by A.G. Booth.

All rights reserved. No part of this publication may be reproduced, distributed, or transmitted in any form or by any means, including photocopying, recording, or other electronic or mechanical methods, without the written consent of the publisher. The only exceptions are for brief quotations included in critical reviews and other noncommercial uses permitted by copyright law.

MILTON & HUGO L.L.C.
4407 Park Ave., Suite 5
Union City, NJ 07087, USA

Website: *www. miltonandhugo.com*
Hotline: *1- 888-778-0033*
Email: *info@miltonandhugo.com*

Ordering Information:
Quantity sales. Special discounts are granted to corporations, associations, and other organizations. For more information on these discounts, please reach out to the publisher using the contact information provided above.

Library of Congress Control Number:	2024922474
ISBN-13: 979-8-89285-341-5	[Paperback Edition]
979-8-89285-340-8	[Digital Edition]

Rev. date: 10/14/2024

For my mom, who always inspires me to forgive

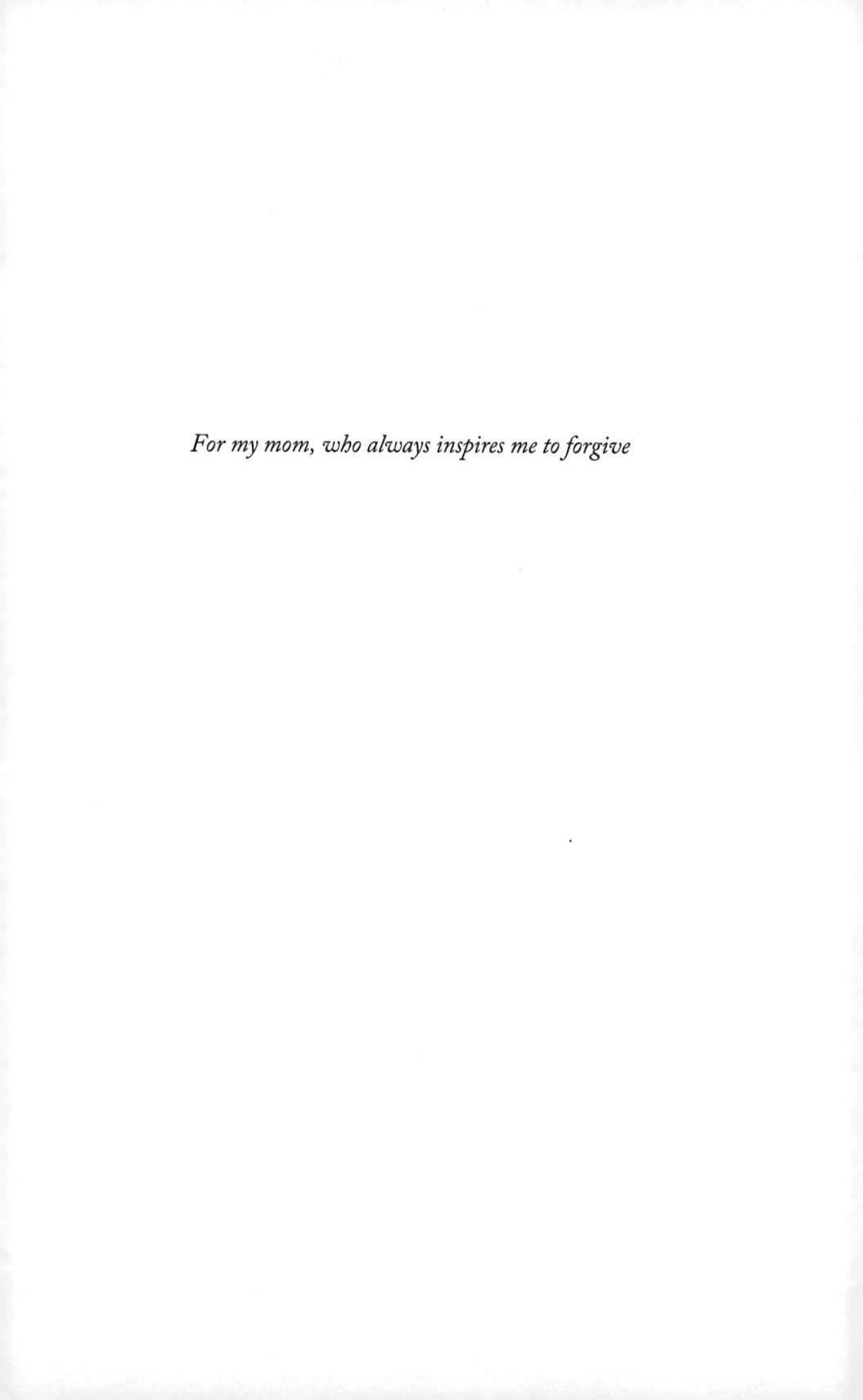

Prologue

Maybe it would always be this way.

Maybe *I* would always be this way.

I crouched on the floor, the iron chains wrapped tightly around my wrists and ankles, allowing me hardly any room to move. I studied the small cuts and bruises peppering my skin. They had become less shocking over time and always healed fairly quickly.

It was the other wounds on my back that took a bit longer.

A sigh shook through my sore lungs and throat and for a moment, I tried to remember what it was like to be free.

I had been here for far too long, at least long enough to forget everything I had once known. Perhaps that was for the best though. I let out a dry laugh and instantly regretted it as the breath scraped painfully out of me.

Anytime now—that's when he would return.

Without fail, I heard the scrape of the cell door being pushed open. The bearded man came into view and I didn't even bother trying to scuffle away or fight him. I had already tried that and used up all of that energy years ago.

Simply put, I had given up.

Instead, I kept my head down and began to tunnel deep inside of myself. I spiraled down into that place where the pain became numb.

I jolted awake from the dream, iron chains rattling. I glanced around in hopes that it had in fact just been some terrible nightmare, but disappointment was ever my companion.

As my mind and surroundings came back to me, I became very aware of my sore limbs and lungs and throat that burned from screaming. I groaned and shifted, realizing that they had left me unchained. The iron that usually wrapped around my wrists and ankles was no longer there.

This had only happened a precious few times in the past, that's how I'd figured out about the onyx frost.

I watched as tiny swirls of darkness spiraled around my fingertips and seemed to dance. The ebony ice designs slowly grew but only slightly before it fluttered away, as if being blown out like a flame.

I wondered how something that could seem so beautiful could also cause such agony. I'd been told I had elven blood in me since that first day where they found me in the boat. I was told I was dangerous, which is why I was kept here. I wiggled my fingers, willing the frost to come back to life.

I had been made to endure pain, to grit my teeth against the torture. I had been forced to learn, to suffer and become numb to it.

I wondered now if a broken part of me enjoyed it?

Maybe it would always be this way and maybe it wouldn't.

Either way, the pain would never cease, it would always be a part of me. After all, it was far too late to heal someone as broken and dark as I was.

CHAPTER

1

I didn't want to be here.

A ripple of shouts and cheers rose to greet my ears, I cringed, fighting the urge to cover them. Glasses clinked together in what I assumed was a toast. Considering the festivities had been going on for a few hours, and there had been a considerable amount of drinking, the group of people screaming could have been toasting to anything.

I turned to survey the throng of people; the same gloating, insufferable faces that were entertained when I killed competitors, met my eyes. The view hadn't changed in years.

Someone snickered near me and I watched as a woman practically threw herself upon a man nearest her, acting as if she'd tripped. Her glass of red wine sloshed over the rim and she apologetically and rather seductively began to wipe it off the poor man's shirt.

I rolled my eyes and turned back to lean on the railing of the ship. The water rippled quietly beneath me and I felt the vessel sway back and forth in the small current circling the docks. The constant movement of the ship wasn't the only thing that sickened me.

I lowered my head and closed my eyes, willing everyone to shut up and end the commemoration so I could leave, even if I would be returning to that dank cell.

I hated big crowds.

A light breeze tousled my golden brown hair and I used my pointer finger and thumb to tuck it back behind my ear. My fingers grazed over the pointed tip of my ear and I almost pulled the strand back to hide them—to hide what I so clearly was.

Ignoring the insecurity, my gaze fell away from the water and wandered to the mountain range that surrounded the lake town of Helmfirth. My eyes warmed with curiosity and wonder at the thought of one day cresting that mountain and seeing what the rest of the world had to offer.

Beyond these parties and frivolous, wasteful things. Beyond the pleasure houses of this filthy, human lake town. Beyond the *Death Pit* that I so often strode into to end yet another life.

All too quickly, my thoughts were *rudely* interrupted by the uproar of more squeals and cheering.

I squeezed my eyes shut. My hands began to shake and I could feel the tightening in my chest once more. It was so loud—too loud. I inhaled in and out and focused on the lap of the water.

I opened my eyes to watch the sun's rays disappear behind the mountain. I found that temporary peace filled my senses once more and I tried to gather as much of it as possible, the rising panic subsiding slightly.

A familiar hand caressed my bandaged back and I stiffened instantly, the peace obliterated with that one touch.

"Not to worry, it's just me Ryn." That voice.

It made me want to vomit and scream and run and claw out my hair all at the same time. Regardless of what I wanted or felt, I turned slightly and stared at him.

Lord Elton Hode of Helmfirth.

The man had graying hair and was at least a few feet taller than me. He wore his brown jacket and slacks with a white shirt beneath. His boots, perfectly polished leather.

"What do you want?" I snapped, unable to control my emotion. I turned back to the water below us.

"*Tsk, tsk*, my dear, have we not talked about that tone you use with me?"

I stilled as his hand continued grazing over the many scars I had. "Apologies, my Lord," I said even as bile rose in my throat. I wanted nothing more than to cut off the hand that was touching me.

"Much better." His breath fell on my ear and made my blood freeze. "How are you enjoying the party?"

I turned around to face the crowds and to get his damned hand off my back. "It is exquisite."

"As it should be. How did your morning go?"

I stiffened at his choice of words and picked a spot in the crowd to stare at and become lost in. "Fine," I replied, terse.

"Good, good." Elton crossed his arms across his chest and casually stated, "I have another competition for you."

I glanced at him, the golden lights on the boat making his gray hair shine. "When?"

"Tonight."

I raised an eyebrow. "And the opponent?"

"Does it matter?" Elton shrugged. "They're inexperienced."

I nodded. It would be an easy kill then. My stomach churned.

The Lord of Helmfirth turned back to me. "Don't be boring about it, either. Make it entertaining."

I just nodded and dipped my head as he took his leave. I didn't miss the way the partygoers gawked at him as he brushed passed, then flicked their jealous, ogling stares at me.

Little did they know the monster in their midst.

The hours waned on and, naturally, so did the party. I was allowed to be excused once the hour of my fight drew near. I had yet to change and ready myself.

With my guard at my side, I was escorted off the boat and onto the darkening docks of Helmfirth. Fishers were just coming in from the hard days work they'd had and I didn't miss the way they lowered their heads when I passed.

If I were them, I wouldn't look myself in the eye either.

I walked nimbly in my dress shoes, knowing exactly which cobblestones to avoid and where the murky puddles would be. I'd walked this path many times afterall. Elton had a celebration every night it seemed. I often wondered if he used his ship for anything else other than hosting ridiculous, annoying parties.

His manor loomed ahead of us now, a three story, thick stone mansion—prison more like. The guard and I both took the steps two at a time and he opened the door for me. I didn't speak or look at him.

Once in the stone structure, we walked down the carpeted hall and ascended a staircase leading to the second story. I entered a room and finally, I was left alone. I leaned against the door and inhaled the silence. However, the long awaited silence would soon be taken from me. I only had minutes to spare if I didn't want to be late to the fight.

I pushed off of the door and retrieved the outfit already waiting for me. It was a long sleeved, brown leather suit. I took off my slippers and dress and donned the armor, careful to not snag my braid as I zipped up the back. When I bent down to pull on my leather boots, my plaited hair fell over my shoulder. I brushed it back as I stood and tucked the two pieces framing my face behind my ears, sweeping the area with my gaze.

This had been my old bedroom, the one Elton had once allowed me to sleep in when I was actually welcome in the manor with him and his son.

The son I had almost killed—by accident of course.

I sighed and glanced at myself in the looking glass. This suit did wonders for my curves and I filled it out rather nicely.

I smirked.

I was night. I was hate. I was death itself.

A knock sounded followed by the opening of the door. I raised an eyebrow at the intruder to find the lord of the land himself staring back at me.

"My, my," he whistled as he shut the door behind him.

I resisted the urge to roll my eyes and went back to admiring myself in the full length mirror. I sensed Elton inching closer and fidgeted, pouring all of my attention into my sleeve cuff.

"How you've grown into a marvelous young woman," he purred over my shoulder, not quite touching me but his breath grazed my neck.

Shivers ran down my spine and I stiffened, nausea coiling in my stomach. "Don't you have anything to say?" he pressed further.

I remained indifferent, just the way he hated and stuck my chin in the air. "I do not."

"Have I done something wrong for you to treat me with such incivility?"

Yes, I wanted to say. Everything. Yet, I swallowed those rising, desperate words down and adjusted my features to become lax. "I need to have a clear mind if I'm to perform my best tonight."

Elton nodded and the hand that had been outstretched towards me fell away. "That's why you're my best champion, Ryn. You never allow yourself to become distracted."

Right.

I allowed my green eyes to sweep over my figure again.

"Are you satisfied?" Elton's voice fell to a whisper, sultry and sweet.

"Satisfied with what?" I asked.

"Yourself."

I moved away from Elton's prying eyes and hot breath and inhaled sharply. "Isn't it time we were leaving?"

He looked at me through cruel, deceiving black eyes. "I suppose it is. Carriage is waiting below."

I snatched the dagger they would take away from me soon enough and followed the Lord of Helmfirth, prick though he was, out the door and to our awaiting transportation.

The carriage ride was quiet, save for the sound of the horses' hooves clacking on the cobblestone and the rumbling of the wheels. Elton sat adjacent from me, ever the picture of perfection with his bear skin cloak wrapped around his broad shoulders. His close cropped hair and freshly trimmed blackish-graying beard.

Elton caught my eyes grazing his appearance and he grinned. "I thought you might approve of the new look." He scratched at his beard lightly and I gave him a small smile, nothing to overthink.

When we arrived, the carriage driver opened the door for us and Elton graciously helped me out. His cracked, dry hands touching mine were enough to send me reeling backward but I stood strong and endured it.

Afterall *he* had taught me to endure.

The tavern in front of us was already filled with the voices of the growing crowd cheering and jeering. A shiver slithered down my spine. I wondered who was in the ring now, fighting for their life.

Elton handed the man at the door our identification slips and he looked me over once. Twice.

Grinning, he handed the papers back. I had no doubt he was enjoying the backside of my outfit as well.

Let him.

Let them all gawk and ogle over me. It was afterrall, another part of the performance.

Inside, the din was even louder than outside and Elton led me through the packed crowds pushing and fighting to get a chance to see the pit themselves. Once we reached the otherside through pure force and Elton's cursing, he led me through the back door.

Opening and shutting it swiftly, he turned to glance me over. "You look ravishing tonight."

"So you've said."

"I think the suit fits you better now."

My jaw clenched as I resisted the urge to gag and simply gave him that smile he loved. I had been *too* young when I started working for him.

"Ready?" he asked with eagerness and bloodlust in his eyes. I was always ready.

I gave him the nod and we walked down the stairs into the dank *Death Pit* as the devotees liked to call it.

The stench was stifling and the air felt thicker down here. We stopped at the bottom of the stairs where the gatekeeper opened the chained entrance and quickly shut it behind us. Iron bars separated us from the sandy pit and the competitors currently in it. Elton wrapped his hands around the iron and peered through the bars at the fight going on. I did the same, save for touching the accursed iron, knowing full well what would happen if I did.

Pushing that thought from my mind I focused on the fight, on the competitors footwork and lunges and stance. The human man was sweating and breathing heavily while the wolf fighting him was licking his lips and snarling at him. I watched as the dog-like creature circled him, his tongue lolling out, maw snapping at the human every so often.

I listened as the crowd—damn them all—booed and shouted in anger, while yet some cheered and screamed for blood. There was no difference between these crowds and the ones who gathered for Elton's parties.

It's why I hated big crowds, they made me want to be sick.

I inhaled and tried to focus on the fight at hand and speculate what was going on, instead of the churning in my gut.

The wolfish creature was taunting the human.

If the poor man knew to go for the creature's haunches, he would get to the most sensitive part and be able to disable the wolf long enough to go for the throat and end it. But the man did not know that, so when the creature finally went for the killing shot, I was not surprised when he tore the human's throat apart right there on the sand in front of the hundreds gathered in the stands.

Deafening cheers and boos erupted in the crowd as the whole arena stood up, either jumping in celebration or throwing things in anger at the contestants.

Elton jerked his head to me, unphased. "You're next."

I nodded and prepared my mind and body, stretching my legs and arms like he had taught me to. The minutes went by far too slowly but when the horn blew, I knew it was time. I was more than ready to get this over with and enter into that calmness that came when I fought.

Before I entered the ring I was patted down and my dagger was taken away. Elton eyed me as if to ask, *why do you insist on always bringing that?* But it was special and sacred to me. A good luck charm and protection that I only got when I wore the suit, even if I never used it..

There had been too many times that I considered shoving it in Elton's throat.

Either I was too scared or there was something else stopping me.

I rolled my neck from side to side and when the iron doors swung open, I strode in, gliding with grace and strength, my hips swaying from side to side. Cheers arose and people pumped their fists in the air. I saluted them by fisting my left arm up and turning in a circle.

It was all a performance, I reminded myself.

The iron doors on the opposite side screeched open and not half as many cheers arose as a man staggered out. He'd been beaten and was already bleeding, although it seemed like they'd tried to clean him up somewhat for the fight tonight.

I willed that calmness into my heart and steadied my mind for the task at hand. Slowly, the cheering and booing of the crowds died away and it became silent in my mind. The man saw me but only circled, assumingly assessing his prey, the same as I was doing.

I flicked my gaze to his feet as he began stepping closer, his shoes were torn and patched. His right foot stepped forward just as he threw the first punch. I side stepped and he stumbled past me. When he turned towards me again, sand spewing behind him, he was angry.

He seethed, jaw clenched tight as he ran at me with full force.

But I was ready, I planted my feet in a fighting stance, bringing my fists up to protect my face. The man ran and leapt at me, throwing a fistful of the sand directly at my face just as he jumped. I whirled, blocking the sand but alas his booted feet planted themselves in my back. We tumbled to the sand with a muffled thud, I felt the pain in my lower spine and felt hands going for my throat from behind. But I was too quick and before the man could block, I elbowed him in the jaw. I heard a crack and used the momentum to flip around.

Just as I did, a fist came crashing down on my skull. I made an X with my forearms and blocked the blow just as I kneed the man from behind and sent him flying over me. I rotated and got to my knees, using his method and tossing sand straight into his eyes.

As he struggled, wiping at them—not as successful as I had been—I leapt on him and pummeled him to the ground. Too fast to think, I snapped his neck with a sickening sound and his head fell at an unnatural angle. His eyes, lifeless and still squeezed shut from the sand, would forever haunt me.

I removed myself from on top of him and brushed off the sand from my suit. I couldn't see past the blur in my vision or hear past the muffled sounds.

But I knew what to do.

I walked to the center of the sandy pit and crossed my ankles, scanning the chaotic crowd through my blurry gaze, I bowed, grinning wide.

A huge, rutting performance.

CHAPTER

2

Torch lights blinded me as I exited the *Death Pit*.

The flames surged towards the twilight sky, the sparks disappearing amongst the stars. Those who could not pay an omission to get into the actual arena, waited outside to hear the news of the contesters. Those who had bid, and lost, paid their dues in an exchange of coins or other manners of payment.

I pushed through the sea of individuals, my guard ever present behind me. Why couldn't he make himself useful and make these people move? I did not utter polite words or weak voiced requests as I burst through the cluster of frantic people. I pushed and shoved my way through, resisting the urge to elbow harder than necessary.

"There she is!" someone shouted, a finger jutted out towards me.

"Lord Hode's champion!" another cheered.

Others began pointing and I hastened my steps. They really needed to find a better way of transporting me after the fights. I rolled my eyes at those who tried to stop me in my path or ask for signatures or plead with me or ask me questions.

I wanted to be left alone.

And I would soon get my wish once I was safely in Elton's manor, in my dark cell, chained to the wall. It was funny how I considered that to be safe. But then again, in this realm of humans who would do anything for money or pleasure, it *was* the safest place for me.

Especially when I carried something that was so valuable.

Once I got through the pressing crowds, I made it to the carriage and the sweet relief of silence washed over me. Only the voices outside of my transportation could be heard and it was easy to block them out.

Except for one; a man began yelling at someone and I leaned forward, listening with my keen hearing.

"How much for her?" The man was Theldarian if my hearing picked up the accent correctly.

"She's not for sale."

I jolted back, realizing the Theldarian was talking to Elton. I sunk further into the cushioned seat of the carriage, hoping no one could see me.

"Name any price." This man was persistent.

"Again, she's not for sale. And you would do well to get out of my realm before I consider your presence here an act of war."

I bit my lip. This was serious then. The carriage jostled and the door opened as Elton joined me. I could tell instantly that he seemed flushed. He banged the ceiling of the carriage and we lurched onward. I didn't dare glance outside at whoever that man might have been.

I glanced at Elton instead, the question burning in my eyes before I spoke, "Who was that?"

He sighed, and pushed back his graying hair. "That, my dear, was someone haggling for you."

My brows twisted in confusion.

"You are very valuable, dear. Have I neglected to tell you? I get offers from Theldar often. This was the first time they actually showed up in person." He glanced out the window as if he could still see the man in the streets.

I turned my gaze away, wondering how the hell other realms knew about me and obtained the knowledge of where I resided. I began counting the minutes until the mansion would loom before us.

"They only want you for your body, Ryn. Don't forget that."

My eyes resisted the urge to roll. Elton also only wanted me for my body. What was the difference?

Once we arrived back at the mansion, the dagger was taken away as it always was. It still saddened me to see it go, it was my one taste of freedom in all of this, even if I wasn't brave enough to use it.

I was escorted upstairs, allowed a bath and a change of clothes before being handed a hardy meal and locked back in my cell. At one point, I had been able to eat with the lord and his son. But when I almost killed his precious son, they deemed it best that I was kept under lock and key unless training or fighting or attending a party.

So here I was, sitting on the damp floor, wrists and ankles shackled in iron that singed my skin, scarfing down my food.

This was my life though, had always been since as long as I could remember. Of course, that wasn't very difficult when I had no memories of my life beforehand.

I pushed the plate and cup of water aside once I was finished and laid my head back against the wall, sighing deeply. I could hear the celebration going on outside of my cell. Even though the walls were thick, it was hard not to be able to hear everything in this small of a lake town. I could practically hear the lapping of the dirty water on the docks and slapping against the ships hulls.

Thank rutting goodness Elton hadn't made me go to another party, he at least could see that I was worn out and would need my strength for the competition tomorrow.

I stood and walked to my cot, trying to find a comfortable position on the thin mattress. Weariness soon took over me and whether I was comfortable or not, I fell asleep.

I was already sitting up, awaiting the opening of my cell door when I heard the guard stomping down the hall, keys jingling from the ring around his waist. I counted his steps until he fumbled with the key, I heard a click after a few seconds and then the cell door opened.

"Let's go," the guard grumbled, leaning down and unlocking my chains.

I pushed myself up off the floor and followed as he led me up the stairs to my old room. I was given privacy to relieve myself and change into my training clothes before heading to the courtyard. I was never offered any meals before training and was only allowed water, so I downed a glass and began my routine of stretches and warming my body up.

The sun was up but hadn't yet crested over the top of the mansion, leaving everything in the courtyard clinging to that little bit of chill and moisture from the night before. Fog curled around the mountains beyond and sat heavily in the training yard. I knew from the past that it would be floating so close to the water, the surface would almost look like glass.

I began my lunges across the entire cobblestoned yard, stretching my aching muscles and waking them up. After a few squat kicks and practice punches, I was ready to begin.

To my dismay, Marcus strutted into the courtyard, shirtless and gleaming with sweat. Rolling my eyes, I gritted my teeth. I did not want to know what kind of exercise he had already done at such an early hour. His cropped blonde hair stuck to his rather large forehead and his eyes glinted with malice.

"Morning, Marcus," I drawled with dripping sarcasm.

Elton's son yanked his head away from me, snatching his hateful gaze away too. The guard stood off to the side, eyeing us both but I ignored the grunts and grumbles of Marcus as he began his exercise routine.

Thus, the morning went on like this, Marcus glancing at me every so often and me glaring back at him. Afterall, I had made him wet his pants all those months ago when I almost killed him. In truth, he had rightly deserved it.

"What do you keep staring at?" Marcus barked from his side of the courtyard.

"Not much!" I snapped back.

His brow furrowed in a poor attempt to glare at me and I stuck my tongue out at him.

"You better start improving in the competitions. I heard about last night and Father is already looking for a replacement."

I almost laughed at Marcus' attempt to jar my confidence. I gave the crowd *entertainment*. That was my job. I wielded a dagger and threw it at the target.

Bullseye.

"If you wanted to *try* and unnerve me you should try using real threats."

"Well, how about the other thing I heard last night?" he drawled, crossing his arms.

I snickered. "Oh? And what would that be? More threats from your daddy dearest?"

"That they are planning to increase your daily *procedures*."

I blinked, the only form of shock I would show. I rolled my neck, trying to calm my thundering heart. I wasn't sure whether to believe him or not. I wasn't sure what to think at all.

Marcus seemed proud of himself as he straightened his shoulders and held his head high. "Indeed. I heard Father talking about it. Seems they can't find what they are looking for so they need—"

"Marcus, Ryn!" Elton's voice boomed over the sound of whatever else Marcus had been about to say.

But a chill was working its way into my bones—my blood.

"How's the training?" Elton glanced between us.

Marcus winked at me in an annoying way and went to talk with his sorry excuse of a father.

I swallowed, trying to remember how to breathe, how to will air into my lungs. How to even think. Almost the entire time I had lived here, these procedures were inflicted upon me. I didn't think I could handle *more* of them.

"Ryn?"

I snapped out of it and turned to my master, nodding as a way of greeting. "I asked, if you're ready for tonight's comp?"

I faked a smile. "Ready as ever." I didn't miss Marcus' smirk or the gleam in his eye as he exited the courtyard.

But I was not *ready as ever*, in fact, the only thing crowding my mind while the sun continued its journey across the sky was what else they were going to do. What else I was going to have to endure?

I was terrified and I willed the day to last longer. But, alas, it did not. And as night fell, I found myself already on the way to another competition.

I flexed my fingers on the other side of the iron bars, awaiting my turn in the arena. My leathers felt especially hot and constricting today and I kept fidgeting with the collar.

Elton stood next to me grinning wildly. "I want you to give them a show, Ryn. This opponent will be nothing more than a pebble in your shoe but try to make it last longer than two minutes."

I said nothing as the iron door creaked open and I sauntered into the ring. But I didn't feel like myself, my mind was elsewhere and was not focused on the fight at hand.

I watched as a nix stumbled into the ring. She was half naked with only scraps of cloth to cover her and her wings were snapped in half. The word *inexperienced* didn't even begin to describe her. I fought the urge to whirl around and yell choice words in Elton's face.

This poor creature shouldn't even be in this ring.

I cracked my knuckles and stood in the middle of the ring, eyeing the creature. I took my gaze away for half of a second to glance at Elton, and that was my first mistake. I felt a sharp sting across my neck and whirled back to the nix, defenses going up. My fingers felt the blood that she had drawn and I tilted my head.

Maybe this wouldn't be as easy as I thought.

We danced around each other for a few more seconds and then I feigned a lunge to the right and dodged swiftly left, snatching her already snapped wing in my hands and yanking her towards me. The nix howled and scraped at my hands with her freakishly long nails but I held firm.

I yanked and pulled and twisted her, hearing the membrane snap and crack beneath the pressure. The female screeched and finally whipped around so fast her wing tore in my hands. She ran at me and I batted at her with her own broken wing, green blood seeped from it and glowed on the sand.

She shrieked something in her language and scratched and clawed her way through the wing I was using as a shield until nothing remained of it. I tossed the pieces in her face but she jumped at me and tackled me at the knees. As we went down and my head slammed into the ground, I caught the look on Elton's face.

The minutes were almost up. I had to act fast.

The nix screamed and thrashed on top of me and her face was a mask of pure terror and rage and bloodlust. I'm sure there was nothing different in my own eyes as I snatched her thin, long hair and yanked her head back. As I did so, she swiped her claws across my face, seconds before I snapped her neck.

I tossed her limp, pale body off of mine and didn't even bother looking at the roaring crowd as I swiped a sleeve over the blood dripping down my cheek and neck. I wanted to vomit at how the din of the crowd deafened my ears. They were so desperate for blood that they would do anything for it.

I ignored them as I walked out of the arena, hoping Elton would be satisfied with my performance. But it turned out, later that evening when we had arrived back at the manor, he was indeed displeased.

"She was *nothing*; a piece of scat from Sodnier! Have I not taught you better?" Elton seethed from across his desk, hands white knuckled as he pressed them into the scarred wood. I sat in a wooden chair across from him and could feel the heat of his stare.

But in truth, his shouts and screams were falling on deaf ears.

"I thought it would be *easy* for you. What the hell happened?" Elton pushed back his hair with his hands in a frustrated motion.

"She was better than you assumed," I retorted.

In fact, I still had her nail scrapes across my skin as proof.

"Or maybe I assumed too much of you," he spoke as he walked around, hands folded behind his back. "You are to train for the rest of the night. No breaks. No refreshments."

I nodded, showing no disappointment or anger. I would spend all night training rather than going beneath the mansion. . .

"Now get out. I don't want to look at you for a second longer!" Elton shooed me away with a flick of his wrist and I gladly slipped out of his office.

Perhaps Marcus had been bluffing after all.

CHAPTER

3

I swore over and over again.

My chest heaving at the loss of breath and the sweat dripping from my body. The sun had long since gone down but I stood in my fighting stance and threw my sets of punches to my invisible opponent.

I ducked and squatted and thrust and punched the air over and over. I would fight past the breaking point.

I leaned to the side and kicked out to where my opponent's waist would have been and then dropped low and swung my legs out as I pivoted. My opponent would have surely gone down and I landed the killing blow in thin air.

Pure perfection.

But not good enough. It would never be good enough for Elton.

As I continued with my routine, the stars growing ever brighter, I thought about what life must have been like before the war. What the world might have been like before the Territorial Treaty was signed. Resulting in every realm barricading themselves from one another. I had been so young when I first showed up on Helmfirth's docks, no memory of where I'd been or how I'd even got there.

I was told the war lasted for almost two years after that but I was kept safe under Lord Elton's supervision. He had been the one to so graciously take me in—at least that's how he put it. I wasn't sure how *gracious* his endeavors were when I endured such mistreatment beneath his cruel hands.

My entire life, I was told I should be grateful for the Territorial Treaty because it gave me an occupation in Helmfirth. It gave me the opportunity to make something of myself. Without the signed treaty, there wouldn't be a *Death Pit*.

Of course, there were always competitors like me who had been trained and brought up for the purpose of becoming champions. But without the wandering trespassers breaking the treaty, there would hardly be enough action to even warrant the pit.

Anyone found within our borders who were guilty of breaking the Territorial Treaty signed by every realm after the war, were given a choice between a trial or their chances in the *Death Pit*. Most chose the pit, knowing that a trial would have them on the next ship sailing for Hell's Keep, governed by Azazel.

Once prisoners were sent to Hell's Keep, they never left unless it was in a wooden coffin, their bodies permanently marked by the atrocities Azazel allowed. It mattered little which option they chose, none of them ever made it out of the pit anyway.

If they, by chance ever did, their victory was short lived. Sooner rather than later there would be news of a horrible accident occurring after their latest victory. Of course, most of us with any sort of wits about us knew exactly what had happened to cause such a horrible *accident*.

"Now *that's* what I want to see next time." I whirled at the sound of his voice.

I hadn't heard him enter the training courtyard and my guard had given me no indication he was here.

I wiped my brow and fully faced Elton. "And when will the next time be?" I squared my shoulders.

"I reserved you for a few fights," he remarked, hands clasped behind his back as he strode forward. "You'll want to prepare for the last fight of the week though."

I cocked my head to the side in a silent question but he only shook his head. He was not one to reveal his secrets outright. I turned and went back to my combo and rhythms. This time I walked over to the wooden plank we often practiced with and threw my fists at it.

"Ryn, yield," Elton growled, seemingly annoyed that I hadn't said more. I ignored him and kept punching, knuckles bleeding in the cracked areas. "Ryn."

I could feel the sting as the wood pierced my skin and tore flesh away but I would not give up. I would endure and last all night if I had to.

"*Ryn.*"

I felt the yank before the slap as Elton sent me reeling to the ground. "When I say yield, you rutting *yield*!"

"You told me no breaks!" I screamed back, my hair splayed out over my eyes and face.

Elton bent directly in front of my face and spat, "And now I'm telling you to stand *down*. You better get your head in these competitions or I will find somebody new!"

Good luck. There was no one else in this blasted town who would get him as much coin as I did.

Elton left me lying on the ground as he exited the courtyard with a single backward glance and the words tossed into the night air, "Get some rest."

My ever present guard escorted me roughly back inside the manor. As I walked, I glimpsed the night sky one last time. The stars twinkled and shone, their beauty unmatched. All too soon, the ceiling of the manor covered whatever else I was able to see and I frowned, a weight crushing my shoulders.

I would not see the stars again until tomorrow night. . .if I was lucky.

And it seemed, I was rather lucky recently. Marcus seemed to be wrong about the procedures. In fact, it seemed as if they were slowing down altogether. Maybe the conversation he had overheard was that they actually *had* found what they had been searching for all these years.

—ɯ—

The following day, a shiver snaked its way down my back as I began dressing in my fighting leathers. I was glancing at my reflection in the mirror when the urge to turn around and examine my back surged over me. And even though I told myself I wouldn't look anymore, I did.

Disappointment coursed through me at the sight of the scars peppering my skin, some large and some smaller. I sighed and had barely begun zipping my leathers back up when the door opened, revealing the man who was behind those scars.

"Just about ready?" he asked, leaning against the wall. I nodded once, beginning to braid my hair.

"You never wear your hair in anything else," Elton whined.

"This is easiest," I replied.

"I want something else for this fight."

I resisted the urge to roll my eyes. "And what would you suggest?"

"Pull it back, and tie it up high." His eyes raked over me and then he opened the door, calling behind him, "Carriage leaves in ten."

I rolled my eyes then and tore the hair out of the plaited braid and, if not a bit violently, pulled it up into a ponytail.

What a self-serving, ugly prick he was.

I laced up my boots, my hair falling over my shoulder and into my face from the high hairstyle. I swiped it away annoyed. With one last glance in the looking glass, I was satisfied with my appearance, for the most part.

I stormed out of the room with a curious look from my guard and was escorted to the awaiting carriage. I sat in my designated seat and noted the way Elton glanced at me, there was a strange gleam in his eyes that I hadn't seen before. I simply ignored him and glanced out my window, content to observe the goings on outside of the carriage.

Once we arrived at the pit, we were escorted inside and Elton and I resumed our familiar positions. The arena seemed especially full tonight and seemed to be anticipating something big.

"Don't forget to leave the best performance for the end of this week," he reminded me.

"As always."

I watched the fight for a few more seconds before my vision became blurry and I relaxed into that killing calm that happened before any fight. Once it was my turn, the dagger was taken away from me, I was searched thoroughly and then once deemed fit to fight, sauntered into the din of applause and cheers.

The fight lasted a total of sixty seconds against another human. The crowd had barely ceased cheering before the man lay dead. I had used his own shirt to choke him.

"What, was it too fast this time?" I asked, swaying my hips back and forth, reentering the space on the other side of the iron bars, sneering at my master.

He grinned at me ruthlessly and his eyes gleamed. "You are truly unmatched!"

And so the week went on like that. I won every competition he signed me up for, gaining Lord Elton Hode more coin than I had in two weeks worth of fights.

At the end of the week, I was stretching and warming up in the courtyard as the sun splashed its hues of orange and pink and purple in its final descent. The sound of a carriage approaching and the neighing of horses echoed and I knew it would be time to depart soon. I brushed off my suit and gave a nod to the bearded guard who escorted me out of the courtyard and through the main halls of the manor.

Elton awaited me in the foyer and we exited the manor arm in arm. Once in the carriage I ventured to ask, "Any hints on who I'll be fighting against?"

He shook his head. "Absolutely none, you know the rules."

I sighed and let a smirk slip. If I could bribe him into telling me anything, it might prove to be worth it. "Not even one teensy one to help me get the advantage?"

Elton grinned deviously. "Oh, you're winning this thing. No matter what."

That was encouraging. I sighed and sank into the cushioned seat. Lord Elton Hode would never let me off the hook, nor would he accept any small amount of failure.

Once inside the more-than-usual packed tavern, I assumed my designated position and waited. Even though there was a fight going on right in front of my eyes, it was not what I saw. I envisioned myself as one of the competitors and made the moves in my head; preparing myself physically and mentally.

The horn blast startled me from my mind vision and I cracked my knuckles and rolled my neck as the iron gate opened. My good luck charm was taken away from me and I entered the ring with no small amount of cheers. I frowned and turned around in a full circle not looking at anyone in particular.

But something was off.

I didn't show it on my face but something felt strange. There was a peculiar scent in the air and I felt that strange tingling in my bones. I heard my opponent's iron gate slide open and I turned to face whomever or whatever they were—

I stopped short, the breath catching in my throat.

A tall, midnight haired male stood before me. He did not stumble or falter in his steps as he strode towards me. In fact, he had a snarl painted across his face. His ocean blue eyes pierced through me as if it were a steel blade.

He was young and he was elven. I could tell because of his pointed ears—because they were the same as mine.

I had never killed one of my own before.

I had never been pitted against any elven kind. I had thought it was pure luck but now, hearing the cheers and the thundering sound of the crowd, I had a good idea that this was planned.

I did not make the same mistake as I had previously when I glared at Elton, although everything in me desperately wanted to. The elven male and I studied each other, unspoken words dancing in both of our eyes. I briefly wondered if *this* was why Elton had wanted my hair up, so that my elven ears were on full display.

What game was he playing?

I didn't have time to think about it any longer because the male began to circle me, my stomach was in my throat and the tingling in my blood had only gotten worse. But this *couldn't* happen. . .not again. The last time I hadn't done exactly what Elton wanted, I had suffered for it.

I shifted my boots through the sand as we began circling closer and closer.

What if I failed to make this last fight worth it? What if what Marcus said ended up being true if I failed?

My stomach hallowed out and I thought I might be sick. How had I not seen this beforehand?

I could not fail him again.

I *had* to kill this elven male—young as he was, of my own blood or not.

I heard a hiss and lunged just in time to miss the dark haired male's strike to my throat. I punched the side of his face and he staggered back. I ran at him but he feigned left and I staggered into thin air, feeling a sharp pain in my head as he yanked my ponytail back. He held it tightly and using the hold he had, I whirled and squatted, kicking my leg out to punch in his knee caps.

He leapt away before I could make the hit and in the process lost the hold on my hair. Out of nowhere, he came reeling back and landed a hard punch straight to my nose. I reeled backward, faceful of sand sticking to my bloodied face. I pushed myself up quickly and reassessed my opponent, wiping my nose with my arm. I dared to steal a glance at where Elton was standing, arms crossed, eyes narrowed.

I had to act fast. It was now or never.

I moved to a squatting position and when the elven male swung his leg to kick my face I grabbed it and yanked him towards me. But before he fully lost his balance he kicked me in the chest with the very leg that I held. I let go of him, wincing as I watched him whirl away.

This was no rutting male, this was a warrior.

I eyed him, willing the ache in my chest to ease, but I knew it wasn't just a physical ache.

We stared at one another as we both rose to our feet and closed the distance in an all out run. We collided with elbows and knees to the face and stomach and whirled away again. The crowd was a deafening cheer now, I sure hoped this was the fight they would all be satisfied with.

I watched as the male ripped a piece of his already torn clothing and twisted it in his hands. He could only have so many plans for a piece of cloth but choking me was most definitely on the list. He tilted his head again as if to communicate what was left unsaid.

Guilt panged through me, he had no idea.

We rushed at one another and I blocked and defended myself and my position. My boots were planted firmly in the ground and I thrust a fist to his throat, he took the hit with a grunt and staggered back.

I pressed on.

I kicked his shin while he was distracted and punched him in the face, whirling just as he retaliated with the piece of cloth trying to wrap it around my hands or neck to get me to stop. But I was a force to be reckoned with. I would not stop, because I wasn't just fighting for my life—I was fighting for my sanity, to protect what I might have to endure after this.

I crouched and glanced over my shoulder, anticipating his next move. He came at me with the cloth stretched and just as he was about to yank it over my throat, I snatched it and with all the strength and brute force that I had, I yanked him forward, throwing him to the ground. My wrist twisted in the cloth he still had and he yanked me towards him, sand and blood covering us both.

The crowd went absolutely silent as I gained the upper hand and pushed my boots against his feet so he couldn't kick me. My wrist was still strangled in his cloth and he was pulling it ever closer to him, but that meant he also didn't have access to his hands.

"I don't want to kill you," I seethed.

He writhed under my weight and the hold I had on him and settled his eyes on me. "Then don't."

"I can't afford that I'm afraid."

"Then you are going to have to choose."

Choose? I was supposed to choose death over killing this elven male?

I sighed and glared at him, my green, gold flecked eyes halting on his frosty blue ones. Bile rose in my throat at the thought of having to snap his neck, of ending his life.

It shouldn't have been this easy. It shouldn't *be* this easy to claim life and send people to the afterworld or. . .wherever deceased people went. Would this male be looked upon with mercy? Would he be taken care of? Would his family miss him?

The sound of chanting and thumping reached my ears and I dared a look at the crowds. . .at Elton. His glare told me it had been too long.

"You always have a choice," the male hissed, glaring now. "We could decide to simply not end each other's lives and walk out of here alive."

I almost laughed. "If such a thing were possible, do you not think I would have done it already?"

"Maybe you don't know it's possible."

I moved my hands, the one still twisted in the cloth and the free one, to his neck. He didn't struggle and I assumed he had accepted his fate. I placed my hands strategically around his neck, in the places where I had been taught that with one swift and cruel move, his neck could be snapped.

"I'm sorry," I choked out right as a stinging etched its way into my heart at the look in his eyes. But it was not fear and it was not hate. . .it was pity.

I felt something in me urging me to let him live. To choose death over killing him.

To choose freedom. . .but that wasn't possible. Elton would never let me go.

Yet, as I looked once more into the piercing blue eyes, I wondered what was so different about this male that he could think such things even in the situation he had been forced into. I groaned, ignoring that urge, that pull to freedom, that desire to remove my hands and help him up and walk out of here together.

"You may find that in the end freedom is possible." His blue eyes flashed as he stared at me.

"There is only freedom in death," I said as I moved my hand so swiftly and so brutally, snapping his neck.

The sound ruptured in my ears and sent icy shivers down my spine.

He was dead. I had killed him. Those ocean blue eyes, leached of all life would forever be imprinted in my mind's eye.

Eruptions of people cheering and clapping and jumping in their seats made my vision hazy. I could barely even hear over the ringing in my ears. I got to my feet and stepped away from the midnight haired male with the pointy ears, his cobalt eyes glazed over and blank in only the way that lifeless eyes can look.

I didn't cry or make any sounds as I stared at him one last time, memorizing his face before I walked away. I didn't *dare* look up at the frenzied crowds or into Elton's face. I could see his mouth moving and felt him reaching for me, but I shoved him away and fled the *Death Pit*. Pushing through the crowds, elbowing people and quite honestly not even caring. I ignored the carriage driver reaching for me and yelling after me and took off in a sprint.

I bolted, trying to get as far away as I could.

I fled past the cobblestones streets, the filthy slums with hell knew what splattered on the walls, the fish markets dead quiet from the days previous events and past that rutting manor. I fled for the docks, for that mountain range cresting the horizon where the clouds still kissed the sky.

I fell to my knees at the edge of the dock and an ear piercing sound expelled from my lips. Spilling out of my lungs, I screamed and cried into the night. I leaned forward on my knees and wept into the salty wood beneath my brow.

Through my closed eyes all I could see were those ocean eyes, the shades of sapphires and sparkling water looking up at me not begging or pleading for life but waiting. . .waiting to see which one I would choose.

I had killed so many people, I thought one more wouldn't matter. But I had *never* killed one of my own race before. I had never felt this before.

Why was it so different? Why was there a dark hole nagging and gaping inside of my chest?

I heard the sound of racing feet behind me and prepared for what might come next. It wouldn't be good, but I deserved it. For the awful things I had done, I deserved whatever came next.

I stayed silent as rough hands grabbed me by the shoulders and dragged me away. I barely felt my legs and feet snagging on the uneven cobblestone, or the sharp nails digging into my skin.

Everything was numb and blurry.

CHAPTER

4

I screamed.

I arched my back against the pain that crackled through my body like a flame. I had been here for hours, strapped down to that table with no way of escaping. I could barely see through my blurry vision and the pain—it was too much to bear. In the end, it hadn't even been worth killing the elven male. In the end, Marcus had been right.

Pain pulsated through me with each strip of skin that was torn away from my body while vials were being filled with my blood. I could feel trickles of it sliding down my bare sides and back, but it wasn't hot.

It was ice cold.

I was shivering so hard my teeth clattered together and the tips of my fingers were covered in black frost. I hissed and bit down on another scream as a thin piece of flesh was carved away.

You will suffer for your failures.

Elton's words when they dragged me back to the manor echoed in my head.

You will suffer for your inability to obey me.

A cold sensation grew in my stomach and threatened to burst out but I shoved it back down.

I gripped the straps and gritted my teeth.

I would not break. I would not yield. I would not fail—I had failed.

"She needs a break my lord," a voice said to my left and the pain subsided for a moment.

Sweet rutting relief.

Elton's voice filled the room and my relief washed away as he barked, "Keep working. Do not stop until we have enough."

Enough of what? My blood? They had already taken so much.

I didn't have time to think another second longer as pain erupted on my back and I felt the prick of that ice begging to be freed. This was worse than any other time I'd been brought down here. I began to feel faint at the loss of blood as the shackles and straps that were keeping me contained turned into frozen shards. Which was quite odd because the iron they usually used kept my magic at bay.

Not this time it would seem.

A scream escaped my lungs, feeling like it was ripping my throat to shreds. My hands broke free as something snapped inside of me and from both palms came a dark frost, erupting and swirling around the occupants of the room.

I pushed myself up and whirled on Elton and the other man. The blood from my back dripped onto the floor as the black ice circled the surgeon and then forced itself into his mouth, his nostrils and I felt something change as he dropped dead on the floor; his skin frozen black.

I turned my green eyes and icy rage to Elton. But he only smiled at me. "So, it is true then."

"Is this what you wanted to see?!" I snarled, the mist-ice circling him.

He remained silent, goading me on. He hadn't put the iron chains on for a reason.

I cocked my head, inching forward. "You wanted this, didn't you? You wanted to see that I am truly the monster you have always believed I am!" I was screaming now and the shadows choked him around the neck, flinging him against the wall.

"Do it, Ryn! Kill me!" he spat out.

I wanted to. How sweet that victory would feel—I could practically taste it.

All the darkness and bitterness in me wanted to desperately choke the life out of him, but I couldn't bring myself to do it. Images flashed of

Lord Elton Hode who had been so cruel to me, had beaten me, tortured me, used me and driven me to my breaking point *so* many times. It was my right to take what he had taken away from me and yet somehow, I could not do it.

Hesitating had been my first mistake.

Elton must have seen the hesitation in my eyes because before I could blink, he punched my throat and I staggered backwards. The black ice retracted and disappeared completely. He backhanded my face and snatched me around the throat lifting me up against the wall.

I screamed mutely against the agony as my open wounds were pressed against the brick, he slid me down and I bordered on unconsciousness as my skin tore and fell away from the brick being scraped across it.

"Guards!" Elton shouted and spittle flew onto my face.

Momentarily, two guards rushed into the room and instantly assessed everything. They each took an arm in hand and I didn't hear what Elton said to them as they dragged me out. I wasn't sure what happened between being dragged from that hell hole to a different one. I felt irons clasped on my wrists and ankles and in a blur, I slumped onto my stomach in an effort to relieve my torn back.

I welcomed the blissful darkness that soon followed and encompassed me, hauling me in and out of pain and relief for how long I did not know. I prayed that death would finally come for me and do me a favor.

But it never did for I awoke to the sounds of screams, perhaps I was truly in hell then. I jolted upright and cried out in pain as the wounds on my back reopened.

Damn it.

I pushed myself up slowly so that I was half kneeling, half propped up on one elbow and wiped at my eyes, trying to clear the dirt and sweat away. I looked up at the small round window that often gave me comfort and grimaced. I could see the glowing of embers flickering in the shadows.

I tried to recall how long I had been asleep or unconscious, I didn't know which, but it was for naught. There was no way I could recount the time since. . .since. . .I swallowed, not wanting to remember the scraping sounds of the tools and the tearing of my very flesh.

Elton's face came to mind and I wanted to vomit. *He* had done this to me.

More screams and shouts came from outside, the sound seeping in through the window. I strained to hear the other sounds; thumping footfalls, the sound of crackling fire and whooshes of wind.

If Helmfirth was in danger they had brought it upon themselves, I only hoped whoever or whatever was out there would have mercy upon me and spare me.

My eyes caught something in the corner and through the round window came drifts of light. It was ember gold and light blue as if straight from the innermost part of a fire. My eyes widened as I watched the mist slither in through the opening and drift down to where I was chained to the wall. I tried to scoot as far back without touching my skin to the wall and held my breath.

Maybe it would bypass me if it couldn't sense me.

The sounds of chaos continued outside as the mist swirled closer and closer to me. It looked the same as what had exploded from me in the torture room except this was golden. Without thinking, I lifted my hand to touch it. It seemed to stop and then it twirled itself around my fingers. It felt smooth and hollow and breathy to touch and I was mesmerized by it.

The door burst open and I jumped back, not only hitting the wounds on my back, but also slamming my head against the stone. I clamped down on my howl and met the gaze of a handsome pointy eared male.

"I found you," he rasped, his auburn hair ruffled from whatever was going on outside. He stepped into my cell and breathlessly said, "We've been searching for you for a very long time."

Words escaped me as I watched the mist trickle away and fade into the male's skin and hands. I met his gaze once more and felt something.

"I'm getting you out of here."

I blinked and felt a clench in my gut. "Who the hell are you and where are you taking me?"

"To the Sol Kingdom," he said, ignoring the part about who he was. He came forward and bent to inspect my chains. His scent smelled of oakwood and sweet sap.

"How can I trust you?" I asked, weakly, my head feeling extremely heavy.

He looked up then and his soft brown eyes met mine once more. "Because you know it's true."

I wasn't sure what he meant. I knew that I was an elven blood but I had no memory of anything before washing up on the docks of Helmfirth.

"Agh!" the male cursed and a blue light flashed from my irons. "Blasted humans! They're iron."

"Well, yes," I said, rather rudely.

"I won't be able to get them off. I'll have to carry you." He glanced down at the chains wrapped around my wrists and ankles.

I scoffed. "Like hell you will."

"Do you want to leave?"

I clamped my mouth shut as he yanked the ring holding my chains around the wall rather impressively. Stone and dust plumed down and I wrinkled my nose. And as I wobbled to my feet, the male put his hand on my back.

I screamed in pain. "Don't touch me!"

And that's when he looked. Whatever was left of my back, however badly it was infected, made his eyes widen and he swore under his breath.

"What did they do to you?"

I shook my head. "Just hold me around my shoulders and I'll be fine."

And he did just that. He wrapped his strong arms under my knees and held me as he hoisted me up and carried me out of my dark cell. He carried me past the dark halls and doors and rooms where I had suffered under the hand of Lord Elton Hode. I turned my face into the oakwood and sweet sap smelling male, wishing to never lay eyes on this hell hole again.

I felt the chill breeze wafting in from Helmfirth Lake and the glow from the fires heated my face. I turned to look as flames licked up the buildings and homes closest to the docks. The white hot flames ate up the wood ravenously and everywhere people were running and screaming.

I turned away from it all; the destruction, the terror, the loss. I wasn't sure what I was feeling but it certainly was nothing akin to pity or sorrow for these people.

"Steady now," the auburn male said close to my ear as orange light surrounded us and a cool breeze wafted by with the scent of smoke.

The world felt as if it was warped and falling, wood groaned and I realized through my hazy vision that I was being put into a boat. It rocked slightly and then it was sailing away from the docks, away from Helmfirth.

I was leaving Helmfirth.

The thought crossed my mind several times in the distance it took us to get from the docks of the lake town to the bottom of the mountain. Ash floated across the rippling waters and melted on the surface. The flames blazed from the laketown and the screams were growing ever fainter.

I did not care where Marcus or Elton or even my guard was. In fact, I hoped they were burning to a crisp in their beds. I hoped the entire *Death Pit* collapsed in flames and ash and rubble too.

The boat knocked against the dock on the opposite side of the town and the elven male nimbly got out, tied the vessel off and reached for me.

"You're going to be okay," he whispered.

I didn't know why he was doing this, whether he was actually rescuing me or delivering me to some other evil.

Staying conscious took every ounce of strength I had left. My eyes were heavy and even though I tried keeping them open as the male took me in his arms—trying his best not to touch my back but failing miserably—they insisted on closing. I was aware of the pain in my back and my head swimming and that it seemed we were ascending the mountain but that was all.

The next moment I gained consciousness again, we stood on the top of the mountain, frost covering the ground beneath us. I lay on something soft and could hear two voices now.

I tilted my neck and blinked, trying to clear my vision. I could see smoke rising from the lake town into the star speckled sky from the several fires burning, the reflection rippling in the lake below.

People were still shouting and I could hear children and women wailing, although extremely faint now.

I ignored them all.

"We need the healer," the auburn haired male ordered.

"They are all back at the palace," someone replied.

"Damn it, why didn't she order them to come along?" the auburn male again. "It is not our job to question what the queen orders."

"Well, she can't walk and if we carry her she very well may bleed out and die on us."

I didn't have the strength to tell them I would heal. I always did in some miraculous or cursed way. They ended up deciding on making a go for it but flipped me onto my stomach so that my back wouldn't rub on whatever stretcher I was lying on.

That was about as much as I remembered before losing consciousness completely.

CHAPTER

5

Sun warmed my face.

Or perhaps that was still the fire from Helmfirth. Maybe we hadn't made it out afterall. A heaviness settled inside of me as this thought traipsed through my mind. I stirred, instantly noting that I was still being carried. As I cracked my eyes open, light flooded in.

Relief washed over me that it wasn't, in fact, the fires, but the sun that warmed my face and body. I could feel some sort of fabric draped across my back but even that was warm. I could feel the sting of my wounds as they had more than likely scabbed and were sensitive to the heat.

Moving my eyes to look down, I could see the grassy path my alleged rescuers or captors walked upon. Grassy knolls filled my vision and the sounds of a waterfall just before it came into sight. The water gushed down into rivers and lakes and pools that rippled elsewhere, leaving a spray of water and sunlight in its wake.

We must have neared the palace because golden gates filled my tilted vision and the sunlight was obscured slightly. The flow from the waterfall must have followed us because we crossed over a bridge made from vines and branches with gushing water running under it.

My vision continued to blur but I instantly began to inspect everything that I could see, even from the awkward angle I was currently in. I briefly glimpsed mint and cream, bronze and gold colored walls, archways, trimming, verandas and polished floors.

But it all blended together and swirled too much as the stretcher was put down. I tensed at the presence of others and wondered what they would do. They began touching me, that fabric that was between them and my wounds was being pulled away.

No, no, no.

I began to shift, opening my eyes in terror. They were going to cut me and prick me with tools and needles and I—

"Damn," someone whispered.

"Bloody hell," the other cursed.

I remained still and silent, but listening intently. "Her wounds...they are healed."

"Get the queen, *now*."

However long it took to get the queen, that's how long I laid there with the auburn haired male at my side and wondered whether my fate would be in good hands or ill advised ones. The male spoke words to me but I did not remember them nor did I respond.

Finally, rushed footsteps could be heard in the cream and gold halls and the auburn haired male straightened, adjusting his armor.

"Good gracious!" someone exclaimed.

I angled my head to try to see who it was but since I was still lying on my back, I could do nothing. I knew it to be the queen although I had not ever set eyes upon her, the presence that filled the room was, without a doubt, of someone royal.

The auburn haired male spoke beside me, "Your Majesty, as you can see, her back was torn to shreds...but it has healed."

"Which one of our healers did this?" the queen, I assumed, asked.

"No, you misunderstand. No one has touched her. We've only just arrived."

Quiet, graceful footsteps moved towards me. "You mean to tell me her magic healed her own fatal wounds?"

"Yes."

What they spoke of was nothing new for me, but I had thought it was normal for all elven bloods. Clearly, it was not.

"Let's get her into a sitting position, are you quite well, dear?"

I didn't know what to say to her and didn't have time to think of a reply as someone helped me sit up on the stretcher, careful not to touch my back. It wouldn't have mattered, it was sore anyway. The scabs stretched a bit and I hissed as the pain was a dull, throbbing ache.

The female who knelt before me was one of beauty and grace. She had flowing dark black hair, deep brown eyes, high cheekbones and long, pointy ears. She was slender but strong and looked quite elegant, even as she knelt before me. She wore a dusty pink gown with beads of cream and thin gold thread lining the hems, sleeves, and the neckline. And her brown gaze. . . filled with compassion.

"Are you well, dear?" she asked again, glancing up at the other males in the room, the ones who had brought me here.

"As well as one can be," I replied, casting my eyes down. I had never been in the presence of such royalty before and still had not decided if they were threats or not.

"Get a glass of water and some food for our guest," she ordered the male behind her and he briskly walked off to do her bidding.

That left me with the queen and the male who'd initially found me. "Why am I here?" I asked, my throat and voice hoarse.

She smiled, eyes bright. "Many reasons, we have been looking for you for quite some time."

I shook my head. "What does that mean?" I gestured up at the auburn male. "You said the same when you found me."

"All in due time," the queen nodded reassuringly. "We have anticipated your arrival."

"The hell does that even mean?" I didn't mean to sound snappy but my entire body ached and my head was beginning to pound.

"For now, I want you to settle in. We will speak more later—"

I snapped, "It's in your best interest to tell me something now."

The queen raised her eyebrows as she stood up. "It is in *your* best interest to do as I say."

A chill raced through me that made me feel uncomfortable.

"I need you fully rested and you've had quite the journey, now is not the time."

I groaned beneath my breath and resisted the urge to roll my eyes, an unsettling feeling sinking in.

"You are safe now. You are free," she said as she glanced at the auburn haired male and turned to leave.

Safe? Free?

Two things I had never been before in my life. So, why didn't it feel exactly how I had always envisioned?

I leaned forward, elbows resting on my knee and brought my forefinger to scrub at my eyebrows, trying to release the tension behind them.

"Let's get you to a hot bath and a room."

I wouldn't argue with that so I allowed the elven male to assist me in standing, we left the foyer of the palace and the male led me through cream and gold halls, rivers ran all throughout the palace; the result of the waterfall I presumed.

We walked up a flight of stairs that I had to rest on due to the dizziness, but we eventually arrived at a cream painted door with gold hinges and a gold door knob. I barely even glanced at the room as he led me to the bathing chambers. Upon entering, I knew this would be the fanciest bath I'd ever taken.

"Should you need anything, I will be in the combatant quarters, ask anyone to point you in that direction and they will aid you."

I nodded my thanks, although I wouldn't be needing help from any of them. As soon as he left, I was locking all of the doors.

"I'll have a meal sent up to you." Locking just the bathing room door then.

After he removed his presence from my new room, I promptly locked the bathing room door and allowed the tub to fill with scalding hot water. It should have been too hot for me, the temperature bordered on burning my skin but it didn't bother me, even as it stung my scabs and cleaned them with a viscous touch.

I blinked. Once. Twice.

And the weight of everything that had happened came crashing in. I squeezed my eyes shut but the images burst their way in unwelcome and haunting.

No, no, no.

I clutched at my throat feeling the pricks and stabs on my back. I felt the chains around my ankles and wrists. I knew this wasn't real but the pain wouldn't stop even as I lay in the tub and sobbed into my hands.

The weight of what I'd done—what had been done to me came in full force and I stifled my cries.

But I could not stop the blue eyes that pierced my mind—

NO!!

I jolted, clutching at my throat just as the nausea hit me and I bolted out of the steaming water, splashing it everywhere. I made it just in time to vomit into the porcelain bowl, holding my hair up. When the heaving ended, I spat the bile out; the only thing my body could bring up from my empty stomach.

I pushed myself to stand and walked over to the sink to wash my face and mouth out. I stared at my reflection, knowing that I shouldn't but being too stubborn to stop myself, I looked over my shoulder and pulled my sopping wet hair back.

They were hideous.

Scars and scabs marred my flesh and spread out in different directions, where Elton and his men had sliced into me.

I tried to stop them but the tears came along with the remembrance of the pain. I tried to convince myself that I didn't care. What did it matter what my back looked like? But deep down I knew I was lying to myself.

It did bother me. And I hated them.

I stepped back into the bath and submerged myself beneath the surface.

Desperately trying to escape the hellish pain inside of me.

I didn't sleep much that night, in fact I never even left the bathing room. The door was still locked, my meal long since gone cold on the other side. What stirred me awake in the morning was the creak of the bedroom door opening and a gasp, then light footsteps to the bathing room door.

"Lady? Are you quite well?"

Everyone kept asking that rutting question and it really unnerved me. According to the previous night, I was not *quite well*, but when had I ever been?

"I'm in here," I replied.

"I've brought you some clothes and. . .I can bring you some fresh food."

"No, thank you. And if the clothes are a dress of any kind, I am not wearing it."

I heard the female stutter and seemed to be trying to find the right words. "How about a tunic?" she finally offered.

"Grand." I rolled my eyes and gave a rude gesture to the shut door.

And then, with the padding of the female's feet exiting the room, I was left alone again. Thank rutting bliss. That was all I wanted, was to be left alone.

But I also wanted answers and I assumed the only way I would find out what I wanted to know was if I actually left the bathing chambers.

More or less my room for that matter.

"Just this way."

My heart flipped and I straightened as I walked behind my escort; a long-haired male with a tunic of green and white-gold hems.

I, myself, wore my brown leathers from Helmfirth and the tunic I'd asked the maid to retrieve. Which she had done as well as leave me with a message stating the queen awaited my presence in the throne room, hence I was headed there currently.

Colors and hues and scents passed by in a whirl and I took all of it in. Everything seemed so vibrant here, it smelled of lilacs and mint and the flowers and trees were blooming in all of the green patches and courtyards to either side of me.

There were many bridges crossing over sparkling rivers both inside the palace and outside. I marveled at the grandeur of the white-gold floors and pillars and sparkling ceilings. They revealed the vines that grew from the trees outside and spread through the windows and open spaces, allowing them to continue to grow along the walls and ceilings.

"My lady."

My Lady. I snapped out of my thoughts and met the eyes of the prestigious elven male. He had stopped and was looking at me now.

I blinked.

"The throne room." He extended a hand out from his body and bowed slightly.

I hadn't even realized that we had arrived and swept my gaze behind me and in front of me before proceeding to follow him through the double gold doors. The freshly polished floor laid out before us, leading all the way to a pure cream and gold entwined throne. Atop it sat a majestic looking female; Queen of the Sol Kingdom.

"High Queen Cressida, it is my great honor and pleasure to announce to you Lady Ryn."

He had asked for my name on the way here but I had refused to give it to him. How the hell had he known? Why even ask me if he already knew the answer. I turned my gaze to him and glared as hard as I dared.

"I am glad to see you looking well. I trust my staff have treated you kindly?" Queen Cressida stepped down from her dais and floated towards me.

"Yes, indeed," I replied, perusing the room with my gaze one last time and giving the male next to me one last glare.

"Come, dear, we shall speak of the things I promised you." She extended her hand to me, her fingers laced with gold rings and nails that were dipped in what looked like bronze paint.

I stepped forward and she took my hand. She was warm and soft and an aroma of vanilla greeted me when she drew closer. We walked away from the guards and to a small balcony just outside the throne room.

"You want to know why you are here, correct?" she asked, turning to me in the golden light of the sun.

I nodded. Obviously.

"You are clearly elven born, you have the ears of our kind and you have the elven blood flowing through your veins, do you not?"

Clever. She was making me confess it to her. She was making me admit something I had long since snuffed out of my mind. But with her brown eyes staring so intently into my own gaze, I spoke in a voice that was hoarse, "I am."

"You are what?"

"I am elven born." There. I said it.

Cressida nodded. "But you do not belong to the elven race of my realm." I tilted my gaze to hers. The rutting hell did she mean?

She looked out over the balcony, gesturing. "There is another realm called the Crescent Kingdom. I believe your powers to be from there, Ryn. That is why I need you. We Sol Bloods do not have this certain power that you have."

Something tingled inside of me and I felt uneasy. Elton had been searching for something in my magic, was Cressida aiming to look for the same thing? The memory of the dark frost exploding from my palms made me cringe. The way it had so easily killed the surgeon—the way *I* had so easily killed the surgeon with it. It wasn't something to be worshiped or used for healing.

It was a weapon.

"I want you to know it is completely your choice, you are a free citizen now. Whether you choose to live here or elsewhere. I would simply be asking you for a favor if you allowed me to have some of your magic."

"What would you use it for?"

"Healing," she spoke as she smiled and looked off into the distance. "There is such struggle and strife out in the world, I want to become the good in this world. Healing what is broken."

Relief washed over me but I remained wary. People often say one thing and mean another. "I will consider it, when do you need an answer?"

"It's on your time, dear. I am in no rush. I am just grateful we were able to find and rescue you from those horrid humans."

I nodded, glancing over the balcony at the flowering gardens and rivers below. "May I just say, I am so sorry you had to endure such horrible treatment."

Tears welled in my eyes but I hid them and glanced away from the greenery, I nodded in appreciation, unable to form any suitable words.

CHAPTER

6

Golden light spilled over my face and coaxed my eyelashes open. I jolted awake when I didn't realize where I was.

Mint green walls loomed before me and I lay in a ginormous bed. I was not accustomed to sleeping in a bed and felt strange amongst the sheets and translucent satin creating a canopy over me. The blankets were warm and soft and the entire room glowed with the sun as the day beckoned.

I realized that night had never come.

I blinked and stared up at the satin canopy, the sun *never* stopped shining here. A brisk knock sounded on my door, momentarily interrupting my wandering thoughts. I leapt to open the door and addressed the female with the turquoise dress and cream belt.

"Good dawning, Lady Ryn. May I come in?" she asked as her eyes sparkled.

I wondered at her choice of words but nodded my approval since I was already at the door. She slipped in with a smile, carrying a copper tray full of ivory dishes with intricate gold designs painted across the surfaces.

"You've been asleep for half the day," she quipped, setting the tray on the desk next to my bed.

I pressed my lips closer together and fiddled with a stray string of fabric on the dark gold bedspread. Or was it copper? I wasn't sure when the sun beamed through the ceiling high windows, making everything appear brighter and richer.

"I've brought you quite the spread of dishes, all still steaming and fresh," she said, taking the lids off of all the bowls and plates. "Have you ever had hot chocolate?"

I shook my head. I hadn't ever had cold chocolate either. She smiled as she picked up a steaming cup of what I assumed was hot chocolate.

"It has vanilla and cinnamon spices and then the chocolate bags are steeped into the milk and ta-da!" She pressed the warm mug into my hands and grinned wider than before, if that was even possible.

I took a small sip and pushed a grim smile onto my face and nodded, giving my approval.

"I'm Iris, by the way. We didn't really get to meet properly and of course you've been through so much and traveled far as I'm sure. And now, you've barely even come home to us and there's so much to prepare for and do. It's all rather exciting!"

I tried to swallow but Iris was. . .overwhelming me to say the least. She was talking way too fast and saying so many things I wasn't even sure what to respond to. My hands shook as I set my mug back on the table and said tersely, "I think I'll eat my breakfast alone."

Iris, mercifully, shut up. She blinked and folded her hands. "I am so sorry if I overstepped."

I shook my head. "I'm just tired."

She inclined her head in a bow and hurriedly left. I noticed her cheeks had a bit of color and I did feel slightly guilty. I sighed again and crossed an arm over my eyes. Birds chirped and sang in the distance and I could hear their small wings fluttering as they flew from one branch and perched on another. The wind rustled the leaves of the weeping willows and I swore I could hear many voices lifted up in a song nearby, I couldn't be sure.

And I didn't care.

I turned over and stuffed a pillow over my exposed ear. I had had enough of birds and elves singing and whatever else this day held for me. I was going back to sleep.

But my failed attempt to fall asleep was interrupted by another knock at the door. I peered above the covers and screeched, "Go away!"

A cough sounded. "It is I, your rescuer!"

Oh, he was wretched. I rolled my eyes. "I do not care, go away."

"The queen has sent me."

Did he have a death wish? I chose to ignore him and when I thought he was finally gone I turned over once more, content to stay in bed all day.

"Lady Ryn?"

Lady. . .I stared at a spot on the wall and glared so hard I thought the wall might turn to ice.

"Queen Cressida has—"

I bolted out of bed and threw the bedroom door open. "Shut your rutting mouth!" I hissed, staring at the auburn haired male standing before me. I inspected his brown leather pants and boots for any concealed weapons. He had on a white long sleeved shirt with a *V* neckline and showing off his tanned skin and chest scars. His boots were a darker brown and laced all the way to his shins. The only weapon in sight was the sheathed sword hanging at his side.

"Just *what* exactly have you annoyed me for. . .?" I realized I didn't know his name and didn't really care either.

"Her Majesty sent me to deliver a message," the male said, straight as an arrow and his eyes locked with my own.

I jerked my head forward. "And?"

"She requests your presence at her personal dining table for the later meal."

"Anything else?"

"You should probably get dressed in something other than your lady things."

Horrified, I looked down and realized I was indeed in my underclothes. Thank the sun and the stars that I had been wearing *something*.

I jerked my head up at the smirking male. "Stop looking, sniveling prick."

"See you at dinner. . .hopefully in something less revealing."

I slammed the door in his face. Prick. Prick. Prick.

I marched after my escort into the dining hall as if it were the *Death Pit* itself. I wore a new white tunic I had asked Iris to find for me and my old brown leathers with the boots Elton had bought for me when I stopped growing.

To my great dismay, the horrid elven male was standing at Queen Cressida's right hand side in the dining hall. He must be important then. I quickly assessed the room, scanning any and all possible exits and how many guards were posted with how many weapons.

Two directly across from one another, each with their own sheathed blades.

I scanned the veranda with its white-gold pillars and the vine wall just beyond; blocking any view eavesdroppers might have of the queen and her honored guests.

Clever.

"Welcome Lady Ryn," Queen Cressida's voice lilted from where she sat at the head of the long table and her smile swept across her lovely face in a perfectly amiable way.

I gave a slight nod and plopped down into my chair. I didn't miss the inquisitive stare I received from the queen or her guard dog of a male.

"Allow me to introduce you to your rescuer, Captain Skandar Galakir."

The captain eyed me and nodded, but not before I glanced at the smirk he wore across his face. I didn't so much as bob my head at him.

Queen Cressida gave a silent command to Skandar and he took his seat on her right side. I, adjacent from him on her left. She looked to the guards on either side of the doorway and they shut the doors, sealing us in the dining room.

As servants trailed in bringing in trays of food and drink, Cressida turned her attention to me, her bound hair braided and pulled back revealing the heritage of her elven blood. Her ears were not the same as mine though, more similar to Iris', longer and adorned with pure gold accessories.

"I hope you have found the Sol Kingdom to your satisfaction, Lady Ryn." Cressida smoothed out the invisible wrinkles of her red and bronze dress, her eyes never leaving mine.

"Quite so," I replied, ignoring the face Captain Skandar made.

The servants finished placing the last of the dishes down, bowed and left. I hadn't had much of an appetite but whatever was beneath the gold lids smelled heavenly. At the wave of Cressida's hand to start the meal, I opened the lid and a waft of smoked, lemon pepper chicken hit me full force. Salted and sauteed greens, leeks and potatoes dressed the plate in color and accented everything wonderfully.

Maybe I was hungry.

I picked up my fork and knife and dug in.

"I am sure you're curious as to why I invited you to dine with me this dusking," Queen Cressida said, daintily holding her wine glass.

What I *was* curious about was the choice of words these elven races kept using. Dawning and Dusking. What the hell did those mean? My eyes flickered to the hedge of vines beyond the pillars and I glimpsed the golden rays of the sun. . .but shouldn't it have already set ages ago?

I cleared my throat and glanced back to the table. "Yes, of course."

Cressida nodded and her eyebrows tilted up slightly. "If you don't mind, I'd love to hear about your life in Helmfirth first. If you have any questions, I will gladly answer them as I am able, or Captain Galakir may aid you in your curiosites as well."

I cringed and hoped he wouldn't be doing any of the talking. I set my fork and knife down and swigged down some wine. I was going to need it. "Well, I don't remember anything before the age of ten. My first memory is vague, I washed up on the docks of Helmfirth in a boat and was taken in by a lord there. He trained me to be his competitor in the *Death Pit* and I became his champion after the treaty was signed. I have killed and fought for him since."

Skandar didn't blink or even move.

Cressida on the other hand reached a hand towards me. "My dear, how awful. You began fighting at such a young age."

I forced a close lipped smile and she squeezed my hand, the scent of her trailing towards me. Whatever the age difference was for elves versus humans, I had still been young. It's rumored the lifespan of an elven male and female is much longer than the average human, but we were not immortal.

Retracting her hand she spoke again, "Did you always know you were of elven heritage?"

I nodded. "Yes. When you are the only race in a realm with strange ears and magic, it makes for interesting conversations."

"How did these...death games come about?" she asked, waving her ringed fingers delicately.

"After the Bloody War between the differentiating realms and the Territorial Treaty was signed several years ago, anyone found in Helmfirth that did not belong, were given a choice between a trial or to fight in the *Death Pit*. There were plenty of trespassers to keep the fight going every week." I swallowed and rubbed the back of my neck not meeting the eyes of the queen or the captain for fear they would see I had killed one of our own.

"How...very human."

I wasn't sure I liked the way she had said that and straightened in my chair. "I am sure you have your own precautions in place if you ever find trespassers in your land?" I watched Cressida closely for a reaction.

She calmly smoothed her already smooth dress. "Of course, we do. I suspect every kingdom does after the atrocities of the near two year war."

"What was the cause of the war anyway?" I found myself asking. Skandar's brow creased for a half second before he masked his expression.

Cressida seemed to glance at me curiously. "What it's always about; domination. Every realm thought they'd be better off ruling the world and of course some did not agree. Thus, the war ensued."

"And do you think the elves are superior? Should they be the ones to rule the world?" I did not take my eyes off of her.

Her lips spread into a small smile and she chuckled softly. "I think you know the answer to that. Who else would be fit enough to rule?"

Skandar cleared his throat and spoke, "You're very lucky that lord found you and made you his champion. Your life would have been a lot harder if he hadn't."

My neck snapped towards him and I glared. "Do not *dare* assume my life was easy because Lord Elton found me. You have no idea what I have endured." There was a crackling of ice in my soul and I struggled to bury it.

Not here. Not now.

"Apologies, Lady Ryn, Captain Skandar meant no harm." I didn't miss the hot glare Cressida sent to the male seated at her right.

I downed my wine and pushed back my plate.

"Now that is settled, how are you finding our home?" Cressida flashed her bejeweled fingers and smiled at me.

"It's interesting," I replied, swallowing down the temper from before. "I do have one question."

"Certainly."

"Why do you all keep saying *dawning* and *dusking*? And why has the sun not disappeared yet?"

Skandar hid his smile and Cressida smiled. "Ah, here in the Sol Kingdom the sun never disappears. We call the beginning of the day Dawn and the end Dusk. There is only Day here, never Night."

"Why?"

"We are the Day Elves; Sol Bloods."

My mind began to wander and Cressida must have seen the questions beginning to surface because she answered, "Then there are, of course, the Crescent Bloods of the Crescent Kingdom, where you are from—according to your powers."

The Crescent Bloods.

My skin prickled and I felt an icy chill crawl down my back. Why had Queen Cressida rescued me from the human realm? If I was indeed a Crescent Blood, why hadn't *they* been the ones to find me?

"Much obliged," was all I replied with.

"If it interests you, there is a library in the palace. You can learn and study all about your heritage, traditions, and rituals."

How I longed to read a good book again. Since being locked away in that cell for nearly killing Marucs I hadn't touched nor smelled one in months.

"I would like that very much."

"Very well. Captain Skandar will escort you tomorrow."

My face fell and the captain and I both glared at one another. Rutting grand.

CHAPTER 7

A knock sounded and I groaned.

I downed the rest of the hot chocolate with cinnamon. Iris continued to bring me a mug at dawn every day. I pulled on my boots and sighed, I had faced many a foe, I could face one annoying elven male. I yanked the door open and glared at him.

"Good dawning," Captain Skandar spoke cheerfully.

I slammed my bedroom door behind me and strode past him, ignoring his morning sentiments.

"I didn't know the lady hated the dawn so much."

I retorted, quickly, "I don't. I just dislike the company."

A scoff from him and a snort from me and we were on our way to the Golden Library, as the Day Elves called it.

Once we reached said library, my breath was stolen away at the sight of the huge double doors. They looked to be made of pure gold, which given the name was very likely. Intricate designs of a forest, a meadow, and rivers were carved all over the face of them.

Skandar opened one of the doors and I strode in, ignoring him completely. However, that was partly because words would never be able to describe the magical feeling that surged through me as I spun around and gazed at the pure beauty of the library.

Cream bookcases with golden trim lined every single wall and shot up towards the high dome capped ceiling. My eyes drifted towards a skylight at the very top where golden rays of sunlight cascaded down to kiss the bookshelves. The light danced amongst the ladders and desks with small lamps and candles; each one complete with a quill and ink writing set. The walls were the same cream with a hint of a sage hues along with gold trim lining every nook and cranny that *could* be seen.

A sweet smell and sound greeted us and I closed my eyes to take it all in. Of course, there was the smell of old, used books but there was also a scent of honey and the lilac that seemed to be everywhere here. The sound of silence greeted me and it was almost enough to make me forget who stood next to me.

I began to wander and walk in and around the tall shelves full of books. I could tell which ones had been used recently and which ones hadn't due to the amount of dust coating the covers. My fingers brushed across the spines of the books and I read each and every title. The library in Elton Hode's manor hadn't been *half* as grand as this one and still, I found myself thinking about it and remembering when he had found me crouched in the corner, hiding. He had yanked me up and screamed at me saying that he was going to beat me—or worse.

And he definitely had done worse.

I blinked and came out of the memory, realizing my hand had stilled on a book. I bottled the pain up and took the book down, opening to the first page.

A hand touched my shoulder and I yelped elbowing whoever had just touched me, the book I had been reading flying from my hands.

"Ryn! It's just me!"

I whipped around at the sound of Skandar's voice and slammed him up against the bookshelf. "Don't sneak up on me like that," I hissed as blood dripped from his nose.

"Get off of me." He pushed me back and wiped his nose. "You've been here for hours, I didn't sneak up on you. If you hadn't been so absorbed in that book then maybe you would have heard me!"

"Right, so it's my fault. Next time just leave me alone, why don't you?"

"Fine."

"Good." I crossed my arms.

"You're absolute hell to be around."

The words stung but I snapped back, "I've been through hell and back, I guess a little rubbed off on me."

Skandar stormed past me and out the library doors. I snatched the book I had thrown and bent the page to keep the spot saved. I heard the library doors shut a little too loudly with how quiet the room was and rolled my eyes. I hadn't noticed the time flying by at all, it felt like I'd just picked up the book when in all reality, I was half way through it. I hooked it under my arm and began my search for others that were written about the history of the Day and Night elves.

If I was going to live here I might as well study up on them and learn all I could even if *some* of them were revolting and annoying to be around. I stopped suddenly and leaned against the bookshelf. The thought hadn't really crossed my mind until now.

I was free.

There would be no more *Death Pit* games or fights. No more bloodshed and no more chains trapping me in dark, small cells. Tears began to gather in my eyes but I didn't blink or wipe them away.

I was free from Lord Elton Hode and his evil games and ideas.

I held onto that feeling for the rest of the day. I barely thought of the annoying captain or anything else other than reading. I had acquired a cup of tea and plate of cookies and was content to remain in the library for the remainder of my life.

But those feelings were all too quickly snatched away when that dusking, while I was lying in bed trying to sleep, nightmares plagued my mind. I tossed and turned trying to get away from Elton and his son as they walked towards me carrying chains and cruel looking devices.

No, no, no.

Dark ice twirled around my fingers but it did nothing against them as they took me and strapped me down onto a table and began to work on me with the devices. I screamed and thrashed but there was nothing and no one to help me.

I jolted up with a scream expelling from my lips. The blankets were entangled around my neck, arms, and legs and it was an effort to get out of them before running to the bathing room to make it in time to vomit. Thus I remained there, head resting against the wall, not daring to fall asleep again.

I huffed. I was a damned fool to think I could have escaped him. A damned fool to believe I was ever truly safe or free.

I spent most of the next few day's reading. Of course, it was hard to tell when the days really ended and began when one was reading for such a lengthy amount of time. It didn't help that the sun never set either.

I read in the library, my ridiculously large bedchambers, the dining areas and ivy covered verandas. I read on the river banks while soaking in the sun and dipping my feet into the cool water. I read on the bridges in the gardens and lying on the grassy knolls.

The only way of escape was through the books that I read. My mind had become wholly silent and still unless I was poring over inky pages. I hated the stillness, it crept up behind me and wrapped its clammy hands around my mouth and suffocated me.

It was usually in that stillness that the memories and flashbacks came crawling back to aid in suffocating me. I barely slept because of the nightmares, thus I distracted myself with the books. What else was there to do in this utterly peaceful kingdom? There were no fights to compete in, no streets full of starving vagrants and no evil lords committing heinous acts of violence.

Even still, I did not know what to do. As much as I had longed for freedom, this was not it. This was not what I'd imagined and it made me rather ill-tempered. Thus, when the annoying and tedious captain poked at my toe moments after having switched to a different history book, it vexed me to say the very least.

"What do *you* want?" I snapped, not looking away from my book, if only so I didn't have to look at him.

"I have been assigned to be your personal escort and guard."

"And? Why must you bother me up close? Go sit by that tree and watch me from there." I nodded my head towards a weeping willow that's branches brushed the river rippling beneath it.

"*Our* queen has ordered me to be within grabbing distance in case of a possible threat."

I hadn't missed the emphasis he put on the word *our* and rolled my eyes. "Why the change?" I hadn't yet decided about the deal she had wanted to offer me, maybe this was her way of telling me to hurry up and make a decision.

"Queen Cressida does not answer to you. She can make changes how she sees fit. And to be honest, you are still an outsider. Perhaps it is *you* that must be watched and not any other possible threats."

I put a hand to my chest as if I were wounded by his assumptions and snapped the book shut. "Very well then, but don't speak to me."

The captain stared me down. "I will speak to whom I please."

"And does speaking to me please you?" I asked, eyeing him finally and staring into his golden brown eyes.

The muscle in his jaw twitched and he absently rested his hand on the hilt of the sword at his side. "If I say no, you win. But if I say yes, you will know I am lying."

"Then I have already won."

"Not if I were to say that it would be a pleasure speaking to you if you weren't so vexing."

I wrinkled my nose at a loss for words. Damn it.

He chuckled and plopped down onto the grassy knoll a few feet away but still close enough. I glared at him and threw a book at his head. To my dismay, he caught it and began looking at it.

"If you're going to be here all day you might as well help me," I said, turning back to the book I already held and opening it back up.

"What are you looking for?"

"Nothing and everything," I said, finding myself amusing.

"Why do you find me so disagreeable?" Skandar suddenly asked in the silence that had settled.

I peered over the spine of my book at him and ignored his question.

"You know, you should be thanking me. I am the one who saved you." He raised his eyebrows and they crawled half way up his forehead.

I rolled my eyes, covering my face with the book.

"Why were you chained up anyway? And. . .what happened to your back? You never told me."

I sucked in breath, the memory of the pain flickering across my mind. I felt uncomfortable in my own skin and didn't know what to do with my hands or face.

"Ryn?"

I snapped, "I don't need to answer your stupid questions, Skandar. You have no right to ask them."

"Fine, I was just trying to get to know you."

"Well don't. I don't want anyone getting to know me. Leave me alone."

I heard a *thunk* and then boots crunching in the grass. I dared a peek and watched as the captain walked away. Step by step doing just as I had asked, leaving me alone, whilst also disobeying the queen's orders.

Later that dusk, after a feast of food, I overlooked the waterfall careening to the depths below from the balcony I stood upon.

Standing next to one of the pillars with my arms wrapped around my waist, my copper dining dress swayed slightly in the light dusk breeze. My leathers had mysteriously disappeared so it was either this or wear nothing.

Out of the corner of my eye, I watched Skandar stride to the pillar next to mine.

"I am sorry about stomping off earlier," he said, crossing his arms and looking directly at me.

I tipped my head slightly to see him better and said, "You don't look it."

Dinner had been positively horrid. Skandar and I didn't say a word to each other which was fine with me but Queen Cressida had joined us to dine and had asked us both so many questions. I think she was trying to get us to talk to one another or better yet, purely humiliate us.

"It's not often that I find a fault and try to make it right—"

"Only when *your* queen demands it of you." I clasped my hands behind my back and stared at the view of tiny lights shimmering and shining in the gardens.

Skandar was quiet but I felt him slide closer to me. "I apologize of my own accord."

"Fine."

"Just fine?"

"Yes." I didn't offer him any more than that.

"What do I have to say to get you to talk to me, Lady Ryn?" Skandar leaned against the pillar and had the most devilish grin splayed across his face. I wanted to smack it right off of him.

"You can start by ending this *Lady Ryn* nonsense." "As you wish."

I rolled my eyes. "And on that note, I think I shall retire to my room." I kept my arms behind me and made to leave when Skandar pushed off of the pillar and strode next to me.

"There's something I'd like to show you before you retire, if that's alright?" His head was cocked to the side and the wind tousled his auburn hair.

"I'm rather tired," I argued.

"It will not be more than a few minutes." Captain Skandar looked down and the next thing I knew, his hand was in mine and he was pulling me down the golden hallways, past the ivy laced walls with various kinds of flowers that smelled of lilacs and sweet honey.

I halted, checking my surroundings. "Where are you taking me?"

"My secret spot," he whispered, looking back at me, an invitation in his eyes.

I stayed still and began searching him for weapons, after realizing what I was doing, I stopped myself. I was not in Helmfirth anymore, I was in the Sol Kingdom where it was peaceful and sunny and beautiful.

I looked around and stepped forward. Why the hell not?

I allowed him to continue to lead the way. I happened to gaze down at the rippling waters below us as we passed a bridge and I could see our reflections whizzing past. The wind whipped through our hair with the gold rays of the sun settling in around us. I realized for the first time that dusk and dawn were very different; when the day turned to dusk the light was so much softer than at dawn. It cast a different type of golden hue that I might have decided was my favorite.

We sprinted under weeping willows, the branches brushing our cheeks and tickling our noses, I wrinkled mine and felt like sneezing. But I felt Skandar slowing down, his grip still tight around my fingers, so I looked past his shoulder and saw what must be his so-called secret spot.

Amongst weeping willows and aspens was a shimmering small lake with a river flowing into it. Across a beautiful bridge lay a grassy knoll where tiny little bobs of light floated around. I could smell something sweet and the sound of the river babbling made me sleepy.

"Well, what do you think?" Skandar finally let go of my hand and leaned his forearms against the railing of the bridge.

I was gaping, I realized and made to shut my mouth just as he laughed. "What?" I asked defensively.

"You just look so shocked!"

"Well, I've never exactly seen anything like this. Are those fireflies?" I stepped forward, inching closer to the small nook of paradise.

"Well, fireflies in the human realm, yes, but here they're called firedragons here."

"You're kidding." I almost snorted.

"Nope," Skandar said, letting out a laugh.

"Who came up with what first?"

"Oh, definitely elves. We've been here *way* longer."

"Hmm." I didn't know what else to say, I didn't even know why I was out here with this giddy auburn haired elven male, and yet, I couldn't think of anywhere else I should be. So I stepped forward and sheepishly walked past Skandar. "Can I go over there?"

"By all means, Lady Ry—"

I shot him a look and he retracted. "Just Ryn," I reminded him.

Captain Skandar blinked as if he wasn't sure he could call me that but I sprawled out on the grass, my dark copper gown hitching somewhere above my knees, but I didn't care. I stuck my arms behind me and cradled my head in them. My eyes were closed when I felt Skandar sit next to me—not too close, but close enough to where I could smell him. His scent was like freshly chopped oak wood and sap.

I opened my eyes to look at him and found him staring at me already. My throat closed up and I suddenly felt uncomfortable and the air got extremely warm. I cleared my throat and made myself look up at the willow branches above us. What was I doing out here? Why was I even taking a dusktime stroll with an elven male who I could barely tolerate?

I groaned inwardly and shielded my eyes.

"What's wrong?" Skandar asked softly, a little too softly.

"I'm just tired." Lie, lie, lie.

"You're sure? You seem upset."

"I'm fine."

"Usually when people say that they're not."

This elven male did not give up. I was growing a bit irritated at his constant presumptions and foolish questions. My room and books were starting to seem a little more inviting by the minute. I was a fool to think I could enjoy this. Who was I to think I deserved this? Skandar didn't *know* me and yet he was trying to be a friend.

And that was the neverending issue; I didn't *have* friends.

I sat up and fixed my gown, saying, "I think I'll retire to my room now."

When I looked towards Skandar he looked hurt and confused but he helped me stand nevertheless.

"I hope it wasn't anything I said," he confessed, looking directly into my eyes.

"It's just. . .it's a lot to adjust to, you know?" I forced a smile to my lips but we both could tell it was forced.

"Of course, Ryn."

Skandar's eyes had become distant and faded and I felt a twinge of regret, but it was foolish of me to think I could pretend to be someone I wasn't.

CHAPTER

8

Once I was back in my room I tore off my gown and tossed it on the floor.

I splashed water on my face and brushed out my hair. Then I slipped on a soft dust pink nightgown before crawling into bed with a book in hand. Before I opened to the page I had been reading earlier, I lay there for a few moments. . .simply thinking.

I thought about the past few days, the conversations, and the walk with Skandar. If it had been different circumstances, maybe we would have enjoyed our time together. Instead, I had to go and ruin it—like I always did. But then again what did it matter?

Brushing the thoughts aside, I opened my book and picked up right where I left off; the scene where the two romantic interests had finally just kissed. I smiled as I read the scene unfold, wholly swallowed by the story, the reality of my own life forgotten.

And within that forgetfulness, dawn came too quickly.

I groaned at the constant stream of day seeping through my windows. I had pulled the drapes closed hoping it would block some of the light but my efforts were in vain. All throughout dusk I couldn't sleep, curtains shut or not. So, I had stayed up and finished the romance novel and started a new one by the time dawn came creeping over the horizon to take over.

I yawned and cursed quietly.

I was just about to get up and bathe or wash my face—something to refresh myself—when I heard a knock. I watched a slip of paper being thrust under the crack of my door. I looked around as if the note might be for someone else other than myself, but then timidly pushed the covers back and stepped out of bed. I reached down to pick the slip of paper up and opened it; the handwriting was delicate, written in inky black:

> *The Sol Kingdom awaits the ~~Lady~~'s. . .my apologies, Ryn's appearance for her official tour of her new home. A very special elven male would like to know if she will be attending?*

I rolled my eyes but a smile turned my lips upward. I crept towards the door and opened it expecting to see him standing there but. . .he was not. I frowned slightly and then my eyes flitted to the note once more. I noticed writing on the back so I flipped it.

> *If the lady in question wishes to tour the kingdom with the said elven male, she will be able to find him waiting in his secret spot.*

My heart did not jump at the words written—it dropped.

I scanned the window behind me for any sign of an escape. My shoulders sagged forward and I sighed, tossing the note away. He would be waiting a long time for me because I would not be joining him.

I walked into the bathing room and shut the door. I stripped off my nightgown and to my surprise, found the bathtub already full of steaming water. The whole room smelled like lemon and mint. Small glass bottles full of teal liquid to wash my hair and body sat at the edge of the tub that never seemed to run low. I covered myself and looked behind me, I even dared look in the small closet that was in the bathing room, but the only thing I found were more glass bottles and cream towels.

Confused, I turned back to the tub and found bubbles now floating to the edge. They floated in the air and popped once they got to the ceiling. I suddenly remembered that I was in an elven kingdom and that they had magic. I sighed and rolled my eyes, of course there would be magical bathtubs! I chuckled to myself and plunged in. The water was absolutely divine.

I lathered myself in the teal soap and scrubbed at my body and hair and face. The liquid soap smelled heavenly and I used almost half the bottle but once I set it down, it refilled itself. I dunked my head under the water and rinsed the soap suds out. I held my breath for as long as I could before breaking the surface of the bath water, it ran off of my face in tiny droplets.

I lay my head against the tub and absently wondered what it would be like to go on the tour with Skandar. Did I dare join him?

Before I knew it, I was drying off with a soft towel and rummaging through my closet that had seemingly filled overnight. Although, I assumed it was most likely Iris trying to coax me into wearing the dresses of the realm. My leathers still hadn't shown themselves and I had a right mind to assume she'd had something to do with their disappearance.

Sapphire blue caught my eye and I pulled the fabric out. This would do quite nicely.

I walked to the place Skandar had shown me, strolling past the branches of the willows and patches of grassy knolls with bubbling streams of water where above, pathways led to bridges for easier access to the other side. I looked down at the dress I had chosen to wear and even though I wasn't quite comfortable with the way I looked or the way my body was, I had felt decent enough.

The sapphire blue of the gown rippled as I walked, it had long sleeves that flared towards the end. The neckline scooped into a *V* and the fabric barely grazed my shoulders, whether it was a tad too big, or it was supposed to be like that I wasn't sure. I had slipped on my old boots but no one would be able to see them underneath the length of the gown.

I had swept my still wet hair up into a rather messy knot atop my head and, as much as I'd coaxed and tempted the shorter pieces to stay put, alas they did not. My cheeks felt rosy from the sun and the fresh air made me smile a little.

Today held the promise of being a good day; one full of new things and excitement. I had not felt this way in awhile, usually the only excitement was when I had been able to see the stars in the night sky of Helmfirth or right before a fight in the *Death Pit*.

I reached where I could see Skandar laying in the grass waiting for me, and a twinge of fear and shame poured over me, suffocating that excitement. I stopped suddenly and wondered if this had all been a very bad idea.

Too late. He had seen me.

From across the bridge he got up and waved in greeting. I felt a smile tug at the corners of my lips and crossed the gateway between him and I.

"You got my note."

It wasn't a question and I raised an eyebrow at him as he tried to kiss my fingers, but I pulled them away saying, "I almost didn't come."

"And why, pray tell, not?"

"You said the undesirable word."

"Ah." Skandar made his eyes big as if in shock. "I was hoping you could forgive me for that error."

"Hm, I'll need some convincing, Captain Skandar." I crossed my arms behind my back and smirked a little.

"I was thinking about breakfast out on the town?"

"Perhaps that will curb my need for revenge." I forced a quick smile.

We laughed together and set off across the bridge and onto a different pathway I had never taken. It was made of white cobblestones and reflected the sun's light extremely well, but was not blinding.

Along the way to wherever we were going, we passed many flower and plant patches of grass and streams upon streams of gurgling blue water running over pebbles and teeming with small fish.

I thought the water looked very similar to the dress I wore. We passed a few people and anytime males passed Skandar they always put a fist over their heart in lieu of greeting.

"You're quiet today," the captain said beside me.

I rolled my eyes, as if this elven male knew me well enough to say that I was being quiet today. "I'm usually quiet."

"You don't seem like the quiet type."

"And how would you know?"

"You read. The readers always appear quiet and then out of nowhere they'll surprise you."

"Are you speaking from experience?"

Skandar twisted his nose, caught off guard; just the way I had planned. I laughed, but not in a joyous way.

"Fine, you win." He scowled down at me.

I shrugged. "I didn't realize there was any other outcome."

Skandar laughed out loud at that and I wondered why he thought it was so funny, after all, I hadn't been joking.

I always won.

We continued walking and I tried to relax. I wasn't even sure why I had really agreed to this, or why I had taken a bath and gotten ready. But if I was being honest with myself. . .it had felt good. It felt good to take a bath and put on a pretty gown and look half decent at least. And then there was the part about it feeling like a grand day. Whether it was from reading all the novels, or pure delusion, I wanted to pretend this had always been my life.

Part of me wanted to keep myself locked up in my room and read all day, but the other part of me couldn't bear to be surrounded by four walls a moment longer. I shivered at the thought and could feel the ice crawling up my spine and neck to haunt me.

Just below us, in the heart of Sol, a roaring waterfall gushed from a cliff's edge and tumbled down in a sparkling teal lake that led into a river that flowed along the market venues, cafés, and shops. It flowed even further through the busier part of the kingdom and then off even further into the trees and pathways where I could just make out thatch roofed homes.

On either side of the huge lake and waterfall were gigantic white stone steps glinting in the sun's brilliance and leading down into the bustling chaos of the town. Over the waterfall was the biggest bridge I had ever seen, but the colors that reflected off of it were like that of a rainbow, but not a rainbow of the human world.

I couldn't believe how magical it looked. How the sun seemed to reflect and shine from Sol itself. I must have been gaping because Skandar looked at me with a twinkle in his eyes. He motioned for us to continue and we walked down the winding path that led to the gigantic steps. We descended every single step and just as we reached the bottom, my legs were aching and protesting against my weight and the effort of climbing down however many stairs that had been.

I glanced over my shoulder, with shame I noticed it was a hell of a lot less stairs than I had originally thought. That's when I realized that with all the reading and lounging around I'd been doing, I was losing the muscle I'd trained every single day for. My gut twisted at the thought and I wasn't even sure what to do with it. I had trained for the competitions, but that was no longer a requirement.

If I wanted to train, I knew a certain captain that would most likely know where the courtyard and equipment was. I bit my lip as we continued walking amongst the throngs of people. Since he was my guard, petitioned by the queen, he would most likely train with me as well. Could I tolerate him?

"Just down this way," he said, gesturing down a packed, white cobblestoned area.

I glanced around at all the people laughing and talking and enjoying themselves. They dined in cafés eating what smelled like delicious food and drinking steaming beverages from mugs.

I hoped we were going to just such a café that had food and drink like that. I was pleasantly surprised when Skandar turned abruptly and chose a seating area outdoors for us. He gestured to someone inside the building and I assumed he was a frequent customer for the workers to be able to recognize him.

Skander pulled my chair out for me and I sat across from him. I watched as someone brought out two glasses of water with mint and lemon garnishes.

"Thank you, Ersin." Skandar nodded his gratitude and the server reciprocated.

I didn't have a chance to thank the elven male before he scurried back indoors to his seemingly bustling shop. I turned back to the table before me and instantly noted that all the tableware was white with deep gold trim around the outermost part of the plates. The mugs were made in much the same way and the silverware was pure gold that glinted with the sun's rays. I chuckled to myself realizing that the silverware here was most definitely goldware.

"What are you smirking about over there?" Skandar asked playfully, he quickly checked himself and straightened his dark teal jacket. "Did I drool or something?"

My eyes twinkled at that and I felt a laugh rising in my chest. "No, I was simply thinking of how the silverware here is actually goldware."

Captain Skandar's brown eyes lit up and his mouth curled upwards into a wide grin. "She makes jokes!" He turned as if he were going to pull someone off the street and yell to them what he had just told me.

"Skandar," I hissed, sheepishly looking around.

He turned back to me and leaned back in his chair. "I didn't know you were funny."

I rolled my eyes. "I'm not."

"Evidence would say otherwise."

I sighed and twirled the fabric of my napkin. My fingers trembled a little with nervousness. I hoped he couldn't see. I glanced around to distract myself and realized how the streets bustled and echoed with the sounds of merry making. It sounded all too similar to the party's that Elton would throw.

I swallowed as my stomach twisted and my palms began to moisten. Maybe it had been a grave mistake to come here.

"So, how many books have you read since being here?" Skandar asked, not seeming to notice the turmoil I was experiencing.

I was glad for a distraction. "I've actually read them all."

His eyes went wide. "What?"

I picked up my glass of water and before taking a sip said again, "I've read every single one of the ones in my room at least."

"I mean, it's a good thing. We will just need to get some more," he said, smoothing out his jacket. "Good thing there's a library."

"I like romances and mysteries if you ever find more," I replied, setting my glass back down on the table.

"I shall keep my eye out for them then."

After our brief conversation about books, Skandar and I talked very little, it wasn't necessarily awkward. I was enjoying being outside with the sun on my face, although I desperately wished the streets would be quiet. Once our food arrived, Skandar dug into his downing three glasses of water and whatever else he had ordered in that huge mug, he had said it was mead.

I, however, picked at my food and sipped my water. It wasn't that the food was bad, quite the opposite, it was delicious. I had been craving just this sort of food, but my appetite was strange and I couldn't help but think how when I had nightmares, my body would rid itself of the food I'd consumed.

I tried to push it aside and was able to take small bites of my platter.

Skandar paid the bill and thanked the café owners on our way out. I had enjoyed sitting there soaking in the sun and conversing with Skandar, even if we hadn't talked much. It was nice to just have someone to sit with other than a book.

We strolled through the streets like all the people I had been watching earlier and I found myself gazing at all the unique little shops along the way. Through the windows I could see clothing shops with more things than I knew existed, galleries full of art and paintings of what were most definitely locations of Sol. There were shops full of pottery objects and I could even see someone at the potter's wheel creating something, his hands, face, and clothes covered in clay.

I stopped to watch and found a smile turning my lips upward. The elven male who sat at the wheel must have felt me staring, because he looked up and smiled at me with crooked teeth and sparkling eyes.

Skandar led the way through the streets, passing more cafés and shops and places where people seemed to be creating and making things. From bakeries to blacksmiths to bars, there was so much to see. Everything smelled of lilacs and mint and fresh grass. I took in a breath of the fresh air and felt the wind tousle my hair.

"I want to take you to one more absolutely gorgeous view, Ryn," he said, looking back at me and that's when I realized I had stopped in the middle of the street. My cheeks grew warm and I quickly caught up to him. He led us out of town and I could tell we had looped back around towards the castle.

A stream of gurgling water rippled to our right beneath weeping willows and the backs of all the shops, cafés, bars, and places of creation lay to our left, the sounds finally muffled. We were on a grassy pathway that angled upwards a little and I wondered where we were going. But as we broke the treeline and I saw stairs looming before us and that beautiful bridge beyond, I knew.

We crossed the bridge and leaned against its glass railing smack dab in the middle. Very few people were on the bridge, so it was mostly Skandar and I. Crossing the bridge had made me realize why it looked like a rainbow. But not any rainbows I had seen in the human world. This. . .this was different.

The bridge was made of glass so it reflected the sun's rays and the sapphire water below sparkling and rippling. If I looked hard enough, I could see life teeming below in the water, and the pebbles at the very bottom were all different colors, which made the rainbow-like effect.

It was truly stunning.

As I leaned my elbows on top of the railing I closed my eyes and breathed in deep, smelling all the scents and taking in the warmth. I would definitely be coming back here, maybe even with a book.

"What do you think?" Skandar asked, staring straight at me.

I looked at him out of the corner of my eye, half because I didn't want to take my eyes off of the lovely sight and half, because I didn't want to face him fully. I drew air into my lungs and said, "It is truly one of the loveliest things I have ever seen." It was the truth, but then again I hadn't *seen* very much of the world.

Skandar seemed proud as a wide grin spread across his face. "I hope that. . .you enjoyed today."

The pause in his words had me holding my breath. I wasn't sure what I had thought he was going to say but my heart hammered against my ribcage. I nodded and flashed him a smile. There was nothing I could think of to say, and even if I had, I am not sure if my dry throat would have allowed me to.

"Shall we head back then?" Skandar held an elbow out to lead us back to the castle and I took it flashing a smile.

I reminded myself that this was not a performance. I could be me here.

As we walked back in companionable silence, I realized that today had proven to be wonderful afterall. My insecurities and concerns had almost let it get the best of me. I cursed Elton for having done this to me. But I was slowly beginning to realize that that was no longer my life.

I hoped at least.

I would always carry the scars of what I'd endured but perhaps there was yet a light to be found. Perhaps I could find it here.

I cringed at the thought of how my muscles had become lax and turned to Skandar as we continued our walk. "Do you think you could show me to the training yards tomorrow?" I asked, if not a bit quietly.

Skandar glanced at me, surprise written across his face. "Of course."

And that was the end of our conversation and the end of our day. He escorted me to my room and bowed dramatically as he left.

However, I found myself smiling as I closed my door.

Not because I felt anything for this male but simply because I had enjoyed this day. . .with a friend.

CHAPTER 9

Hands strangled me.

Strong, forceful hands wrapped around my throat and pushed me further into the bedframe. I tried to scream but my throat was silent. I tried to kick and claw but the hand was relentless. There was no face that I could see but I knew who it was.

My head hit the headboard and this time my throat allowed a pathetic cry to escape. My vision faded in waves of black and I could see the face now, the smiling, hateful face of Lord Elton Hode, strangling me.

Air, I needed air— "Ryn!!"

I jolted awake, blankets flying, head smarting, and vision blurry. I scrambled away from him, my hair covering my face so that I could barely see through it.

"Ryn, you were screaming, I thought someone was in here!" I knew that voice. It was the captain.

I inhaled, took a heavy breath and swiped my hair away from my blurry eyes. I rubbed at them and realized I had been sobbing. My face and lashes were soaked.

"Are you quite alright?"

Skandar came into view, kneeling beside me on the bed, hands in the air as if I'd tried to hit him perhaps. I breathed again. No, I was clearly not alright. I was a fool to think I could ever actually enjoy what I had without the damned man who'd ruined me.

I sighed, sobs still wracking my body.

"Can I do anything?" he tried again.

"No," I muttered. I struggled out of the sheets trapping me and rushed to the bathing room where I emptied the contents of my stomach. Heat filled my face at the fact that Skandar could probably hear everything.

"I'll be out in just a minute. Would you ask Iris for my leather's back please?" I leaned my head against the wall and listened as the sound of his boots paused outside of the bathing room door and then left.

I sighed and I must have drifted somewhere deep into my mind because not too long after, Skandar returned with my leather trousers. Now freshly cleaned and with a new white tunic and belt. I took them gratefully and changed in the bathing chamber, coming out into the room to sit on the bed and lace up my boots.

"Are you sure you're okay?" Skandar leaned against the bedpost and was looking at me, curiously.

I shrugged his comments off. "Yes. It's nothing."

"It doesn't seem that way. I hear you screaming from out in the hall. You hardly ate yesterday, you're vomiting it up and now you're saying it's nothing?" His eyebrows were raised and he seemed to be judging me.

I hated the way I felt under his scrutiny. "I'll be fine," I snapped, sauntering out of the room, putting the performer side of myself in charge. If anything, so that I could actually get through the day and pretend I was fine.

However, it did little to fool the captain. The entire time we practiced and trained, he kept looking at me. At first, I thought it was because he was impressed with how much I knew about exercising, but that thought seemed rather prideful. He glanced at me with worry and concern, not admiration.

I was nothing but a nuisance and a guest to *escort* around, this was technically his job. Queen Cressida had ordered him to keep an eye on me so that I didn't escape. She needed me—needed my magic.

But all my life I had been used for my magic. Whether it was for a good cause or evil intention, I didn't think I wanted to give it up anymore. I had decided that I'd like to keep it to myself.

The sun beamed down on us in the training courtyard. Sweat trickled down my brow, back, and arms. I wiped it off on my tunic every so often so it would quit stinging my eyes. I was in the midst of my usual routine that I used to do in Helmfirth when I felt eyes watching me.

I continued doing the routine but slowly slid my gaze to where Skandar was fighting an invisible opponent with a long sword. But he wasn't looking at me, he was intently focused on his training. Ice cracked in my veins and shivers ran down my spine. Slowly, I stopped what I was doing and glanced over my shoulder.

Queen Cressida stared down at me from a balcony, two guards were positioned at her side. When our eyes met she did not look away, nor did she smile. She wore different apparel to what I'd seen her wear in the past, from where I was on the training ground I couldn't see much but it almost looked like travel garb.

"Your Majesty," Skandar said, bowing. He must have just noticed she was standing there watching us.

I bowed respectfully, but couldn't help feeling strange.

"It is good to see you are enjoying your time here, Ryn. I trust you have become well acquainted with your new home?"

"Yes, quite, thank you." Shivers ran up and down my arms.

"I depart in just a few minutes but wish to bid you farewell," Cressida spoke, inclining her head to me. "I trust you will have made your decision when I return?"

Fear coursed through me and something told me to keep quiet about the decision I had made. So, I just nodded my head, plastering a smile across my face. This was just another performance.

"I leave you in charge, Captain." She raised her eyebrows and then nodded to her guards. "Until I return."

Then she was gone.

I glanced at Skandar but he had returned to his training, sweat glistening in the light. He seemed perfectly unbothered while I felt nauseous and cold, as if clouds had passed over the sun.

Hours later, Skandar escorted me back to my rooms and bid me good day after asking if I needed anything. He'd offered to bring me a morsel to eat and now I was regretting snapping at him to leave me alone, because I was famished.

I had tried to read to distract myself but to no avail as my stomach growled extremely loudly. Thus, I braved the world outside of my room and snuck through the halls to find my way to the kitchen. It was after several minutes of wandering around that I finally came to the realization that I would not be able to find it without help.

Reluctantly, I began searching for the captain instead. I had thought it would be easier to find him but even that proved to be an impossible task. Once I felt that I had searched the palace to its entirety, I wandered outside. The glow of the dusk sun set everything in a brilliant warm hue and made everything appear golden.

I smelled lilac bushes and the sweet scent of willow trees swaying in the wind and I could have sworn I smelled something sweet baking. However, just as I reached a bridge and began walking over the gurgling stream below it, I heard a whip crack. I instantly hit the floor and held my breath.

A loud scream followed the sound of another lash of the whip. I flinched, memories flashing in my own mind of times that I had endured the cruelness of that particular punishment. But why the hell was someone being whipped here?

Another *crack* and I glanced over my shoulder. The sound that emanated from the female was gut wrenching, all thoughts of finding something to eat completely vanished from my mind as I went into survival mode.

I whirled around, brushing my loose hair out of my face and behind my back as I crawled towards a rose bush that was about as high as the tops of my knees. I peered over the hedge and beheld a sight that twisted my gut.

People—elves—were chained together, being pulled and pushed along by two guards at the front and two at the back. One female in particular, had fallen and was now being whipped by a guard clad in black leather—not the usual dress of the Sol Bloods, or so that I had seen.

I squinted closer and felt something nudge my shoulder as if to encourage me to go and help the poor female but I stood my ground. It would do me no good to get caught. But something froze my blood at what was happening here.

I watched as they finally stopped whipping the female and yanked her up, her dress fell off of her shoulders revealing her bare breasts and horribly torn and bleeding back.

I knew what that felt like. My gut clenched.

I should go help.

I swallowed and watched as she fell in line behind the rest, finally submissive and humiliated enough. They marched around the side of the palace wall and disappeared out of sight, the cries and the clang of chains disappearing with them.

I sat back on my heels and stared into nothing. I should have helped her—helped all of them.

I *had* magic. Why hadn't I just killed the guards and freed the poor souls?

Coward.

The word floated towards me and I tried swatting it away from my mind. Coward, coward, coward.

I groaned and looked back to where the line of elves and their guards had disappeared. I knew what I was about to do regardless if my brain and heart aligned.

I slunk behind the corner of the building to a well worn path leading to an iron door.

Damn. It had to be iron.

Greenery and underbrush pressed up against me as I stood back to assess the door.

It had no handles and glinted in the dusk light. I crossed my arms and fought the urge to just go knocking on the door and simply say the queen had sent me. In the end, I decided that that would be a foolish idea for when she returned they might ask her and find out I had lied. Before I could think of another option, the iron door hissed open. I ducked behind the bushes and crouched low.

Two of the four guards walked out. Now.

It was now or never.

As soon as the guards walked far enough away, I darted for the iron door that was slowly closing behind them. Careful of their peripheral vision and the casualties of the iron, I slipped through the slight opening as it got smaller and smaller. It singed my arm as I burst through and I had to silence the cry that threatened to escape my throat.

The smell hit me first. I gagged and clamped a hand over my nose and mouth. I knew that smell all too well; it was death and blood and human waste.

I crouched against the wall as the iron door clicked shut and angled myself in the shadows along the walls, listening. Distant chains rattled and clanked and the sound of muffled sobs floated towards me.

What the hell was this place? And why was it in the Sol Kingdom? I had seen nothing but peace and light and brilliance, but now, to see something that felt so evil and so wrong, nauseated me.

I swallowed the fear that rose up in me and checked my surroundings. The walls and floors were made of stone, there was no light in this place and no windows or sconces. I peered into the dark and could make out a hallway with stone walls on either side, nothing more.

I looked back at the iron door, there was nothing for it but to see what lay past the hall. One more look and I was creeping along the wall making no sound whatsoever. I kept my hand running alongside the stone as my eyes adjusted to the dimness. Once it did, I trailed the drops of blood along the floor, some of the splatters old and some fresh.

Whispers of evil and musty air met my face as I came to a split in the hallway. The blood trail led to the right and I felt a twinge of something strange and yet familiar down that way even though I had never set foot here before.

I turned to look down the left tunnel and before I could fully look, was slammed into the stone wall by a brute force. My nails scraped against the stone as I tried to catch myself and before I could even turn around, a heavy fist came crashing into my lungs from behind. I clenched my mouth shut and whirled, blocking the third blow with my crossed forearms, pushing myself into my attacker.

"Thought you'd sneak around for a bit, eh?"

The raspy voice of the guard didn't sound human and it certainly didn't sound elven. I stared into the black hole that was his face and squinted to see through his hood, it only earned me his jaw crashing into the side of my head and I stumbled back, open and vulnerable.

I needed to get it together.

The man or male, whatever he was, ran at me and brought his elbow down into my windpipe. I gasped for air as it rushed out of me and brought my legs up to kick the guard in the shins. He swore loudly and I noticed he started favoring the other leg. Another swoop of his leather covered arm and I ducked, rolling away even as my chest barked in pain. I finally dragged air through my nose and rose to my feet, battle stance ready just like in the *Death Pit*.

The guard came at me again but I was ready this time and swung my own punch to the side of his face and just as he went to block it, punched the other side of his face with the other knuckle that was waiting to strike. I didn't give him time to think as I jabbed his unblocked throat and then went for the gut. Just when I was about to bring my knuckle up to send his nose into his skull, he grabbed my hands and spread them so far apart I thought they'd rip off. I kicked and thrashed, trying to get out of his grip but he was too strong.

"Pity you'll die the same as the other low lives down here." His voice sent shivers through me and made me sick to my stomach.

"And what way would that be?" I spat, trying to get him to talk.

But he only yanked my arms further and kneed me in the stomach. I bent over in pain, darkness creeping at the corners of my vision. I shook my head and blinked and saw the only chance I might have to survive this. The guard loosened his hold for a split second to reach for his dagger, but it was already in my hands. I sliced his throat too fast for him to even notice until he was falling to the stone floor a second later, his blood pooling beneath him.

I coughed and doubled over, hands on my knees as I wretched from the punch I'd received to my gut. I wiped my mouth and uncoiled, coughing a bit. I stuffed the dagger in my boot and turned back to the door.

If they had guards at every corner, even if I had the element of surprise, someone would start asking questions about who was spilling their blood. All too soon Queen Cressida and Skandar would get involved and I couldn't risk it.

I would have to find a different way to explore this hell hole.

I slipped back through the iron door, kicking it shut with my dagger-concealed boot. Instead of going around the corner in case anyone saw me, I pushed past the underbrush and stepped through the greenery. My hair snagged on the low hanging branches and I ducked to avoid them.

Insects buzzed around me and I swatted them away just in time to see that my hand was covered in blood—black blood. I turned it over to inspect it and realized my clothes were covered in that *things* blood as well. I jerked my head up and scanned the area for running water.

I heard it before I spotted it and dashed in that direction, stepping out of the foliage. It would be no good for someone to see me with black blood covering every inch of me. I spotted the water and kicked my boots off slipping the dagger in the left one, then shucked my shirt and pants off and dove into the rippling river, remaining only in my underclothes. I broke the surface of the water and scrubbed everything on me; my face, my arms, my hands, my hair.

The sky split and spread from rose and lavender hues to golden and blue hues seeping in through the trees. I could just barely make out a few stars—the only form of night the Sol Kingdom would ever see—as they twinkled into existence.

I scrubbed at my scalp and rung the river water from my hair. The cool droplets fell over my bare skin and I assumed it would have felt refreshing, if it didn't feel like blood. I had thought my days of killing, of threats and fights were over but according to what had just occurred, that was far from the truth.

I would find out just what the hell was happening here, at whatever cost. Queen Cressida was not who she said she was and I was starting to wonder if Skandar fell in that category with her.

"Hello there."

I whirled around clutching my hair in my hands. Captain Skandar looked down at me with those warm brown eyes of his that seemed to glow in the dimming light and was smirking.

"How long have you been there?" I snapped, glancing around. My bloody clothes were still on the bank and I flicked my gaze away from them instantly so as not to draw attention to them.

"Not long. I just saw you and was very curious as to what you were doing. Is your bathtub broken?"

I rolled my eyes, my thundering heart skidding around. "No."

"Then what, pray tell, are you doing out here?" Skandar shucked off his jacket and began unbuttoning his slacks.

"What are *you* doing?" I averted my eyes as he pulled his tunic off and revealed a very muscled and tan chest. I didn't want him here. I did not trust him nor did I want him to see how shaken up I was. For all I knew, he oversaw what was happening.

"It just so happens I need a bath. . .and I'm already here." Skandar, now stripped down to his underclothes, waded ever so slowly into the river.

I finished ringing out my hair and ducked underwater again to give it a good rinse, just to make sure it was clean. When I came up out of the water Skandar was much closer than before and my breathing hitched.

"Your eyes are huge," he said, tipping his head to the side with that cocky grin of his.

"My eyes are perfectly normal," I bit back. Glancing behind him as I planned my way of escape.

"Yes, yes they are *Lady* Ryn. I've never seen more beautiful eyes."

"Really? Is that what you tell all the females around here?" I gave his shoulder a slight push, trying to act normal. "And don't call me lady."

"I'll do as I please." He swam away and kicked water in my face.

I grimaced, wiping it away and splashed water back in his own face. "Oh. . .oh *now* you've done it, Lady Ryn!"

Skandar laughed and pushed a wave of water at me but I ducked under the water to miss it and swam away. I popped up on the other side of him closer to the bank and splashed him from behind. He lunged for me and grabbed my foot dragging me through the water. Bubbles shoved themselves up my nose and once I surfaced I couldn't stop sneezing or coughing.

"Don't—*achoo*—don't ever do that—" I rubbed my nose and coughed again. "Don't do that ever again!"

But we looked at each other and he began laughing as I glared at him. My underclothes were soaked through and becoming a little too loose for comfort. My stomach was still in knots over what had happened and the water felt like I was swimming in a pool of blood. I wanted to leave.

But Skandar continued swimming and splashing and was now floating on his back. I thought this might be the perfect opportunity to slip away.

"What are you thinking about?" he asked, breaking the silence.

"Just the beauty of the sky," I lied.

"Ah, a true wonder to behold."

"Indeed."

A sound of water rippling and a few seconds later I felt the presence of the captain beside me as he treaded in the water.

I tensed.

"Are you ever going to tell me what happened to you?"

I dragged my gaze toward him and began treading water lightly brushing my hands through the cool ripples. "I don't know."

Definitely not now.

"I want you to trust me, Ryn," he whispered.

My heart stopped. "I can't." I would never trust anyone ever again, especially not these people.

"Why?"

"I hardly know you."

"Liar."

I leveled my gaze at him. "I am. I'm a liar and a fighter and a killer. You don't want me to trust you."

And with that I stepped out of the water that sent a chill spreading through my bones and my very blood. I snatched my clothes up and didn't bother to put them on as I walked away, leaving the captain in his own undergarments in the river.

CHAPTER 10

I snuck back through the same foliage path I had taken yesterday. I sighed and pushed a forearm over my head to block a low hanging branch. I wore my old boots, different brown leather slacks Iris had graciously given me since mine were still soaked, and a deep olive green long sleeve tunic. I still had the male's knife, whom I killed yesterday. It wasn't the same as my lucky charm back in Helmfirth but it was a weapon nonetheless.

I waited, making sure no one was coming or going through the iron door and made my move. A few bounds and I was hunched next to the door, dagger in hand and already edging it in next to the latch. Good thing I sharpened the blade this morning.

After a few horrendous scratching sounds, and even a few blue sparks flying as soon as my skin touched the iron, I had wiggled my blade in between whatever was keeping this door latched and twisted it in. It made a clicking sound and hissed open.

I quickly nudged it open with my boot and then slipped inside. My fingers still burned from where the iron had singed me but I ignored it. They would only turn into more scars and calluses I could add to the list.

Once the door shut I began my venture deeper into this hellhole. I passed the split in the hallway where I'd killed that male—his blood still staining the ground—and took the right pathway even as I felt a tug to go left. That same blood from the day before had left a trail to the right and I followed it. I wanted to see what they were doing with these people.

I passed stone doors on either side of the hallway that were sealed shut, I knew because I'd tried to open them. I held my hand near the cracks of one and could feel something both icy and hot emanating forth. It made frost coat my fingertips and my magic thrum in my veins. I took my hand away and the frost melted back into my fingers.

Interesting.

I heard the rattling of chains and the sobs and moans of females and males. I instantly crouched and crawled towards the opening—a ledge more like. Stone steps on either side trailed down into a stone cathedral or pit of some sorts. The ceiling was domed and made a full circle the same as the floor beneath it. Every inch of the walls below were covered with chains. . .and people hanging from those chains.

I caught the breath in my throat before it released and gazed at each and every face of the captives; young, old, female, male. The manacles wrapped around each of their wrists and ankles and they were all linked together and chained to one big bolt at the very center of the ceiling. It would be impossible to set them all free without freezing or sawing their very hands and feet to get the cuffs off.

I remembered what those iron cuffs felt like; the burning sensation whenever they came on or off.

I seethed under my breath and cursed. What the hell *were* they doing?

I scanned the stone arena once more and noted that some of the elves looked a lot paler, if not bluish-gray compared to the others. Some looked as if they had the very life sucked out of their bones while others still looked normal, as normal as one can look whilst chained to a ceiling.

I didn't see anything else that would help me, no exits, no windows, no openings to aid in an escape so I silently backed away and uncoiled to a standing position once I got far enough away. I leaned against the wall, dagger still in hand and laid my head back.

A wave of nausea hit me and I tried to stop the flashbacks but they came far too quickly. Maybe it was seeing those people chained up, hopeless and alone. Maybe it was the smell in this place that smelled so familiar and so awful. Maybe it was the fact that I was about to leave them all down there and couldn't do anything about it.

Not now at least.

There was so much to think about, so much to act on and yet I was just one person.

How could I be enough to save them all?

I slunk away, unwanted tears brimming in my eyes.

Once I reached the path in the halls I went left. I wanted to see what was calling to me and tugging at me. But as soon as I set foot down the hall I knew something was wrong. Frost coated my fingertips, my lips, my nose. My magic was responding to something down here and as I continued, my head started pounding.

I tried to focus on the hall before me, my feet moving and dagger in hand but there was such a dull thudding in my head that it pierced through and made me wince in pain. I looked down the hall a little ways and could only make out faint stone walls and more chains...or perhaps a cage. I heard snarls and hisses but my vision blurred so viciously that I couldn't see the floor in front of me.

A hand pressed to my pounding head I stumbled back the way I'd come. The further away I got from the left hall, the more my vision returned and the pounding ceased. At the entrance I slumped against the wall and regained my composure.

What the hell was in there? What secrets was the Sol Kingdom, and perhaps their queen, keeping down here?

I heard stifled cries down the other hallway where the prisoners chained to the walls were and another vicious snarl from the one I'd just come from. I decided I couldn't do anything for any of them leaning against the wall so I slipped out of this hellhole to find other answers.

"Ryn, what the bloody hell are you doing in there?"

I jumped away from the iron door I'd just slipped through and came face to face with Captain Skandar. My throat and lungs stopped working and I stared at him. I didn't know whether I was afraid, deeply curious or fuming with rage at the fact that the captain knew about this place. Out of my three options, I assumed it was fuming rage as frost bit at my fingertips and a cold breath of air expelled from my mouth as I opened it.

"You *know* about this place?" I spat.

Skandar looked at the now closed iron door behind me and then flicked his gaze back to me. "Yes."

I scoffed, nothing but a humorless laugh coming out. "So *this* is what the queen has planned for me, is it?" I fidgeted with the dagger at my side.

"Ryn, we don't need to go through all of this now. I'll say I never saw you here and you'll say the same." He went to grab me but I jerked my hand away.

"I'll say no such thing. What are they doing with the prisoners in there?"

"You're not really in a position to be asking questions."

I flicked my knife out before he could blink and pressed it to his throat. "How about now?"

His eyes grew wide and he seemed to have halted his breathing.

"Care to tell me why there are *people* chained to the ceiling?" A shiver slithered through my body at the words. Yes, I had fought and killed for an audience so that they would find their bloodlust curbed. But I *knew* what it was to be chained and to be treated like an animal. This type of cruelty I would not stand for.

It enraged me that this was happening to others, that I had been taken away from Helmfirth, given a supposedly perfect life, only to be like a pig for slaughter.

I poked the edge of the dagger closer to Skandar's throat and hissed through my teeth, "Tell me now, Captain."

"Go to hell."

"I probably already am. Try something new."

He rolled his eyes and I pricked his skin just enough to scare him but he stepped forward, pressing the sharp point into his own throat. It caught me off guard and I loosened the grip, not wanting to slice him. . .just yet.

"What's the matter? Not so confident anymore are you?" Skandar continued pressing me back but I slackened the blade so it barely grazed him.

That was my second mistake, my first being the fact that I spared him when I should have just sliced him, ear to rutting ear.

My back barked in pain as the captain slammed me against the iron door and in pain the knife fell away from his exposed neck, a slight trickle of blood dribbling down. I cringed and opened my mouth to let out a cry of pain but clamped my teeth together. I welcomed the hurt so that I could squat and grab the hilt of my knife and slash Skandar across the face. He yelled and fell away, I jumped away from the door, angling the dagger for a fight.

"You—"

I ignored the nasty name he called me and bared my teeth at him. The cut went deep across his jaw, barely missing his ear. The blood trickled down and he growled at me.

"Next time don't push me," I snapped, my words dripping with bitterness and death. But a part of me felt sorrow, I had wanted to trust that Skandar wasn't a part of this. It seemed I had hoped in vain. "Are you going to answer me or not?"

"I will not forget what you've done and I think you already know what is going on."

"And *I* will not forget this." I waved my hand back at the iron door, indicating his effort at burning me and the captives locked deep in the dark halls.

"You better watch your back." Skandar backed away into the foliage, glaring at me.

I tipped my head back and laughed. "You better watch *yours*."

CHAPTER 11

Things had changed since finding the captives and the incident with Captain Skandar.

I hadn't seen him since and he hadn't come to kill me when the light was at its lowest. Even though I stayed up nearly every night waiting for him. Due to the lack of sleep, I had finally thought of creating a trap if ever someone were to come barging in during the wee hours of dawn or dusk.

No one came to ask questions and the queen had still yet to return. Which was the perfect time to execute my plan. I needed to get out but I wasn't going to be foolish about it.

"Iris, would you mind getting me some more ink and parchment paper?" I asked, sipping from my mug and biting into a crispy piece of toast.

"Out of all your sketching supplies so soon?" Iris crooned as she neatly placed a throw over the couch.

"Indeed," I mumbled over my toast.

"I shall return shortly then." And with that, the door clicked shut behind the ever clueless servant girl.

I snatched up another piece of toast and slathered butter across it. The drapes fluttered in the warm wind and I finished my breakfast staring out the window. Summer had come to full bloom here and the flowers and trees were all bright with their assorted colors. But it all looked rather dull and ugly to me knowing there were people far below me who were suffering; their very magic and quite literally their lives being drained from them.

Such evil being done in such a beautiful and peaceful place was strange and made me feel hollow inside. Or maybe that feeling had always been there; this was just a lovely reminder of all the things I'd endured.

I shut my eyes against those memories and focused on the task at hand.

"Here we are!" Iris spoke cheerily, bursting in through the door with a bottle of ink and an assortment of different color parchments.

"On the desk will do." I walked over to where one of the papers was drying on the floor and studied my work. What an excellent drawing it was too.

"I love the flowers and how the river looks like it's actually running," the servant girl said over my shoulder.

Ignoring her compliment, I grazed one eye over her. "That will be all."

Iris straightened suddenly and nodded, taking her leave. Truly, the girl could be such a pest. Once I could no longer hear her light footsteps, I scrambled to the bathing room and took out of the cupboard the other parchment papers—the real ones I had been working on. I spread them across the floor and placed the empty plate of toast on one corner and the half empty mug on the other.

My masterpiece.

Kneeling down, I peered closer to the part that was unfinished and began to sketch the layout of the iron halls that led to the prisoners. I carefully marked which pathway to take with a symbol and began sketching the lines of any and all possible exits.

Which were none. . .except back through the iron door.

I sighed and drank the rest of my now-cold hot chocolate. I needed to scout out more escape routes if I was going to do this. I waved a hand over the fresh ink and blew on it to encourage it to dry.

Sprinting up I snatched my black trousers and dark green shirt and quickly went to change in the bathing room. Coming out again I glanced down at the ink and pulled half of my hair back so it was out of my face but still allowing the full waves to fall down to my waist.

I sat on the floor next to the map and laced up my boots over my wool socks and tested the ink to see if it was dry.

It was.

I rolled it up and stuffed it in the storage area in the bathing room and checked to make sure everything was as it should be. My eyes snagged on the sketch that I was supposed to be working on and I added a few more lines to the river and some birds in the branches and then swiped a few flowers in the field, in case Iris came in and expected something to look different.

I passed very few people but, those I did come across, dipped their heads in respect and hurried about their day. I heard whispers that the queen might be returning soon and that everything needed to be in tip top shape. I heard nothing about a certain captain or the new scar he had running down the side of his face.

How interesting. It seemed as if the captain had gone into hiding.

I smirked and held my chin high as I crossed over multiple bridges, through courtyards and vineyards and grass pathways. I arrived at the massive bridge passing over the sapphire lake that flowed right from the Sol Palace itself and gazed at it for a moment. The wind tousled my hair, sending it spinning this way and that.

It truly was such a magnificent place—*was*—because no place could ever hold beauty when such evil lurked in its depths.

My brow furrowed in anger and I inhaled and began my crossing over the bridge. I needed time and space to plan out my next moves and to commit every inch of this place to memory. This was simply another *Death Pit* with yet another opponent to conquer.

I sat back on a bench surrounded by grassy patches and knolls and gardens full of sweet smelling flowers and buzzing bees. I could hear a brook babbling nearby and the breeze swept by in a graceful motion. Tall willow trees swayed around me and golden light spilled through the branches, splashing upon my suntanned face.

It made me nauseous, I hated the way the lilac smelled and the sound of the running water. I rolled my eyes and turned my gaze to study the palace from afar. I could just barely hear the sounds of the cobblestone streets where vendors and cafés were opening up and hurrying about their workload for the day. I knew there would be no way of escape through town with hollow faced victims trailing behind me.

I scanned the guards posted on the parapets and towers that would be able to see for miles upon miles, especially with their keen elven senses. My eyes snagged on the waterfall that cascaded down from the cliff edge just above the palace. A thought waltzed into my mind and I instantly stood. If I could just. . .

Yes. It might just work.

I strode back down the cobblestone pathway and nodded at the guards as I walked out of the palace grounds. The gates stayed open behind me with vines and flowers weaving in and out of the crevices.

I despised the fresh air that greeted me and could not wait to be rid of this place. The sooner the better. I began the climb up the grassy knoll to the top of the cliff with little struggle. Perhaps all the days spent training had paid off, afterall.

When I reached the summit, mist from the waterfall floated up towards me and caressed my skin and hair. The droplets of water clung to my eyelashes and I ever so carefully looked over the edge. The water careened down and down until it met with a small river that flowed right through the heart of the palace and wound all the way through and under the great bridge just at the edge of the town.

The sun's rays shone down upon me and glinted in the river, blinding me with its reflection. As far as my elven eyes could see rolling fields and hills of green and yellow expanded for miles and miles. A grouping of tall trees surrounded the edges of the fields and stretched even farther. Behind me, I could just make out the shapes of dark mountains with roiling dark clouds above them.

I sighed and shoved my hands in my pockets. There was hardly anywhere to hide, to escape the elven senses. I made to sit down on a flat rock next to the river when I sensed something—someone behind me.

I slowly reached for the dagger in my boot when he spoke. "Scouting out the grounds are you?"

I slowly turned and faced him, the male with the auburn hair and the fresh scab running along his face. "Taking a stroll actually," I lied.

"Don't let me stop you then."

"But you already have."

Skandar squinted at me, his hands folded behind his back. He must have noticed me staring at his cut because he said rather bitterly, "Enjoying seeing what you did to me?"

"Hmm, that can't be bitterness that I hear, Captain?" I strode to the left a little, away from the river and felt the familiar prick of my magic deep down.

"Not bitterness," Skandar huffed a laugh. "Regret."

"As is often the emotion people feel when they cross me." I smirked. "Regret at not killing you."

"I've been waiting for you."

"You'll be waiting for a long time, I'm afraid."

My throat closed and something icy slid into my gut. I remained calm and kept my face neutral. "Meaning?"

"You need to be kept alive," he snarled, moving his hands from behind his back. "But as soon as she's done with you, you're mine."

A flash of iron and I whirled away.

Frost nipped at my fingertips and swirled in my palms.

Skandar made a move towards me but I stepped back, away from the river once more.

"Don't even *think* about coming closer," I hissed as ice crackled and sizzled in the summer's warmth.

"This will be so much easier if you just come quietly and calmly," Skandar said, taking calculated strides towards me.

I laughed with no humor. "Then you, *Captain,* do not know me at all. I do not just come quietly and calmly."

"Then you'll have hell to pay."

"I already told you, I've been through hell and back." I grinned as the dark ice swirled around my fingertips to kiss the sweet air. "Get the hell away from me," I seethed as Skandar continued his approach.

"I'm under orders."

"Your orders mean nothing to me. *Get back!*"

Light formed at Skandar's fingertips and red and orange flame burst forth. I dodged it and sent a burst of my own magic towards him. He seethed as it grazed his shoulder but nothing else.

"Tell me, Ryn, did you never wonder what the humans were doing to you everyday? Why they were so curious about you?"

I tried to ignore his words and focus on the heavy weight in my hands and blew my hair out of my face. I should have braided it.

"For the glorious charade you put on for everyone, you're not very bright."

Dark ice shot straight for the captain's stupid mouth, but he melted it away with his blaze of heat.

"At a loss of words are you?" Skandar allowed his hands to drop for a single moment and that's when I struck. A wave so cunning and so cold to knock him off his feet. He went flailing and landed on his face in the grass that was now scorched.

A flash of metal caught my peripheral as Skandar threw one of the cuffs at me and I blocked it with a burst of ice. It froze midair, then fell to the ground.

"Nice try," I spat as I put even more distance between me and this accursed male. Skandar stood quickly, wiping at his brow the other iron cuff in his hands.

"Was any of it real?" I asked, refusing to let emotion show on my face. But then, giving him no time to reply, I demanded, "Why *did* you come and rescue me from Helmfirth? Was this Queen Cressida's plan all along?"

"Oh, you foolish girl," Skandar spat, eyeing me with such bloodlust and something else that I couldn't pinpoint. "You don't even know how long the very deity's have been planning this. Do you not know how much you can offer this kingdom? You can finally put that darkness in you to good use."

I jerked my head back. "By snuffing it out? By being chained just like the rest of the lost souls down there?" I don't know if I was screaming or hissing but something in me snapped. "I would rather *end* my own life than go back into slavery, to that hell I endured!"

Skandar *tsked* and stepped ever so carefully towards me. A calculated move if I had not been paying attention. "You are dangerous. You should be locked up. Your magic should be snuffed out because all it is. . .is darkness. It's evil."

"Do you also call the night evil because it is dark? Just because it is not of the Sol Kingdom does not make it evil." A calm had come over me, one I knew all too well. I prepared myself for what was about to happen and let the ice in my blood coat my veins, my bones as it made to pounce.

"There is no mistaking the darkness that lurks in your heart."

I snapped. I had had enough of listening to this annoying males retorts. I unleashed myself and such a roaring filled my head that I fell to my knees, my arms outstretched towards the captain. Black, gushing night spilled from my hands and filled Skandar's mouth, nose and eyes. He choked and fell back so hard I flung his body against the flat rock near the river. I heard a sickening *snap* but kept pouring my magic, my darkness, my evil into him.

I heard screaming and I wasn't sure if it was from him or me but when it was over I fell to my knees, the darkness swirling around me and then dissipating into me.

I refused to look at him.

The male who I had thought could be a friend.

I refused to look at the Sol Kingdom just below me as I stood up. The place I had thought of was my home.

Lies. Lies. Lies.

And maybe it made a monster out of me for what I'd done, but I would not go back in chains. I would *not* submit myself to torture again. Not when I knew what the queen had asked him to do to me, not when I knew very well something darker and cruel was happening here.

Without wasting another moment, I fled.

CHAPTER

12

I never looked back at the Sol Kingdom.

My boots couldn't take me away fast enough. I had refused myself the feeling of sorrow or regret and kept my tears tightly tucked away.

I was walking now. Walking fast and far away from the horrid stench of evil that filled that place. I didn't allow myself to think about what they would do when they found his body. Nor the conclusion they would come to when they found me missing next.

The image of Skandar's body and the bodies of all the others I'd killed in the *Death Pit* blended together and swarmed around me to remind me of what I'd done.

I hated myself for it, but what else could I have done?

I heard the sound of a river running and changed my direction. It would feel good to wash the heat of the sun away and refresh my mind. When the stream came into view I found a rock to set my shoes and socks and clothes on. The sun pricked my bare skin and as I waded into the river, I could tell it had been warming the water all day.

I ducked my head under the surface and stayed there for a minute. If only water could do to my memories what it did to the dirt and sweat on my body. I blew all my air out and rose to the top again. The sun reflected off of the water as I emerged and I brushed my hair back from my face, the water running off of me in tiny droplets.

I sighed as I finished scrubbing myself and arose out of the stream and back onto the bank. I needed only a few minutes to dry off so I lay, bare skinned and all, in the dry grass. But as soon as I closed my eyes *they* were there, haunting me. I tried to shove the thoughts away by squeezing my eyes tighter but my efforts were in vain. I finally forced them open and stared at the sky.

Nothing would help this horrible ache in my chest or the visions that plagued me.

All I saw were the broken and dead bodies slumped against the ground, their blood spilling out in bright red pools onto the sand beneath them. Their necks bent in unnatural angles. A body broken against a rock with tendrils of darkness still leaking from him. And those ocean blue eyes, filled with pity—pity for me.

I groaned and covered my face. I screamed into my cold hands and felt the prick of emotion at the corners of my eyes. I couldn't keep the tears back anymore.

My throat was raw and dry by the time the tears faded and the anger turned into numbness.

I didn't know which was better.

I barely remember getting dressed but I was on my way walking again before I knew it. I had no direction and no plans and quite frankly, didn't care. If I died of starvation or some wild creature got to me before I would welcome death with open arms.

I fell against a rock and laid my head to rest on the cool surface. I was so very tired and had no idea how long I had been walking. Whether it had been a few days or just a mere few hours. The night sky full of the twinkling stars—

My eyes shot open. The night sky?

I jolted upright and realized with a rising panic that I was surrounded by darkness. I was on my feet and circling to see if there was anyone around or if perhaps this was a strange dream. But indeed, I was surrounded by a dark blanket full of stars blinking and shining. It was so bright it reminded me of the early mornings back in Helmfirth where the sky would fill with darker and lighter hues of the first signs of the sun rising. There was no color except for that twilight blue glow.

My pulse quickened and I felt sick to my stomach. Even though I was never going back to Sol, the light had been comforting.

The Crescent Bloods of the Crescent Kingdom.

I heard the voice in my head as if it was being spoken out loud. I glanced around and wondered if I had walked as far as the Crescent Kingdom, where the Crescent Bloods resided.

If this was indeed the Crescent Kingdom I wasn't safe anywhere. I was going to have to find places to hide while I continued my journey. I thought briefly about going back to Helmfirth but that thought had quickly been tossed out. I was not *that* foolish.

I lifted my eyes to the sky and watched a shooting star fly across the dark blanket. I hadn't realized how much I had actually missed the stars and even the coolness that the night brought.

I heard something crunch and whirled around. The only thing that met my gaze were shadows and more darkness. I tried to slow my breathing and relax. I closed my eyes but I was on high alert all throughout the night.

Sometime during my light sleep, Skandar, the female nix, and the elven boy with the blue eyes had come to greet me. Their faces were all twisted in pain and anger and their backs and necks were bent in unnatural ways. They seemed to be slumbering towards me, reaching out for me. But when I scrambled back in my dream, I hit a thick wall and could not escape their ghostly fingers and nails as they scraped them across my skin—

I awoke, soaked with sweat and instantly stood, brushing my clothes and face off. I could still feel the nails scraping across my skin and shuddered. I had no idea how long I'd been asleep but I figured it had been long enough so I began to walk again.

But after fifteen minutes, I knew I was being followed.

I didn't look back so as not to alert my predator. But I could tell someone—or something—was hunting me. The forest had gone dead quiet; no birds singing or chirping and no creatures scurrying around. And the shadows that lurked behind me seemed unnatural.

So I made a plan.

I decided I wouldn't outrun whatever or whoever was following me, instead, I would try to lose them in the thick brush. I changed my direction to the left, to go deeper into the forest. The branches were so low I had to duck and the evergreen growth at my feet seemed to trip me every few steps. The trunks of the trees were growing closer and closer together and I risked a glance behind me.

I couldn't see those strange shadows anywhere. Maybe I had actually lost them.

But my joy was quickly snapped in half when I heard a *crack* and I felt myself surge into the air. I screamed and jostled around in the air and as I began to fall back down something coarse and full of holes caught me.

A net.

Both my legs stuck through one of the holes and my arm was hooked through another high over my head. I cursed loudly and tried to free myself, but all I did was make it worse, continuing to wrap the cords around my limbs.

I looked down with heavy breaths and saw that the ground wasn't that far away.

An idea sprang to life in my head and I tried to reach for my boot with the dagger but heard a snap as my shoulder popped painfully.

Too far then.

"Well, well, well," drawled a male's voice from below.

I glanced down moving only my eyes and glared at the two males staring up at me with devilish smirks.

"Good to see the old traps still work, eh?" said a blonde male, inching closer, gawking up at me.

They wore midnight black leather armor with belts full of knives and swords at their hips and on their backs. I wondered if they always wore this or if it was just to hunt me down.

"Does she speak?" crooned the dark haired one, stepping forward and staring up at me. I swung the leg that was sticking out of the hole and he dodged it. "Hey! No need to be nasty, love. We bested you and caught you fair and square."

"Oh yes! Two armed males stalking a girl through the forest at night. *That* sure doesn't seem fair to me." I crossed my arms and bared my teeth to them.

The blonde warrior looked to his comrade. "You seem like a grown ass female to me." He cocked his head to the side and looked me up and down.

I rolled my eyes and felt them draw nearer.

"Where do you hail from?" the darker haired one asked.

"Nowhere," I muttered. It was true, technically.

"Where are you *coming* from?" The same one demanded drawing his sword.

"Over that way." I pointed with a sly smirk on my face.

But before I could put my hand down, the male swung the blade directly at me. I squeezed my eyes shut and prepared for the blow but instead felt a whoosh of air above me and then I was falling.

Thud!

I yelped and opened my eyes. I was sprawled out on the ground, the two elven warriors staring down at me. My rear end protested against the fall and my spine stung. I glanced behind the males quickly and realized if I could make it past them I could run so fast and so far they'd never catch up.

But they were staring at me so intently that I hesitated. They glanced at each other as if having some sort of unspoken conversation.

Why were they staring at me like that?

Deciding to hell with it all, I leapt up and dashed between the both of them.

The edge of the forest was just in sight and they would surely be slowed down by all the low hanging branches. However, when I broke the tree line I felt a presence on either side of me.

Not another trap I hoped.

But when I looked left and then right, the two elven males were smiling like fools running right next to me. The blonde haired waved at me on my left and I rolled my eyes.

I slowed down and waved my hands at them. "Okay fine! Take me! Put me in chains and take me to wherever it is you take trespassers. And stop smiling like that!"

The dark haired one was the first one to stop smiling and he did actually take my arm a little roughly but not enough to hurt. The blonde with the gold eyes just continued walking on my left. I looked between the both of them, their massive muscular bodies towering at least two feet above mine.

"No chains?" I asked.

"You wouldn't be able to escape either way, love. Why bother putting them on if we can just run and catch you?" the dark haired with hazel eyes commented, adding a smirk and a wink. "But I will take this." He bent down and snatched the dagger from my boot.

I wanted so badly to punch his face. My cheeks were hot from humiliation at the fact that I was such easy prey and it put me in a foul mood. The entire time they escorted me to wherever it was we were going, they chatted away and told jokes and laughed like fools. I was already past the point of being annoyed and crossed my arms, sighing loudly.

"Where *are* you taking me?" I demanded angrily.

"Hell's Keep," said the dark haired one.

My heart stopped and I could feel the color drain from my face. I didn't care if they saw or not. I knew what a deathly place Hell's Keep was and, even deadlier, the ruler of the keep. I had heard stories from the fishermen. Stories I never wished I'd heard about that forsaken place. Azazel was deemed the ruler over the prison and everyone knew that death would be a much kinder damnation than being sent to his domain.

I managed to ask in a hoarse voice, "Don't I get a trial of some sort first?"

The light haired one on the left smirked and glanced at his comrade. "He's playing with you. We're bringing you to the king for a trial as the law states."

Relief flooded through me and I wouldn't be surprised if they could sense it with their all too keen elven noses.

"Or we *can* execute said trespasser right here. . .right now." The elven male with the dark hair and sparkling hazel eyes sneered at me. But it was that strange sparkle in his eye that made me realize, somehow, that he was joking. But I knew better than to trust them.

I swallowed and continued walking in between them.

My heart had begun to pound in irregular beats and I began to shake. Twice, the two elven warriors had glanced at me and then at each other as if having some silent conversation but I didn't care.

Let them gawk.

Eventually, when the Crescent Palace came into view, it was *I* who gawked. If I had thought the Sol Palace was wonderful and magical—this was completely otherworldly and terrible and great all at once.

While the Sol Palace had been a complete replica of the sun and everything bright and warm, whether it was a ploy or not, the palace that loomed before me now was exactly the opposite. The spikes that crested the top of the midnight dark castle pierced the starry sky. They cascaded down into obsidian stone that made up the entirety of the outside walls. Shards of the moon glinted off of the obsidian, making the palace shine with a dark blue hue.

There were three main towers with windows overlooking each direction, I assumed lookouts for trespassers or attackers. The view that surrounded them was a massive dark ocean that stretched out to the ends of the world if I had to guess. The sky seemed to have been flipped upside down in the still salty water. The only indication that it wasn't actually the sky was the occasional ripple of the waves when a breeze brushed by.

Looking back to the three towers, I noticed they were sectioned equally between the entire palace. Two were at the end and one was in the middle. And the terribly majestic foundation of the palace itself was brilliant. The obsidian walls led to many roofless balconies and windows that plunged straight down towards the massive black glass gates.

As we approached, I noticed bridges with no railings led to all sorts of different entrances. None were as grand as the one we were about to enter but I noticed them nonetheless, in case an escape needed to be made of course.

With a groaning sound the gates opened. We walked in and were flanked by two more guards on either side instantly. They all exchanged looks and then glanced at me quickly. I squared my shoulders and stood up straighter, making it a point to ignore their gazes.

I took in my surroundings and the absolute grandeur of the castle. The floors and walls and ceilings were flawlessly, polished onyx with rough edged arches placed every few hallways and anterooms. When I glanced up at the ceiling, I noticed I could see the stars in the sky twinkling above. When I blinked they faded in and out and I wondered if it was just a trick of the light or if they really were stars. There were no portraits hanging on the walls but instead weapons and artifacts and trophies and after that, just midnight black empty walls.

We turned down a long hallway and at the end stood two massive doors with the same blue hue as the exterior. The guards who had flanked us went ahead and opened the doors, one entered and bowed low and in a loud voice announced, "Your Majesty, King Haleth, we have found a trespasser in the woods. Would you like to trial them now or at a more convenient time?"

The voice that replied made the hair on the back of my neck raise. "Enter!"

I briefly thought about running but there were too many guards and I didn't stand a chance. I would have to face this trial and accept whatever fate befell me. In all honesty, I had been wandering the fields, forests, hills, and plains goading death to come and snatch me. To take me to where the deity and divine might judge me, or simply toss me into whatever awaited beyond.

I kept my head high and assessed every exit the minute I stepped into the throne room. My legs felt like lead and my heart even heavier. I had no home, no family, nothing. And I had killed yet *another* elven male.

I was nothing, a nobody who had no purpose in life except for people to use me.

Walking further into the room, I raised my eyes to meet the gaze of the king. He had short cropped graying hair and kind green eyes with a ring of gold in the middle. His wrinkles were smoothed out in a frown as he sat atop an obsidian throne that was so smooth it could have been black glass.

Whorls and twirls of the obsidian were etched all around the walls and came up in three long spikes at the back and came to rest on either side of the king as arm rests. Tall windows stretched out behind him distorting the stars and the ocean view beyond in ripples.

It was in those windows that I could see myself standing in the throne room. In the distorted reflection, I could just make out my own green eyes with the same ring of gold as the king.

No. . .

"What is *she* doing here?" King Haleth barked, his voice shaking slightly, pointing a crooked finger at me.

I watched as he descended the steps towards me and it bothered me how much it reminded me of Queen Cressida. His black tunic and robe shifted with him, sparkling in the blue hue of the moon and the chandelier above us. I briefly stared at it blinking as each tiny teardrop of light shifted and fluttered in an unfelt wind. Dragging my gaze from the momentary distraction I turned back to the king and watched as each step he took down from the dais sent my heart into a panic.

I stumbled back. "How do you know me?" The scent of ashy chocolate shoved itself up my nose as he loomed closer.

"Where did you find her?" he demanded, glancing at the males behind me.

My head was spinning and my heart was beating so fast, I felt sick. Why wasn't he answering me? With him so close, I could really see his eyes now and they were the *exact* same as mine.

"We found her in the woods, Your Majesty."

"Then why didn't you leave her there?"

I jerked my neck back at the absolute disgust written on this king's face. All remorse for myself had vanished, who was he to talk about me like this? And then it dawned on me.

"No. . ." I backed away as someone said something behind me but everything had become muffled. "You aren't. . .you can't be."

Haleth finally turned to me. "I am."

My brows creased, finding this extremely difficult. The world spun and I felt as if I were in a glass bowl, words and sounds completely drowned out. I froze and put a hand to my throat.

"You are Princess Ryn Noireis, Crescent Blood and heir to the Crescent Kingdom."

"You're my father?" I asked.

He swallowed and nodded, glancing at someone behind me as if I was not even worth looking at for longer than mere seconds.

"Where have you been the last ten years?" I yelled.

Someone gripped my arm tighter and I watched as the king's face distorted into rage.

"Take her away! I do not wish to look upon her any longer." He simply flicked his wrist and turned away.

Was there never an end to the rejection and betrayals? I barely felt myself being pulled away and certainly could not see for the blurriness obscuring my view.

What the hell just happened?

Two things entered my mind while I was being mindlessly led through the palace. One, was that the king, my *father*, was a bastard. And two, was that I might very well have walked into another trap.

I squeezed my eyes shut and held my temples with my thumb and forefinger. I realized that the world had stopped moving and so had my legs. The elven male must have asked me a question because he was staring at me, his hazel eyes pulled into a squint.

"What?" I snapped, crossing my arms over my chest.

"Well, I asked if you were going to be alright but if you're going to have an attitude with me then I withdraw my inquiry."

"You're a real treat, you know that?"

He shrugged, hazel eyes flashing. "That is what all the ladies tell me."

"Leave me alone," I groaned.

"As you wish." He turned away and I watched as he walked down the hall. He called over his shoulder, "If you need anything, I'll be around."

My brows squinted. There was no way in hell I was staying here after all of that just happened. I waited until he disappeared down the hall then followed him. I tried to recall the way back to the front gates but everything was so distorted. I groaned in frustration at yet another dead end, another roofless veranda, and doors that led to nowhere.

I was exhausted, emotionally and physically. My body and heart ached. And so, after stepping into a hall that simply led into a garden with strange looking hedges, I slid against an onyx pillar, hitting the floor. I put my head in my hands and broke down into sobs that wracked my body.

"Still want to be left alone?"

I groaned into my hands. "Go away!" I screamed.

"It seems you're in need of some help."

"Yes, kindly show me the way out." I lifted my head and tear stained face to the hazel eyed male, glaring at him.

"I don't think I'm allowed to do that but I can show you to your chambers." He had a foot propped up on the wall and was examining his finger nails, casually.

"I just want to leave."

"And go where?"

"Anywhere," I said more to myself than him.

"Here you're at least safe from prowling creatures, you have a bed, bath, food?"

I squinted at him. He wasn't wrong, which I hated. But did I really want to go out into the wild forest in a strange land I'd never been in before? As much as I hated it, I stood up and gestured for him to lead the way. I would be no good to myself if I were dead.

We walked back down the halls and pathways and came to the door he had originally left me at.

"Rest."

He waited for me to slip inside the room and I did, shutting the door behind me. I slid down the center of it, burying my face in my hands. I didn't even take the time to look at my surroundings as uncontrollable sobs slipped from my lips and tears fell through my eyelashes.

An overwhelming sense of loss and pain filled me and wracked my body. Sob after sob threatened to come forth and swallow me whole, eventually making things worse as a lump formed in my throat.

I brushed the tears away angrily and gritted my teeth.

I wanted to know just where the hell was my supposed-father when I was being *strapped* down to a table to be experimented on. I wanted to know where he was when I was *chained* to a wall and tortured. I wanted to know where he was when I was *forced* to kill in a ring for the pleasure of others.

I banged my head against the door and let the tears fall. I didn't care if someone could hear me or if that dark haired male was still on the other side of the door.

I did not care.

CHAPTER 13

Silver light streamed across the floor and splashed in my eyes. I rubbed them and slowly sat up. Where the hell was I?

I jolted upright and midnight blue walls spread out before me and dark wood floors greeted me. A dark velvet couch was placed in front of ceiling high windows letting the starlight and moonlight spill in.

My gaze snagged to my right as I glanced over a lush armchair that could have swallowed me whole if it truly wanted to. Next to it was a basket full of what looked to be the softest blankets in the whole world. On the other side of the huge armchair was a coat rack.

Crescent Kingdom. That's where I was.

I slowly stood up realizing I must have fallen asleep on the floor. Next to the now closed door was a white sheet of paper. I reached down to snatch it up and read it.

I snorted. The king wanted an audience with me. He'd be fortunate if I ever left this room. I crumpled the piece of paper and threw it against the wall.

I looked around the room and spotted three small steps to the left that led straight into another small chamber. After descending, I found a black silk canopy bed placed in the center. The sheets and the bedspread were a dark silver that seemed to sparkle and shift in the light.

I stepped further into the bedroom and noticed the wall adjacent to the bed had a cold fireplace and a bookshelf filled to the brim with all sorts of books. On the other side was a writing desk with paper, ink, and quills. A door was placed ajar in the corner next to a bureau. I stepped towards curtains that kept the silver light out of the room and flung them open.

An exquisite view of absolutely nothing but my own reflection greeted me.

I sighed and turned away. My mind felt so shattered I didn't want to think anymore. I pressed a trembling hand to my brow and sat at the edge of the bed.

Minutes or hours later, I stepped out of my clothes and crawled beneath the heavy duvet cover and sunk into the silk sheets. I had ignored a bath and any sort of washing up entirely and fallen into a fitful, terrible sleep. One where my dreams too quickly turned to nightmares and the faces of those I had killed came to haunt me.

And yet, no sooner had I drifted off, I woke up again. I expected to be greeted by golden light flooding in but no. . .it was just a never ending night. Amidst being plagued with night terrors and shaking with the sweats and chills, awakening to the pure darkness completely unnerved me.

I flung the covers back and got out of bed several different times. I even took a bath in the wee hours of whatever time it was. It was hard to grow accustomed to this dark blanket peppered with stars when I was used to the soft glow of the sun every hour of the day.

I dressed in my normal attire, dirty as they were. Brushing my hair with the soft comb I'd found in the bathing room, I focused on the *drip, drip, drip,* of the water. It fell from my hair and splashed onto the cold floor.

Pushing away the feelings and the thoughts trying to crowd themselves in my mind, I stepped out of the bathing room just as some sort of light stretched across the sky. The stars were dimmer now, if not completely gone and a blue light cascaded through the clouds, it looked like the hours before the sun would rise in Helmfirth.

A knock on the door had me freezing and glancing around for a place to hide myself. No sooner had the knock sounded that someone entered. Was there no privacy in this realm?

Hands on my hips, a sour expression on my face I demanded, "You were not invited in."

It was the male with the hazel eyes who towered in the door frame of my bedroom. "I don't need an invitation when my king demands an audience with you."

I tilted my head back and laughed. "He's no king of mine. Get out."

"You will come."

"I will not." Indignation covered my entire face.

The male stepped forward and *dared* to grab my arm. I whirled away from him, punching him in the jaw. He did not even flinch.

"Do you want me to drag you, kicking and screaming or would you rather come quietly and calmly?"

What this male did not know was that I did not come *quietly* and *calmly*. I spat a few choice words at him but he remained unphased.

"His Majesty does not wait for anyone, the longer you prolong this meeting, the more you will regret it."

"What does he want with me? He didn't seem too pleased that I was here in the first place. You'd do better to drop me off where you found me."

"And leave you to die?" The male raised his eyebrows at me. I shrugged. Would that be so bad?

His stern face seemed to soften and he extended an arm. "I would like to escort you to meet with your father. Would you care to join me?"

My brows creased. "Do I have a choice?"

He nodded. "Of course. But I have warned you that it will not go well for you if you deny."

Did I really want to anger the king? My father? What if he was anything like Lord Elton? I had appeased that bastard my entire life to avoid any complications or punishments. Perhaps I could do the same now.

I sighed through my nose and roughly took the elven male's arm. "I'm Adaner."

I ignored him.

We walked silently throughout the halls and I tried not to fidget with my hands or clothes. But I was nervous. I didn't know what to expect or even how to act. And there was such a rage within me that I didn't know what to do.

Brushing these thoughts from my mind, I focused instead on my surroundings. I quickly realized that this palace was much different from the Sol Palace. Where Sol had vines crawling up the walls, flowers blooming, and trees swaying in the wind with their lilac scents wafting through the air; the Crescent Palace had constellations, moons, and stars lining the onyx walls and floors. The scent of the sea wafted in on the light breezes and glass candle lit orbs hung from the ceiling everywhere.

It was simple and grand all at once.

There were seating areas and balconies that looked out over the dark ocean and the forest. A blanket of star speckled ceilings looked down upon rooms furnished with dark silk couches, black velvet armchairs next to bookcases and long tables with onyx, marble tea sets. Pianos and fiddles and weapon cases and fluffy rugs filled the empty spaces of the rooms. Marble fireplaces occupied each area with streaks of that same blue hue from the exterior of the palace.

In fact, everything in the Crescent Kingdom was obsidian and inky with a midnight blue hue swirling into one final color. I noticed right away there were flights of spiral staircases everywhere with black glinting steel railings winding up and up until I couldn't see them any more. I briefly wondered where they might lead as I passed another one. I felt the salty breeze cascade down to kiss my cheeks and, surprising myself, I stopped for a moment to breathe it in.

The wind carried a lovely salt and pine smell of the Crescent Palace and I closed my eyes, imagining the feel of the ocean's tide on my feet.

Adaner spoke, "Are you well?"

I opened my eyes, my moment of solitude gone. I continued walking with him without uttering a word. Mere seconds later, we exited the shelter of the corridor halls and walked down a few steps into what seemed like a courtyard. Tall hedges loomed above us in every direction and in the hazy light of twilight, they shifted and groaned and seemed to reflect a sort of beryl color amongst the black stones of the pathway.

"The terrace is set and King Haleth awaits you." Adaner gestured down a single pathway and halted.

I looked down the path but I was not admiring it, no, I was planning my escape. "I will take my leave here, the table is just beyond this hedge."

I blinked with cold eyes but the view was blocked by the greenery. Without saying another word, I nodded and stepped forth to face him. I didn't smile. I didn't frown. It was something in between that meant so much more. My eyes scanned the table briefly and flitted over a silver tea kettle, a glass pour over, and silverware; plates, bowls, cups, cutlery, etchings of some sort swirled on the silver in black ink.

"I do appreciate your efforts in meeting me here," Haleth spoke as he stood, probably waiting for me to quit staring at the table like a fool and speak.

But I didn't speak. I took my chair and crossed my arms, not caring if it was improper or not. I felt guarded and safe this way.

"Tea?" he offered. I declined.

He poured himself a cup of dark tea, stirred in cream and sugar and then leaned back in his chair. He seemed to glance past me but when a brush of wind tousled my hair, it seemed to bring his attention back to me. "I must say, I am very surprised to see you."

"And why would that be? Am I not your long lost daughter?" The words came out far too quickly for me to even stop them.

"I do not like your tone."

"And I didn't like being orphaned. Did you know I was in Helmfirth all this time?"

He swallowed. "You were sent away for your safety."

He hadn't really answered my question but I assumed what he'd said was answer enough.

"Why? What was so dangerous here?" I shrugged.

King Haleth sipped from his mug. "There was an inside threat, it was for the best that you left the kingdom."

I scoffed. "Do you even know what I endured at the hands of the lord who found me?"

He shook his head. "I do not nor do I care to know. That is in the past."

I blanched, I glanced around at the scenery trying to distract myself from the sinking feeling deep inside of me. I had always wondered if I had a Father or Mother, but *this* is not what I had envisioned them to be like.

"You are welcome to stay, that is all I wanted to talk with you about."

I stared at him. "That's all?"

King Haleth raised an eyebrow. "Did you expect there to be more?"

"What of my memories?"

He shrugged, flicking something off his shoulder. "What about them?"

I blinked. "I do not recall anything before being found in the boat."

"That is because they were stolen and you will not be getting them back."

I seethed, "Like hell I will. They are rightfully mine."

"Like I said, they are stolen. You should be grateful I am even allowing you to stay, it puts my own kingdom in great jeopardy. Anything else you would like to add?" Haleth glanced at his fingernails, oblivious to my rage.

I glared at him. What an idiot. I had an idiot for a father—a poor excuse for one. "If it puts your kingdom in such jeopardy, why let me stay in the first place?"

"I have a duty as a father, do I not? There may come a time when this can no longer be a home for you. But for now, make yourself as comfortable if you must." He shrugged and sipped his tea once more, the picture of nonchalant indignation.

I blinked. Once. Before I huffed and pushed away from the table not wishing to look at his rutting face any longer. Without a second glance, I left him sitting there with his cup of tea still in hand.

Foolish, selfish prick.

I stormed back into the castle, leaving the beryl colored hedges and ill fated conversation behind. I had long since learned to tuck away any emotions that arose unwanted, but this time was different. I found myself beneath one of the steel staircases, gazing up at it and wondering where it led. Without waiting another moment, I ascended.

I took the steps one at a time. Placing my hand on the railing and letting the cold metal bite into my skin. It was smooth and cool and reminded me of stones that had been lapped over in a river for so long they were now soft.

At the top, a breeze swept past me, it was stronger than below on the lower level. Pillars stood every ten or so feet apart and connected to archways that circled around the entire space and as I tilted my neck, I realized the sky replaced the ceiling above me. In between some of the spaces of the pillars there were balconies extending out into thin air. Some had tables and chairs and some had benches while others had nothing.

I glanced around and stepped away from the opening of the stairwell. I appeared to be the only one up here. Although, the pillars and balconies extended around the corner and I couldn't quite see around it, meaning there could very well be people sharing this space with me.

Placing my hands behind my back I walked forward to one of the balconies with nothing on it. I had to admit, the view was breathtaking; the ocean waves stretched as far as the horizon, the sky mimicking the same color as the dark blue of the water. I could just barely hear the audible sound of the waves crashing on the shore and watched as they receded back, leaving the sand an even darker color.

I inhaled and breathed in the smell of the salt and pine air. I didn't want to feel the emotion rising in my chest but it came, unwanted and unabashed. I did not feel welcome here but where else could I go? I did not feel safe but I knew I certainly would not be safe on my own with no money and hardly any weapons.

Haleth had made no mention of my mother and I wondered about that. He had seemed content to leave me in the dark about quite a few things. I had briefly wondered if I should find her and perhaps she led a normal, good life and I could share that with her.

I shifted as I stood, for now, this was all I had. I certainly wouldn't go back to the Sol Kingdom. At this very moment they might be finding Skandar's body.

I sucked in air. How horrid everything had turned out to be.

Ruckus laughter filled the air and I jolted out of my deep thoughts. I looked over my shoulder slightly to see two males pushing each other around, laughing so hard they doubled over. I recognized them, Adaner, and the other with the short blonde mop atop his head.

My captors.

They must have caught me staring because Adaner, the prick he was, smiled and raised a hand in greeting. I gave him a glare in return and turned back to the view of the ocean waves crashing on the shore.

"Hello love," drawled Adaner.

I rolled my eyes, not even bothering to turn around or even speak to either of them.

"Oi, you wouldn't happen to still be cranky at us?" asked the other male, with the blonde mop.

I shut my eyes. What an imbecile.

"Oi? Can you speak?"

"Enough!" I whipped around. "Do me a favor and keep walking."

"But the view is such a lovely one from this specific balcony," the dark haired male crooned, hazel eyes alight with a fierce glow.

"Then I shall leave." I got up and tried to push my way past them but they moved simultaneously and barred the way so that I was eye level with their shoulders. *"Move,"* I hissed.

"Make us. . .oh wait, you can't," said the blonde this time, sneering down at me.

"What do you mean I can't? I can do whatever the hell I want."

"Oh, can you now?" taunted Adaner.

"Want me to prove it?" I could feel the dark ice accumulating in the very blood that flowed hot through my veins.

"You already know my name but this is Cadeyn." Adaner gestured to his comrade as he grinned wide.

"I don't care."

"A pity, truly. For you might never know how fine our company is," mocked Cadeyn.

"I think I can tell how poor it would be." I crossed my arms, still fuming.

"Why don't you give me a chance, love and I'll show you how thrilling it can be." Adaner tried to reach for my hand or my waist, I wasn't sure, but fast as lightning I jolted out of his reach and the sound of ice cracking filled my mind.

"I can see that you grow weary of us." Adaner straightened his lapels and broke eye contact to look me up and down. "Have a good eventide, Princess."

That's when it happened. I snapped.

I threw a punch straight for his face. He dodged it but not before I skimmed his cheekbone. When I spun out of reach of his grasping hands, I aimed for his gut and just as I went to throw the punch I felt my arm bark in pain as it twisted behind me and I was slammed chest and shoulders first straight into a pillar.

Hot breath poured down my neck and near my ear as the scent of amber and citrus filled my nostrils. "Don't ever try that again."

I fidgeted but stopped when my arm, twisted around and up my back, protested with stinging pain as if it were being pulled out of the socket.

"Your heart is beating quite fast," he hummed with his thickly, accented voice.

"Get your rutting hands off of me!"

I could feel it.

Rising in me like the ocean waves beyond the pillar I was pushed up against. Before I could blink a blast came out of me, pushing both me and Adaner off of the pillar and spilling onto the tiled floor. Amidst the ice particles we slid across the floor, landing in a heap.

Adaner only laughed. "Quite a show, love."

I said something very vile to both of them and stormed away, almost slipping down the onyx staircase in my rush of anger.

CHAPTER

14

I needed to cool off.

I hated this place already.

I pushed my way past many elves lurking in the halls going about their normal activities. I wasn't sure if they had heard that nasty exchange above but I was confident that if they were to see me again, they would run far away. I could see the fear coating the whites of their very eyes at the pure fury that leaked from me.

Good. Let them fear me.

I could still feel the ice beneath my skin and felt my frosty, gold flecked eyes burning with anger as I stormed out of the palace. I burst through one of the garden exits and found myself walking down cobblestone stairs, towards a sandy beach and the rolling waves beyond. It was glorious and huge and dark all at once. The waves crashed onto the sand only to retreat seconds later, repeating the motion again and again. The half-light glow of the sky wasn't quite fading yet and my body ached with exhaustion from the events of the day—night.

Bloody hell.

This realm seemed to only be lit by the moon and the stars during the evening and a soft blue hue during what I could only assume was twilight, which in the Sol Kingdom would have been known as *morning*.

I scrubbed at my face and groaned. There were so many conversations and voices rattling off inside my head that I needed to escape to find solace and to just shut them up for a bit.

The salty tide pooled around my bare feet and then surged back into the ocean to gather more energy and reinforcements for another wave. My hair whipped back and forth in the sea breeze and I felt the spray of the water as it crashed yet again against the sand and the rocks. I had long since abandoned my shoes at the top of the grassy ridge, along with my shirt. I wore only my pants rolled to my ankles, and my pearly colored undertop that stretched to my navel and wrapped under my arms to cover my breasts.

I climbed atop the massive black rocks stretching out into the sea and nimbled over it, barefeet and all. Finding the smoothest edge to sit on I obliged myself and pulled my knees up to my chest, staring out over the darkening expanse; how great and wide it was. Far greater than the lake in Helmfirth that now seemed rather small.

I'd longed to break free and to crest that mountain for my entire life growing up there. And yet, the world wasn't at all how I'd imagined. I had even more questions than answers and my life was far more complicated and confusing.

And still without all of my memories.

I ground my teeth at that thought. Elton had tried explaining it was trauma but deep down, I had always known it was something bigger. I had always known there was a mental block that was preventing me from remembering. But it wasn't the kind of mental block that one chooses. It was the kind that's forced.

My fists clenched so tightly around my legs that my nails bit into my skin.

King Haleth claimed I would never have my memories back because they were stolen. Stolen my whom? Stolen how? He knew something but wasn't telling me.

I sighed and rested my forehead on my knees. I would find them.

I *had* to know what happened to me before Helmfirth. I *had* to know if I was always this broken or if there was still a part of me that maybe I could find again. . .if it wasn't lost for good.

But as I stared out to sea and watched dark clouds roll in over the waves, something inside of me told me it was already too late. Something told me I was too far gone. Lost in the darkness of what I'd done, and the darkness of my magic to ever hope to find a way to heal the splintered shards of my soul.

A few droplets of rain splattered on my face and hands and pelted the rock I sat on. The cold wetness reminded me of things I had tried to forget over and over again. I looked back up the grassy ridge and to the Crescent Palace looming in the distance.

There was still much to be done, much yet to be answered. I laid back on the rock and let the rain fall on me. It splattered and splashed on and around me and I welcomed and cursed every raindrop that glided over my skin.

Would I stay? I thought about this several times while I just lay there. Where else could I go? Cressida would eventually find me, Elton might come looking for me. Would I perhaps be safer in a realm with a lousy father who did not care about me that much? At least *he* wasn't trying to use or abuse me for my magic. He had seemed to not have a care in the realms for my magic.

I blinked away the rainwater as it dripped into my eyes. Perhaps this was the safest and smartest option for me, currently. Even as much as I hated it.

I must have dozed off for some time because I jolted awake suddenly and swiftly sat up. My eyes scanned the area around me and I noted that the rain had ceased. The rock around where I had been laying was completely soaked but where my body had been covering the rock was lighter color and completely dry.

I tuned my pointed ears to glean any nearby sounds; something had woken me up.

I scanned the water and found nothing. The only sounds emanating forth were the now calmed waves and the flock of occasional birds flying overhead.

I bit my lip and turned my head back towards the beach. I squinted and spotted something floating in the water near the shore. I leaned forward onto my knees, trying to get a better vantage point.

A body. . .it was a body; dark hair floated loosely about the head and the arms and legs were limp in the water.

I scurried off of my rock and dove head first into the cold salt water. How long had the body been floating? Would I even be able to revive them? Gliding through the ocean and surging myself forward, I surfaced and inhaled air a few feet from the floating male.

For it was a male; shirtless and tan and shoulder length hair— No. . .

Before I could change my mind or swim away, the male moved, flipping his hair behind his head in a graceful and effortless move, inhaling deeply and sharply.

I clamped down on the scream that threatened to expel from my lungs and tried to mask my shock and fear.

"Well, hello there love. This is quite the surprise." Adaner.

Still fuming from earlier, all I could do was glare at him. "What, did your little nap not improve your mood?"

"Well, *someone* woke me up," I shot back.

"I was trying my best to stay quiet but your elven ears must have picked up when I belly flopped off of the rock."

"The rock I was sleeping on?"

"Yeah, last I checked the rock was on Crescent territory," he snapped as he began treading water in a circle around me.

"While I was sleeping?" I pressed, following his movement with my frosty green gaze.

"That is what I said, maybe your elven hearing isn't as good as I thought."

I rolled my eyes. "What would you know? You've known me for all of half a night."

"That is quite long enough to gather a bit of knowledge. Besides, we've all heard about you. We've been waiting for you."

A memory flashed through my mind of Skandar saying something very similar when he first burst into my cell.

Adaner pooled water in and around his hands and gazed down at it casually. "I just didn't think you'd be falling asleep half naked in the rain when you got here." A smirk splayed across his face and, intending on wiping it away, I splashed water at him.

"Oi!" he moaned. "That's not very royal!"

"Just stop!" I screamed, marking him again with the sea. "I am *not* the princess!"

Adaner swiped salty water out of his eyes and groaned. Then, looking at me through his hair curling in front of his eyes, said in a much deeper tone, "Maybe you're right. Maybe you've let us all down."

I didn't let him show how much his comment hurt but I think he could already tell as he started swimming away. Not being able to contain myself I shouted after him, "Why do you keep saying that?"

"Saying what, love?" he questioned, without turning around. That damned name he kept calling me. It set fire to my bones.

I swam after him furiously. "Why do you keep saying that you've all been waiting for me? I don't even remember *living* here."

He stopped then, the only movement were his arms keeping him afloat. I watched his back muscles twitch and he rotated to look at me.

I couldn't read the look on his face. "What?" I demanded.

"Nothing, nothing at all." He turned away.

"Prick."

"My ego boosts everytime someone calls me that. Thank you," he called over his shoulder.

"You're not welcome." I swam past him and didn't bother sparing him a glare. Everyone liked their secrets in this place it seemed.

And this male—Adaner—vexed me.

"Nice talking to you, love! Oh, and watching you sleep!"

I shuddered at the rage that coiled through me and fought the urge to whip around and freeze him to the ocean floor.

—⚏—

That evening, when the sky was as black as could be, I twisted and turned in my satin sheets. I couldn't find it in me to fall asleep peacefully. Sure, I had dozed off here and there but I was always awakened by this tightening in my chest. It was so tight that I found it hard to breathe. It was as if some monster with gangly fingers was reaching into my chest and up my ribcage to squeeze my heart.

It was at this moment that those gangly fingers were at work again and I yelled in frustration. I swung my legs over the side of the bed and sat up, trying to catch a breath.

Breathe.

Just breathe.

But as I tried to inhale once more a sharp pain shot up my chest and down my arms. I winced this time because of the pain and fell forward. I clutched at my throat but absolutely no air would come in or out.

I was suffocating.

I knelt on the floor now and grasped and scratched at my throat, clawing for air. As if in an answer of aid or by some deity above, a breeze swept by, tickling my cheeks. My head snapped up and I stumbled to my feet, rushing to the balcony doors inside my bedchambers. Grasping at the handles I yanked them open and fell onto the deck. The air was filled with salt, pine and the scent as if it might rain.

I wheezed, my lungs gulping down air one breath at a time. I laid my head back still kneeling and let the star freckled sky greet me.

Sweet breath.

I inhaled and exhaled.

I leaned forward pressing my forehead to the deck and wept. I was tired of this. Tired of all the nightmares, the images, the bodies, the constant feeling of guilt, the ever pressing feeling of not wanting to exist any longer.

My tears spilled down my cheeks; the ugly, unwanted tears that I was ashamed of and hated myself for.

The next morning—blast it all to Hell's Keep—twilight, the sapphire hue cascaded down from the heavens and spilled over the tempestuous sea waters. I leaned against the balcony railing having not gone back inside my bedchambers to fall asleep. I had dozed in and out of sleep but mostly had gazed at the stars peeking in and out of the clouds. Judging by the scent of rain and the roiling dark clouds, another storm was brewing.

I inhaled through my nose and allowed the sea, pine and rain air to fill my nostrils and lungs.

I needed to move my body.

I turned back to my room and without another thought I left. I had no idea where the training yard would be in this palace. That is, hoping they had one. I still wore my ragged dark pants and green shirt from when I first got here and enclosed my fists around the extra fabric of the blouse's sleeves in a nervous gesture.

Passing a glass door that was propped open, I paused to peek in. It revealed a round table with daggers of all sizes lined perfectly in a circle and all pointing directly to the middle.

One look to the left and right showed no signs of anyone. So, I took the liberty and stepped in, leaving the door ajar. I walked around the table, admiring the various weapons. My dagger, which had still not been returned to me, could not compare to these ones. None of them were the same, but they all had intricate designs; whirls and twirls, spikes and spokes.

I ran my finger down one of the handles, feeling the etched engravings beneath my skin. These were pure artwork. What I wouldn't give to handle one of these.

On second thought, I raised my eyebrows and quickly assessed the room. Still, no one had come in to stop me. No one seemed bothered by the fact I was in here. I wrapped my fingers around the onyx handle, it glittered with jade and topaz and came down to a longer, thinner blade.

I twirled it in my hand and grabbed the handle loosely enough to maneuver it into any move *or* to strike at any given time. I spun on my heel and dropped low, throwing the dagger up I watched it glint and shine in the light and snagging it out of the air I finished my spin and jabbed it straight into—

A hand seized mine before the blade could pierce their chest and with a flick of the wrist was trained back at me—the tip resting near my throat.

I held my breath and looked into my opponents eyes. . .his piercing ocean blue eyes. I inhaled sharply, spiraling down into my memories. A flash of sand, of people cheering, of the pointed ears so similar to mine, midnight black hair and. . .ocean blue eyes.

My spine crunched against the wall behind me but I barely felt it as I stared into a different elven male's face, but with the same eyes as the boy I had killed in that arena.

I cursed and swallowed, feeling the tip of the knife bob on my throat. "Well, this is amusing," he spoke like liquid ink.

I couldn't speak. All I could do was stare, dumb founded at this male. I was surprised he couldn't hear the pounding of my heart as it hammered inside of me.

"Does the elven lady speak?" he questioned, raising one of his dark eyebrows, his hair cropped short near his ears and neck.

I tried to inhale but it got stuck coming out of my throat. I swept my eyes over his face and snagged on his blue eyes again. He was speaking again but it was muffled. All I could hear were the words of the elven boy before I snapped his neck.

Then you are going to have to choose.

And I did choose. I chose to live and to forever pay the price of that choice. "Oi!"

That voice, smooth and dark, snapped me out of it and with one blink of the eyes I slipped back to reality.

"What the hell are you doing to her?" Adaner?

I hadn't even realized the blue eyed male was shaking me but when he stopped and pulled away the lack of movement felt odd.

"Bloody hell mate, you don't treat a female like that!" Adaner stalked up to the other male and went nose to nose with him.

"She was unresponsive, get off me!"

"Rutting hell, Tolden, you have such a bloody attitude," Adaner grumbled and turned towards me.

I wasn't entirely sure why I felt instantly safer with Adaner, because just recently *he* was the one antagonizing me. I pushed air out of my lungs and brushed back my hair from my face. I looked towards the male Adaner had called Tolden and still felt shaken up.

"Are you alright?" Adaner asked me in his thickly accented voice.

"Like it matters to you," I fired back.

He threw his hands up in the air in what looked like mock surprise and growled, "Damn it all if I ever save your ass again!"

"My ass didn't need saving, you lug."

"Sure," Adaner lowered his voice and leaned closer towards me, "princess."

Anger sparked inside me and that's when I remembered the round table full of daggers. Adaner and Tolden followed my gaze but Tolden just put the dagger I had originally been holding back and wiped his hands on his slacks.

"None of us should even be in here, let's go," Tolden spoke with authority and even stood a little straighter as he started walking.

"Why was the door ajar then?" I quipped, feeling the need to rebel against this unspoken leadership steaming off of him.

"Because this is the king's private weapons room. He does what he wishes." My stomach jolted and I felt queasy. Haleth?

I glanced around once more and felt something inside of me twinge. He favored daggers as well? Seeing as he did have an entire collection to prove it, it was likely.

"Come on," said Tolden in a more rude tone this time.

The three of us filed out and the door was slammed shut by Adaner who came out last. I watched Tolden continue walking, watched the way he sauntered away and bile rose in my throat.

"What exactly happened in there, love?"

I turned to find Adaner leaning against the wall, his black leather glinting as if it had just been cleaned or as if rain had been spilling down it. Even his dark hair was wet and some pieces stuck to his neck.

"It's none of your business," I snapped, crossing my arms.

"Oh, so he's already got you in the palm of his hand? You don't even *know* that male."

"And *you* don't even know me so don't presume anything." I whipped around, my hair flying with me, and swayed my hips down the hall; the same way I used to do walking into the *Death Pit*—it always made the men stare.

"You should try finding new clothes to wear, love. You look ghastly!"

I rolled my eyes. I guess that trick didn't work on elven males.

CHAPTER 15

I wandered around the rutting Crescent Palace for longer than I wished to admit.

After being unsuccessful in finding the training yard, I returned to my room. I hadn't bothered to ask where it might be and had the horrid vision of exercising in front of the three elven brutes. Slamming the door to my room, I trudged in, grumpy and dizzy from the many flights of stairs I had descended and ascended and from all the halls and rooms I had wandered in and out of.

I groaned and flopped on the top of my bed. Staring at the ceiling, I let the events of the twilight wash over me. Tears began to brim in my eyes and I wasn't entirely sure why. I was stronger than this. Yet, salty streams fell down my face and left streaks. This emptiness, this feeling of loss settled in my soul and wouldn't go away.

I briefly thought about Haleth's room of daggers and the scenario that had unfolded. An oily, cold sensation slithered inside of me and dark thoughts penetrated my mind. I squeezed my eyes shut willing the harmful memories to dissipate but they only became more clear.

I made myself sit up, aiming to distract myself and noticed something leaning in the corner; several silver packages were set against the wardrobe all tied closed with the same silver string. I picked them up in one armful and I set them on the bed, one by one I opened them up, grateful for the temporary distraction.

The first was a gown made from the softest emerald silk lined with gold lace and beads and corset laces up the back with a plunging neckline. I held it up against my body and it spilled over me and the floor in waves of green and deep gold.

Turning to the next package it revealed a deep twilight blue dress, almost the same color as the sky outside. This one was more simple and not as grand or luptuous. And the neckline was more rounded. I glanced at the bed and there were four more packages.

How many dresses did a female need?

Tearing the rest of them open, the packages revealed three more gowns the colors of a long sleeved ambrosia, deep violet; so dark it was almost the color of coffee with tiny sparkles like stars. The last gown was complete in silver satin with beads of tiny bluebell flowers spread across it with straps for sleeves.

The fourth package revealed what looked to be training leathers and for those, I almost began weeping. I had begun to fret, fearfully worrying I would have to remain in lace and satin gowns for the rest of my life.

Picking up each dress and holding it against my body I spun around, allowing the fabric to sway and swirl around me in billows of soft and velvety billows. They weren't *so* bad. I turned to lay the rusty orange one back and noticed that neatly tucked in each package was a pair of lace and satin underthings, whole sets of them.

I picked them up and gasped at how luxurious they were. Curious, I picked the leathers up and sure enough there were ones to go with that outfit as well.

I couldn't lie, they looked and *felt* heavenly.

Eager to try them on and realizing that a bath might do me good, I shucked my clothes on the floor and started filling up the huge onyx marble tub. The black marble was cold, but as the clear warm water started filling it up it grew steamy. To the point that it fogged up the oval looking glass above the matching onyx marble countertop.

I sighed and sank further into the water. The tub was big enough for two people to sit or lay comfortably. I dunked myself beneath the heated water even though it only made it worse. I held my breath and scrubbed at my face and body, I massaged my scalp and felt my hair drifting every which way. Emerging I wiped the droplets from my eyes and searched for some soap.

There was an assortment of forest green bottles sitting on the edge and I ran a finger on each, studying them. There was hair, body *and* face soaps—all of them separate—and then the last container was body oil.

I scrunched my nose in confusion. But I reached for each one and poured the contents into my palm, applying it to its specific place on my body. Each one smelled marvelous and contrasting from the others.

My whole bathing room was awash in the scents of pear, ambroxan, seasalt and apricot. Come to think of it, they smelled just like the whole of the Crescent Palace.

Of course.

This place—this kingdom *was* magic, just as Sol had been. Of course everything would smell heavenly. I splashed water on my face and wondered if I would ever get used to the way of the elven realms.

I had known I was an elven blood ever since Lord Elton Hode told me very early on in my training in the human realm. But I had never guessed I would actually live here. I had barely even dappled in my own magic.

It had lain dormant in my soul for a very long time.

I scrubbed at my arms and shoulders, the smell of ambery hitting me.

Maybe that was why my magic was dark. . .because it had lain dormant for so long it hadn't had time to be used and made to be stronger. It had festered inside of me, utterly useless.

I swallowed, remembering all the days and nights of screaming and thrashing about while being strapped to a table and had my body poked and prodded and stuck with needles. I remember the other horrible things Elton had done to me; the abuse and trauma.

The first time he had hit me.

The first time he and Marcus had done abhorrent things.

I remember when I was first dragged, half bleeding to death, to my cell and I had been there every day until Skandar rescued me.

I shuddered despite the warmth of the bathwater. Skandar.

The water around me started to feel a little too similar to the blood of the people I had killed. I finished washing and quickly got out, wrapping a towel around me before I could look at the hideous scars on my back.

No, Helmfirth had never really been home. Neither had the Sol Kingdom. But they were all I had known at the time. I tried to swallow and realized it had become difficult, a lump had formed in my throat and my cheeks were wet and sticky.

I didn't have much hope for the Crescent Kingdom. I didn't have much hope left for me.

I lathered the body oil all over me and rubbed it in until I felt smooth and porcelain. Using the towel that had been drying my body, I scrunch my hair up in it and let the dripping coils soak into the fabric.

I sighed, avoiding looking at my image in the looking glass. I truly didn't know if I could handle seeing the female who gazed back.

I think I hated her.

So I gravitated to the thing that aided the most; distractions.

I picked the black leathers and the black satin underthings to dress in and marveled at how they fit perfectly. But of course, there was magic here, so I really couldn't be surprised now could I?

As I braided my wet hair in a long plait down my back I formed an idea in my head. A lovely distraction *and* plan that involved books.

I was going to get my memories back.

I despised the idea of simply idling about, for that was when the dangerous thoughts consumed me.

A good bit later, after wandering around and finally seeking aid from a brown eyed elven female who wore a long silver gown, I was pointed in the right direction. Apparently the library was *beneath* this level. I had no idea there could be so many levels in a castle.

It made me question how many more there were in Sol too as I descended. The air became cooler down here and there seemed to be an unknown draft. I ran my hand along the wall of the stairwell and was suddenly stricken with an image.

An elven being, colorless and lifeless, hung from the ceiling by their wrists. I tripped on one of the steps going down to the lower level and caught myself on the railing, jerking my body.

I blinked and glanced around. There was nothing and no one in this lower level hall and I dismissed the imagery as a memory, triggered by the air around me.

Yes, that had to be it.

I tried to recall it, the way the empty room looked in my mind's eye, but there had been only one body remaining. I couldn't see whose it was though.

I shook it off, tucking the image away so I could think on it later. For now, I had to keep to the task at hand.

Once I descended the flight of steel staircases, I came to the level with lit sconces and a ceiling that seemed to be a reflection of the very sky at eventide; just as the brown eyed female had said.

I let my eyes roam the ceiling and realized the few mirrored stars moved as I moved. They took shape—my shape and followed me.

I smiled as I lifted my arm and the stars did the same.

Ahead, I could see the glow of more firelight or starlight coming from an open doorway. Stepping into the light filled room, I beheld a glorious seating area with rows and rows of bookshelves stretching far back into the room. The sound and warmth of crackling fireplaces greeted me and I noticed that this ceiling was similar to the one in the sconcelit hallway.

"Hello there," said a chippery voice to my left.

I turned and a small female with jeweled hands and pointed ears smiled at me. She even had two jewels in her teeth.

"Hello," I replied.

"Is there anything I can help you with or do you know the way?" The female had on a long gray coat covering her deep blue gown.

I folded my hands awkwardly behind my back. "I've never been here before but I am looking for the section about spells or magic or anything like that." I smiled, trying to seem innocent and curious. I wasn't sure why I had an odd feeling inside my stomach. I looked behind my shoulder as if someone would be lurking in the shadows.

"Of, course let me guide you in the right direction."

A few bookshelves back and the bedazzled female turned right, she stopped and extended her arm, the rings flashing in the starlight. "Here we are! This will be everything from how to cast spells and use and sense your magic to revoking your spells and even your magic."

My brow furrowed and I peeked down the aisle. "You mean to say you can take away someone's magic?"

"Quite right, but it is a horrendous ritual and one that we have *never* done here and will *never* do since it is against the law."

"But it's been done in other places?"

"I should sincerely hope not!" The female's voice went an octave higher and I winced.

Duly noted.

Once she left, I started on the top row and made my way across it. The tip of my finger soon became coated in dust but I allowed my magic to melt it away with a little bit of ice.

I continued to scan the rows until I came across a book titled *Head And Heart Incantations*. I snagged it and tossed it on the pile of books growing larger by the second. Once I was satisfied I had covered every inch of this library section, I took my books and dumped them onto one of the desks towards the back.

The desk was made out of some sort of black wood and had hardly any scratches or dents. Three small candles sat dormant in the corner and as I sat in the swiveling velvet chair I looked in the drawers. Snatching out the match I'd hoped to find, I lit all three of the wicks. I watched the match's smoke plume after I'd blown it out and placed it in the ashtray where a few others were as well.

I picked up the *Head And Heart Incantations* book first. The cover was thick and intricate with swirls of inky etchings written across the top. It shimmered in the starlight and firelight and the words seemed to move as if in water.

I unfastened the latch that secured it and turned to the first page. My forest green gaze sweeping over it, I noticed it was written in poem form;

> *The reader must know, that no matter a head or heart of snow, the truth will forever be sown.*

My brow furrowed and as I read it over in my mind again I felt a tingling at the edges of my fingertips. My gaze brushed over the library, only the sound of the wood popping in the fireplaces could be heard.

I returned to the book and flipped to the next page. Similar formats of longer and shorter spells were written in all different places and fonts all over the coarse paper. I wondered if these had anything to do with memories or if it was all just a hoax.

As I was flipping through the pages my finger snagged on one of the edges, slicing the delicate skin on the side open. I winced and popped my finger in my mouth to stop the tiny trickle of blood that had appeared. As I raised my hand to my mouth, the tiniest bit of blood dripped onto the page.

I tried to wipe it away but I just smeared it even worse in the process. To my horror, black ice spread across the incantation book and crawled across the pages like a glass web. The icy pages began to flip on their own, sending bits of dark chunks spewing this way and that. And then it was all over. The pages stopped turning and fell open to a spell towards the back.

I snapped my head up to see if anyone had seen, but there was no noise from the bedazzled female and everything seemed as it was before.

My eyes scanned the spell and I silently read it;

> *Recollection sought, eradication fought. Though never truly forgot, yet exiled into Oblivion.*

My brows inched closer together in concentration. What the hell was that supposed to mean? And how come the page froze to this distinct one?

I sighed, sections of my hair drifting with the breath, through the strands of golden brown my eyes snagged on ocean eyes and raven black hair.

My heart stalled and my throat caught in a swallow.

Tolden slipped in between two bookshelves a few feet from my desk and I instantly picked up another book in my pile to become occupied with. But as I stared at the pages all I saw was bloodied sand, my hands around the elven boy's neck, the sound of it snapping—

No. No. No.

I would not go there.

I made myself swallow the bile rising in my throat and set the book down. Not wanting anyone to know what I was up to or that I was checking books out, I opened the drawers full of quill pens, ink and thin pieces of paper. As I began to scribble down the two poems that I'd read I felt my cheeks heat.

Someone was watching me.

Flicking my eyes up I noticed another pair staring at me through the bookshelf spaces. I instantly looked back at my paper but didn't write anything.

I cleared my throat and blinked a couple times. This was not the elven boy from Helmfirth.

Elves sometimes looked similar. I was being foolish.

"You seem to have lost your train of thought there." The drip of mockery in his voice scratched the insides of my ears and made me shiver.

I lifted my eyes to glare at Tolden. "You flatter yourself."

He leaned against the bookcase, the perfect image of smug and arrogant elven male pride shining in his eyes and on his face. "That's rich coming from you."

"Meaning?"

"Nothing. . .*Princess*." Tolden's cocky attitude and grin told me all I needed to know.

He knew who I was. Of course he did, so why was I surprised? Nevertheless, it made my blood boil beneath my very skin.

"Don't ever call me that again," I hissed, fingers itching with an icy tinge.

"Why? What are you going to do?" Tolden pushed off of the bookcase and winked at me as he turned to go, a book tucked under his arm.

I shot up from my chair and glared at the back of his head. Willing him to turn around so I could punch him? Throw ice at his jerkish face? I didn't have a rutting clue.

I seethed and bit my lip so hard I felt a prick of pain.

But tears began to well in my eyes and I blinked them away bitterly. There was no end to this madness. To this darkness leaking inside of me.

CHAPTER 16

It had been hours since. . .that interaction in the library.

I couldn't get what Tolden said out of my head. He had called me by my royalty outright and had seemed so angry.

I had gone over the scene in my head again and again and I couldn't tell why he had been so upset. Perhaps he had not been upset at all and was simply joking and wanted to confuse me.

Which in this case, he had very well succeeded.

I put my thumb in my mouth as I traipsed around my room, walking one way and then turning sharply to walk the other.

And bloody hell! His *tone* really edged its way beneath my skin! I sounded like a selfish prick—maybe I was.

Turning to the glass balcony door I found my reflection in the pane and evergreen eyes stared back with that ring of gold. But I saw so much deeper than just the color or the details of my irises.

I saw memories of pain, of being tortured, of being forced to do horrible things. I saw a little girl of barely ten curled up in a corner, crying because she thought her family abandoned her. I saw an even older girl screaming and struggling to free herself as men dragged her into a cell and chained her up. I saw men laughing at her as she lay, strapped to a table; so afraid that she had wet herself.

I saw the first time the young girl had killed a living being.

I saw her sobbing and banging her head in her cell that same night. I saw many things. . .and remembered them all.

I blinked and realized I was crying. I wiped my tears away and folded my arms around myself for comfort. I had a lot of memories, some I wished to be taken away and some that I wished to get back.

Which is precisely what I planned to do.

But first, I had to figure out what the poem meant.

I found myself in the library again, this time I remembered the way and came across it much easier. I even grabbed a cranberry scone from one of the tables in the rooms I passed on my way. This room in particular had been decorated with seashells and jars of sand with conch shaped chairs and couches. Sparkles seemed to glitter on the floor and walls and I wondered if they had plastered sand into them.

Munching on my scone while I descended into the abyss that was the library I squared my shoulders. I couldn't just hide in my room for the rest of my time here. Whether Tolden was here or not I *had* to find out about this Oblivion place. I needed to stop freezing whenever he was around. . .he just. . .

He looked so much like that young boy. I hadn't realized, but I'd stopped in the middle of the staircase, scone still in hand.

I clenched my other fist.

Flashes of images came back from my time in Helmfirth, the bloody arena, the cheering and booing crowds.

I heaved a sigh so heavy it rattled my lungs. I just needed time, and then I would heal.

I would be fine.

Stepping down the rest of the way I stood straight and inhaled and walked into the library with that swagger I knew all too well.

"Hello again!" the female at the front desk chirped.

I smiled.

"Didn't get your fill the first time?"

"Never," I said as I slipped my scone that I'd lost my appetite for into the little bin by her desk.

"Well, what are you here to read about now?"

"Oblivion," I said bluntly.

The female's eyes flickered and brightened and then went dull again. The smile returned to her face and those two jewels appeared.

"I certainly have many books on oblivion, but they are all different definitions. I am not too sure if we will have the right one."

"Doesn't matter, any will suffice." Truth.

"This way then."

And she was back to leading me down aisles and shelves full of books. This time, I noticed we went in a different direction than last time and even passed under an archway that glistened with that onyx color that was everywhere here.

I flashed my eyes upward and caught my reflection gazing back, green and gold and black mixed together and it sent chills crawling down my spine. My magic awakened in answer, crackling to life and I swallowed to keep it down.

"Just over here!" The elven female called to me, having noticed I had stopped following her. I picked up my pace and peeked around the shelf she was gesturing towards.

It was small.

Smaller than I expected.

"Not too much here, but it's all we have."

"Thank you. . ." I paused, realizing I didn't know her name.

"Rosita."

"And I'm—"

"Oh, I know who you are, Lady Ryn."

Black ice crackled at the corners of my vision and I clenched my fist. I pursed my lips together and Rosita inclined her head to me. . .almost in a bow.

I turned to watch her go and warmed the frost that had begun to creep inside of me. The never ending black frost always edging closer.

I sighed, and I swore I saw my breath come out in a puff.

Now, to the task at hand. I brushed by the books until I came to the very top of the first shelf, standing on my tip toes and just barely reached it. Angling my head so I could read the titles and authors, I began my search.

It turned out it wasn't a very long hunt since this aisle wasn't very large. But I had read enough of mushrooms causing oblivion, and the history of the elves who'd drunk themselves into oblivion to recite them in my sleep.

I breathed a breath of relief when I'd found a book of a different sort. It had a plain cover except for a mountain range across the top of it. I brushed the dust off and admired it. Squinting a bit closer it looked as if something was shimmering and moving at the crest of the mountaintop. I blinked and shook my head, it must be from reading about all those mushrooms.

I smirked and sat, my back resting against the bookshelf. Opening to the first page I glanced over the summary of the book and the page numbers and flipped through all the boring first pages. Some of the words and ink had faded but as I glanced closer at one of them spread across the parched paper it looked familiar. Or the formation did at least.

Shrugging, I turned to the beginning. But to my surprise there weren't any words or faded ink spots; there were paintings and drawings sprawled across the parched yellow pages. Paintings of horrific creatures with ghastly looks smeared across their faces and hollow eyes and mouths. Some of them with just sockets, no teeth, no hair.

They were hideous things.

Turning the next few pages, there were images of the beings floating and reaching out for something. . .or someone that was not there. Flipping through even more there were caves filled to the brim with glowing objects that the floating creatures seemed to be searching for, or guarding.

Whether it was magic or my imagination I swore I could hear them wailing and moaning, some even screaming.

A shudder ran down my spine and I made to close the book when a finger stopped the pages from shutting. My neck snapped up in an attempt to locate where the finger had come from.

My eyes locked onto hazel ones. I scowled.

"Look who took my advice and actually looks decent!" Adaner winked at me, crouched in front of me with his pointer finger still in the middle of my book.

"Shut up."

"I have a few ideas of—"

I stared so hard at him I started seeing icicles forming.

"Alright, alright." He lifted his hands in the air, letting go of the book and allowing the pages to fall shut.

I slammed it closed and got to my feet to put it back but before I could Adaner snatched it from me and held it too high for me to even reach.

"What are you studying?" He peered over his nose to look at the pages and flipped through a couple. "Ghastly creatures, they are."

"Do you know of them?" I asked, warily.

"Who doesn't?"

I swallowed and looked away.

"Oh, I see. The princess doesn't even know the history of her own elven land."

My frosty gaze swept towards him, words nipped at the edge of my tongue but I held them back. A lot of good it did for me to talk back to Tolden. Instead, I simply asked, "What of it?"

"The history? Well, these creatures live in Oblivion." Adaner stopped there but I had so many more questions.

"What do you mean live in Oblivion?" A memory sparked in my mindseye and I pictured that frozen poem.

"Mount Oblivion? Golly, girl have you really never heard of it?'

"I've been in the human realm these past years, so you'll forgive me if I don't know anything about this one," sarcasm dripped from my tongue, I was in no way actually asking for forgiveness.

Adaner smirked and flipped the book a couple of pages back. "See here?" He pointed to a painting of a cold, misty mountain. Its edges were jagged and dark and fog floated around the crest of the mount. "That there is Mount Oblivion and it's where all the lost minds, or memories are sent."

Something snapped in me upon hearing his words. Lost memories?

I tried to not look too intrigued and bit one of my fingernails. "So, the creatures that are floating around in there are lost minds?"

"Aye. They're the ones who were unsalvageable after the war."

"Are they still alive?"

"No, they don't even really have an existence. They are simply minds that have been lost, and they are sent to guard the lost memories stolen from others."

Like me. I wanted to say, but kept silent.

Adaner flipped through the pages until he got to the last one. I peered over his shoulder to look and found a map gazing back. I smirked inwardly. He had just given me my free ticket there.

"It's one of the most dangerous roads to travel on, but it's the only way to get there. Not many return from the Glandor Gap."

I glanced at Adaner for half a second. The teasing and mockery had ceased, for a little bit at least. He was actually helping me, but he didn't know—couldn't know—what I planned to do. He was probably just stating a fact.

I cleared my throat and straightened. "Well, I think my history lesson is over."

"That it is, Princess." He winked and I resisted the urge to smack him. "If ever you need a history teacher to aid you in your lessons, never hesitate to call for me." Adaner reached above me, returning the book to its place and pinning me against the bookshelf in the process. "There's a lot I could teach you, I'm sure."

A very visible shudder shivered its way down my spine and Adaner's hazel eyes glowed. I was sure my own eyes shone back with frost and bitterness as I placed a hand on his chest and pushed him away.

Without a word, I watched him leave the library, smirking and swaggering with that cocky confidence of his. I wasn't watching him for the reason he thought albeit, I was waiting for him to leave so that I could rip the page from the back of that book and be on my way to find my memories.

With the crumpled piece of paper enclosed in my fist I waited for a heartbeat of a moment before I, too, left the library. I nodded in farewell towards Rosita and she flashed me a jeweled grin.

Back in my elaborate bedchambers, I sprawled across my bed, dresses shoved aside and map in hand. I studied it, identifying all the roads and paths and forests leading to the Glandor Gap. I tried to imagine what mishaps would happen but quickly tucked those thoughts deep inside my heart. They would not suffice.

I thought back to what Adaner had said about the Glandor Gap. He had warned that it was quite a dangerous road and that not many survived it. Had he been trying to warn me?

No. He couldn't have known.

Seeing as it was the only way to get to Oblivion, I was going to have to take it. I inhaled, held it for a few heartbeats then exhaled. I would leave tomorrow. For now, I needed to find the kitchen and infirmary for supplies—which proved to be a lot harder than I previously imagined.

No one was allowed into the kitchens, or perhaps it was just me, *Lady Ryn,* who was not allowed in. Regardless, the way was barred by a very tall female with hair slicked back so tight it looked as if she didn't have any.

"I've said it once and I'll say it once more, Lady Ryn, no member of this court will be stepping a single toe in my kitchen. Not today, not ever." The female placed her slender hands on her slender hips and stared down her nose at me.

I made a pouting face. "But I'm famished."

"And you will continue to be famished. Go fetch yourself an apple from one of the gardens, or even better fetch yourself some patience."

I resisted the urge to give her a vulgar gesture and almost, *almost* used the *'but I'm the princess'* excuse but immediately thought better of it.

My guts twisted at the thought of even mentioning that out loud.

The female harrumphed and whipped around, the swinging door to the kitchen moving furiously.

I sighed. I would have to steal the food from the tables in some of the rooms then.

Hopefully the infirmary had a better outcome.

Thankfully, it did.

Once I was finished, I went along my way. I was leaving tonight, with or without enough supplies. It was foolish, I knew that. But I had gone days without food or water, I could do it again.

I had been taught to survive, so survive was what I would do.

CHAPTER 17

The night air felt crisp against my skin as it wafted by.

It tousled loose strands of my braided plait in my face as I tucked it inside my shirt, feeling the hair snaking down my back. No need for it to be a distraction tonight.

I stood on my balcony overlooking the ocean cliffs and the roaring sea beneath and inhaled the salty air. Who knew when I would smell it again?

I had mapped out my journey. I knew how far Oblivion was. I knew I didn't have the supplies for it and I certainly knew it was nigh on impossible for me to ever return to the Crescent Kingdom.

That excited me and I did not let myself wonder why. I felt as if this was my one last adventure to be had. There was nothing for me here anyway.

I inhaled once more and grimly scanned the horizon. That twilight hue was just barely beginning to show. Everyone would be awakening for their early training soon.

Shouldering the pack that I had made out of my satin pillowcase with the *very* small amount of supplies I had, I slipped back through my balcony door and out of my elaborate bedchambers altogether. The door clicked quietly shut behind me and I began to walk swiftly but silently down the halls.

I passed no one and heard not a peep of a sound. Good. Brilliant even.

But when I reached the cobblestone pathways leading away from the civilian houses and the palace, I began to feel as if someone were watching me. I shrugged it away and labeled it as paranoia. Yet even as I left the perimeter of the palace grounds and took the cobbled steps leading to the sandy shore below, I turned around slowly.

I spotted a figure, dark hair blowing in the wind standing atop a balcony, the same wing as my own bedroom. I squinted, acting as if I were looking at anything else, not wanting whoever it was to know I was looking at them. I feared it was too late though as the sensation of two eyes meeting across a great distance spread all over my body.

I swallowed visibly and whipped back around. I controlled my steps as I leisurely descended to the shore. Soon the balconies were out of sight and I hoped I was too.

Something told me inside that it didn't matter.

Crouching low on the sand I took the map out and scanned the route once more. Glancing north I assessed the path I would be taking and allowed myself no other thoughts as I rose and headed on the journey. It would take two weeks on foot to get there, according to others who had taken this same route, which was the only route. Or so Adaner had said.

I cursed. He had better have been telling the truth because if there was an easier way—I would be livid.

Brushing back my hair I stuffed the map back in the satchel at my side. Something like excitement brimmed inside of me. It hadn't been too long ago that I'd set out on a trek, but this time I knew where I was headed. I had a destination, instead of running away. Whether it was the same or different this time, I did not care. I had a purpose and I had the right mind to fulfill it.

But that excitement soon slithered away almost three nights later, as if melting through the cracks of a kingdom's worn cobblestones.

I heaved a breath in and out, again and again as I trudged up a steep hill. The grass beneath my feet was slippery from the dew of the night and I kept tripping and splattering dirt and grass all over me.

I stuck my booted foot on a sturdy looking rock and pulled myself up only to feel the rock give way. I slipped and felt myself falling before slamming my face into the muddy ground.

Cursing and spitting the watery earth out of my mouth I wiped at the corners. Blast it all; this place, this land, the bloody rain!

I swatted at the flies buzzing around me and sat there on my rump. I probably looked hideous—felt hideous at this point.

There was no turning around, nor giving up and I certainly wasn't planning to but the route could have been a little more accessible. I had quite a few words for whoever had mapped it. I had already trekked across sandy beaches, sometimes having to swim through the salty water to get across the coves and caverns that continuously tried to suck me into certain death.

Now, there was this massive hill to crest.

Wiping my hands on my already muddy and wet leathers, I rose to my feet and crawl-slipped my way up the hill. Once I crested the top I let out a sigh of relief, about bloody time. But as I turned to adjust the satchel on my back and get the map out, the rock my boot was resting on gave way and I went careening down the slope, not the way I'd come, but the way I was headed.

The muddy hillside was steep and covered in boulders, sticks and other things I couldn't tell but each one bit into my skin and tore at it. I screamed as I kept tumbling, head over heels, hair flying from the plait, mud and blood mixing together.

I yelped as I landed at the bottom and was suddenly submerged. Trying to gasp for air resulted in me swallowing salty water. I frantically began to kick my legs and pump my arms to reach the top—wherever it was. It was dark and the water stung my new cuts.

I felt the surface of the water approaching and kicked one last time. Emerging out of the water I gulped the muggy air down. Immediately, I began to cough and spit what felt like half the ocean out of my mouth.

I groaned and pushed back my wet hair from my face, aiming to get my bearings. I swam towards the bank and pulled myself out and laid on my back, my chest heaving up and down.

My hands instantly went to my satchel and I cursed colorfully when I found the map and everything in my bag was soaked through. Squinting at the parchment in the dim light of the stars and moon I could read a load of nothing.

"Great," I mumbled.

But when out of the darkness, across whatever body of water I had just fallen into, a deep grating sound rumbled and every hair on my neck and arms rose, I realized I had issues tremendously larger than a wet satchel.

I scrambled back even further up the bank and limped all the way to the bottom of the muddy slope I had just fallen down. Quickly glancing back up it, I mentally noted that there would be no way of escaping the way I'd come.

The snarling sound continued and my ears strained to hear the other sound. I steadied my breathing and listened. My heart began to beat faster when I realized it was the sound of the water rippling.

I pressed my back as far into the muddy slope as I could and even tried getting a little higher but to no avail as every time I gained ground, I fell closer to the water than I was previously. I unsheathed the sword strapped across my back, my neck sore from banging against it during my fall.

I didn't dare take my eyes off of the water and with careful, practiced training, I adjusted my breathing. Rings of water rippled towards me and I could still hear that grating, rumbling sound. I watched as a layer of spikes attached to a massive wormlike body emerged out of the water and submerged again.

I adjusted the grip on my sword and waited, heart hammering against my rib cage.

Claws that scratched against stone echoed through the damp night and my breathing hitched slightly. The claws hesitated as if sensing something.

I held my breath.

It could sense my fear.

I closed my eyes and went through my breathing exercise once more.

A huge wave of water crashed down upon me and I flung my eyes open. They filled with sea water and I pushed my back even further into the muddy slope, holding myself upright by planting my heels in the slippery mud, but to no avail. They would not stop bloody slipping in the accursed wet earth.

The sea monster dove back into the water, having not sensed me perhaps. Except if I was honest with myself, it was more than likely taunting me. Struggling on the slope and failing in all my attempts to hold myself upright, I began slipping down the hill. Ripples began to appear once more in the water and I dug my nails into the earth, grabbing only fistfuls of mud. A gasp escaped my lungs as I slipped further down the hill, boots hitting the water just as the sea monster burst out of the rippling current and made a decent attempt at snapping my body in half.

Attempt being the key word.

I leapt upward with all my strength, sticking my sword into the muck. It held true and firm as I hung tightly with my left hand. I curled my leg towards me and snatched my dagger from my boot, angling the blade down.

"Not today, demon!" I snarled right back at it as it snapped its jaws at me, just inches from my feet. If I were to slip, even the tiniest bit. . .

I adjusted my grip on the sword and prepared to strike. I would take out its eyes first. In one swift motion as the sea worm angled its head back and thrust it forward to, no doubt eat me whole, I thrust my dagger into its left eye, down to the hilt.

It squealed and squirmed and jerked away, snapping its jaw and almost pulling me with it as it tossed its head every which way. I yanked my dagger out before it could yank me off the hill, blood oozing all over my hands. Slipping slightly, I pulled myself back up on my sword.

This time the spiked worm flung itself back and disappeared in the water.

"Damn it," I cursed. My hand was continually slipping on the hilt of this sword. I couldn't last much longer. Silence flowed through the night and I was able to focus on my breathing, anything to keep my mind off of the growing ache in my left hand and arm. I counted the minutes and listened for the ripple of the water.

My eyes were closed, giving me the full advantage of my hearing and that's when I heard it; the tiniest rustle of the current. It was headed for me again. I felt a little smug at the fact that the monster would still find me hanging here, but also a little offended it hadn't given me more time; as if it thought I wouldn't last that long.

In truth, I wasn't sure I would either.

The sea worm rammed right into the side of the muddy hill and it rattled my teeth, blood, water and mud flying everywhere. I yelped and grasped onto the sword with both hands. I glanced down. It was about to strike again and I braced myself.

SLAM.

Right beneath me.

My eyes flicked to where the blade of my sword was stuck in the mud and I noticed it was starting to loosen.

I groaned through my teeth and felt them rattle a third time. This was just another day at the *Death Pit*.

Just another creature. I was the champion.

I was going to have to do this a different way.

Allowing the worm to continue to ram its ugly head into the side of the hill I began to wiggle the sword loose. My arm ached and protested against me but I kept at it.

I continued glancing down at where the creature was and timed his attacks.

One. . .two. . .three. . .

The sword tipped down as it became unstuck and I tensed. I counted until the creature pulled away again and then—

Yanking the sword out completely I held it and my dagger up high as I careened towards the monstrous sea creature below.

Before it knew what hit it, my blade and dagger were embedded in its skull down to the hilt. Blood and other liquids squirted up at me and sprayed across my face and hands.

The sea worm reared up and screeched so loudly I wanted to cover my ears. It echoed off the water and bounced back. Grimacing, I felt the warmth of his blood and brains spilling all over me.

Before I could react and twist the hilt in further to make sure he was dead I felt myself falling. . .or rather the creature I was kneeling upon had succumbed to death and was now falling. Salt water swallowed me and filled my nose, mouth, and eyes. They burned but I ignored it as I placed a foot on the worm's head and tried to yank my sword out of its head. But it was deep. I had done my job too well, it seemed.

The water kept swirling around us and it became darker and darker as we tumbled to the bottom of the bay. After all, I was holding onto dead weight. Except I was *not* about to drown after having survived a sea monster attack. There was no way in Hell's Keep.

After trying and failing to pull the sword out of the worm's head a second and third time, I forfeited it and snatched my dagger back instead. Pushing off of the dead creature's body, I kicked and swam wildly for the surface.

Breaking through the water I gasped and inhaled the muggy air. Immediately, I began coughing, my lungs and throat burned with the ache of having had no air and the sting of the salt. Turning in circles, I realized I was unable to see where I was. It felt like I was in the middle of the water with no land on either side. And goodness only knew what else would be in here. I didn't want to stall and give some other monster a chance for supper.

Treading water, I closed my eyes and allowed myself to decide the direction. The wind blew past me and blew my hair out of my face, guiding me with the current. If I remembered correctly, which I usually did, the wind had been tousling my hair *into* my face at the palace from a slight angle and throughout my entire journey the wind had been at my back most of the time.

I circled around, feeling the breeze push against the back of my wet hair, plastered to the back of my head.

This way should do.

I began to swim, not caring that I couldn't see land. Not caring that I very well could be leading myself *away* from shore. I had to trust my instincts.

After what seemed like hours, I finally reached the blessed land.

I scrambled out in an extremely ungraceful manner and laid flat on my back, drawing air into my lungs and blowing it out again. I coughed and turned to my side, spitting the water from my mouth. I shuddered and didn't allow myself to think what else could be lurking in the water. I was out now. That's all that mattered.

Standing to my feet I opened my soaked through pack and didn't dare touch the map. It was so wet it needed time to dry or one touch and it would turn to clumps of long lost parchment and ink. I cursed and tossed it gently behind my back again. I felt it thumping against my hip and dripping water down my pant leg. It didn't matter all that much seeing as I was just as drenched.

As the stars shifted, revealing that time was passing, I crested the top of a lush green field, one that was much different than the muddy slope I'd taken a tumble down earlier. Wildflowers speckled the terrain and I could see the sparkling glint of water in the dim light.

I made my way down the hill and into the field of wildflowers and tall emerald blades. Practically sprinting, I reached the glorious flowing stream and plunged in after hastily tossing my satchel to the bank.

I scrubbed and scrubbed every part of me. I wanted this salty swamp stench gone. I ran my fingers through my hair and scrubbed at my face. Surfacing again, I took a breath and watched the wretched seaweed, mud, and blood and other particles float off of me downstream.

Good riddance.

I shivered as a cool breeze wafted past and glancing over myself, I decided I was clean enough. Swimming through the water I reached the bank, snatched up my pack and went to find a spot where I might dry off. Not bothering to peel off my clothes I sprawled beneath the stars.

I hadn't realized how much I'd missed the sun. How the absence of it affected me more than I thought but now laying under a blanket of night I wished for the warm rays of the sun more than ever.

Part of me wished the Crescent Kingdom had sun, or had some days where there was sun. I rolled my eyes. It mattered not, seeing as I would not be returning.

I stuffed my hand in my satchel and fished out the apple I had taken from one of the midnight glass bowls in a room with seashells and scales hanging all over the walls. I inspected it beneath the starlight and after washing it off for good measure, devoured it.

I lifted my hand to take another bite but my torn and broken nails caught my attention, flashing in the dim light of the sky. A few had completely splintered and were much shorter than before. They stung slightly but not as bad as being eaten or chewed on by a behemoth sea monster.

As the time began to pass I was almost completely dry. The stars were in completely different sections of the sky now and there was even a different hue to the black expanse of sky.

I had long since tossed away the core of my apple and now began on my way again. For the rest of the night the blue hue grew darker and the moon traveled a little higher, stars peaked out here and there. I trudged on, always following the map I took out every so often to make sure I was on the right path. I was grateful it had dried well enough, although pieces had ripped off and it was extremely wrinkled.

When night officially fell and the moon had long since been high in the sky, I climbed into a lone tree and nodded off. Never fully falling asleep for fear of some other monstrous creature finding me. I had good reason too, all throughout the darkness there were strange, ominous sounds. At one point I even heard screams.

I sighed.

It was going to be a long two weeks.

CHAPTER

18

Upon awakening, I found the moon to be in the same bloody spot.

I couldn't stand this. My back ached, my neck ached—everything rutting ached! I jumped from the tree and stretched. I wasn't even sure as to how much sleep I had actually gotten. My guess would have been a mere few hours.

It didn't matter. I shouldered my pack and I set out once more. I crossed bright green fields peppered with tall plants, walked through forests buzzing with insects and whispers of singsong voices, passed many streams leading into lakes and even came across a couple towns.

I never crossed through the towns for fear of too many questions being asked. Even though I knew I was still in the Crescent territory I didn't want any unnecessary attention. As I walked along the ridges of a third small town I watched it bustle about. It was quaint, barely even had enough houses or structures to be called a town.

It was more of an outpost.

I watched elven males standing guard at the borders. I noticed children running in and out of the homes, there seemed to be fields of grain growing where elven females could be seen working and carrying bundles to carts pulled by horses.

I wondered what it would be like to grow up in such a place as this. I stopped for a moment and peeked over the ridge so as not to be seen. What would it be like to live in a place so quaint and simple that everyone knew each other? To come home to a family and enjoy a home cooked meal and read books by the fire?

Something wet fell onto my cheek and I wiped it away with a finger. I had not realized I'd begun crying. Pushing myself up off the ground, I tucked this scene into my memory to save for when I was feeling lonely and wiped my tears on the dirt-stained pants of my leg.

Nights passed and I came across very little. The terrain was becoming rockier and barren. It was twilight when I came across the mountain ranges.

Weary and dusty from my journey, I took a moment to look at how grand they were. My eyes glanced from the path I was walking on up the mountain side and I saw steps. Taking my map out I glanced over it and sure enough, those steps were my path. I breathed in and out and stuffed the parchment back.

It was while I was half way up the steps when I heard a deep rumbling sound.

I halted completely and listened. It sounded like a herd of animals racing across the rocky terrain. I slipped my dagger into my hand and crouched low, waiting.

Snarls and growls ripped across the range and the thundering of the things running echoed all around me. Those steps would be the actual death of me if I did not get off of them right the hell now.

I glanced up to the side of the mountain, but only gray slate stared back. There was nothing to hold onto, nothing to get out of the way.

And I didn't have time for out of nowhere goblins with gangly limbs came crawling from over the side of the mountain, heading straight for me. There were at least thirty of them.

I wasted no time and took off back down the steps, my feet could barely keep up with how fast I was half falling, half running down stone. I tried to think if maybe this had been the wrong way. . .but Adaner's warning came back to mind.

This must be Glandor Gap.

The sound of snarls and the thundering of the goblins chasing me snapped me back to reality and I just barely caught myself before completely careening off of the steps. I desperately looked to the left and the right, looking for a place to hide or squeeze into or maybe even a ledge I could jump on—there!

Without thinking, I veered right and jumped off of the steps onto a harsh jagged ledge. I felt myself falling and tried to will myself closer, but then a blast of dark ice poured out of my palms, creating phantom steps for me to step on to the ledge awaiting me below.

I quickly ran across them, barely registering that it was *my* magic. The steps melted before the goblins could even think about going across them. But they were already crawling around the side of the mountain to get to me. They snarled with jagged teeth and had claws for hands and feet. They were naked, bony, nasty looking creatures with pale bluish skin.

Holding my dagger in one hand and readying the other to blast dark ice, I prepared myself. Two goblins jumped, trying in vain to get to me. I shed no remorse as they quickly fell to their deaths at the bottom of the gap.

I heard their claws on the stone behind me as three more goblins lunged for me from above. I sliced one right across the neck and blasted the other two with my dark ice. With not much training, the first blast actually hit the goblin, the second one veered too far to the left to even come close to hitting the last one.

Groaning as it reached out with its claws I slashed my dagger across its hand. It screeched so loud I screamed. But it still came after me, clawing the ground, its blue blood pouring everywhere. I kicked its face and slashed my dagger across its neck.

Its last squeal died on the frigid wind of the mountain range. But there was still more racing towards me.

I inhaled and crouched low, ready for them. But with each one I killed, more seemed to appear from the very crevices of the mountain.

They were swarming me now.

My magic and dagger weren't good enough as I sliced and slashed and stabbed. From the extensive use of my power, I was beginning to feel faint. My vision blurred as a goblin reached for my arm and slashed its blue claws across the tender skin. The next one dug its claws into the skin of my thigh.

I screamed with each claw that punctured my skin.

I stabbed one in the head and it careened off of the ledge. I stabbed—no, I realized my dagger was no longer in my hand but in the head of the goblin that was now falling to his death in the gap below.

I ground out a yell and summoned more black ice to the surface. I began to shiver and feel numb but kept fighting. I would not go down lying on my back. I would go down fighting.

I felt a coppery tang of blood in my mouth and could smell it in the air as five goblins raced towards me and toppled me to the ground. Their slashing, gnashing teeth came so close to my face. I pressed my back as far into the cold stone as possible and held them at bay with a ring of ice around me. But with each pound and claw and snarl the ice became thinner and thinner.

Tears formed in my eyes from the stinging of my wounds and the struggle to keep my magic working. I felt the thud of three more goblins jump over the gap and readied myself for the end.

I would not make it past the Glandor Gap, just like Adaner had said.

And now, I realized he had been trying to warn me. How foolish I had been.

The power shield that I had around me shattered and dark ice splintered all over me. I closed my eyes and prepared to feel the pain of gnashing teeth and ripping claws, but I did not.

The goblins started screeching and screaming and scattering away. Bright white magic surged past me and the sound of metal slicing into goblin flesh echoed all around. Three figures who looked vaguely familiar fought and killed the creatures.

Dots danced before my blurry vision and I felt my hand snap against the stone of the mountain before I felt hands—strong hands—pulling me from under my arms. I let myself be dragged and didn't even bother to try to defend myself.

I was so very tired and my vision kept going in and out in blurry waves, making me nauseous. I expected to feel the sharp, clawing talons of the goblins grasping at me, but instead I felt muscular arms carrying me and pressing me against a leather and smoke scented chest.

A male scent that was so familiar.

That was the last thing I remember thinking before the blissful darkness took me and with it all the pain.

I jolted awake, searing pain lancing up my leg.

I screamed and lashed out but chains held me back—chains? I thrashed and thrashed. How could I have gone back to Helmfirth? Pain reverberated through my thigh and my arm and I let out another scream.

Maybe it had all been a dream, no, some horrid nightmare.

I began sweating but felt cold and hot all at once. The pain like lightning surging through me.

Maybe I had never truly left in the first place.

"Hold her *still*!" a voice commanded in a thick accent.

"*What* do you think I'm doing?" another snarled back.

"Not a very good job."

I had heard these male voices before. . .in these same tones arguing in a room.

My head swam and swam and my vision began to unblur, though not all the way.

Pain ruptured again and then relief as something was taken out of my thigh.

I blinked through the tears and blur as warm light penetrated my vision. Three male figures leaned above me and as I blinked again just before my vision fully cleared, unimaginable pain spliced through my arm as I felt them *pull* something out. I gritted my teeth but could not stop the scream that expelled from my lungs.

"*Hold her!*"

And that's when I knew; they had come to rescue me. . .however they had known.

Adaner's face was the first I focused on. His thick accented voice brought me back to reality and his face, covered in blood, was staring down at me.

I was not in Helmfirth.

I squeezed my eyes and then opened them again. That's when I saw the male with shoulder length blonde hair, Cadeyn. He leaned over me and I could feel a strong grip on my legs.

"You basically had them all slaughtered before we even got there," he joked, even though his gold eyes were filled with. . .concern.

I choked on a laugh that didn't quite make it out when I saw who else was there; Tolden, his blue eyes staring down at me as he applied pressure to my arm.

Suddenly, splicing pain shot up and down the arm he was holding and I managed to clamp down on my cry as I looked down to survey the damage.

Bile rose in my throat.

My skin was pulled back at the edges of a deadly looking wound. My skin was burnt and decayed. Inside the flesh of my arm, I could still see the remnants of the blue blood that had seeped beneath my skin. Two of the goblins claws that had undoubtedly been *embedded* in my skin as well, now lay discarded on a cloth.

Adaner glanced at me watching him and spoke, "The Glandor goblins are some of the most dangerous monsters out there, love. Their claws drip with poison and they embed them into their prey so that they can feast on them while they slowly die."

I swallowed.

"When I said not many people return from the Gap. . .I meant it. You should have listened, love." He sighed through his nose and went back to mending the wound on my leg.

I opted to remain silent and looked away from them all.

Adaner continued mending my wounds. He had some sort of bottle that smelled strongly of cinnamon and peppermint and something else that I couldn't quite decipher. It stung as he dabbed it on the wound with a cloth but I made no sounds.

I looked at the ceiling and studied it. It looked as if we were in a cave of some sort with blackened walls leading into a dark ceiling with speckles of openings here and there to reveal the dark sky.

Stars appeared here and there amongst the fog and I tried to count them but searing, stinging pain shot up my thigh and I lurched forward with a cry of pain. I hadn't realized it but I grabbed Adaner's forearm and clung tightly to him.

"Hold tight."

A scream escaped my lips. I wasn't sure what was happening but it hurt like hell. Tears slipped down my cheeks and someone pried my grip away from Adaner, I'm assuming so he could keep working unhindered.

I could feel myself slipping. Not into unconsciousness, which I would have preferred. No, it was in the part of my mind that I didn't like to visit. And it was never my choice to go there. I squeezed my eyes shut trying to make the images go away. Trying to send the memories fleeing. . .but failed.

Adaner's hand became Lord Elton's. Tolden and Cadeyn became the torturer who brought in the tools and the guard who would drag me to my doom.

I clawed even harder into Elton's arm—no, someone else's arm—and cried out, "Please. Please don't, Elton!"

Elton looked at me and with a blink he disappeared and it was Cadeyn who faced me now. His golden brown eyes were coated with worry and I realized Adaner and Tolden's faces were masked in strife as well.

I peeled my fingernails away from Cadeyn's arm and saw that I had left tiny indents in his leather.

I inhaled roughly. I needed to get away from them.

I didn't want to be here anymore.

All three males glanced at one another and it was like a silent code was going on amongst them. No one really knew what had happened to me in Helmfirth. I didn't want anyone to know. It was my own burden and past that I had to carry. No one else needed to be burdened with it.

I laid back down and covered my eyes with my arm. Why? Why had King Haleth sent me away?

None of this would have happened. I wouldn't have become Helmfirths Champion in the *Death Pit*. I wouldn't have been treated like an animal and had things done to me no human should have to endure.

I bit my lip and held back a sob. I would be fine.

I always had to be. I would endure.

CHAPTER 19

"Unfortunately, there is a possibility of you being crippled."

"Permanently?" I barely dared to ask.

Adaner glanced down at my leg then trailed the length of it up to my face again. "I don't think so. I think we got the poison out in time. You might experience pain permanently in the future but it's too soon to know."

I nodded and lowered my eyes.

Clothes rustled as if someone were standing and then a hand appeared before me. "Can I speak with you?"

I stared unblinkingly at Adaner. "I don't bite, love," he teased.

"Not unless you ask him to!" quipped Cadeyn from in the corner.

Tolden glared at the both of them from his side of the cave as he sharpened his weapon.

Adaners hazel eyes glowed and a smile spread across his face for a split second. He winked at me and I allowed him to put his arm under mine and help me out of the cave, but not before rolling my eyes at both him and Cadeyn.

Pain spliced up my leg but I gritted my teeth and bore down on it as we ducked to get out of the cave's mouth. The frosty breeze nipped at me and I shuddered. I instantly went on high alert for any goblins that might come roaring out of the crevices of the overhanging stone edge above us.

We were higher up than I had been when the creatures attacked me and layers of snow could be seen below and even a few flakes falling from the sky here and there. Adaner guided me to lean against the wall and I was able to prop my leg up on a tiny rock jutting out. I didn't feel as faint as I had earlier, the pain in my leg subsiding a little quicker.

I crossed my arms and glared at him. "Why are you being so agreeable to me?"

"Am I not allowed to treat a lady kindly?" He didn't even bother turning to look at me.

I rolled my eyes and looked away. If that's how it was going to be I wouldn't waste my breath.

"In truth," Adaner breathed in a sigh, "we almost lost you." His voice sounded genuine. None of the cocky mockery I had experienced with him.

"What do you mean?"

"You. . .died. Your heart stopped beating." Adaner still looked to the snowy view beyond.

Strange sensations flowed through my body and I wasn't sure how to react to them. Was it relief or regret that I had lived? Pushing my confusing thoughts aside I asked, tentatively, "How did you bring me back?"

He turned to me then. "We didn't. Your magic did." I swallowed hard enough to hear.

"At first I began trying to get your heart pumping again and breathing life back into you but you were fading too fast. We're not healers so we couldn't stop you from dying. But out of nowhere your magic started glowing from inside of you and brought you back to life." Adaner ran his hands through his hair and his face looked distraught.

"I've never seen anyone with that kind of power. With that *strength* of power," he pondered.

"What does it mean?"

He shook his head.

I slumped against the wall further, allowing the cold granite to bite into my spine. "I don't know what to say," I muttered.

"How exactly did you come to be in Helmfirth?" Adaner's words were careful, precise even.

My gaze flickered across his hazel eyes, then moved to the snow flakes falling behind his shoulder. "I was sent there."

"Where were you before that? What was your home?"

"Why are you asking me this? You know that I'm the heir of Crescent. You only remind me of it *every* damn time you call me princess."

"I want to hear it from you."

"Well you're out of luck." I shuddered against the cold.

"You said you didn't remember living in Crescent." Adaner's eyes glowed with realization. "Are you trying to retrieve lost memories. . .*your* lost memories?"

I simply nodded. "They were stolen."

It wasn't a question but I nodded in confirmation anyway.

Adaner turned away and faced the mountain view. His muscles in his back seemed to tense and he inhaled a deep breath.

"Did all three of you *really* just follow me or did someone send you?" I had my assumptions but wanted—needed—to know.

Still facing the mountains he replied, "Haleth wanted to keep an eye on you."

Anger boiled inside of me. "Haleth?"

He turned slightly towards me.

"What the hell, Adaner? The king sent you here to follow me? How the hell did he know?" I was yelling and didn't really care if any of the goblins could hear me. I had pushed off of the wall and began limping towards the male in front of me.

"It's his order, we have to follow him." His gaze flicked across me and glanced at the wound on my leg.

"Why the rutting hell didn't you tell me?!"

Adaner's eyes changed and he stood taller, a whole head taller than me as I craned my neck to look up at him.

"First of all, I don't owe you anything, *Princess*, so don't for one second come at me with your feisty attitude when you would be rutting *dead* right now if it weren't for King Haleth sending us out here to follow you!"

I was livid now. Boiling anger flowed through me and I felt dark ice pricking me everywhere. "I don't care! You could have left me for dead and I wouldn't have cared! Besides, my magic would have healed me."

"Perhaps, perhaps not. You were still poisoned!"

"I had accepted death!"

"Just because you accept it doesn't mean it has to be." Adaner stepped away from me and cursed colorfully, "Damn you're impossible to talk to!"

"And you're so easy yourself?"

"No, I'm not! But we almost lost you in there and. . ." Adaner hesitated and violently pushed his hair out of his eyes.

"And *what?*" I snapped.

"And King Haleth would have had our heads on a platter if we returned without you," he spat.

"Oh, I see. You're just here to follow orders. So you're damn lucky my powers saved me, otherwise what kind of a hellhole of a mess would you be in now?"

"What other reason would you have me here for? I don't know why you're making this such an extensive affair," Adaner growled and stepped towards the frosty edge looking out at the snowy mountain again, fists tightly clenched.

A gust of wind blew at my face and I welcomed it. I was hot and tired and fuming. As I glared at Adaner's back, I realized my error. I had revealed too much and shown my vulnerability; that I had actually wanted them here. I *had* been relieved to see them and when I found out they had come to save me, somewhere deep down in me wished it was because they actually cared enough—*someone* cared enough to follow me and help me of their own accord. That I wasn't just another task or command to be obeyed.

A stinging thought crashed into me and I tried to push it away but like the frosty wind pelting my face it burst through.

King Haleth cared.

But did he care enough because I was his daughter or simply because if I disappeared, he would be in a lot more of an unfortunate circumstance than he already was with harboring me?

I groaned and tried to turn around when splicing pain licked up my leg. I fell with a cry and hammered my fist into the ground.

"Damn it," I hissed, biting on the scream that threatened to break loose. I fought the tears trying to slip from my eyes and kept beating the stone ground trying to rid myself of the humiliation and pain shooting up and down my leg.

Adaner tried to reach down to help me but I shoved him away and tried to push myself up. My arm and my thigh burned with pain and I growled in frustration.

"Let me help," Adaner commanded. "I don't *need* your help."

"Clearly. Since you're just laying on the ground throwing a tantrum."

I'd had enough.

I whipped around and punched Adaner in the face—or would have if he hadn't deflected my blow with a flick of his wrist.

"Agh! Damn you!" I tried to get up again and this time Adaner thrust me to my feet and held me firmly under the arm.

"Better, love?"

"No!"

Suddenly my back was against the wall, pinned between Adaner's strong, very male body and a cold wall.

"I am going to say this once so *listen up*; you are going to have to learn how to ask for help. You are going to have to learn to rutting accept that help or. . . You. Won't. Survive."

"What if I don't want to!" I screamed in his face, spit flying from my mouth.

"That's a lie. I saw the relief in your face when you saw us coming to save you from the death awaiting you in the goblins hands. I saw your relief when you awoke and realized it was us."

I was done.

Done trying to argue.

Done trying to prove myself. I had given up.

I crumpled in Adaner's grip and he helped me slip to the floor. I didn't care that tears were spilling down my face. I didn't know whether I was sobbing or screaming or just crying. . .but I didn't care.

The darkness, whatever brokenness this was, could have me.

Again, I felt the iron clasps wrap around my ankles and wrists. I wasn't sure if they would ever go away. However phantom they were.

Different sorts of iron chains were wrapped around me now. The ones in my mind and heart.

And they were almost worse.

I was sobbing now and clutched my knees close to my chest. My thigh and arm protested against it but I ignored them. The pain reminded me I was alive.

I was alive.

CHAPTER

20

Eventually, Cadeyn and Tolden came to find Adaner and I.

They found us both leaning against the stonewall. My face must have been pale and gaunt for Tolden and Cadeyn to look at me the way they did. I ignored their question filled gaze and absently looked at Adaner.

He seemed to be sleeping as his head rested against the rock and his eyes were closed. I wondered why he'd done what he did. Why he'd bothered to stay. It angered me and frustrated me and I wasn't entirely sure of the reason.

Confusion wrapped around me as I grunted and rose to my feet. I realized my limp was nowhere near as painful as before. I moved my arm around and it had the same result.

Adaner stirred and rose without saying a word. He didn't even spare a glance towards any of us as he sauntered away.

"Are you alright?" Cadeyn questioned as Tolden followed Adaner inside the mouth of the cave.

"Fine." I stared after the two males and Cadeyn continued talking about something that I paid no heed to. "Since I am healed, can we make our way to Oblivion Mountain?" I asked rather blatantly.

Cadeyn, mid sentence, closed his mouth then opened it again, speaking, "Of course, my lady."

"Don't start with that name," I seethed.

"Sorry." His gold eyes glowed with sarcasm and a grin started to appear on his face.

"You should be." I glared at him but knew he could see I was jesting. . .at least a little bit.

He snickered but I was already heading back through the cave opening. My limp was getting better by the second. When I stepped through to the corner of the cave, where the supplies were set up, Adaner and Tolden both watched me and their eyes dragged down my body, to my leg and back up to my arm.

Beneath both of their stares I wanted to crumple to the floor and disappear through the cracks in it. "What?" I snapped.

"Your leg. . ." Tolden paused.

"It's healed," finished Adaner.

"Upset that your medical verdict was wrong?" I quipped, crossing my arms staring hard at Adaner.

His eyes squinted ever so slightly and the glint of hazel disappeared for a second. "Overjoyed actually."

I snorted. "That tone of voice convinces me all the more."

Adaner turned away and began packing up what satchels they'd brought.

Tolden spoke up, "That limp could have inflicted you for the rest of your life."

I snatched up my satchel and slung it over my shoulder.

Tolden continued, "I have never seen anyone heal that quickly. Especially from wounds such as yours."

"Indeed," Cadeyn piped in.

I turned to all three of the elven males. "As Adaner has already mentioned to me. But what does it mean?"

"It could mean a few different things. You could have healer blood or powers in you. . .or just that you have extremely powerful magic," Adaner answered me, not even turning around but I could see he pushed his hair back from his forehead, only for it to fall once more in the exact same way.

Flashbacks of conversations I had once overheard drifted in and out of my mind. I could never really piece them together in Helmfirth because after Lord Elton and his evil doers were done working on me, I was always bobbing in and out of reality and dreams; constantly fighting consciousness.

"Ryn?"

I blinked and was unwillingly whooshed back to the present. I focused my gaze on the three males, one of which had called my name.

"We're heading back to Crescent. You're to come with us."

A merciless chuckle escaped my lips as I glared at Adaner. "Like hell I am."

He groaned and shoulder his pack. "Like hell you are, *actually*."

"You can't make me."

"I can toss you over my shoulder and carry you all the way back."

A snort from Cadeyn had my blood boiling.

Something like fear shot up inside me and I looked around for an escape. I *was* going to Mount Oblivion. I had come all this way, I wasn't about to let three brutes stop me.

"I'm going to Mount Oblivion and if you so much as dare to touch me," I desperately wished I had my dagger in hand. But instead I just glared at him and angled my head to the side. "You'll have hell to pay and I'm not afraid of the consequences."

Adaner's eyes darkened. "We were ordered to keep you safe. So keeping you safe is what we will do."

"Perfect!" I exclaimed, turning around to the cave opening. "Then you all can come with." I walked out of the cave. It would be up to them if they wanted to obey the king's orders and follow me to keep me safe.

I rolled my eyes. Like I needed it.

Only moments later, I felt three presences behind me, following me, if not a bit begrudgingly.

Flicking my braided hair behind my shoulder, I dared a glance. "Glad you could join me!" I jeered.

"You're the one who should be glad," Adaner mumbled. "We saved your damn life."

"Again," I hissed. "I never asked for it."

"A simple thank you would suffice."

"I'll say it when I think you deserve it. Need I remind you that my magic saved me?"

I heard a chortle from Cadeyn and I could practically feel Tolden's piercing blue gaze boring into the back of my head. Adaner's hazel eyes were no doubt dark and filled with frustration.

Halting half way through our trek I unshouldered my satchel and dug through my belongings. My heart began to race when I didn't find what I was looking for.

Alarmed, I dumped my bag upside down and shook everything out. When I still had yet to find what I sought I began to look around on the snow covered ground. How had I lost it?

"What are you searching for?" Adaner asked, one eyebrow raised in a comical arc.

"My rutting map!"

A rustling of paper and Adaner's booted feet came into view while I searched my empty bag frantically. I glared up at him only to have a piece of parchment shoved in my face.

I snatched it and to my relief, it was the very map I was searching for. "You could have told me a bit sooner," I harrumphed and stuffed my scattered belongings back into my bag. "Saved me the trouble of *this*."

"And the trouble of dealing with your attitude," he grumbled as he stormed past me.

I stuck my tongue out at him.

"Besides, I know these lands well. We don't need a map. . .at least *I* don't."

Adaner turned back ever so slightly to smirk at me.

I made a face that Tolden glared, and Cadeyn snickered at.

I was starting to like Cadeyn. He found me comical, however much I'd love to punch them all in the face, Cadeyn had been the most agreeable. Even if he had helped Adaner in turning me into the king.

I sighed. What a turn of events.

Shouldering my pack once more I somehow ended at the back of the line. With the three elven males towering ahead of me, there wasn't much of a view—not one that counted at least.

Since the cadre I was traveling with were the silent type of travelers I decided to look down the obscenely dangerous edge of the pass we walked on. Slightly leaning over to see, I became dizzy at the height. The fall itself would be enough to kill the unfortunate person who slipped. I leaned a little farther and spotted patches of gray where the snow had already melted or not been able to quite reach.

It was so strange to think of all the territory I had crossed through and to now be trekking a mountain covered in snow. The very mountain that held memories—*my* memories. I inhaled and realized the males were already way ahead and I needed to catch up.

I sprinted after them up a rather steep slope. When I reached the top, huffing next to Adaner, my breath coming out in puffs of air, he simply looked at me from the corner of his eye. I couldn't help but feel small beneath his scrutinous side eye.

"We've arrived," he announced.

I tore my gaze away from his judgemental one and followed their line of sight; massive oak doors with etchings in a different language stretched out below us in a snowy gorge. The mountain rose up on either side of the small valley covered in a fresh layer of snowflakes. It was perfectly white with nothing marring it. The snow had ceased a little and seemed to slow just for us as we made our way through the gap.

I looked behind us at the footprints we left behind and wondered what I would know when I came back out of this palace. With the knowledge that I would learn, would I change? My stomach began to twist and I squeezed my hands tightly, fingernails biting into my skin.

When we reached the oak doors, Tolden stepped forward and ran his hand along the edge, his mouth was moving as if he was speaking to it and then suddenly a loud crack sounded and the doors rumbled open. Snow was swept away with the grand opening of the entrance and all three males drew their swords.

My mouth was left agape. How the hell would I have entered? Tolden had seemed to know a secret code to get in. Would I always be this clueless and helpless?

"Is it dangerous?" I asked, pushing away my own personal thoughts.

"The creatures usually mind their own business but we want them to know we mean business too. We take no chances." Adaner didn't look at me as he answered my question but I nodded anyway.

I followed Tolden and Cadeyn in while Adaner trailed behind, insisting I be in the middle. It was the first time I realized how weaponless I was. I had lost both my sword and dagger, left with naught but my bare hands.

That didn't sit well with me.

I leaned forward to ask Cadeyn if he might lend me a weapon when I heard a shrill moaning sound. The hair on my arms and neck rose and I turned towards the sound. To my horror, a ghostly creature, almost exactly like the drawings I had seen in the book back in the Crescent Palace, floated above us. I clamped my mouth shut and watched it move around as if looking for something and yet it was completely expressionless.

I shivered and dragged my gaze away from the ghastly creature to examine the rest of the cave. There were long tunnels leading into even darker areas where the those creatures were weaving in and out of. Some carried those glowing bottles, while others didn't. There were jagged rocks reaching towards us from the roof of the mountain and it seemed like they were prepared to pierce any one who lingered a bit too long.

We took a turn and the dark shadows began to disappear with the glow of a warm ambient light. Taking a corner we were met with the sight of several stories of shelves filled with glowing bottles and vases, all different shapes and sizes. My mouth fell open with how far the expanse of the shelves were.

"How do we know where to look?" I asked.

"Your name, love," Adaner drawled.

I rolled my eyes and lifted a hand. "What, so we're just supposed to ask one of these ghosts where my memories might be?"

"They have logs."

I looked at Tolden who had spoken. "Well, that's very organized."

"Yes. It is."

Neither Adaner nor Tolden sounded very impressed with me and I hated the way it made me feel. I sidled next to Cadeyn and waited for them to show me what to do or for them to just *do* something.

It's a good thing I hadn't ended up here alone, though I would never admit that aloud.

"Princess Ryn Noireis, Crescent Blood." Adaner's voice echoed beneath the mountain and the way he said my name sent shivers down my spine.

Not because I liked it. No, I hated it.

"Don't ever say that again," I seethed. He just looked me over and glared.

One of the flighty creatures began moving in the direction of the glowing shelf wall and went up, up and up, until I couldn't see it anymore. We waited a few moments before we could see it again. It was carrying the smallest ball of light I'd ever seen. Once it reached us it stared blankly at Adaner and held the ball of light out. He took it and handed it to me.

Just like that.

I breathed in deep.

"Now, just look into it and say your name."

I nodded and walked a few steps away. Leaning close to the small jar I held in my palms, I whispered, "Ryn."

Nothing.

No magic, no sparks, no memories. I cleared my throat, "Ryn Noireis." Still nothing.

"You're going to have to say your full name," Adaner said, picking at his fingernails.

"That *is* my full name."

"And I'm the king of the human realm." He stretched out his hand and admired it.

"Hell. To hell with you and—"

"And what, Princess?"

Anger. That's all I could feel boiling inside of me. I whipped around and mumbled the same words he had, "Princess Ryn Noireis, Crescent Blood."

Something began to happen. Even smaller spheres of light began to detach themselves from the larger one and began floating towards me. I watched until they disappeared from view, feeling them as they fell onto my forehead and temples. It was a strange cooling sensation that turned into stillness and yet the feeling of falling all at once.

A vision took hold of me, I felt like I was transported in time as I watched a young girl play in the sand. She was laughing and smiling while a maid watched her a few feet away. The stars shone overhead and the ocean was calm.

Suddenly, the young girl froze as she stared down at the sand she'd been playing with. It was now completely frozen over. The young girl looked at her maid and the fear in her eyes could not be hidden.

I felt jerked forward as a vision of the young girl and a female appeared. The older female was bent over the younger one, beating her. Then she was grabbing her ear and yelling into it. Blood trailed down the young girl's arms and back. Tears streamed down her face.

A third vision felt like it pushed me forward as the young girl stumbled into the throne room, being dragged by the older female. The young girl watched the female and the male argue. I could feel her desperation as she tried to hear what they were saying but the female was yelling so loudly, the young girl covered her ears.

The next thing I saw was the last memory. I watched as Haleth put the young girl in a boat and sent her down the river. He did not say goodbye, he didn't kiss her forehead, he didn't even wait to see her off. The young girl cried in the boat, all alone, cold and afraid.

Then the world went dark.

—⚡︎—

Something was shaking me. No, not something—*someone*.

I peeled my eyes open and looked up at the gazes of three concerned males, all of whom had knit-together brows and creased lines by their mouths from their frowns.

I didn't say or do anything. I simply lay there while Tolden or Adaner or Cadeyn stopped shaking me. I could barely hear their voices. I still felt far away. Everything was still a bit muffled.

Except for my thoughts. My mind was running rampant. I couldn't believe it. . .I had. . .she had. . .

I was going to be sick.

I pushed Adaner or Tolden—whoever—away from me and lurched forward just in time to heave my guts up, crouched on my knees, over and over again.

I heaved again and again as tears began to roll down my face. I wasn't sure if they were from the vomiting or the memories that had been replaced.

I started to cry and then my throat felt hoarse as if I was screaming. I banged my fist into the ground over and over until I could feel something warm and stinging trickling down my wrist. But I didn't care.

It was too much. All of this was too much. I didn't even know how to process it or even say it aloud.

One thing I did know was, Haleth had lied. That was the first thing that came to mind, my own father had lied saying I could never get my memories back. . .and more. He had clearly not wanted me to know what had happened. Who it had happened with. Why it had happened.

Things were starting to make sense now. At least a fraction of a bit.

My stomach began to ache again and I clutched it. There wasn't anything else to throw up so I got to my feet and began walking out. I didn't care about the moaning ghosts above me or whatever else might be living in this dank place.

I simply walked out.

To hell with it all. My three companions could follow me or stay, I didn't give a rutting damn.

I kept walking and did not look back. I could feel the presence of the three males behind me but I did not utter a word. Back down the snow covered mountain, my satchel across my back I descended the steps where the goblins had attacked me. In fact, their remains were still there. I didn't even give them a second glance.

I heard one of the males call my name but didn't respond. I had to get back. Two weeks was a long time and even then I might still be too late.

CHAPTER 21

Night fell across the Crescent Kingdom in a blanket of stars and wispy clouds reaching out to the seashore.

It took us a little less than two weeks to get back. We rested only when absolutely necessary, with one of us always rotating a watch throughout the night. I hadn't spoken a word since I got my memories back. I'd been so busy devising a plan and trying to process everything that I often forgot there were three males traveling with me. Not that I wanted to talk to them anyway.

No one told me that when my memories were replaced I would have to dive deep to find them and really remember them again. Some of them were fuzzier than others. They were like any memories any child would have from the ages one to ten. Some were blurry but some were very vivid.

I could see the vivid ones now. I knew what I had to do. Things were starting to fall into place.

I stopped on the sandy cliff overlooking the Crescent Palace and inhaled a deep breath. I could sense the three males come up beside me. I didn't know how I felt about them just yet. They were crude and annoying, always telling me what to do and what not to do. Fighting amongst themselves and constantly commenting about me and calling me *princess*.

And yet, they had saved my life, magic healing powers or not. In truth, if they hadn't shown up when they did when my shield was failing, my body would not have had time to heal itself because there would have been goblins tearing into it.

A rather gruesome thought.

I glanced back at them, glaring. I was starting to realize that whether it had been a job or not, they had saved me. That was worth something right? It was strange how a person could feel a bond to another when they'd saved your life.

"What are you staring at?" Adaner demanded.

"Not much," I muttered. So much for that bond I was thinking of.

"I need a bath," Cadeyn complained, smelling his armpit and nearly gagging.

"Your butt smells worse than your pits."

I stifled my unexpected laugh at Tolden's retort.

"And yours smells so much better, eh?" Cadeyn made a face at Tolden and I decided before they broke out in a fight it would be best to ask them the favor I had been plotting.

"I need your help," I started to say. The three of them trained their focus on me, eyebrows cocked, jaws set like stone. "I'm going to the Sol Kingdom."

Silence. Utter silence.

Then the staring started, lips parted in silent shock as they studied me. I am sure trying to glean if this was some sort of joke.

"Okay." Cadeyn shifted on his feet and walked towards me. "I'm in." I felt lighter at his eager willingness to aid me.

"Like hell you are," Tolden argued, no surprises there. I crossed my arms. "Like hell I am."

"Why?" Adaner demanded, exchanging a look with his brethren.

I bit my lip. I wasn't sure if they would believe me. Flashes of Skandar lying dead on the ground protruded my mind. Other flashes of what I'd seen elbow the Sol Palace broke their way through and I squeezed my eyes shut for a moment, willing them to leave me alone.

But they wouldn't leave me alone. My conscience could not take anymore of their haunting imagery. So I opened my mouth and said, "There are prisoners beneath Queen Cressida's palace. I need to save them."

"And how do you know this?" Adaner asked, brushing back his hair.

I felt a little defensive. "I saw them with my own eyes."

"How can we trust this? What if you're just leading us into a trap?" Tolden's ocean eyes were set on me and I could feel the icy rage.

I shrugged. "Guess you'll just have to see." I turned on my heel without a second glance and headed up the sandy pathway to the palace waiting beyond. "I leave at twilight," I called over my shoulder.

I didn't sleep a wink.

I washed nearly four weeks of filth off of me and inspected my arm and leg while in the bath. All that was left of the goblin wounds were vertical scars running the length of my thigh. The one on my arm was a little different, the marks wrapped around my forearm in vein-like strokes, I turned it to get a better look.

I wiggled my toes and fingers. No pain.

I finished in the bath and hopped out, draining the water. No limp.

I glanced at myself in the mirror as I dried off with a velvet black towel. I cocked my head to one side as I ran the fabric up my neck and down again. I was sore everywhere.

I caught the reflection of my own eyes in the looking glass and just stared at them. How strange it was to have just been trekking through the terrain of a kingdom that was supposed to be my home for weeks on end. Almost dying twice, to then being saved by elves I didn't particularly like. Yet, all of a sudden being back in the palace that was supposed to be my home growing up, bathing in a tub bigger than my cell in Helmfirth and soon to be setting out again.

Setting out to the Sol Kingdom where. . .

I couldn't see my reflection anymore. Something blurry was gathering in my eyes and made it impossible to see.

I blinked.

The tears fell, warm and salty on my face. I closed my eyes and wrapped the towel around my body. I would need to be strong. Only when it was done would I be able to let my guard down and cry.

I inhaled and held it in for a few heartbeats.

Exhaling, I tossed the velvet towel aside and slipped into clean underthings. Then dressed in my dirty leathers. I would have to ask for another pair.

I combed and braided my wet hair and flicked it over my shoulder. When I glanced at the lotion jar sitting at the edge of the tub I sighed and lathered my face with it.

It was so dry and chapped from the ice and snow and wind. It stung a little on the small cuts, especially the one on my lip, but barely enough to notice.

The moisture felt good honestly.

I grabbed my leather jacket and swung it over my head, slipping both arms into it.

It was tight fitting but perfect to my size.

Slipping out of my room, I silently walked down the halls and listened with my keen elven ears for any sound. I lifted a hand to brush back loose hair that had fallen out of my braid and glanced at a gazebo area. I slowed my steps and watched as King Haleth sat in one of the obsidian chairs, sipping his coffee while the world lightened beneath our very gazes.

I expertly hid myself behind a pillar and watched him. He picked up the glass cup and brought it to his lips. He seemed to be smelling it and then took a sip. The sky was filled with the blue twilight hue that would remain until night fell again. Very few stars were left as the sky began to brighten and brighten.

I sighed through my nose and then instantly regretted it. Haleth turned his gaze in my direction but not before I skillfully moved back behind the pillar, I hoped.

I held my breath.

I heard the sound of his glass cup being set on the glass table and the scrape of a chair scooting back on the patio. My eyes darted in every direction, trying to find the easiest way of escape.

"King Haleth, may I trouble you to look over this list for the Constellation Eve Holiday?" a crisp voice asked, piercing through the silence and saving me in the process. I could hear the fall of the elven male's steps as he entered the patio.

Thank the fading stars. "Of course, Bastian."

I heard the sound of the chair scraping back in place and papers rustling. I peered from behind the pillar and bolted at the sight of Haleth and the elven male named Bastian leaning over the papers. I sprinted down the hallways and out the back kitchen door. I had noticed it when I requested a morsel to eat from the cook who had barred the way. Beneath her jutted elbow, I had spotted it though.

I glanced both ways before sprinting down the steps and towards the gate that would lead me out and to the Sol Kingdom. I had stolen two daggers and a longsword strapped to my back and was sure no one would miss them. Glancing behind me once more, I looked at the kitchen doorway, willing any one of the three males to walk through. I had high hopes that Cadeyn would be joining. But as I walked through the gates I didn't see him.

I sighed and began my trek not looking back at the gates or the palace, so when someone came up beside me and spoke, I drew my dagger and whirled around.

"Off without us, eh?"

Not only was Cadeyn there, hands in his pockets and grinning devilishly, but Adaner and Tolden were too. The latter without a smile on his face.

"Decided to believe me, eh?" I asked, mimicking them, sheathing my dagger.

"Couldn't let you have all the fun," Cadeyn teased.

"Or go off dying again," Tolden mused.

I rolled my eyes. Adaner came closer to me, studying the sword at my back. I cringed inwardly, hoping it somehow wasn't his. He reached behind me and shifted the scabbard it sat in. Moving behind me I felt his hands adjusting it and tightening the belt.

"Excuse me?" I pulled away. "The hell are you doing?"

"Helping you." He shrugged. "You have it all the wrong way." He reached between my back and the scabbard and I felt his hand brush across my lower back as he fixed whatever it was he had deemed unfit for the journey. I pulled away as soon as he was done and glared at him.

"Off we go then." Cadeyn was cheery for such early hours but I wondered if any of us had gotten any sleep. Perhaps he was running off pure adrenaline.

For the first few hours as twilight became brighter and brighter, none of us spoke. My thoughts were plagued by the constant images of what we were about to face again. If we were caught, there wouldn't just be hell to pay—no, we would pay with our lives. I tripped, my hand going to my throat as I felt it wanting to close up. I tried to swallow but in vain.

A hand at my back snapped me back to reality and I flinched away. Glancing over my shoulder, I trailed the elven male's body up to his eyes. I only came up to his chest. Glowing hazel iris' met my own.

"Can I help you?" I inquired.

"Can I help *you*? You're the one tripping over your own feet." He winked and lowered his hand.

I swallowed, successful this time, and looked away blinking. "I'm fine. Do not worry yourself."

I could see it now. How all the pain leading up to this almost made sense in a way. It made me want to hurt people. Hurt *her*. But I needed to be strong. There was no room for failure or emotions. I clenched my fist and forced it back down at my side.

"What exactly should we be expecting when we get to our destination?" Adaner asked, having remained by my side while the others followed behind.

"Sun."

"Pardon?"

I flicked my gaze over his then back to the road. "You can expect there to be sun."

"And what of the mission? To rescue the prisoners?"

"We must be as stealthy and discreet as possible."

Adaner's brow crinkled in the middle. "That's all the plan you have?"

I snapped my eyes to him and glared, of course I had a plan more detailed than that, I was simply. . .perfecting it. Adaner glared right back at me and we left the conversation alone. I thought I heard Cadeyn snicker and Tolden groan but I wasn't about to look behind me to find out. My cheeks were already warm from tripping and the doubt in Adaner's eyes.

But I didn't need to prove myself to them. Right?

"It will be a few days' walk to get to the Sol border but there are taverns along the way that we can sleep in. Once we get closer, we will be sleeping under the stars," Adaner rattled off this information casually.

"Taverns? But we have no coin?" Even as the words were slipping out I wished I could take them back.

Adaner grinned at me and patted a coin bag attached to his hip. Of course. I rolled my eyes and he just chuckled. I should be grateful but I was damning myself for not thinking of that. My mind had been so set on just getting the prisoners out.

When I realized I was walking along the road alone, I turned back to see what the hold up was. I caught a look exchanged between Adaner and Cadeyn. The latters gold eyes flicked towards mine and then Adaner's as he flashed me a grin.

A cover up if I ever saw one.

I whipped back around and flicked my braid over my shoulder to rest down my back. Tolden was saying something else about the taverns and how he hoped they had good ale.

It turned out, the Whitetail Tavern did.

We arrived about an hour ago and finally our ale, soup and bread turned up. We guzzled down our meals and Tolden signaled to the tavern workers for a second helping.

We had plenty of coppers for it—thanks to Adaner.

A band of jovial elves had begun playing an out of tune strum stick and fiddle. The tavern guests began gathering together to dance in the corner. I watched as they clapped and laughed together, sharing smiles. I think we were the only table that wasn't joining in on the festivities.

I began tapping my foot to the beat and humming along. I took another swig of ale and bit into a slice of bread. I caught Adaner watching me curiously and stuck my tongue out at him. His face remained neutral but his eyes twinkled.

I turned back to the music and began to sway back and forth in my seat, wanting to forget the memory that kept plaguing me from at the top of the mountain. I had confessed things to Adaner in the heat of my anger and pain that I wished I could take back.

"Are you itching to join them?" Cadeyn questioned.

I looked around, female and male elves jumping around wildly, laughing and smiling, dancing jigs that were completely off beat, breathless and merry.

"Yes, I am." I smiled.

Cadeyn jumped up. "Do me the honors."

"She's a princess," Adaner interrupted.

I glared at him. "And?"

Adaner shrugged. "I wouldn't want to be caught dead doing a jig in a tavern."

"Shame." I stuck my lip out in a mock pity pout and rushed off with Cadeyn. I could feel Tolden and Adaner's scowls on our backs the whole time.

I didn't care.

Cadeyn spun me around and we twirled and danced and laughed and smiled. We moved with the tune of the melody and the others around us did the same. Soon, we had the entire tavern clapping and stomping their feet, with the exception of the two moody males in the corner booth.

It was refreshing. Life giving.

I hadn't felt that joyful in a long time. It made me forget everything.

So I danced and drank and sang with Cadeyn until the music faded away and everyone either went back to their tables to drink some more or retired to their rooms to end their night.

Cadeyn and I stumbled back to the table where Adaner and Tolden leaned back in their seats.

"Having fun?" I poked at them, swiping another piece of bread. It had gone cold by now.

"Riveting," Tolden stumbled. Adaner rolled his eyes.

"They only had two rooms left," Adaner spoke as he stood and adjusted his scabbard.

"Two rooms?" My stomach sank. . .who would I be so lucky to share a room with, I wondered.

"You'll be rooming with me."

I glanced back at Adaner wondering who he was speaking to and then realized he was looking straight at me.

"Hope you don't snore." Adaner smirked and made his way up the tavern's wooden staircase—up to our room.

"If you'd rather room with someone else—" Cadeyn began but shut his mouth at the look Tolden gave him.

"I'm not rooming with grumpy Adaner or you. He's all yours." Tolden backed away with his hands up as he ascended the staircase.

I snorted, following them up the wooden staircase. "He can't be *that* bad."

The looks Cadeyn and Tolden gave me before disappearing were none too convincing. At the top of the stairs, I noticed a door that was left slightly ajar and walked toward it. Through the crack, I could see Adaner's scabbard leaned against a chair in the corner. When I opened the creaky door wider, I watched as Adaner shucked off his boots and placed them neatly next to his scabbard.

He seemed far less intimidating in his socks.

I snickered to myself and shut the door, making sure to lock it. Taverns were notorious for being dangerous places, at least the ones in Helmfirth were. When my eyes flicked across the room, my stomach dropped and my cheeks grew a bit warm.

There was only one rutting bed.

I cleared my throat and leaned my back against the door. My braid had fallen over one shoulder and loose pieces of hair now framed my warming face.

Adaner was facing the wall and I watched as he took off his leather armored jacket and then grasped his white undershirt at the base of his neck and pulled it over his head. It ruffled his dark hair a bit and made my breath hitch in my throat.

I cleared it again, still leaning against the door.

"Something in your throat?" Adaner questioned, not even turning around as I watched him unclasp his belt and slip it off.

"I guess room availability is sparse in the Crescent Kingdom."

"Be grateful you aren't sharing a bed with all three of us, Cadeyn farts in his sleep and Tolden is selfish enough to steal the blankets. You got the better end of the bargain."

"Someone's ego is busting." I smirked and slowly walked toward the bed. "Do I want to know how you know that Tolden steals the blankets?"

Adaner's back went rigid and he slowly turned to look at me. My eyes went wide, because this was the first time I'd actually seen how muscular and tan he was. My gaze bounced away but I could still feel him staring at me.

"If you must know, I've shared a bed with the same female as him *at* separate times mind you. She was the one to tell me."

My stomach twisted and I hated the way I squinted at him, trying to glean if it was the truth. "Are there not enough females in the realm for you to have your own bed mates?" The words were scarcely out before I regretted them. I bit my lip, silently cursing myself.

"Is your mind always in the gutter?" He raised his eyebrows at me, fully facing me now.

"Why are you so grumpy?" I deflected as I unlaced my boots, sitting at the edge of the rather small bed.

"What gave you that impression?"

"Your face did."

"Oh, I'm sorry, is this better?"

I glanced up and Adaner had plastered on a fake smile and gave me a rather rude gesture.

"Lovely," I mouthed, kicking my shoes to the otherside of the room and watched as Adaner's jaw twitched.

"You're not going to put them somewhere a little neater?" he asked. I shook my head, rather amused.

Adaner strode over, shirtless, in his socks and with ruffled hair, bent down to pick my boots up and placed them next to his, perfectly aligned.

I rolled my eyes and laid back on the bed still fully dressed. Without much to look at besides the low hanging ceiling, my thoughts roamed freely and I began to feel a gnawing deep inside of me.

What if it was too late to save the prisoners? What if I saw Cressida? Would we fight? Would all four of us be strong enough to take her and her army on? The answer to the latter was obvious.

I sighed and rubbed a hand down my face in exhaustion. I should at least try to get some sleep. I sat up again and began to take my weapons off. Laying down with a scabbard poking me in the back wasn't very comfortable.

I walked over to where Adaner had placed his sword and set mine next to his, and just to be a little spiteful I angled it crookedly. I then slipped the belt that held my daggers and laid them on the chair.

"You can put those on the dresser," he crooned.

I looked up, my fingers barely grazing the daggers. "I thought we were putting all our weapons here? I was just trying to make it look *neat.*"

"Well, that happens to be my bed." I glanced down at the chair.

Realization hit.

"You can sleep in the bed, Adaner."

He was facing the window that the curtains didn't quite cover enough. His arms were crossed over his chest and I could see the rise and fall of it as he inhaled and exhaled.

"It's alright. I'd like to keep watch anyway."

Stubborn. "Adaner," I spoke softly as I left my daggers on the chair and stepped toward him. I could see the reflection of his face in the window pane. "I need you all to be well rested so that we can face whatever awaits in the Sol Kingdom at our very strongest."

I was tempted to reach out and touch his shoulder but refrained. Instead, I wrapped my arms around myself. When he turned to face me, his hazel eyes brushing over mine, I could see all the unasked questions just brimming beneath the surface.

I'm sure my eyes looked the same and just to break the tension I said, "Don't get the wrong idea and think I *want* to share this bed with you. But it would be rather selfish of me to have it all to myself."

I turned away, taking off my jacket. I would sleep in my undershirt and leather pants even though they had enough filth on them to scare away goblins.

"I hope you don't mind sharing a bed with sea creature and goblin guts." I laid my jacket over the back of the chair.

Adaner chuckled. "By the way, I didn't share the female's bed for immoral reasons. It was during the war and the temperatures were near freezing. We needed the body heat."

I bit my lip but didn't say anything. I wondered why he'd felt the need to explain that particular situation to me. Our gazes met from across the room and I nodded before I walked to the bed. I pulled back the blanket and fluffed the pillow. Slipping into the clean sheets I laid on my back and stared at the ceiling.

Adaner followed suit and when I felt the weight of the mattress shift when he laid down, I felt something. I didn't know how to explain it though, it was nothing romantic.

I sighed and pulled the scratchy blankets up to my chin. "What did Elton do to you?"

Adaner's question struck such hatred and shock in me that I froze. I stopped breathing, stopped thinking, stopped everything.

When I didn't say anything he continued, "When we were tending your wounds, you screamed at us to stop. But you weren't shouting our names. You were screaming his."

A sob lodged itself in my throat and I couldn't stop the tears rolling down. I just shook my head and in a barely audible whisper said, "I'm not ready."

Adaner said nothing after that. But I knew he understood because beneath the blankets he intertwined our fingers together and squeezed my hand.

And when I fell asleep with my knees curled up to my chest and tears staining my cheeks, I had the flicker of a memory that someone brushed my hair out of my face as I slept.

But perhaps it was only a dream.

CHAPTER 22

Blue hues covered the entire sky, spreading like inky trails gathering in the clouds.

I awoke before Adaner to find his hand resting on my pillow. I got out of the bed slowly, adorning my jacket and weapons. After having stubbed my toe when I lost balance putting on my boots, I now stood facing the window. It was a miracle I hadn't woken Adaner. I glanced back and a curve of a smile splayed across my lips as I watched his chest rise and fall, his mouth slightly open and his curly hair flopping everywhere.

Some vicious warrior he was.

I turned back to the window, wiping the smile off my face for fear he would wake beneath my stare. In a few more days, we would be walking beneath the sun; something none of us were very accustomed to. As I looked out at the ever brightening sky, gooseflesh rose. I didn't miss the Sol Kingdom but I sure did miss the sun.

I heard rustling behind me and turned slightly. Adaner was sitting up and rubbing his eyes. His hair was unruly and falling all over his forehead, but his face looked as if he had gotten some good rest. But I wasn't looking at his face, my eyes were fixed on his heavily muscled chest.

Our eyes met and I swallowed very visibly. I cleared my throat. "Have a restful sleep?"

"Yeah, actually," he said, pulling the blankets back and adjusting his pants as he stood up.

I turned back to the window, silently cursing myself for staring. "You?"

"Not horrible." I shrugged.

"Good."

The silence became taut, tension I could cut with a dull blade, so I suggested I go find out what they served for breakfast and left him to get dressed. I didn't know why we seemed to have meaningful conversations for a moment and the next it was like it had never happened. I sighed and leaned against the shut door for a heartbeat, rubbing at my temples.

"Heyo!"

I looked up at the sound of Cadeyn's voice and grinned, his hair was absolutely everywhere and the two small braids connecting at the back were a little lopsided today.

"Hello," I replied.

"So, how was your *night*?" He looked at me expectantly and I punched his arm.

"How was *yours*? I hear you snore," I teased.

"Oh, I slept like a log. I think Tolden's in a mood though."

"When is he not?"

Cadeyn and I shared a laugh as we descended the stairs to scrounge up a meal. Which turned out to be porridge. My eyes lit up when I saw the sugar, I dumped spoonfuls of it into my bowl and took it to the same table we sat at the night before.

Adaner and Tolden appeared at the same time and we all ate in companionable silence. One in which I made it my mission to not make eye contact with Adaner. Once we finished, we gave our thanks to the tavern owner and his wife and were on our way again.

I followed the cadre out of the small town and glanced around, assessing my surroundings. The cobblestoned streets were lined with bars, inns, bakeries with delicious smelling baked goods, shops with an assorted amount of items and rows of homes that looked identical.

Chimneys puffed with smoke from fireplaces, no doubt families cooking their twilight meal. Children ran amongst themselves in the street, jumping out of the way of the male elves riding in on horses. It must have rained in the night for everything had a dewy look and scent.

I hadn't realized I'd stopped until Cadeyn called my name. I waved him off and looked back at the town one last time. I didn't know what it was about towns like these that made my chest hurt. These towns weren't much different from the one I'd grown up in.

I scoffed. Who was I kidding? *Everything* was different.

"Ryn, make haste!"

I cursed Tolden's name beneath my breath and turned to follow them up the grassy path. At the top of the grassy knoll, I stopped to read the name carved on a wooden board: *Silvendale*.

"The next town is out of the way from Sol so we might have to set up camp tonight," Tolden said matter of factly.

"I don't mind sleeping under the stars," I replied.

"I bet it's better than sharing a bed with old mate Adaner here," Tolden snickered.

But when I met Adaner's hazel gaze it was like we were frozen for a moment. I recalled a soft voice and a gentle hand. My heart leapt in my throat and I flicked my eyes down, my face warming.

What the hell was I thinking?

For most of the journey there weren't too many conversations happening. I enjoyed the silence, as it gave me time to go over and process the plan inside my head. As we grew closer and closer to the Sol Kingdom, I could feel the dread and throat closing fear gripping me from the inside.

Fear was a dangerous thing. I had no time and no room for it.

That evening, after hours of simply trudging through the sandy paths along the Crescent coast, we made camp away from the road in a spot of grove of trees. I busied myself with gathering kindling for a fire. The forest smelled of sweet sap that stuck to my fingers and clothes and I took my time piling the sticks and branches into my arms.

As the night wore on, I stilled, watching the fireflies buzz around the grass littering the forest floor. My fingers barely grazed a stick that some of the bugs were nestled on and when I disrupted their sleep they flew off in a tizzy.

The fireflies—firedragons—reminded me of the Sol Kingdom and...Skandar. I swallowed and tried to shake away the feeling.

Alas, I was unsuccessful.

I sighed and leaned against a tree with bark that poked into my back and arms, I blamed the tree for the tears that blocked my vision. I had thought Skandar was a friend—a good friend.

I glanced at the three other silhouettes walking amongst the trees, bending to pick kindling up, turning to one another to poke fun or share a crude joke. I watched as Cadeyn snuck up behind Tolden and smeared something across his back. He turned in a fury, log raised to strike but Cadeyn was long gone, having sprinted away.

I caught myself smiling. These strong, ill tempered warriors knew how to have fun and joke. The first time I officially met Adaner and Cadeyn they were laughing so hard they were toppling all over each other—a little mead might have helped with it—but having fun nonetheless.

Tolden was a bit of a different story. But I couldn't blame him for the anxiety I felt every time I looked at him. It wasn't his fault he looked so similar to the young boy I'd killed.

I didn't know what they were to me. My friends? Companions? They felt like it sometimes. Even though they annoyed the hell out of me more often than not.

"Oi, quit standing around, we need firewood!" Cadeyn's voice bellowed through the forest and I knew he was talking to me.

I grinned, having just proved my own point. "Will you shut up?" Adaner hissed.

"What's going to hear me? The whales in the ocean?"

"Fool, I hope they do and then come and swallow you. But *just* you."

"Why? So you can finally be alone with Miss Ryn over there?"

I stilled when I heard Cadeyn say that. I watched Adaner hit Cadeyn upside the head and then snarl something in his ear. He pushed Cadeyn away from him and scanned the forest for where I was.

Or I assumed he did, for out of pure reaction, I'd hid behind a thick tree.

I heard their footsteps absently get quieter and knew they had more than likely gone back to our camp spot. I slid down the side of the tree and rested my hands on my knees. I let the firewood drop to my side and wondered what the hell that was supposed to be about. They were always jesting so it was probably another one of their stupid jokes.

I laid my head against the tree trunk and listened to the faint voices of Adaner and Cadeyn fighting. I scoffed as I rolled my eyes, making up my mind to break up the fight. Wondering what the hell Cadeyn had meant by saying what he had. Just as I stood up I caught eye contact with Tolden across the way. Had he just been staring at me? I cleared my throat and forced a smile to my lips. I started to turn away but he walked towards me.

"Are you alright?" he asked.

I blanched. When had he ever asked that? I nodded. "Indeed."

We started walking back each with our own bundles of firewood in our arms.

"I don't know what memories were returned to you, Ryn, but I know they were taken away for a reason. Whether that was a good or bad reason is up to you."

My brow furrowed. I stared straight ahead. "It was a bad reason, I already know that."

Tolden shrugged. I didn't like the way he was acting.

"You have no idea what it was even about," I said a little bitterly.

"You are more than welcome to tell us." He gestured to the others.

But I stared at him, wondering what it was that made him so disagreeable. I didn't say anything after that. Tolden had no clue what he was asking me to reveal. He had no idea just how much trauma was tucked into the few memories that were returned, or how they even fit into my past. They would know soon enough, I wouldn't be able to hide it forever.

When we came upon the grove of trees where our camp was set up Adaner instantly looked at the two of us. He seemed to stiffen and his eyes darkened. He walked towards me and took the armful of kindling and set it in a neat pile. His eyes scanned mine and then darted back to Tolden. There must have been a lot of tension coming from us then. Even Cadeyn was silent—and that was rare.

When the fire was lit and sparks flickered into the starry sky, we divided some of the stale jerky and dried fruits that we'd packed, washing it down with our waterskins. With very little conversation being made, we retired for the night.

I volunteered for the first watch and even though I could tell Tolden and Adaner wanted to argue with me, I stood my ground. I wouldn't be able to sleep unless I finished processing my plan anyway.

I watched the sparks from the fire crackle and pop and float into the forest above. Wisps of smoke from the fire rose through the tree line and made the stars above look foggy. I could hear the slow breathing of the cadre around me and the snap of the logs as they burned. I met my back with the log behind me and exhaled.

Minutes went by and I sat up straighter. There was a strange sound coming from the direction of the road. I fisted my dagger a little tighter and crouched on my knees. I could see shadows running along the road. They weren't coming towards us but I didn't like the way the forest had gone absolutely still and silent.

I crept up and silently sprinted to the trees closest to the edge to see if I could get a better look. I peeked from behind one and kept my dagger low. The shadows were large and humped and seemed to have either a ton of fur or capes adorned. I squinted and saw flashes of something metal in their hands. Weapons?

I listened and could absently hear the sound of clinking. Not weapons then—chains. I would know that sound anywhere. I released the breath I'd been holding. One of the shadow creatures stopped and turned towards the forest, towards where I was.

I held my breath once more. It sniffed.

A few other black masses followed suit and they started creeping towards the edge of the forest, but in the dead silent, star-filled night a piercing cry broke through from the front of the line. I watched as they perked up and instantly went back to the path, like sheep to their herder.

A shiver snaked its way up my spine as well as a hand on my shoulder. I jolted and sliced my dagger towards the intruder.

"I'd like to keep my hand."

I rolled my eyes. "Then don't sneak up on me."

"I didn't. I let you know I was there."

I scoffed, but it came out sounding more like a cough. "What are you doing awake anyways?" I could see Adaner's hazel eyes in the moonlight and could tell that he hadn't ever gone to sleep.

"It's my turn for the night watch," he answered.

I glanced at the moon and could tell it was still early. "I don't think I'd be able to fall asleep after seeing those." A lie, of sorts.

"I have never seen those creatures before," Adaner breathed, crossing his arms and looking me up and down in the moonlight.

I flicked my gaze towards him and then back to the shadows. "They make the air feel tight and the light feel colder."

He nodded, his lips thinning.

I bit my lip. "They're headed towards Sol."

He nodded again.

We sat in silence for a while until the herd of shadows had disappeared. They made me feel extremely uneasy. Unlike the male standing next to me.

"So," Adaner cleared his throat. "What were you and Tolden talking about earlier?"

I turned to look into those hazel eyes but they were looking down at the ground. I glanced up at the stars and my brow crinkled.

"Nothing, really. I guess he just wanted me to know that King Haleth had his reasons for stealing my memories." I could hear the bitterness in my tone but didn't care that much.

"He said that to you?"

I glanced back at the surprise in Adaner's deep accented voice. I nodded in confirmation.

"I think that's rutting wrong. He should never have stolen those memories from you."

I tried to hide my smile. "Golly, sounds like you're siding with me there, Adaner." "Maybe I am, Princess."

I snorted. It was true though. King Haleth should never have obliterated them. I sighed and looked down at my booted feet. "If you weren't under Haleth's orders to follow me when I went to Mount Oblivion, would you have followed me anyway?"

Adaner's eyes burned with something I didn't recognize in them and I couldn't catch it before he looked down again. "I'm sure you would have been fine, so no. I was simply following orders."

"Lie." I scarcely said the words before they had escaped. My heart pitter-pattered and I clenched my fists.

"Come again?"

"I smell a lie on you." I turned to him, arms crossed. "I would have been dead if you hadn't saved me from those goblins."

He stepped forward, forcing my back against a tree and angled his head close to my ear. "Careful, it almost sounds like you're thanking me."

"Maybe I am." I turned my head to look directly into his eyes, not realizing how close we actually were, a smile appeared at the corners of my lips.

Adaner lifted his arm and braced it against the tree trunk, glancing down at my lips for half of a second. "Tell me, did you ever expect to come back?"

His question caught me off guard and I swallowed. His eyes dipped down to watch my throat bob.

"Did you even want to come back?" he pressed.

My eyes widened and I suddenly realized how close he was and it felt like he was getting closer. "I should try to get some sleep," I offered, pushing off of the tree and forcing him away. When I turned away he didn't follow me and I didn't look back until I reached the campfire.

When I glanced up at him he was looking out over the view of the road and the starry sky. I laid down and glared at him until sleep overtook me.

CHAPTER

23

Day and night shone overhead.

It was one of the most wonderful and strangest things I'd ever seen.

The cadre and I stood on the coast where across the cliff we could still see the night sky with faint stars blinking and the moon setting, giving way to twilight slowly to the north. But then on the side of the cliff we were closest to, the sun was shining blindly, setting everything bright and green and looking warm.

We were in between both of the elven realms.

It was still and quiet, no wind blew, no birds chirped. It simply was.

I did not remember seeing this in between place when I fled the Sol Kingdom the first time, but then again I didn't even remember crossing the Crescent Border. Night had surrounded me without me noticing.

When we walked through, fully stepping into the Sol Kingdom, nothing changed.

There was no warping or blurred edges as I had imagined, just thin air.

"We must be on high alert now. We are in enemy territory," Adaner cautioned, his fists hanging calmly but expectantly at his sides.

My fingers itched to use my own blades. But in the heat of the Sol Kingdom my Crescent leathers were going to be the death of me. I had forgotten how warm it was here. The climate of Crescent was slightly cooler, being close to the coast and the only light being that of the moon and all.

I wiped at my brow constantly as we trudged through the grassy plains and hills and footpaths. My mind was set on the task at hand so when we stopped for water I almost argued that we should keep going. But we would be no good to one another if we were dehydrated. I knelt on the bank, the fabric covering my knees becoming soaked and cupped water into my mouth. I couldn't help but wonder if this was the same river I had stopped at when I'd run away.

My breathing hitched and I choked on the water running down my throat. I needed to be fully present, so I tucked the memories and thoughts away. I would be able to fully unpack and process everything later.

After I did this. After I saved them.

"How much further do you think it is?" Cadeyn asked nobody in particular.

"I'd say from this stream to the border, a few more hours," I responded after splashing my face full of water. "Fill up your canteens, this will be the last time we stop."

The last stretch of the journey was the hardest. With each step I took I could tell we were getting close. I wasn't nervous.

I was thrilled.

A calmness had come over me, one I knew all too well and welcomed in the *Death Pit*.

We were crawling on our stomachs now. I could see the spew of the waterfall leading into the Sol Kingdom and see the very tallest spikes of the towers where, no doubt, scouts were looking in every direction.

I crawled in front of Adaner, Tolden and Cadeyn and made my way to the spot where I had last been a few months ago. I held in my panic as I spotted the rock and the river where Skandar and I had fought.

My eyes darted in search of his body but it was foolish of me to think they wouldn't have searched for him everywhere. I kept crawling past the rock and river, the grass leaving its stain on my hands and wrists. When I reached the very edge where the river ran into the waterfall I stopped and peeked over the edge.

The waterfall gushed over the rocks and pummeled all the way down to the clear teal surface below. It foamed and steam billowed upwards from the intensity of the plummet.

I raised my eyebrows at the cadre.

"No way." Tolden shook his head, his eyes wide in denial. I nodded.

"This is our *only* way in."

I watched Cadeyn's throat move as he swallowed but he looked at me and smiled. "I'm in."

I looked at Adaner. "It's risky, I know. But if we jump straight and hit the water with our boots, we might be fine."

"Might?" Adaner raised his eyebrows but then shrugged. "Agh, to hell with it. Let's go."

I grinned. "Good, because I really did not want to have to fight our way through the front gates."

"Yeah, you and whose army?" Tolden scoffed.

I gestured towards the three of them. "I have my army." I felt a sense of pride gush forth but tried to hide the grin that spread across my face.

"I'll go first." I moved towards the edge but I felt a hand on my waist.

"Wait." Adaner was so close I could feel his breath on my neck. I felt his hands remove my scabbard with my longsword attached and then unbuckle the belt that held my daggers.

"You don't want them strangling you or hitting you when you break the water." He handed them to me and his fingers grazed mine gently.

I blinked and looked away, nodding. Clutching my weapons in either of my hands I turned and smiled. "See you at the bottom."

I stepped towards the ledge, the steam from the waterfall rising to kiss my cheeks. My heart hammered against my chest. Refusing to allow the fear a place in my mind, I looked forward and pushing off of the solid grass ground, I jumped.

I was flying.

Flying through air, steam, water, the very rays of the sun.

I could feel my stomach lurch into my throat and my braid whipping every which way as the water below rose and rose up to meet me. The teal water foamed and bubbled and I closed my eyes right before my feet hit the surface of the water and dragged me below.

Cold surrounded me and I held the breath I had taken right before the water encircled me. I shot straight to the bottom but instantly started kicking for the surface. The current was strong and I did not want to get stuck under the pummel of the waterfall. My leathers grew heavy and it was hard to swim when my hands were full of my weapons but I kicked harder.

When I broke the surface of the water I sucked air into my lungs. Water fell from my hair and dripped into my eyes but I kept kicking away from the under current.

Glancing up towards the ledge I brought my scabbard over my head and rested it across my back.

I watched as Adaner jumped next and held my breath. He plummeted down straight as an arrow, his arms at his sides and his feet pressed together. When he hit the water it splashed up around him and he was gone. Seconds later he surfaced, his sword raised high in the air.

I grinned and then watched as Cadcyn jumped. He wobbled ever so slightly and his arms flailed. My heart lodged in my throat. He needed to be straight as an arrow or the force of the fall and the water would hurt like hell—could even be calamitous.

He hit the water with a thud and I instantly began swimming to where he'd landed. One too many seconds went by and I had just inhaled air into my lungs to dive to find him when he surfaced, coughing and gasping for air.

"You good?" Adaner shouted at him and to my relief—and I am sure Adaner's—he nodded, smiling of all things.

Bloody idiot.

Tolden hesitated for a mere second before he jumped. He hit the water with a plume of water cascading around him and surfaced seconds later much like Adaner had.

"Everyone good?" I asked in a low voice, glancing at the males once they'd all caught their breath.

They nodded, strapping on their weapons again as the current pulled us to the channel. As we swam with the current I tried to remember exactly where the river ran through. I knew it would carry us straight through the palace. I had walked over the very bridges that were built over the water. I also knew it was clear blue, so anyone would be able to see us floating by.

I began searching for areas that we could get out safely.

"Go under!" Adaner hissed and then my mouth, my eyes and nostrils filled with water as he pulled me to him. My lungs began to burn with the need for air and the fact that river water was just shoved down my throat.

I felt Adaner let go of me and we bobbed to the surface. I coughed and coughed trying to rid my throat of the horrible scratchy feeling.

"Sorry," he muttered near my ear. "There were children running by."

I nodded. The palace loomed closer and closer and I could make out the elven warriors standing at the entrances.

"We're going to need to get out. *Fast*," I warned.

He met my gaze and realization played out in his eyes. The current was getting stronger and faster. If we got out on the bank we would need to crawl to some sort of coverage or the elven warriors would be able to see us.

I wiped water out of my eyes and slung my dagger belt over my shoulder. I grasped at the bank but only got a fistful of sand and reeds thrown back at me.

"Get out now!" Adaner shouted in a whisper.

I dug my nails deeper into the grassy bank and pulled myself out of the current. With one leg up I dragged the other out of the water and rolled away from the soft ground. I could hear the cadre breathing heavily and searched for their faces.

We all lay flat on our stomachs, just breathing.

Tolden made the first move and began crawling towards a bridge. The rest of us followed suit right after him. Grass and dirt stuck to my face and hair and hands but I kept crawling. I didn't hear any shouts or hear any arrows whizzing towards us. Once we made it to the bridge we met our backs with the brick.

I dared a glance around the side. Everything seemed quiet. I scanned the terrain and recognized it. I saw the grove of trees where the iron door lay behind.

"The iron door is around the corner there." I pointed away from the river's entrance into the palace. "Be on guard. Do not engage unless you have to."

"Understood," all three males said in unison.

"We'll go in pairs of two. Adaner with me?" Our eyes flicked across one anothers.

He nodded in response and we bolted from our hiding spot. We sprinted, our heads low and our bodies crouched. As we ran I cinched my belt back on my waist.

The thick foliage loomed before us and we ran right into it. I slowed down and crept through the underbrush in case anyone was guarding the iron door.

The leaves scratched at my face and hands but I kept walking. I could see the iron door through the green leaves.

I inhaled.

I could feel my magic responding to the iron. I still didn't fully understand how my magic worked, but I knew enough to open this door.

I heard Cadeyn and Tolden behind us and began to freeze the hinges and the handle. They were covered in dark ice by the time I was done. When I stopped I was out of breath and dizzy.

Adaner stepped forward and kicked the hinges and handle. It took a few tries to get them loose but then he grabbed the door and twisted it open violently. He brought his hands back and hissed.

"You alright?" I asked, glancing at his now singed palms.

"He'll be fine," Tolden snapped as he pushed past both of us and crawled over the door and into the yawning darkness.

I followed after him and when I stepped over the door the full weight of the horrible stench greeted me in the form of stale air and rotting flesh.

"Disgusting," Cadeyn swore, covering his nose with his arm.

I led the way through the catacombs after listening for any guards. I strode through the one that led to the prisoners hanging from the ceiling but when I sprinted down the stone hallway and saw the opening of the domed tomb I stopped hard in my tracks.

"No."

I stumbled forward, not caring about the smell or the dried blood everywhere. They were gone.

All the prisoners were gone. Their chains were left hanging. *Empty.*

"What the hell?" I yelled, running down the stone steps into the abyss of dried blood and chains and filth.

"Ryn!"

I briefly heard Adaner call me but ignored him. The chains were hanging from the ceiling just as I had seen before. They didn't move in the stagnant air of the catacombs. I looked around my eyes filled with hot tears.

"I'm too late." I felt my knees buckle and steadied myself against the stone wall. My shaking hands reached for my throat. It felt like someone was ripping the air out of my very windpipe and lungs.

"I'm too late," I breathed again, barely audible. I watched Tolden, Cadeyn and Adaner search the domed tomb through my blurry vision.

A strange hollowness seeped inside of me and made itself known. I blinked and wiped angrily at my face. If I had just rescued them the day I saw them this wouldn't have happened. Why had I left them here?

I was so selfish and so afraid that I just left. What if I could have saved them with my magic? Froze the chains and helped them escape? We could have sought refuge in the Crescent Kingdom, Haleth would have taken them in.

No he wouldn't have. But I would have *found* a way.

I hit the stone wall with my fist in frustration. "Damn it."

"Ryn."

I looked up at Adaner, his hazel eyes were filled with sorrow and anger as he walked towards me.

I shook my head. "I shouldn't have left them."

"How could you have saved them?"

I pushed off of the stone wall. "I'm the one who made this whole plan. I could have done this by myself! I don't know why I turned my back and *left* them."

"And where exactly would you have taken them?" Adaner crossed his arms and his eyes hardened.

"Crescent Palace?"

"Ryn, you didn't even know where it was or that it was your home. You would never have thought of that." Adaner put both of his hands on my shoulders and he took a deep breath. "I know that it is so much easier to think of the what ifs and plan what you *could* have done. But it is dangerous too, don't go down that road. You would not have been able to do this by yourself."

Our eyes locked and I could see the truth in them. I just didn't want to accept it. "We should get out of here. The longer we stay the better chances they have of finding us," Tolden warned as he marched back up the stone steps.

"He's right." Adaner eyed me and let go of my shoulders but not before running his hands lightly down my arms. His fingers grazed mine and I swore he squeezed them in reassurance.

Cadeyn looked up at the chains hanging from the ceiling and questioned, "What were they doing to them? How is this linked to your memories?"

A shudder ran through me and I looked away from them all. "Unspeakable things."

We walked back up the steps in defeat and when we came back to the spot where the catacombs split, one way leading left and the other leading right, I turned.

"When I was here last time, there were snarls and horrible sounds coming from this way. When I got closer, my head started to hurt so bad that I had to turn around. Any clue as to what it could have been?"

Adaner walked towards the catacomb entrance and stilled, as if he were listening.

Tolden and Cadeyn stopped halfway down the hallway leading to the door. "I have no idea, Ryn. I don't hear anything now?"

I shrugged. I was tired and defeated.

I should have just inspected more when I was here the last time. I should have endured the pain. I should have rescued them while I had the chance.

Even if it would have been near impossible alone, I should have tried.

"We need to go."

Tolden and Cadeyn looked back at me and Adaner and motioned for us to follow.

They disappeared from view a few moments later but I felt frozen. "You did all you could. You came back," Adaner encouraged.

"But it wasn't enough. I wasn't enough."

"Listen Ryn, you don't get to put this on you. I don't want to hear anymore about it. We can still track them and try to figure out where they were taken." Adaner lifted my chin up and stared at me intently. "This isn't over. Don't give up."

I opened my mouth to say something but Adaner covered my lips with his finger.

It was calloused and yet somehow still soft.

"Don't give up," he whispered and he came so close to me, his finger still covering my mouth.

Our eyes locked and I felt a sensation wash over me. I was swimming in a sea of hazel eyes that were so fierce a moment ago but now were soft and kind. Adaner removed his finger, grazing my lips ever so gently. He lingered there for a moment and I held my breath.

"Adaner," I cautioned. I didn't know what was happening but it felt different. "What is this?"

He took his hand away and stuffed it into his leather pockets. His face and eyes darkened and he glanced away from me. I didn't know what to say or do so I just brushed past him and walked out of the catacombs.

When I looked back he was running his fingers through his hair. My heart hammered against my chest and I placed a hand there to calm it.

What the bloody hell was I thinking?

CHAPTER 24

"Guys, we need to go now!"

I whipped my head back up the steps to where Tolden was motioning us to move. I glanced back at Adaner once before taking the steps two at a time. Matters of the heart—or whatever this was—would have to wait.

Leaving the empty catacombs behind, we shut the iron door. I reached down and felt my magic awakening as I tried to replace the iron handle and lock. If I positioned it to where it seemed as if it were still intact it might buy us some time before anyone noticed it. Seeing as the prisoners were no longer being kept in there, I hoped guards would not frequent this place.

"*Ryn*," Adaner warned as the three of them began slinking back through the grass.

"Shut up," I hissed over my shoulder. Muttering a curse I stepped away from the door and knew I would have to leave it as it was. I couldn't waste precious time making sure it was perfect.

I sprinted to catch up with the three males and crouched low. The thing that I had failed to realize when jumping from a waterfall was the mountain we would have to scale just to make it out.

"How are everyone's mountain scaling skills?" I cursed, my eyes running up the length of the falls. I glanced at the others to glimpse their reactions.

Cadeyn simply grinned like a wild animal.

Tolden rolled his eyes.

Adaner shook his head.

"One at a time, we need to crawl back into the water and make our way to the waterfall. We'll have to scale the rocks on either side," I explained, although I knew they already knew it.

Adaner glanced over his shoulder, his hair flopping over his forehead. "Be mindful of the guards that we saw, they will more than likely be able to spot us. We should be out of range for their arrows."

"*Should* doesn't guarantee us anything," Tolden bit out.

"Would you rather we stay here?" I snapped, pinning him with a death glare.

"Quit it, you two." Cadeyn began crawling before we could say anything else.

I watched as he used his elbows and knees to push himself further through the tall grass and to the muddy bank of the river. Without a single sound, he slipped into the water and disappeared from my sight.

I followed suit, knowing Tolden and Adaner would not be far behind.

The grass scratched at my face and hands and stuck to my hair. My nails bit into the damp ground as I crawled towards the edge of the river. Glancing to my left, I could pinpoint where the elven males stood guard over the bridge. They were still yards away though.

I inhaled a deep breath filled with the moist air of the water and smell of grass and quietly slipped into the river. The first shock of cold woke my body up and I could feel the mud and grass washing off of me. I dove deep into the water, kicking my legs and moving my arms, gliding towards the waterfall.

The only problem was the current I now swam against. I kicked and surged forward with my arms but it felt like I was going nowhere. My lungs began burning for air and I opened my eyes to try to see how far I was from the waterfall. If the current was any indication, I was not close.

Closer to the waterfall should be a sort of pull, currently I was still fighting just to stay in place. I could see the dark form ahead that was Cadeyn but he was still so far ahead of me. I glanced back, continuing to kick as hard as I could and stroking the water with my arms to propel my body forward.

But I wasn't moving.

My lungs burned even more and now my eyes began stinging from the water I had allowed to seep in.

I could take one breath.

I angled towards the surface and inhaled the sweet, moist air, but without the momentum of my body constantly working against the current, it cost me. The water took me and pushed me further away from the waterfall.

Bloody rutting hell.

I began kicking harder than ever and cupped my hands to push more water past me. I finally felt my body getting closer to the waterfall and relief flooded me.

That is until an arrow whizzed past my ear.

Without so much as a glance behind me, I dove into the water to become a harder target to hit. Finally, I felt the surge of the waterfall and could feel it pulling me towards it now. I swam to the surface once more and through watery vision, saw that Cadeyn was already up on the wall, scaling it. Adaner and Tolden had caught up to me and all three of us were struggling not to be taken under the force of the water and the whirlpool it was creating.

Tolden made it to the rocks and pulled himself out.

I barely heard the shouts of the guards over the noise of the falls as I continued swimming. My legs, arms, and back all began to ache and felt like they were locking up.

Adaner was just ahead and glanced over his shoulder at me. Something flashed in his eyes but I didn't have time to really dissect it because the damned waterfall kept pulling me towards it and my body was giving out.

I cursed and tossed out a surge of my magic, black ice shot from my palm and instantly froze the water. It cracked and hissed, starting from the base of the falls and crawling its way up in spider-like veins. Steam rose from where the water was frozen, hissing and spreading towards me.

Which also meant the current wasn't as strong.

Breathing a sigh of relief, I pulled myself onto the rocks on the side of the waterfall and instantly began searching for hand and foot holds. Adaner, Tolden and Cadeyn were already a decent way up.

The rocks were wet and slick with lichen and moss, proving to be difficult to hold onto but not impossible. The falls continued gushing down, where my ice had not quite reached and steam and foam rose to kiss my face. With the force of the water pelting the ice below, it began to crack and float away.

My arms burned and shook and my cold hands struggled to find purchase. I inhaled and exhaled, trying to calm myself but it did little when my adrenaline coursed through me. Not daring to look behind nor upwards, I placed my foot on a moss covered rock and it slipped. I cried out as my arms held the full weight of my body and my ribs banged against the cliff.

"Ryn!" I heard Adaner yell but couldn't reply, could he not see that I was bloody busy?

An arrow hit the rock where my boot had just been and I cursed. I guess they *were* in range. Struggling, I pulled myself up, arms shaking, threatening to dislocate. I lifted my leg and placed it on a wet stone but clear of any moss. Little by little, I began pulling and lifting and stepping.

I tried to keep moving as quickly as possible so as not to be an easy target. I heard the whizz of another arrow and the sound of it clattering against the rock as it tumbled down. It fell past my face and I ducked to miss it just in time to see a stream of white light heading straight for me.

"Watch out!" someone yelled above me.

A stream of white fire found purchase somewhere above me, rock cascading down. Pieces of stone tumbled towards me, hitting my hands, my face, my head. Another stream of fire hit the rock but this time it was right above me and the entire wall shuddered. I lost my grip from the explosion and felt myself tumbling, my back, legs and arms hit against the wet rocks as the icy water below rushed up towards me.

I flung a desperate shot of my power out, trying to grasp onto anything but found nothing. The dark ice only made the wall more treacherous. I reached my arm out and grasped hold onto a piece of rock jutting out.

I screamed in pain as my nails splintered and my arm popped out of place. Gritting my teeth as I swung back and forth, I tried to steady myself. Arrow after arrow fell around me as the movement of my fall made it hard for them to hit me.

Without another minute to waste, I began climbing once more. I did not dare look up to see how far I had left. For all I knew, this very wall might be the death of me. I noticed familiar rocks where I had previously pulled myself up and did much the same this time, completely ignoring my dislocated arm. I grunted as everything in me either was pounding, aching or stinging with pain.

But I was made to endure. . .so I would.

The fire and the arrows had ceased and I was half tempted to look behind me to see why, but something in me would not allow me. I climbed all the way up to the spot where they had blasted the rocks. Everything was loose and crumbling, so I angled myself closer to the water.

Reaching out with my dislocated arm so I could still have a good hold on the mountain, I aimed my dark ice over the entire waterfall. That way the force would not pull me down to my death. Breathing heavily, I ignored the piercing pain of my dislocated arm and shredded fingernails. With aching and protesting muscles, I pulled myself up and stepped on the last rock before strong arms wrapped under mine and dragged me the rest of the way up.

"Bloody hell, Ryn!" Adaner cursed.

"Quick, over here," ushered Cadeyn.

They carried me away from the edge and laid me down. I held up my good arm to demand they give me a minute. My head swam and my body shook with the cold and adrenaline.

"We need to go," Tolden commanded and I had half a mind to freeze that tongue of his. This entire mission I swore that's the only thing he'd said.

"My arm—" I winced in pain. "Can you reset it?" I pushed myself into a sitting position.

Adaner didn't hesitate for a minute and instantly placed his hands on my shoulder and back. "Breathe in."

Before I'd even taken a breath he twisted and set the arm back into the socket. I cried out in pain and instantly bit my lip to keep quiet. I rolled my neck and kept my arm close to my chest to protect it.

Standing, I glanced back towards the iced over waterfall. That's when I felt it. An oily feeling slivered its way down my spine and into my stomach. There on the bridge, among her guards, was Queen Cressida.

Anger coursed through, replacing the pain in my body. We were too far away to see her face, but I knew it was her.

"Let's go!"

I heard my comrades footsteps falling away and with one last look at the Queen of the Sol Kingdom, I too, turned and followed suit.

Hours later, we still hadn't stopped running, not until we knew we weren't being followed. By the time we stopped to rest, my lungs, legs, arms, feet and face burned. I bent over at the waist and placed my hands on my knees. Trying to drag what air I could to my exhausted airways.

Leather boots came into my blurry vision and I straightened to find Adaner standing over me.

"Are you quite well?" he asked, his eyes scanning mine.

I nodded, not able to even utter words. I straightened, still holding my previously dislocated arm to my heaving chest. I watched as he cast his eyes down and inhaled deeply, brushing back his hair before meeting my gaze once more.

"I thought we almost lost you back there," he whispered.

"Me too," I panted.

We glanced at one another, that same strange feeling from in the catacombs returning.

He broke the silence. "How's your arm?"

I scoffed, shaking my pounding head. "Do not worry yourself, I will heal quickly."

In a different situation I imagined Adaner might have laughed but this time, he did not. He simply nodded and rubbed the back of his neck.

"Let's rest a bit." He forced a smile at me and walked away to speak with Tolden and Cadeyn.

Grateful, for the opportunity, I laid back on the grass and let the sun shine on my face, warming me from head to toe. I didn't feel warm though. I felt an endless chill creeping up my spine and settled inside to haunt me.

I could still feel the iron chains wrapping around my own wrists. Still feel them ripping my skin away. I could still feel the blood pouring down my back.

All for my magic.

They had wanted to steal my magic. All those times I had been forced to endure such torture at a young age, they were trying to rip it from my body.

But it did not work.

For years they tried and seemingly failed. Adaner said that my magic was stronger than any he had ever seen. I vaguely remembered a conversation I had with Rosita in the library. She had said something about the evil practice of taking away someone's magic. I asked her if that had ever been done before and she looked horrified.

How little I had known; that very practice was why I had been tortured in Helmfirth. That very practice was the same one those poor elven prisoners were being tortured with.

I felt tears streaming down my face and got up from where I was laying. I walked away, taking deep breaths. I sighed and hugged myself. I wasn't sure I was ready to admit the worst part my memories had revealed to me.

So instead of admitting it, I tucked it away to think about another time. Placed it in the part of my mind that would soon need to be processed, for it was beginning to become quite full.

I shook the feeling away and ignored it.

That part was easy for me.

CHAPTER 25

When we arrived back at Crescent, the first thing I did was bathe. After thanking the three males for aiding me and briefly speaking about what to do about the situation at hand, that is.

The worst part had been making my way into the palace. I stopped and asked a servant if she wouldn't mind bringing up whatever they had that was hot to eat and drink to my room and she seemed more than happy to oblige. The next few moments had been filled with agony trying to make it to my room. Every muscle in my body ached and my legs shook as I walked. I had a pounding headache and my throat was parched from the lack of water.

But all that was past me now as I laid in the steamy bathwater, eyes closed and struggling to keep awake.

I was exhausted.

But I would not rest until I was clean. Thus I began the task of washing the grime off of me and scrubbing at my skin. I had to empty and refill the tub twice because the water had turned murky. I heard a knock on my door and invited the maid to come in. She appeared at the bathroom door a moment later.

"Thank you so much," I showered her with praise and greedily took the tray from her. I didn't even hear her leave, I was too busy devouring the food she'd given me.

Moments after the food and delicious hot chocolate with a thick cream on top were devoured, I rinsed off and fell into my satin sheets, hair and body still wet.

Hours later I awoke. It could have even been the next night, I wasn't exactly sure.

All I knew was I was still naked and my hair was dry.

I crawled out of bed and rummaged around in my drawers for something to wear. I found some lovely underthings, a soft forest green sweater and black pants that were the softest things I'd ever felt. Whoever had made them and brought them here deserved everything they ever asked for.

I slipped into my soft clothes and then opened the curtains to my balcony. Stepping out I tucked my hair behind my ears and made to sit on one of the chairs but someone was already sitting in one.

I looked closer and realized it was Adaner. . .and he was asleep. I looked back in my room and then at him again.

Fear rose up in my chest, I had just been *naked* in my bed, completely asleep.

When had he gotten there?

"Adaner?" I whispered and poked him in his arm. He jolted awake and we made eye contact.

"What are you doing up here?" I crossed my arms and looked at the balcony ledge. "How did you even get in?"

"Your door was unlocked."

My eyes widened and I gripped my arms tighter, the one that had been dislocated aching with soreness. "I was asleep, you can't just barge in my room!"

"I'm sorry I wanted to make sure you were alright after. . .everything."

"I was naked!"

"I didn't know that." Adaner's cheeks grew rosy and he stood up a little fast. "I swear I didn't look at you, I mean I *did* look at you to make sure you were okay but then I just sat out here. You were under your blankets." He held his arms up in a shrug and looked so nervous that I grinned slightly.

"Next time, how about you knock or something." I sat down across from the chair he had previously been in and motioned for him to do the same.

He sat and glanced at me with a sidelong smirk. "I *did* knock."

"Shut up," I laughed and reached over to punch his arm playfully but paid the price when my own arm barked in pain. When I leaned back to rest against the chair I curled my legs underneath me and looked out at the balcony floor. I wasn't sure what was happening between me and Adaner but it seemed like we were getting closer.

"So, are you well? Honestly?" Adaner picked at a piece of invisible fluff on his leathers but didn't look at me.

"Just fine." Lies.

"I can tell you're lying," he warned, looking at me.

I flicked my gaze towards his hazel eyes and then looked down at his jawline, then his neck. I watched him swallow and felt my throat do the same. In fact, my throat felt like it was closing up. Tears threatened to gather in my eyes but I willed them to stop.

"Things have just been a lot lately. It hasn't exactly been easy."

"I understand."

I nodded but my brow creased in confusion. "Adaner, are you just looking out for me because Haleth ordered you to?" It was a question that I *needed* answered.

Adaner's hazel eyes flickered with something, an emotion he wouldn't quite show me because he looked away too quickly. "No, Ryn. I'm not."

"Then why? Since the day I arrived here you've acted as if you hate me. And the next minute you and the others are saving my life, but only because your king ordered you to do so. But when I asked you to go on that rescue mission not one of you hesitated and you went with me. And now...well, here you are waiting for me to wake up to make sure I'm okay."

Adaner shifted in his seat and leaned forward, placing his elbows on his knees. He was looking forward but then angled his head to look at me. "It's true that King Haleth has ordered all three of us to keep an eye on you. So, of course we went willingly with you. We weren't just going to let you go venturing across the kingdoms without aid," he paused and glanced down at his intertwined hands. "But I am here of my own accord. I wanted to see you."

My heart felt like it sprung into my throat and my hand massaged the lump away.

It didn't help. "You wanted to see me?"

"Yes."

I grew defensive. "Well, now you've seen me. I'm fine, I'm alive." Idiot. I raised my eyebrows, feeling my walls going back up.

"You don't intimidate me, Ryn. You can cut the act."

"What? There is no act, Adaner. I'm fine."

"But are you?" He looked at me in such a way that I felt like I could tell him what I saw. *"Are* you okay? Because I saw the way you acted in the Glandor Gap. You were ready to die, you *wanted* to die. You were screaming the Lord of Helmfirth's name with absolute fear and horror in your eyes. I know you might not be ready to talk about it and that's fine but I just want you to know that I am *here*. Here for anything you might need, you just have to ask for help."

"So we're friends then?" I asked, trying to lighten the tension I was feeling and ignore the things he was bringing up.

Adaner laughed and sat back in his chair. "Friends. Cadre. Companions. Whatever you want to call it."

I'd never had the companionship he spoke of. It was so foreign to me I was scared I'd mess it up.

"I still plan on mocking everything about you, Princess."

I glared at him. "Now, *that's* unforgivable."

"Good thing I don't need your forgiveness." Adaner leaned forward and playfully punched my knee.

We stared at one another for far too many heart beats and I rose from my seat to look out over the ledge. I heard Adaner follow me and then felt his presence next to me.

I inhaled deeply and then breathed out sincerity, "In truth, I did want to die in Glandor. I've wanted to die a long time before that too." I watched the waves crash against the sand and watched as a few specks of stars twinkled in the night sky. "I realize it is selfish. There is so much to do now. I feel like I have a reason to live, whereas before I didn't."

"What was before? What made you hate your life so much?"

I didn't want to tell him. What if he thought differently of me? The things I had done and were done to me were unspeakable. I had *killed* for people's entertainment.

That was truly unforgivable.

"I just don't want to slip back into that. I don't want to lose my reason to live."

"Then you have to find it and fight for it every day."

I turned my head to look at the dark haired elven male standing next to me. "Will you help me do that?"

Adaner's hazel eyes flickered down to my lips then back to my own eyes. "I think I can find time somewhere in my night to help you." He smirked and reached up to tuck some of my hair behind my ear, but then decided not to and brought his hand back down. "But that means you have to get up early in the twilight and train with me and Tolden and Cadeyn."

I groaned and bent over the railing, resting my head on my good arm.

"It will be good for you." Adaner turned his back to the railing and crossed his arms. "Besides, you need to get stronger and train your body and mind to wield your magic."

I looked at him from where I was still laying my head on my arm and stuck my tongue out. "Only if I must," I whined. But I knew it would be good for me to train again. It had been so long since I trained my body physically. And I definitely had never trained my magic.

"If you want to track and rescue those prisoners you're going to have to."

I nodded. There was truth to what he said.

"We'll start at twilight tomorrow then?" Adaner asked. "And after that we can begin our search for the prisoners."

I stood straight making my way to the balcony door. "I'll be there." I opened it and stepped inside, leaving it open as an invitation for Adaner to enter. I spun and sat at the edge of my bed. "Guess I'll see you tomorrow then."

"You know, I'm meeting Cadeyn and Tolden for a bite to eat." He motioned to the stairs leading to my bedroom door. "We usually eat together, if you want to join?"

I smiled. "I could eat."

Adaner grinned back. "We better hurry before they devour everything then."

I nodded and slipped on some socks and my boots. When I glanced around for my leathers that I had tossed in the corner I noticed they were gone. At least that saved me some embarrassment. I tried not to think of Adaner walking in here while I was asleep and seeing my messy area, not to mention my unmentionables.

I shut the door behind me and Adaner and I walked side by side down the marble hallways. We scaled the marble staircase and took a left through a different series of hallways and antechambers, passing obsidian pillars overlooking open gazebo areas. We passed gardens with hanging jasmine, purple hydrangeas, and budding primroses. Amongst the gardens were stone pathways with benches placed for citizens to sit on and have a moment of peace, I assumed.

The Crescent Palace always smelled of the sea and salt and pine air. Because it was so open with the pillars and balconies and open ceilings the sea air drifted in and out at its own leisure. I glanced up at the open ceiling and saw a few stars blinking back at me from behind a few clouds.

I wasn't sure where the dining hall was since I'd only ever eaten in a gazebo or in my bedroom. In fact, I had only been to a few places in the palace, everything still felt so new but I wanted to explore everything. The gardens looked like a good place to read a book with a cup of tea.

I took two steps for Adaners one and clasped my hands behind my back, looking up at him I spoke, "Where is your room?"

He glanced at me with a flash of hazel. "In the palace."

I snorted. "Yes, as is mine. It isn't fair you know where mine is and I don't know where yours is."

"Why? Plan on sneaking in at some point?"

My face flushed. "You're impossible."

"Takes one to know one."

I rolled my eyes but could not think of a retaliation.

We rounded a corner with marble pillars set strategically overlooking the sea and the Crescent Square below. I glanced out over the marble ledges and could see glowing lights strung up over the cobblestone streets. Elven male and females were mingling in various sized crowds and I could just barely hear the sound of live music and laughter wafting up into the palace.

"Looks riveting," I voiced, leaning over the banister.

"Rather."

I noticed the banners and decorations that seemed a bit out of place for a daily presence in the square but remembered the Constellation Eve Holiday that everyone kept talking about.

"When is Constellation Eve?" I questioned, looking back at Adaner.

"In a few nights actually."

I nodded, pushing away from the ledge and following him again to the dining hall. I could hear the sound of chatter and the sounds of a hearth crackling and popping. Double marble doors stood on obsidian hinges in front of us, one of the doors was propped open, swinging inwards to allow entrance to any wanting to enter.

My eyes were instantly drawn to the massive fireplace in the middle of the room. The fire was encased by black marble and the logs crackled and popped sending sparks flying towards the ceiling. My eyes scanned the room and I glanced over the many wooden tables and chairs littering the hall in straight lines.

Some tables were full while others had only a few sitting by themselves. Adaner led me to the table Cadeyn and Tolden sat at and the amount of food placed in front of them was laugh worthy.

"We heard you were famished," Cadyen tittered, stuffing his mouth with a buttered roll.

"Oh, surely you speak of this one?" I gestured towards Adaner as he straddled a chair, leaning forward to snatch a slice of roasted apple.

"But of course!" Cadeyn slapped his brethren on the shoulder.

Adaner slapped him with a green bean in return. "Watch it!"

I took the seat next to Tolden and offered a smile. He held a pint of ale in front of him and barely glanced up at me. Something caught my eye near the roof and I watched as a spark from the fire floated up towards the antler chandeliers. I hadn't noticed them at first, they were sleek and black and had pointed tips. The light from them cast a warm glow across the faces in the room.

"Thought you could eat?" Adaner's voice drew my attention back and I smirked.

"I can." I reached over and piled my plate full with the assortment of foods. Salted green beans with bacon bits inside, buttered squash with rosemary, buttered rolls, slabs of meat with honey glaze over them. Cadeyn poured me a glass of honeyed wine and I drank it invitingly.

"We have a new recruit to train with us now," Adaner bragged, raising his mug to his lips and sipping his bourbon ale, his eyes had a mischievous glow in them as he wiggled his brows.

Tolden's blue eyes flicked to mine and Cadeyn slapped the table.

"You?" Cadeyn bellowed.

"You?" Tolden asked, almost in shock.

"Me." I smiled and bit into my buttered roll. It was delicious.

"She starts tomorrow." Adaner glanced at me and I felt myself flush and looked away, focusing on anything but that hazel gaze.

"There must be merry making!" Cadeyn insisted, holding his fork and knife up. "She hasn't been to Crescent Square yet has she?"

"No, she hasn't," I clarified. "She was looking at it earlier though, it looked entertaining."

They laughed at the use of my words and I sipped more of my wine.

"I say we take you to the square, get drinks and maybe go dancing?" Cadeyn offered, shrugging excitedly.

He seemed so thrilled that it made me want to go all the more. However, at the mention of dancing, I hesitated. "I've never danced in my life," I admitted.

"That's going to change tonight." Adaner winked seductively and we finished the rest of our food before leaving to execute our plans.

And it was brilliant.

Golden lights were strung up everywhere to illuminate our path. I could just barely hear the ocean lapping at the shore over the sounds of the live music and the laughter and chatter. I followed Adaner, Cadeyn and Tolden down the smooth obsidian pavement and let my eyes wander over all the buildings.

Open taverns with music, cheers and jeers drifted out towards us. Shops and eateries with their windows and doors propped open to allow the salty breeze waft through. I noticed gardens with the same hedges that were in the palace placed strategically around Crescent Square to make it in the shape of a square.

Clever.

I peeked above one as we passed it and saw people dancing, painting and playing instruments amongst fountains with running water and statues. My eyes widened at some of the outfits the dancers were wearing and even still what some of the artists were painting but I quickly looked away when someone snickered at me.

"I've always wanted my portrait painted," Cadeyn said rather solemnly.

"I could paint it for you, you imbecile," smirked Adaner.

"Yeah, but you'd probably draw me fat, you'd take away my hardwon abs." Cadeyn patted his stomach and I held back a laugh, wondering if there even were any abs beneath his dark tunic.

"What about you, Ryn?" Adaner asked, leaning towards me.

"I've never been drawn or painted before and have no desire to either." A smug look spread across my face as I looked them up and down. "But I bet I could have a go at painting you two. Maybe three," I added glancing over at Tolden who stood glaring at us. "I've sketched in the past."

"We've an artist amongst us! Heyo, we've got—"

"Shut up, would you?" I rushed to Cadeyns side and meant to punch him or slap him when I realized just how tall he was. I looked up at him and felt small and weak. The space between the top of my head and his was massive. I turned to look at Adaner and for the first time wondered if this is what bugs felt like.

"What do you guys eat?" I asked in disbelief.

"Beetles and saltless bread." Cadeyn licked his fingers for effect. I made a gagging sound and Adaner chortled.

Tolden brushed past me, his jacket lapels grazing over my legs. "You all are impossible to be around."

I followed him with my eyes as he looked around and chose a taphouse to walk into. He was tall and sturdy and his black leathers glinted off of the light in the square. His hair was cropped short but those blue eyes flashed, judging everyone that got in his way or simply walked by his path.

"What's wrong with him?" I asked as we walked into the lively establishment, but I never got an answer because suddenly all sounds were drowned out with the chaos of the music and the elves dancing and swaying to the music. Adaner went up to the counter and returned with two drinks in hand.

He handed one to me. "Drink up."

We clinked glasses and then tipped the bottoms up. The drink tasted sour at first then turned sweet and warm as it went down.

"Charming," I agreed, nodding my head and tipping it to the side. I scanned the room for Tolden and noticed he'd taken a booth in the back. Cadeyn already had a lovely elven female in his arms and was swinging her around.

"Shall we?" Adaner asked just as I was about to go sit in the booth and mull with Tolden.

"I'm really no good," I insisted.

"I'll teach you." Adaner's smooth cool toned voice slithered across the distance between and seemed to pull us together. I was drawn to it.

I sighed, drink in hand and the other holding onto Adaner as he led us to the dance floor. There was a cheerful flute and violin ensemble floating over the crowd and it made my bones feel alive and merry.

Adaner spun me gently so as not to spill my drink and I took a sip as we swayed our hips back and forth to the rhythm of the music. Once the golden liquid was gone, I set my glass on the counter next to Adaner's. Then I let him fully take me in his arms as we danced and moved our bodies across the floor.

I felt warm inside and the music seemed to be breathing life into me. Of course, it wasn't *just* the music and the dancing. Although it was hard to be sure.

"Are you enjoying yourself?" Adaner asked as he spun me out and then in towards himself.

"I am," I declared. Curling into him, I could feel his warmth and smell the smoky leather of his scent every time I drew near. His dark curly hair bounced with every twirl and I watched the sparkle glow from his eyes.

"You look dashing."

"Oh yes, in my sweater and pants." I chortled, I hadn't exactly thought to change and didn't exactly care.

My eyes peeled away from the hazel ones glancing over me and I surveyed the room. Tolden was still in the corner with his third ale in hand, some females lingered around the table but none seemed brave enough to speak with him. Cadeyn was sitting in a booth on the opposite side speaking with a dark haired female with kohl lining her eyes and cherry red lips.

He caught me watching and shooed me with his hand under the table. I laughed. "What amuses you?"

I brought my gaze back towards the dark haired male in front of me. "Nothing."

"Nothing at all?"

"Depends. Sometimes all you *can* do is look at life with an amused mindset and that's the only way to get through it. Other times it's different."

Adaner became silent as if he understood and nothing more needed to be said. I found myself wanting to rest my head on his chest and sway with the softer music that was being played now. My fingers itched to spread across his back in a hug and bring him towards me. Alarmed at just how quickly those feelings and desires started to become unbearable, I pushed away from him all too quickly.

"I think I need some water," I lied, bringing my hand up to my throat for effect.

"I'll get us some." And with that he was gone, disappeared through the crowd towards the marble counter.

I scanned the crowd and made my way to the booth Tolden sat at. When I sat down across from him, his gaze swept over me and lingered on my eyes for a moment.

"Adaner seems to be warming up to you," he stated, blue eyes moving to his mug of ale.

I cocked my head. "If that's what you want to call it."

"I just did."

"Good for you. Want a reward?" I rolled my eyes, Tolden got on my nerves and quickly at that.

He squinted his eyes and stared right at me. "I don't trust you. You have secrets you're hiding."

"And you don't?" I shot back.

He shrugged. "I've lived here my whole life. You came here and suddenly have my friends wrapped around your pinky finger."

"How dare you?" I spat the words out perhaps a little foolishly and was about to leave when Adaner returned with our waters.

When Tolden saw that there were two glasses, he glanced back at me and shot me a look that spoke worlds about what he was thinking.

"For the record," I stated, leaning forward as Adaner slid into the booth next to Tolden, "you all have made my life a living hell at times. You two the most, Cadeyn's been alright. But when you came and saved me, orders or not, that's when it changed and felt like we were in this together. *That's* the difference between you and Adaner. He actually seems to care in his own rutting way, instead of just sitting in the corner and moping and being an ass to everyone around them." I got up from the table, drowned the water in two gulps and sauntered out of the lively building.

I didn't look to see if anyone followed, I hoped they didn't.

CHAPTER 26

I stormed out of Crescent Square.

Past the artists in the courtyard and past some buildings that seemed closed for the night. The warm glow of the fires and the stars overhead provided an ample amount of light to see. I heard the running water of a river before I saw it and followed the sound. I stepped off of the cobblestone path and onto soft grass that looked black in the shadows.

I reached the running river and noticed how it flowed towards the direction of the ocean. It flowed over pebblestones and plants in the water and even went beneath a black iron bridge. I stepped up on the bridge and when I reached the middle, leaned over it.

I inhaled and exhaled a few breaths and let the shaky adrenaline wash away with the river running beneath me. I extended my arms out on the railing and laid my head beneath them.

I shouldn't have let what Tolden said irk me, but it did. What had he meant when he said I had secrets I was hiding? Or that Cadeyn and Adaner were wrapped around my finger? He wasn't wrong about the secrets, I had plenty of those.

But didn't everyone?

I certainly wasn't trying to manipulate Adaner or Cadeyn, they seemed to be more agreeable than Tolden. They were the first males I'd met and in fact the ones who had turned me into the king.

I groaned and ran my hands through my hair, sighing frustratingly. In the silence I could hear the sound of the waves crashing against the shore. I lifted my head up and made the decision to move and keep walking instead of sitting in this confusion.

I followed the river out of Crescent Square, past a few homes alongside the cobblestone streets of the kingdom and found my way down to the sandy stairs leading down to the beach and salt water.

I inhaled the scent of the ocean and pine wind and kicked my boots and socks off, burying my toes in the soft, cool sand. The moon was high overhead casting a glow almost as bright as the sun. Angling my head so I could look at the sky, I spotted a few stars across the dark expanse.

They twinkled at me and I brought my gaze back down to the shore, sitting down in the cool sand. I could hear the footsteps of someone behind me in the sand and knew he had been following me. Maybe that's why I'd come down here in the first place.

"You know you really should stop following me, your friend has made his dislike for me very clear," I commented, not turning around.

"That he has."

I whipped my head around in confusion and found Tolden sitting in the sand next to me. I had half a mind to get up and leave, he was the one person I least expected to see. But something held me back and made me stay seated in the sand.

I scoffed and turned away. "What are you doing, Tolden?"

"I'm not here to apologize so don't worry about that."

"Good, I don't think I'd be able to stay upright if you did."

Tolden sighed and ran his hands through his thick dark hair. His blue eyes flicked towards the ocean and then glanced back at me. "I don't owe you anything."

"No, you don't."

Tolden inhaled and brought his knees up to rest under his elbows. His head hung between them as he confessed, "I lost someone. And I haven't been the same since."

My heart started to beat fast and I tried to swallow but my throat was very dry.

"I wish I could be as welcoming as Cadeyn, Adaner included, even though he's had his moments. I have a hard time trusting people. I'm not apologizing or asking for pity. Simply your respect in this time of grieving."

"I would ask the same of you then," I said in a hoarse tone. "We don't know each other very well and I'm sorry for your loss but you have no idea the things I am grieving about. I don't say this for sympathy or pity either, just an understanding, perhaps?"

"Do you think we could have mutual respect and understanding for one another then?" Tolden glanced at me and I found myself nodding.

We sat in silence then, nothing more needing to be said. I felt a twinge of something beginning. As if my mind were piecing something together that I didn't quite yet know or understand.

"I am who I am and that doesn't change very easily," Tolden said, his gaze flicking towards me. "Don't ask me to change."

"I wasn't planning to."

When we returned, Adaner and Cadeyn were at a different pub but this time it was outside with lights strung all across the courtyard dance floor. Grass peeked out of the cracks in the square as people swayed and spun and moved their bodies to the rhythm.

As Tolden and I rejoined the group I caught the quick flicker of Adaner's hazel eyes on us. I wasn't quite sure what the look had meant because it was gone before it was really there.

I rubbed my temples. I needed a drink.

I asked for a honeyed, blueberry wine, it seemed to be my favorite here. Accepting the glass, I sauntered over to where the males were leaning against the brick wall, smirking and laughing.

"We're making bets," Cadyen explained, "whoever can get the prettiest female to dance with them doesn't have to do twice the amount of training exercises tomorrow."

I turned and scanned the crowd. "What about me? What if I can get the prettiest female to dance with me?"

The males crooned with laughter. "You can pick a male."

I grinned and started scanning the crowd. "Do we decide on one together or just choose for ourselves?"

"We all have to agree," Adaner clarified, his deep accent had become raspier.

We all leaned against the wall, sipping our individual drinks of choice and scanned the crowd for the poor soul who was going to be dragged into our bet.

"How about her?" I suggested pointing to a lithe female with flowing blonde hair down to her ankles. She wore a blue dress that had a slit down one of her creamy thighs.

"I would trip on her hair!" Cadeyn sniggered and the other two agreed.

"How about the female in the pants?" Adaner asked.

I searched the crowd looking for her, but everyone seemed to be wearing dresses. "I don't see anyone wearing pants, Adaner."

No one said anything and when I looked back at the cadre they were all staring at me. Maybe the wine had gone to my head because I was extremely confused.

Cadeyn had a smug look across his face and Tolden had his usual frown. When I looked at Adaner, his eyes were sparkling as he looked at me from over the rim of his mug.

Heat flushed my face then. "No! Guys, not me! I can't *be* the female you win the bet with."

"You can decline," Adaner offered, stepping closer to me. "But then you would be forfeiting your end of the bargain too."

I scoffed. "You think you're the most attractive male?"

"Aren't I?" His fingers grazed mine as he tugged on the sleeve of my shirt, raising one eyebrow.

"Are you guys hearing this?" I turned to Cadeyn and Tolden and they were both smiling now. "Was this a set up?" I backed away pointing at them, a smile tugging at my own lips.

"I guess you'll have to choose which one of us attractive males you want to dance with. And the other two will have to do twice the amount of exercises tomorrow," said Tolden.

"You're choosing *me* as the female? Honestly you three." I was flushed and laughing.

"You have to choose," Cadeyn pressed.

"You all are impossible! I choose Cadeyn."

Cadeyn cheered and grabbed my hand while Tolden and Adaner groaned and hurled insults at me.

"You dragged yourselves into this!" I yelled back as Cadeyn dragged me to the grassy dance floor. Somewhere along the way I lost my wine glass and didn't quite care all that much.

He wrapped his hands around my waist as I slipped mine over his shoulder, our other hands clasped together as we swayed to the live fiddle, violin and harp ensemble, harmonizing together.

I glanced over where Tolden and Adaner were still leaning against the wall, glaring at us and stuck my tongue out at them.

"I guess we will be the only ones not working our asses off tomorrow," I laughed.

"Oh, I am sure we will still be sweating and training just as hard," Cadeyn countered, grinning down at me.

I groaned, "I should have known."

"Do you really think I'm the most attractive out of the three of us?"

"What kind of a question is that?" I felt nervous at the thought of answering the silly question. What did it really matter?

"Well, you *did* pick me," Cadeyn bragged, winking at me.

I glanced back over at Adaner and then Tolden. "I'm not going to answer that. It feels like a trap."

Cadeyn threw his head back in laughter. "You *are* impossible."

"I prefer to remain that way."

Cadeyn spun me out away from him as the music ended and as I twirled back into his arms he lowered me and dipped me close to the ground.

"How very dramatic," I crooned as he brought me back up and we left the grass.

"That's me!" he said, bowing.

We walked back to join Adaner and Tolden and they smiled and jeered at us. "What a pair you two make!" Tolden crooned, seemingly a little drunk.

I cringed at his words and unlinked Cadeyn and I's arms.

"She wouldn't even tell me who she *actually* thought was the most attractive!" Cadyen whined.

I covered my face with my hands and laughed into them. "Stop!"

I felt someone inch closer to me and felt his hot breath. "Who *does* the princess think is the most charming?"

Adaner's cool, thick tone was even deeper with the drinks we'd all had. I could smell the ale on his breath. I felt him move closer and then felt his warm fingers pulling mine away from my face.

"She's blushing!" Tolden cackled and bent over.

"How much have you both had to drink?" Cadeyn asked, glancing at Tolden bent over next to him.

My eyes met Adaner's hazel ones and I could see that they were glazed over. I pulled his hand away from mine and stepped away, smirking deviously. "You all think that I would willingly choose one of you as the most charming? The most attractive?" I pushed hair out of my face and grinned. "I choose *myself*. I'm the most charming and certainly have the best looks in the group!"

The groans and moans and complaints that I received for putting myself up on a pedestal were many and echoed on into the night. But I simply flicked my hair across my back and strutted out of the grassy courtyard.

I heard the steps of the cadre following me and could still hear their laughter. They were drunk and ridiculous. When we made it inside the palace, Tolden was half walking half being dragged by Cadeyn while Adaner was trying to keep up with me.

"You have long legs," he stated, glancing down at them.

"Thank you. They help me walk."

"You're angry?" he looked hurt and his brows pulled together in concern.

"No. Witty. It's called being sardonic."

"Ah."

I glanced over at Adaner and tried to hide my smile. His dark hair was unruly and a lock of it kept falling into his eyes. His shirt was rumpled from dancing and the buttons at the top were undone, revealing a tanned muscled chest.

"What are you staring at?" Adaner questioned, leaning closer.

I laughed. "Your unruliness."

"Oh, do you find it attractive?" He winked at me and I got the feeling he wasn't as drunk as the others. I could still see those hazel eyes reflecting concern and centuries of things untold.

"You're staring at me, love."

I cleared my throat and looked away. When I looked behind my shoulder, Tolden and Cadeyn were nowhere to be found.

I glanced back at Adaner and smiled. "We'd better get to bed. Training tomorrow right?"

"Is that an invitation?"

My heart fluttered at his question and I felt my back press up against the wall.

Adaner leaned close towards me and placed his hand on the wall next to my head. "An invitation for what?" I whispered.

His eyes changed suddenly and that glow reflecting in the hazel hues disappeared. He looked down and when he looked back he was smiling but it was almost an apologetic one.

"An invitation to escort you to your room? May I?" He held out an elbow and I took it, rather confused.

Once we reached the obsidian staircase leading up to the wing with my bedroom, Adaner let go of my arm and bid me goodnight. I watched him go. Why had he changed so quickly? What had I done, if anything?

When he was out of sight I climbed back up the stairs. The wine and the events of the night had probably gone to my head and were not helping me make sense of things.

Opening my bedroom door, I shuffled in and clicked it shut. Taking off my sweater and leggings I crawled into my black satin night clothes and splashed water on my face. Then I slipped beneath my cozy sheets and heavy blanket and laid down on my side.

My eyelids were heavy but I didn't fall asleep for a little while. My brain was too busy thinking about training tomorrow. About the prisoners. About what Tolden had said on the beach. And damn it all I kept thinking about the way Adaner's demeanor had changed.

Eventually, I fell asleep and allowed my thoughts to drift away. I would think about them later.

Tomorrow maybe.

CHAPTER 27

Twilight came in a burst of blues and violets with the moon setting beyond the sea.

I awoke with a pounding headache. Which I assumed could only be from the wine I had consumed. So, instead of getting out of bed I pulled the covers over my head and fell back asleep. Shortly after, I was rudely awakened by those same covers being torn off of my warm body and thrust to the floor.

"What in the—" I bolted upright but stopped, seeing Adaner and Cadeyn staring at me. I shot them a glare that should have sent them running.

"I will not have any tardiness amongst my trainees," Adaner quipped rather cheerfully.

I groaned and put an arm over my eyes. "How many times do I have to tell you not to barge in here!"

"I did knock this time." Adaner grinned deviously and I glanced at Cadeyn.

"It is true," he confirmed.

"Tolden is already waiting for us in the courtyard, get decent," ordered Adaner as he walked to the window where the balcony was.

"What, this isn't decent enough?" I snapped back, smirking behind their backs.

"The *only* thing indecent about you is your wild hair sticking out every which way." Adaner yanked the blinds open and light from the few stars remaining and the twilight hue flooded in.

Cadeyn laughed.

"So the rest of me is decent? I can train in this?" I pulled at my night clothes, looking down and the satin caught in the glowing light.

Adaner's hazel eyes flicked over my body and with an unchanging glare he breathed, "You have two minutes."

I got up to my knees and pointed a finger at him, opening my mouth to argue.

"Wanna make it thirty seconds?"

I heard Cadeyn snicker in the corner. Groaning loudly, I rolled off of my bed. Snatching my freshly cleaned leathers roughly, I walked into the bathroom. When I caught sight of my reflection I gasped at just how horrendous it was. I heard Adaner and Cadeyn chortle but didn't have time to hear what they jeered at me because I slammed the door shut.

I dressed in new underthings and pulled on the leather pants. They fit snugly but comfortably. I tugged the leather short sleeved shirt over my head and liked how it tucked neatly into the pants. Since we'd be training I thought the short sleeved would be the better option.

Glancing at the mirror again, I snatched my brush up and yanked it through the rats nest. I winced at the pain it caused and gritted my teeth.

"Hurry up, love!" called Adaner from the other room in a sniveling tone.

I stuck my tongue out at the door and kept brushing until my hair was a smooth but frizzy mess. I brushed it back and skillfully separated it into three strands and then braided it down my back. Before I opened the door I glanced over my reflection and winked at myself. I didn't look half bad.

Opening the door once more, I glared at the two males. They were just standing in the middle of my room, arms crossed and scowls etched in their brows. I found socks in a drawer, slipped them on, pulled on my boots and laced them up quicker than I ever had.

"Two minutes gone and still counting." Adaner bent his knees and groaned gazing up at the ceiling. Before he could move, I snatched his wrist and whipped him around, shoving him up the small steps leading into the antichamber.

"Go! Just go! I'm ready now and you can be grateful for it!"

I slammed my door shut and Adaner, Cadeyn and I walked through the halls, down the marble staircase and turned left, towards the dining area.

"Aren't we going to train?" I questioned, falling behind.

Cadeyn glanced over his shoulder. "Yes. Food is essential to training your mind and body."

"You guys really take your food seriously here."

Adaner turned around but kept walking. "But of course, love. How else are we to fuel ourselves?"

I shrugged and threw my arms out at the sides. "I thought it came naturally to you two."

They both laughed and muttered something I couldn't hear under their breath.

Once we entered the huge dining hall, I noticed the grand fireplace was not lit. The room was still and quiet and only Tolden sat at a table with a few lit candles in ornate, obsidian holders placed around the seating.

"It's about damn time," Tolden muttered as I sat down.

I didn't bother smiling at him and started placing food on my plate. There was yet again an exquisite array of food; steamy bread rolls, sliced white cheese, whole sausages and slabs of bacon, a pot of steaming scrambled eggs, bowls of berries and oranges and jars of jams and butters.

They did indeed take their food entirely seriously.

I buttered a roll and added what looked to be some sort of berry jam. I took a few fruits and pieces of sausage and Cadeyn poured me a mug of hot black coffee. I still wasn't used to it but. . .I was getting there.

I took a sip. Maybe.

"There's cream and sugar you know." Tolden reached across the table and plopped a dish of white tiny crystals and an even smaller pitcher of white milk.

"Oh, thank the divine!" I spooned the sugar and milk into the black liquid, turning it golden and a sigh of relief expelled my lungs. "*Thank you,*" I praised as I sipped on it.

After breakfast we walked to the training courtyard. I had never been in this part of the palace but we'd walked out a set of doors attached to the dining hall and into the crisp air. A path of cobblestone accompanied by hedges of that same, strange dark beryl color lined the walkway.

The cobblestones with the hedges opened up and led us to steps leading away from the palace and into a deeper area consisting of more hedges, statues, wells and fountains. The steps were long and wide and there was a fountain directly in the middle of the stairs every thirty yards or so.

The sky was fully awake with the deep blue hue and light streaks of violet in the sky, which cast more than enough light to see by. A few stars still sparkled here and there and I expected they'd never shy away from the twilight glow. Whenever I looked there were always at least three stars that shined brighter than the rest even when it was completely black.

We rounded a corner and an open courtyard surrounded by obsidian stone lay before us. The stone wrapped around the entire space making a wide circle, breaking only for the entrance we just walked through.

Weapons were stacked neatly in one corner tucked away into a large metal case. Two tables were placed on either side of it completely clear of clutter with boxes of even more weapons, ropes and chains piled into them. The courtyard was made up of patches of both cobblestone and grass. Most likely so the warriors could train on either source of ground and be used to it.

Glancing around while the three males began to spread out and stretch I caught the sight of a pool of water at the far end of the training area. My lip and chin turned down in concentration and I briefly wondered what sort of training that would be for.

"Impressed?" Adaner asked from his position on the ground.

"Sure." I winked and joined them on the grass. I laid flat on my back and stretched my arms above my head. It felt good to stretch my sleeping muscles. It had been too long since I trained or moved my body in this way.

Outstretched on the dewy grass, I gazed at the blue hue above me. Small wisps of clouds floated by and I could just barely hear the crash of the tide miles away.

It felt so good to just lay here and. . .breathe.

I inhaled and exhaled, sitting up and stretching my back by reaching for my toes. This kind of training was so different from what I was used to. This was to help keep my muscles and core strong, this kind of training could be put to good use instead of becoming a murderer in an arena for people's enjoyment.

I turned to the side and lifted one leg up. My gaze swept over the three elven males doing similar stretches a few yards away and I wondered how they would react if I told them the truth. If I told them what I really was and what I had done.

They would hate me.

I exhaled again, this time more in a frustrated groan and stood up. These thoughts were not going to help me in combat today. They would only drag up memories that were better forgotten.

"Ready to start?" Adaner questioned as he too rose from his place on the grass.

I nodded, then cracked my neck and knuckles.

"Cadeyn, match with Adaner first. Show us what you got," Tolden said from the weapons table as he glanced over polished blades and hilts.

I walked to the table and sat crossed legged on top of it. I swung my legs and watched as Adaner and Cadeyn both shucked their shirts off and Adaner swiped his hair out of his eyes.

Both elven males held their hands open in a curl, ready to close into a fist and strike at the first sign. Cadeyn made the first move and Adaner swung, missing his opponent's head and then quickly blocked a clenched fist headed straight for his gut.

"Easy there!" Adaner chided.

I snickered and absently picked at a loose thread on my shirt. "You're supposed to be watching."

I slowly moved my eyes to glare at Tolden, but he wasn't even looking at me. I stuck my tongue out at him and watched the males spar.

They bobbed back and forth, taking steps forward, then taking steps back. All the while, stepping in a slow circle. It gave me all the good vantage points to where I could watch both of their faces equally. Cadeyn was definitely on fire and was making all the first moves and striking hard and fast, but Adaner blocked every single one of them.

They knew each other's weak and strong points and not one of them had hit the other. I expected the only way someone would take a hit was if the other *let* them.

So I assumed that was what happened when Cadeyn's fist collided with Adaner's jaw. Something in me lurched at the sight and I wanted to shout to make sure he was alright.

When Adaner turned his head back, he was grinning. "Have another go!"

Cadeyn came at him with a force so strong I almost jolted from the table to stop them. But this was just sport to them. One after the other Adaner took a hit to the lip, to the other side of his jaw, to the side of his temple to other places I couldn't even keep track of because there were too many.

But Cadeyn wasn't the only one dishing them out. Adaner came right back at him with the same force and amount of hits. They were both bleeding and breathless and to finish it off Adaner tripped Cadeyn and they both collided in a roll of grass, fists, elbows and knees still kicking and hitting.

Too quick for my eyes to catch, Adaner pinned Cadeyn beneath him and had his bulky arm wrapped around his neck. Cadeyn began to turn a different color and I prepared to jump from the table I sat atop. Just as I unfolded my legs to spring forth Cadeyn tapped Adaner's hand and he let him go.

I sighed in relief.

Adaner was the first to stand up and lend a hand to his friend. They turned to me laughing and grinning. Both of their lips were cut and bleeding and they had numerous cuts and scratches along their cheeks and temples.

One of them was so close to Adaner's eye that as I walked toward them, I found myself reaching up to inspect it. He swatted my hand away playfully.

"One would think you were worried for us, love?" Adaner crowed.

I punched his arm. "Never."

"Your eyes and face plead a different case." Adaner ran his tongue over the cut on his lip and a smile crept its way across his face.

Infuriating.

I turned away and looked at Tolden. "Are we next then?"

Tolden laughed, his arms were crossed as he pushed off of the table. "Funny."

I exchanged looks with Adaner and Cadeyn, then back to Tolden. "What is?"

"You think you could fight me?"

"You think I can't?" I crossed my arms and faced him. I'm sure my face was all stern and serious, eyebrows raised and all.

"Okay. Let's see if you last thirty seconds." Tolden rolled his sleeves up and strutted to where Cadeyn and Adaner just were on the grass.

"Bet." I matched his step and stood across from him.

"What on?"

"What's most valuable to you?"

"My magic." A flash of blue glittered in Tolden's eyes.

I hadn't learned much magic. In fact, I would say I had learned none at all. I just exploded when feeling strong emotions more often than not. I would need someone experienced to teach me. Tolden seemed like the perfect instructor. "Teach me how to use mine," I replied evenly.

"So if I lose, I teach you how to use your magic?" he asked, cocking his head to the side.

"Yes. What are your terms?"

"If you lose you have to answer any question I ask."

My heart jumped at that and for a moment, I hesitated. It didn't seem like a very good idea to agree to his terms. But I wasn't about to back down now.

"Agreed," I breathed.

"Agreed," he repeated.

With that, we bent our knees and began circling one another, our fists raised half curled much like Adaner and Cadeyn's had been. I noticed right away Tolden favored his left leg and leaned on it more than his right. Which meant he would hit with his right hand. His mouth twitched upward and he struck.

I dodged his hit both left and right and on the third one I ducked, squatting and sweeping my left leg to unbalance him but he saw it and whirled away before I could make the hit. I rose again and watched as his mouth twitched once more and he threw a punch head straight for my gut.

I stepped to the side and brought my arm down on his wrist and threw a backhanded punch to his throat. He blocked it with his other hand and twisted my arm, twirling me and curling it behind my back. I cringed in pain but elbowed him in the stomach. He grunted and fell back.

I instantly whipped around to face him again but he was already coming after me. He barreled into my stomach and we hit the grass with a thud. My skull smacked against the ground and I felt dizzy. I felt his hands going to pin mine down at my sides and knew I couldn't let that happen.

He was strong. I needed to get on top.

Without wasting another moment, I brought my knee up to kick him between his legs. I didn't do it as hard as I normally would but he still yelled and fell forward. I quickly maneuvered myself and using my legs and arms, twisted us so that he was on the bottom. I immediately put the full weight of my forearm on his throat and used my leg to keep his foot from kicking me. My other arm kept his right one, the stronger one, pinned to the grass.

"Does this mean I win?" I asked, gloating.

"It would seem so," Tolden muttered, making eye contact with me.

"Guess you'll have to win those questions next time." I grinned and helped him up.

"Where in the hell did you even learn to dodge and fight like that?"

"You'll have to beat me next time to find out." I wiggled my brows, even as an oily feeling coiled in my gut.

Lord Elton had worked me from dawn to dusk. Had whipped me when it wasn't enough or wasn't exactly what he wanted. Had me dragged to a room where they tried to steal my magic from me for half of my life. Had me forced into an arena to fight to the death for humans' entertainment.

I shook my head. I didn't want to remember.

Someone touched my shoulder and I flinched. I met hazel eyes and instantly felt calmer.

"I could have taught you how to use your magic, Ryn." Adaner looked solemn, his eyes less bright.

I smiled at him. "I know! But what fun, I won a bet!"

"I would have taught you without having to have lost a bet."

"And I thank you. You can fill in anything he leaves out."

Adaner turned away with a gleam in his eyes I could not quite decipher. "Of course," he muttered beneath his breath.

I watched him walk away but shouted, "Don't forget you and Tolden have to do double the exercises!"

He groaned and Cadeyn and I snickered at one another.

I felt someone come up next to me and when I turned I wasn't surprised to see Tolden. "You have to do double too. Don't shy away."

"We begin now," he muttered.

"Begin what?"

"Your training."

"Ah, so soon?" I extended my arms out and gave him a smile. I fully expected him to lead me in a series of exercises to allow my magic to flow through me, but was surprised when he shouted at me instead.

"Show me your magic!" He stood a few feet away from me with his hands clasped behind his back, but his face was solid anger.

I scoffed. "You're meant to guide me."

"Show me your magic!" he repeated.

I felt stupid just standing in front of him with Adaner and Cadeyn glancing at us from the weapons table. My gaze flickered back to Tolden and I opened my mouth to object. "My magic doesn't just appear, Tolden I—"

"What's wrong? Can't do it? *Won't* do it?" The hate and judgment in Tolden's blue eyes was so threateningly intense.

"No," I argued, stepping forward. "I want to, I just. . ." I opened my hands, palms facing up and tried extremely hard to conjure something up.

Tolden spoke, crossing his arms, "Something's holding you back, Ryn and *you* have to figure out what it is. You are powerful. Use your magic, don't be afraid of it."

"I'm not afraid of it."

"That's a bloody lie. Either you're afraid of yourself or your magic and I'm willing to bet it's your magic. I can see in your eyes that you hold some sort of resentment towards it. It caused something horrible in your life. It took something away."

"Stop," I breathed, feeling my heart race.

"No matter what it is or was, its over and you need to let it go. Stop letting it have a hold on you."

I blinked and felt the world swirling around me. Tolden didn't know what he was talking about. How could he? But deep down I felt a stirring.

A frosty awakening that spiraled from my very core and upwards. I felt the black frost on my fingertips and watched as the pure night shadows swirled around my fingertips. I felt ice on my breath and tongue and felt it from every pore of my being.

"That's it. You're doing it!" Tolden unfolded his arms and I felt a shift in the air. I could sense his magic rallying to counter mine.

I had done this before. With Skandar. Skandar.

Fear shot through me and black ice blew up in my face and speared straight for Tolden's head. He ducked and shouted something.

But I didn't hear him.

All I could see was death. The deaths *I* had caused.

A cold sweat began to form on my brow and trickle down my back.

Something lodged in my throat and anger burst forth in the form of obsidian night pouring from my hands. It poured out of me like shadows and slithered at a fast pace in every direction. I heard shouts and yells and the sound of something crumbling. I sensed something flying towards me but didn't have time to duck before it scraped the side of my head.

I flinched and was thrown off balance by trying to duck. Breathing heavily, I watched the black mist melt into the air and gave way to the destruction I had caused.

My mouth fell agape as I stared at the north wall. . .or what was left of it.

My hand flew to my mouth. The *entire* north part of the training ground lay in crumbles. Black mist still swirling in columns like dust. A few pieces of the bricks that had once been securely part of the structure fell and toppled to the cobblestones, knocking over a rack full of bows and arrows.

"What the hell?" Tolden yelled and I thought he was mad at me but when our gazes collided, I soon realized that shock was written all over his face.

"Bloody stars," I heard Cadeyn whisper.

I whipped my neck back and forth between the three of them. "What? What is it?" They all exchanged looks and their silence infuriated me.

"Tell me!" I insisted.

Without a single word, Adaner lifted his hand and a small ball of ice formed there.

Real, *white* ice. Not black ice.

The words I had been about to utter died on my tongue and were replaced with confusion and shock.

"What does it mean?" asked Cadeyn, the only one who had spoken so far.

Tolden shook his head. "I don't know."

I felt stupid and out of control and like a spectacle they were just picking apart. Without a single other word or glance behind me, I whipped around and stormed out of the courtyard. I didn't know where I was going. I just knew I had to leave their shocked and condemning faces behind.

CHAPTER 28

Hours later, Tolden found me by the water.

The minute I heard his boots on the sand, I rolled my eyes and made it my mission to ignore him. They had all stared at me like some foreign creature and it had humiliated me. I could still feel it burning my cheeks.

My elbows rested in the sand as I leaned back. Tolden sat next to me—a good distance away. We were silent, not companionable silence but rather of the kind where one was waiting for the other to speak.

I caved.

"Why did you bait me to get my magic to react?" It had bothered me ever since it happened.

He glanced at me, piercing blue eyes grazing my green ones. His eyebrow raised slightly and his jaw twitched. "I wanted to show you that it's crucial to learn how to control your magic or results like what you suffered can happen."

"I could have told you that. You didn't have to demonstrate." I looked away from him, annoyed.

"Would you have?"

"Have what?"

"Told me."

"What's that supposed to mean?"

"You don't talk, Ryn. You never tell anyone anything. How was I supposed to know? I was starting with the basics."

I nodded and sat up. Rubbing my temples with my forefingers. "You're one to talk."

Tolden shook his head but I heard a chuckle escape him. "We're similar, you and I."

"Is that why we don't get along?"

"Something like that."

We glanced at each other and a smile began to form on Tolden's lips. I rolled my eyes and tossed sand at him. He deflected with his magic, the cursed light ice magic that I allegedly did not have.

At the glance of his piercing ocean blue eyes, I quickly averted my gaze and inhaled. They reminded me so much of the young boy in the arena. I wrung my hands and drew my knees up to my chest.

"Why is my magic dark?" I whispered. I didn't look at him but I could tell he was thinking.

"I've never seen a Crescent Blood with dark ice powers. We all have. . .well ice and Sol Bloods have fire."

That wasn't helping. "I should go." I stood up and brushed the sand off of my pants.

"Training tomorrow? Same time and place?" Tolden's eyes held more silent questions than the one he'd just asked.

I nodded in confirmation.

And for the next few months, that is what we did. I scarcely knew anything else.

I trained with Tolden, Adaner and Cadeyn. Oftentimes, all together, other times one on one. I was growing to like my magic, I liked learning how to wield and control it. It gave me a sense of strength and control I'd never felt in my life before.

We were still trying to figure out how I had dark ice magic but quickly learned that information or any history about that kind of power was non-existent. As for our search for the prisoners, we had come up completely empty. After training, we would oftentimes ride to the border, scout out to see if we found anything suspicious.

Alas, we had no luck. But we had passed on word to others. The entire kingdom was keeping a sharp eye out for any unusual activity or sightings.

After an especially draining night of training, I began the search for a delicious cup of steaming hot tea, a good book and a bench to read the said book.

I didn't have to look for very long. I already knew where the kitchens were and when I appeared all the wide eyed cooks and servants did everything for me. It was quite aggravating. But at least they did what I requested, the head cook must not have been there today.

I recalled the last time I had asked for a similar favor and she'd turned me away at the door.

When I reached for a mug, a wide eyed female snatched it from me and muttered something inaudible. I stepped around a rather large male to put a kettle on to boil, but he plucked it right out of my hands.

Nevertheless, the result of being waited upon and served was the perfect mug of honeyed tea with steaming swirls and a plate of cranberry scones. I smirked as I walked out of the kitchen. The prize had been attained.

After wandering around and peeking in at all the different alcoves of peace and sanity, I finally chose a quiet spot. It was a grand gazebo shape with a view of a small waterfall and pond with greenery and obsidian pillars and tiles.

I chose a cold, black bench and held my mug of tea in both hands. I allowed the steam to swirl around me and heat my face. It smelled of blueberries and spices. Opening the book I'd swiped from the library on the way, I settled back and began to read.

I occasionally sipped from my steaming mug and nibbled on the scones and plunged into the world and characters of the book before me. It was only a matter of time before I'd chosen my favorite characters and already had theories about the plot.

Flipping page after page and taking sip after sip, pausing only to refill my mug of tea and plate of scones, I remained there until I finished the book.

I laid back on the bench and studied the open gazebo rooftop. I could see speckles of the three stars which told me I'd spent most of twilight here. I thought about the book and its characters and how it had all unfolded. It was quite entertaining to say the least. My mind drifted once more to the prisoners who no doubt were being tortured and killed at this very moment and I could not help the surge of shame that took over me.

I rubbed my face with my hand. I needed to remember there wasn't much that I alone could do—or could have done. Still, no matter what I told myself that gnawing persisted.

"Oh," I heard a small voice exclaim.

I moved my eyes away from the starry sky and saw a female standing in the doorway. She held a mug of tea in her hand and clutched a book close to her chest. She was small with wide but attentive violet eyes and flowing blonde hair that was curled over her shoulders.

"I'm sorry, I didn't mean to disrupt you," she said, as she glanced around as if looking for a different bench but I already knew there weren't any.

I didn't exactly feel like giving up my spot but I was done with my book and had run out of tea again.

"You're not disturbing me." I swung my legs and let them hit the ground. "Please, sit."

"I couldn't intrude—"

"If you say anything about me being royalty I will steal that tea of yours." I smirked and the blonde female sheepishly grinned back.

She edged forward and sat down, placing her mug and book on the bench in between us. "Thanks."

I waved her off and began gathering my things.

"What are you reading?" she asked, as if aiming to start a conversation.

"I just finished this." I presented the book to her and her eyes went wide.

"That is one of my favorites! This is a close second." She tapped the book laying on the bench and I turned my head to read the title.

"I'll have to read that next," I commented, standing up and making to leave.

"You could read it now? Perhaps we could trade? I looked in the library for that one," she gestured to the one in my hand, "now I know where it went."

I shrugged. "If you don't want to read that one, I'll gladly take it!"

"I've read it a thousand times."

"Done deal!"

We traded books and smiled at one another. Pleased with our efforts of sharing coveted copies.

"I'm Thea, by the way." Thea smiled and a small dimple under her left eye appeared. She was intriguing and beautiful.

"Ryn," I offered back.

She nodded, unfazed by my name or who my father was. I liked her already.

"Mind if I stay and read awhile?" I gestured back to the bench and she nodded eagerly.

"We might as well get a tea pot and the whole pan of cookies!" I jested, but when I glanced at Thea she shrugged and we bolted for the kitchen to do just that.

All the cooks stared at us in disbelief when we took a whole steel pot of boiling water and tea bags and a whole platter of cookies, fresh from the oven. We laughed and giggled the whole way back.

After we consumed as much food and tea as we could, we packed up our books and Thea showed me where her room was. I pointed out my door as we passed it and she commented on how that room had stayed empty for centuries. I wondered if it was always meant to be my room—if I had grown up in the palace.

I shoved those thoughts away as she directed us down one more hall from mine and we came to a stop. She opened her door and let me in. It wasn't as big as mine and didn't have the little living area before the bedroom but it was still grand. Her bed had the same sheets and duvet as mine and she had a small bookshelf resting against the adjoining wall. A few lamps were lit, giving the room a warm and comforting glow. I glimpsed the bathing room as we passed it and noted it was painted a bright blue color.

"I heard about your arrival and wondered when I'd run into you. I did not think it would be months," Thea commented, sitting at the edge of her bed.

I nodded, feeling only slightly uncomfortable. "I've been kept busy. I don't wander much."

"You train with the boys, don't you?"

"Yes," I chuckled.

"Do you know them?"

"Everyone knows them," she laughed and a blush covered her cheeks for a moment. "Cadeyn was telling me about you."

I raised my eyebrows. "I see."

"I don't wander much either, my studies keep me quite occupied."

"What do you study?" I leaned slightly against the bed she sat on.

"Botany."

"How interesting!" I knew very little about plants.

She nodded then asked, "So, how are you finding the Crescent Kingdom thus far?"

"It's beautiful. I love the ocean." It was far better than the rotting fish hole I used to live in, but I did not say that.

"As do I. I leave my doors and windows open every night so I can hear the waves."

I tilted my head to the side, that was a really good idea. "I might have to do that now."

Thea laughed and her purple eyes sparkled once more. She propped a leg up on the bed and patted next to her. "You can sit."

So I did. "Are you related to anyone in the palace?" I asked.

She shook her head, glancing away. "My family was killed in the Bloody War. King Haleth took me in after his Crescent Warriors found me."

"I'm so sorry. I shouldn't have asked." I thought it odd that Haleth would be so kind, I didn't think he had it in his soul.

Thea shrugged and looked down. "I like talking about them. It keeps their memory alive."

I liked that. It was a good way to describe it.

"If you don't mind, I'd like to hear more about this Bloody War. I was young when it happened obviously and I wasn't currently in the Crescent Realm. What was it like here?" I inquired.

I briefly recalled the conversation I'd had with Queen Cressida and how shocked she had been about the Death Pit and how the humans had treated trespassers. It made me queasy to think about how she had lied to me. About the truth that lay beneath her Sol Palace.

Thea leaned back and looked toward her ceiling as if pondering. "I was young too but they say you always keep the more negative and traumatic events of your past more than the good."

A sad and broken thought but one that remained true.

"I remember how scared I was whenever Father would leave. I remember crying with Mother if he returned late because we were so relieved that he was alive. I remember the screams from my village when it burned." Thea wiped absently at the corner of her eye and she looked directly at my face.

"I remember the day Father didn't come home and our worst fears had come true. But nothing will compare to the sorrow I felt when they ransacked our house and Mother helped me escape out the window." She looked down and in a quiet voice said, "She didn't make it. But, Haleth took me in and treated me like one of his own."

That comment stung. I fought the anger rising in my chest. Haleth had replaced me with her. I swallowed the venom like words that threatened to come out and instead said, "That sounds awful, I'm sorry you had to go through that."

Thea shrugged. "I'm sorry for getting all emotional."

I shook my head. "There's never a reason to apologize for that. I asked about the war and you told me about what it was like for you."

"What about you? What was it like where you were?"

I swallowed. Did I dare share the truth or lie? "It was no better. I was a prisoner so I didn't get out much." It was at least a half truth.

"A prisoner of war? At such a young age? I thought they had rules against that."

"Not in the human realm it would seem." A selective truth.

"I've heard horrible things about Helmfirth. Especially about Lord Elton Hode. Did you ever meet him while you were there?"

If she only knew the questions she was asking. The memory of his hands and eyes on me against my will came crashing into my mind. I huffed a laugh without any real humor in it and got up from the bed.

"Yes, I met him a few times." It took everything in me to not spiral down into that place of numbness. That place where I didn't have to *feel*.

Thea must have sensed the change in my attitude because she became silent. I turned to her and asked, "All of the realms were involved?"

"Yes, for a while. It was the first time in history that all the realms had warred against one another, well, excluding Hell's Keep and the witches. But differentiating realms allied with one another. Sol and Crescent, Helmfirth and Theldar, LeiHaven and Sodnier. I don't remember much, I'm just repeating what I've been told." Thea looked down again and I walked back towards her.

I nodded, thinking. I didn't remember much at all about the war. I had been so young and imprisoned in a lake town during the entirety of it.

"Technically, we're at peace now with all the realms and we have been for the last seven years," Thea stated, swinging her legs off the side of the bed.

"If you can call it that," I scoffed.

She turned to me. "What do you mean?"

"Well, we're only at peace because of the Territorial Treaty. If anyone not belonging to a certain realm crosses the border without permission there are serious penalties. Some of which include being sent to Hells' Keep."

"That sounds ghastly. I guess I don't remember that since I was so young." She glanced around her room and then offered, "Maybe that's what happened to Tolden's brother."

My heart stammered. Tolden told me he'd had a loss he was dealing with, I had not known it was a brother.

Thea watched me and when I didn't say anything she elaborated, "Rayken went missing awhile ago and he still hasn't returned. Of course, everyone assumes the worst, but I still hold onto a shrivel of hope. I refuse to believe he's dead. . .we can still rescue him if he's been sent to Hell's Keep, right?"

I swallowed, feeling an aching inside my chest. I shoved it deep down and ignored it. "I'm really not sure. I've heard prisoners will take their own lives before submitting to the torment that Azazel permits in Hell's Keep."

Thea's eyes went wide and I felt as if I'd stolen the last bit of hope she held onto. I struggled for the right words to say, "That is, if he's not out somewhere having a grand adventure and there's nothing to worry about." I forced a smile and she returned the gesture.

"I have a painting I did of them, do you want to see it?" Her eyes glowed and before I even had time to reply she bounded off the bed and opened a drawer, where she took out a thick parchment.

When she handed me the painting, I already knew I had taken all of her hopes and crushed them until there was nothing left. That familiar raw aching opened up the hole in my chest and I realized that all this time it hadn't ever been gone. I had been ignoring it.

I hadn't wanted it to be true.

Tears welled up in my eyes and I felt sick.

Tolden and his brothers piercing blue eyes stared at me from the painting.

I knew those ocean eyes all too well because they were the very same ocean eyes on the face of the boy I had killed in Helmfirth.

CHAPTER 29

I didn't know how to react.

Other than plastering a very broken smile onto my lips and muttering about how beautiful the handy work of the painting was. Thea smiled and opened her mouth to say something else but I knew if I didn't leave right that moment, I was going to vomit all over her and her floor.

"I'm so sorry, I have to go. I'm late for training."

I raced out of her room leaving her wide eyed and confused. But nothing else mattered except getting away. I raced down the hall and barely made it into my bathing room before I vomited in the toilet. Over and over again.

Tears mixed with saliva and snot covered my face as I wept and screamed until my throat felt raw.

It should have been me. It should have been me.

I should have offered myself instead of killing him. I killed Tolden's brother.

The next few moments were a blur of anger and hatred and punching the wall and banging my fists into my head to stop my racing mind.

Anything to rid myself of these horrid memories and regrets. I don't remember slipping but I felt a rush of pain shoot up my foot and then I was falling. Piercing pain sliced across my wrists and arms and legs and then I snapped my head against something cold and hard.

Sweet, silent darkness opened its arms and swallowed me whole. And I welcomed it, gladly.

—⚔—

I didn't want to regain awareness, but I could feel my body dragging me out of the coma like bliss I had fallen into. I shivered as my mind came into consciousness and slowly my body came after.

Something wet and sticky covered my body and when I opened my eyes, my head pounded. In the blur that was my vision, I barely made out the crimson color dashed across my arms and feet and hands. As my brain became more aware, so did the part that allowed me to feel pain.

Which is all I felt now. Externally and internally.

I sat up slowly and addressed the situation, not remembering clearly what had happened other than tripping and falling. Glass littered the floor where I lay and I could tell some of it was in my skin.

I needed to get help.

I grasped the side of the porcelain bathtub and dragged myself to my knees. I heard the crackling of glass beneath my weight but ignored the pain it caused.

Medical attention. Help.

Now.

Something trickled down my ankles, wrists and neck with the effort of standing and I stumbled into my bedroom. Everything swayed but I continued walking. I made it out into the hallway and watched as the hallway went in and out of blur. I didn't know where the infirmary was. But I knew where the kitchen and the dining hall was.

I started stumbling in the direction of the dining hall hoping there would be at least one person in there who could help. I had no idea what time it was but with what hope and strength I had left I made it.

The fire crackled in the hearth, sending a million sparks to the ceiling. I stumbled into the doorway and glanced around in the darkness.

There was no one there.

I tried to turn away but was caught off balance and fell against the door. With a groan and a small cry, I slid down it.

"Oi? Is someone there?"

I didn't deserve help. Why had I gone looking for it in the first place? After everything I had done. After everyone I had slaughtered, I was the last person who deserved to live. So even though I knew to whom that dark and smooth voice belonged, I didn't utter a sound.

"Hello?" I heard the sound of Adaner's footsteps as he stumbled upon me and with a puff of air, knelt down and inspected me. "Ryn? What the hell?"

I remember he picked me up and I asked to be left there. I believe I asked him to let me die but he whispered so sweetly and quietly in my ear as he carried me, "I won't let that happen. I will protect you, Ryn. I always will."

I mumbled something but I didn't think Adaner could understand me. I focused on his footsteps as he walked and tried counting each one. My head was tucked into the shoulder blade of the male who smelled of smoky leather and I gladly breathed it in.

It was a comforting smell.

"Here we are." Adaner set me down on something velvety and so soft that I sank right into it. He was gone for a moment and while his footsteps faded I moved my eyes, glancing around the room.

He hadn't in fact brought me to the infirmary, but to his bedchamber I could only assume. Lights hung above me and cast a warm glow across the room. I could hear the crackling of a fireplace and assumed that's why it was so warm.

Adaner returned and our eyes snagged on one another. His hazel eyes warmed me from the inside out, I didn't need a fire for that.

He knelt beside me and opened the box he held. Rummaging around in it and, after grabbing what he needed, he looked me in the eyes. "What happened, Ryn?"

Tears pricked at my eyes and I closed them, not wanting to remember. I had been so angry and so hurt. I wasn't sure why the glass was there. I didn't remember breaking it but in my rage I very well could have.

The only thing I said was, "I slipped."

His eyebrows rose as he dabbed a bit of liquid from a vial onto a white linen. He started by examining my head which apparently I had hit pretty hard. He said there was some bleeding from a cut and there was sure to be some bruising. I closed my eyes and didn't say anything.

It stung when he began cleaning my wrists and arms and ankles but I just kept my eyes shut. Sometimes, he picked bits of glass out of my skin and placed them on another cloth but still we never spoke.

Finally, after he had carefully inspected every inch of me to be sure I was taken care of, he slipped his fingers into mine and squeezed.

"Better, love?"

I nodded but then squinted at the pain it caused.

I felt his strong hands slip under my knees and brace my head as he once again carried me. This time he laid me on top of something even softer but with pillows.

"Adaner," I cautioned.

"Shh." He laid me in his blankets and tucked me in gently. "Rest now, love. You're safe."

Warm, soft lips pressed to my forehead and gave me chills straight down to my toes. If he only knew whose forehead he kissed. The kind of person that I was. He would back away so fast, anger would fill his kind hazel eyes and he would hate me.

I didn't want to be saved and yet once more, Adaner had done just that. The look in his eyes told me he knew that but we wouldn't speak of it until I was ready.

So I nestled down in the blankets and when I felt the mattress dip, smiled ever so slightly to myself. Some time during the night, our hands found one another and we intertwined our fingers together, falling asleep like that.

I awoke before it was quite twilight, the blue hue barely peeking through his curtains. I could feel him tracing designs on the inside of my palm and upon opening my eyes, I found him gazing at me.

"Hello, love," he spoke softly, the early twilight making his voice raspier. I allowed a small smile to creep across my lips.

"Did you sleep well?"

"I did." I glanced down, bashful that we were sharing such an intimate moment. "Thank you for. . .everything." My eyes flickered towards him and the kindness that lay behind them made my heart swell.

"Seems you owe me for all the times I've saved you."

"I'll agree to that," I laughed.

"Ryn," Adaner's voice grew much deeper and he shifted to look at me better. "What happened?"

I could feel my heart beginning to race and pulled my hand away from him. I didn't want to talk or even think about the previous events.

"Please don't shut down." Adaner shook his head. "You always do this, you pull away and disappear into a husk of yourself. *You* asked me to help you fight for a reason to live. I'm not letting you out of this one so easily."

"Adaner, please, I don't want to talk about it."

"You have to fight." Adaner propped himself up on an elbow. "I didn't say it was going to be easy. Hell, in fact fighting is far harder than just giving up but I'm not going to watch you crumple up. I just won't."

Tears began to prick at my eyes and I tried blinking them away.

"You find that shred of hope and I will be right here with you finding my own and together we will find our way."

I nodded and breathed in again. I was not able to vocalize a single word so I allowed the tears to fall instead.

"Feeling is good, Ryn. Don't push it down so far that you lose yourself in the pain."

I allowed Adaner to comfort me by brushing my hair out of my face and staying near me while I cried. He didn't say anything else but he didn't need to.

He was right.

When I cried all the tears I had in me, I turned into the warm embrace of Adaner. "Do you remember when we were in Glandor Gap?" I asked, quietly.

Adaner nodded in confirmation. "I do."

"Do you remember when you stayed by my side while I cried and. . .felt all the pain that had built up?"

"Yes."

"Thank you," I whispered. "I never got to say it, but thank you for then and for now."

"Always, Ryn."

I breathed in and out, inhaling the scent of smoky leather and citrus. I looked up and our eyes met. A mix of his hazel and my green dancing across one another's faces, searching and memorizing.

I noticed that he had the tiniest bit of green in his eyes and I'm sure he was noticing the gold specks in mine. I felt his hand drift up my arm and come to rest at the base of my neck, his fingers entwining with my hair.

"You are so beautiful," he whispered.

My eyes drifted towards his lips and he slowly tilted his head, drawing closer. And in such an effortless and careful way he brushed his lips over mine. They were soft and full of warmth as our breath mingled.

It wasn't a helpless and fast kiss, it was slow and savored and meaningful.

When we parted, we both smiled at one another as if that had been something we'd wanted to do for a long time.

And maybe it had been.

Adaner's hand rested between my cheek and jaw and his thumb brushed over my lips that he'd just been kissing.

"I want to let you in," I confessed. "I just need time."

"Take all the time you need, love. You needn't shy away just because you're not ready or you're scared. We all have things we wish to never speak of or recall. I trust that you'll tell me when you're ready." He kissed me again but this time it wasn't as long.

I felt my cheeks blush.

"Do you feel well enough to train? I expect Tolden will notice you're missing soon."

My heart skipped at the mention of Tolden's name. My body ached, especially my head. "I think I'd like to stay here for now."

"Here as in my bed?"

"If that's alright. I don't feel like leaving."

"You stay as long as you wish. Are you sure you'll be alright left alone?"

I appreciated the sincerity in his voice. I felt emotions and feelings I'd never felt before. I nodded my head. "I think so. I'd be even better if books and tea and treats were brought to me as well."

Adaner laughed softly and brushed his lips over my cheek. "Then you shall have them."

When he rose out of bed, still dressed in the clothes from the night before he looked at me before he exited his room. "You're sure you'll be well?"

I smiled. It would take time to heal, to process and to be ready to talk about the past and whatever else came with it but right now, I felt as if I could see that speck of light in the dark. I felt as if I could feel that thread of hope, small as it might be.

"Yes," I said, nodding my head. "With time, I will be."

CHAPTER

30

Two days passed.

I spent most of them in Adaner's bed.

He brought me sustenance in the form of tea, coffee with lots of cream and sugar, and savory meats and cheeses. Although, my favorite were the fluffy pancakes with butter and honey. Towards eventide, when he returned from the Southwatch tower, where he told me he spent most of his time when he was gone, oftentimes he would bring chocolate and wine.

And of course books. Lots and lots of books.

When we slept we talked, we however did not share any more kisses. In fact, he often curled me into his chest and we fell asleep like that. I wasn't sure if I was overstaying or if he wanted me here for a while longer.

I felt safe.

All this without truly knowing what had happened and why it had gone that far. I had a lot of time to think and process. I had spent hours sitting on Adaner's balcony wrapped in a blanket with a hot mug and treats.

Sometimes I would look out over the view and just allow the thoughts in my head to find their places. The view from Adaner's balcony was different from mine. His was faced more towards the rolling hills of northeast Crescent where the mountain peaks lay scattered with the roaring sea more to the west, which given the direction, was more where my room faced.

I loved watching the clouds travel across the sky and watch as the light would change from twilight violet blue to starry black with a drape of stars behind it.

That's where I stood now. Leaning against the railing, allowing the salty, pine breeze to drift by me. I smelled sweet grass, sand, waves and a hint of snow off the mountains.

I closed my eyes.

There were a lot of things I regretted. A lot of things that I didn't know if I could ever forgive myself for. And yet there were also a lot of wrongs done to me that I couldn't blame myself for. Even still, there were steps I needed to take towards owning the wrongs that I had committed, and taking responsibility for them.

It would take time.

I inhaled and opened my eyes.

I could hear the sounds of chatter and laughter wafting up to my place on the balcony from below. The view of the city was on the opposite side of where the balcony faced but I could still faintly hear the frenzy. Adaner had told me Constellation Eve was tonight and the whole palace and city was preparing for it.

It was apparently supposed to be quite the event. I could hear musicians tuning their instruments, the melodies drifting through the air and into the sky beyond.

I walked back inside Adaner's room and prepared to bathe. My dress for the festivities had been delivered to me steamed and freshly pressed. It now hung on the wall adjacent to his bed. It looked ravishing and deep down I was nervous to put it on. I had thought long and hard about showing my face at this festival.

I couldn't stay in Adaner's room forever. I certainly couldn't just disappear. The others would ask questions and I had already been absent long enough. I wondered if Thea would put two and two together but part of me doubted that she would.

I bent to start the bath water and looked through the cupboards for scented soap and bubbles. Adaner didn't have much, which didn't surprise me, but I did find a stash of unopened jars. Twisting the lid off of one I sniffed it.

Blueberry?

I instantly tightened the lid and chose a different one. This smelled of citrus and there was a third that smelled of bergamot. I poured a good bit into the tub and set it on the ledge to use later. After I tested the water and it was almost full to the brim, I slipped off my clothes and placed them in a neat pile on the counter. The door was shut but I didn't lock it.

Wafts of steam drifted around me and fogged up the looking glass above the marble sink bowl. I allowed the water to pool around me and the citrus bubbles clung to me. I dipped my hand and circled a finger in and around tracing designs in the white fizz.

Washing my hair, I lathered it with the bergamot smelling soap and scrubbed it. I dipped my head underwater and came up again letting the soapy water and my hair cascade down my back.

Something in the looking glass caught my attention and I turned, looking over my shoulder. Adaner stood in the doorway, gazing at me. I was thankful there were a lot of bubbles to shield me.

"Where did you get them?" he asked, solemnly.

"Get what?" I asked in return, even though I knew.

"The scars."

I glanced down, my chin resting near my shoulder. I knew what they looked like. I had hated the sight of them since the first time I looked.

"Helmfirth," I said softly.

"I will kill them all. Whoever did this to you." He came towards me and knelt down.

"You can kill him after I do."

Adaner and I locked eyes and the softness that reflected in him made my heart hurt. I think it was a good kind of hurt though.

"Elton Hode?" he questioned, his voice low as he traced a finger on my shoulder blade.

I surprised myself by nodding. I had never told anyone. He sighed. "He's already a dead man, Ryn."

Silence fell and then Adaner whispered in a smooth but quiet tone. "I'm sorry I couldn't be there for you."

I glanced up into his eyes to see that they were red rimmed. "This isn't your fault, Adaner."

"No, but no one was there for you. . .and for that I am sorry. You were alone."

I could feel the tears rising in my own chest and throat and they were the kind that were painful and throat constricting unless they were released. Adaner brought his forehead to mine and we rested against one another, our tears and sorrow becoming one.

"You're not alone now. I'm not leaving you. I never will." Adaner's smooth voice poured over me like the coolness of river water running down a mountain. I could feel his hand rubbing my back in gentle circles and feel his warm breath mixing with my own.

I felt his breath hitch and I opened my eyes briefly before he pressed his lips into mine. It was soft and passionate and I relished the feel of him. The sparks that exploded inside of me were hard to ignore.

Adaner's hands roamed up my back and came to cup my face, his thumbs absently touching my cheeks.

"I think I am very fond of you," he whispered and we smiled as we came together again and kissed.

But there was still something inside of me that pulled back. I wonder if it would ever truly go away unless the truth was brought to life and the lies were laid to rest.

"I should finish my bath, the festivities are soon are they not?" I spoke, physically pulling away.

"I was hoping I would gain an invitation?" Adaner's eyes were aglow with passion.

I could feel the heat rise to my cheeks and core, I wasn't ready for that. I wasn't even sure I was ready for whatever *this* was. He could see my hesitation and instantly regretted his suggestion.

"I overstepped, I apologize."

I assured him that I was fine and sighed when the door clicked shut. I didn't know how I felt about Adaner yet. I rested my head on the rim of the obsidian porcelain and closed my eyes. The past few nights had been lovely. Adaner had saved me in many ways that I'm sure he did not yet know, but even still there was this pulling away.

It was like a ship that was setting sail and had no other choice but to follow the way of the tide. That was how I felt. But the current felt like it pulled away from this intimacy with Adaner.

I dunked myself underneath the bubbles and soapy water and finished washing myself. My fingers and toes were crinkled like raisins but I was extremely soft. I toweled dry and slathered scented oil all over my skin. I combed my hair with my fingers after looking for a brush and finding none.

My hair was still wet when I walked out with the towel wrapped around my body to cover myself. I didn't know if Adaner would be lingering about or if some unsuspecting citizen might be able to see through the windows.

"Adaner?" I called, waiting for an answer but it seemed he'd left.

I turned to the dress I was meant to wear and just stared at it. The thing was large and looked a bit heavy. I turned and searched for some of the clothes Adaner had snatched from my room while I camped out here.

Luckily, he had picked out a few underthings that would work excellently with this dress. I slipped them on and this time wrapped my hair in the towel. It wouldn't do to have it dripping all over the dress.

I briefly thought of Thea and wondered if she might be able to help me with my hair. The thought of seeing her again brought memories of the painting of Tolden and his brother, Rayken.

How would she react to seeing me again? After I'd disappeared rather rudely and was nowhere to be found for *nights*. I bit down on my lip and charged through the thoughts. I couldn't stay in Adaner's chambers hiding forever.

Donning the dress, I slipped it over my feet and pulled it upwards. The fabric was a dark teal, long sleeved gown that had gaps on the shoulders so they were bare with a thin piece of fabric to hold it up. It fell around me in folds of teal spilling everywhere. I caught specks of gold here and there sparkling through the candlelight.

The neckline dipped low but not low enough to be considered indecent. The sleeves were a sort of transparent silk and I could see the shade of my freshly oiled skin beneath. When I looked behind my shoulders and felt the loose fabric, I concluded that there were tiny buttons leading up to the bottom of my waist and it ended there.

My heart skipped a few beats.

I picked up the dress and walked myself and the folds of fabric to the bathing chamber. When I turned around to inspect the back of the dress, sure enough it only buttoned up so far.

Fumbling around with them I managed to get them all buttoned. My shoulders slumped a little realizing my scars would be visible for all to see. Maybe I should pick out a different one.

I turned and examined the front, I found that it fit perfectly.

The fabric cinched my waist wonderfully and kept my breasts in place without being too revealing. And the skirt of the dress was simply divine, it swished and twirled and made rustling sounds when I moved.

Did I really want to go through the trouble of changing when it was already on?

Did my scars have that much of a hold on me?

I decided I would wear the dress, but that I would keep my hair down to make myself feel better.

I uncoiled my hair from the linen and began to scrunch it dry. Since it was long and thick it would take awhile. I ended up braiding it loosely so it would have a bit of a curl to it and help it air dry.

Peeking out of the bathing chambers once more, I noted that Adaner was nowhere to be seen still. I slipped out and gathered all of the things he had brought over in the attempt to make me feel welcome and comfortable.

It was time to return to my own chambers.

Carrying everything in my arms, I discarded the idea of wearing shoes and went barefoot. Walking down the halls, I remembered Adaner's room faced the northeast and mine was more west so I began walking in what I thought could be the right direction. But after meandering through halls and creeping around corners so as not to be seen, I realized I was lost.

It didn't help that my arms were full of clothes and books. "My gracious, isn't this a sight!"

My heart stammered, making my throat close up and my tongue like sandpaper. I turned around, ashamed at the sound of Thea's voice.

Seeing her face struck no small amount of anxiety in my heart and I tried to swallow it down. I forced a smile to my lips. "I fear I'm lost," I stated.

"I'll say. Where've you been the last few nights? I went to your chambers and it looked like you hadn't been there at all. The maids said there was glass all over your bathing room. Are you quite well?" While Thea ranted she began stepping closer to me, examining me. "Here, let me take some of this from you."

I gratefully handed over some clothes but was unsure of what to say. "Will you point me in the right direction of my room?"

She gave a small chuckle. "It's just this way."

Once we arrived at the door of my room I realized I hadn't been *too* far off. Just an entire floor off course.

I huffed as I reached for the handle and shoved the door open. "Thank you." I placed the books on the floor and motioned for Thea to toss the clothes wherever. She raised an eyebrow at me and walked to place them in the bin where I assumed I should have been putting my dirty clothes the entire time.

"So, are you going to tell me where you've been? You kind of bolted the last time I saw you. What are these?" Thea's eyes roamed over me and spotted a few of the healing knicks from the glass.

I instinctively pulled away and felt my walls going up. I cleared my throat and said, "I just needed some time alone. I am sorry for leaving the way I did."

Thea eyed me but then her eyes fell on the dress I wore and my still wet hair. "This dress is stunning!" She circled me, tapping a finger to her full pink lips. "But. . .your hair might need some work."

I scoffed. "Have any suggestions?"

"I just might. Come, let's go to my room. I have lots of cosmetics!"

Thus, we left my room immediately and went to hers where she bade me sit in a velvet chair while she rummaged around and gathered the so-called *cosmetics*.

My heart hammered against my rib cage and I constantly picked at my nails and the skin around them. All I kept thinking about was Rayken. About how I had been the one to take the life of a fellow kin, of Tolden's brother. He had clearly been dear to him and Thea, probably Cadeyn and Adaner too.

I was a complete outsider here. I did not belong with them. I did not deserve to even be here.

I winced as I pulled off a piece of skin by my nail and it began to bleed. I popped it into my mouth and didn't dare meet my own gaze in the looking glass before me.

A squeal of delight pulled me back to the present moment and my neck whipped around. "Are you alright?" I called to Thea.

"Sure am!" was her reply.

I sighed and dared a peek at my reflection. I *looked* guilty. If I left now, Thea would know there was something wrong. She would ask questions and I would not be able to stop them. She would find out and then they would *all* find out. So if sitting in her chair, letting her apply whatever the hell cosmetics were, and enduring the guilt that was eating me raw would keep my secrets hidden, then that's what I had to do.

It was what I was best at; what I had been trained to do since I could walk. "Alright, I've got all the things!" Thea came out of the bathing room arms full of brushes, combs, tubes and palettes of sparkles and. . .strands of linen?

I didn't say a word as she began to unbraid my still wet hair. Then taking sections of my hair, she rolled them into the strips of linen.

"This will help your hair have lots of volume and curl once it dries! And we still have plenty of time before the holiday officially begins."

I nodded, feeling my chest tighten. I'd never had anyone do my hair before. I didn't think anyone had ever really touched it except to yank it or use it as a punishment. Thea was so careful. I watched her in the looking glass before me. When she focused intently, she would bite her bottom lip or run her tongue over her lips. Other times, she would scrunch up her brows and redo a curl that she seemingly was unsatisfied with.

When she was finished with my hair she turned to stand in front of me and brought a small brush out and dusted my eyelids with a gold powder. Next she took a fluffy, large brush and dabbed my cheeks with a rose colored cream. She used that same cream and smeared it across my lips. After that, she told me to blink a few times while she used an onyx cosmetic to darken my lashes.

"You have such long lashes!" she exploded, smiling wide.

"Is that a good thing?"

"Ryn, surely you jest."

"Sometimes they get in the way." A sly smirk made its way across my face.

She playfully slapped my knee. "Never, *never*, complain about such a beauteous asset again."

I chuckled, although it sounded more like a cough had gotten stuck in my throat.

After Thea finished beautifying me, even though she said I didn't need much help in that area, she stood back and admired her work.

She squealed. "Adaner will be falling head over heels for you."

I blushed, whatever did she mean by that? How could she know? She must have seen the blush because suddenly her jaw dropped.

"Wait. . .do you share his attraction for you?"

"I often am attracted to myself, yes," I deflected, heart hammering.

"Ryn!" she squealed. "Have you guys. . .?"

"Thea! It's none of your business."

"I say it is." She plopped down next to me, hands resting on her chin. "Tell me all."

I sighed and felt a smile forming on my lips, accompanied with the sensation of confusion and excitement. "We've kissed."

A squeal-scream exploded from Thea's lips and she clapped her hands. "Was it dreamy?"

"That's enough! Now, is my hair dry yet? These linens are itching my head."

Thea eyed me knowing I was diverting the conversation but she tested one of the linens wrapped around my hair. "Actually, I think it may yet be done."

Then began the process of unraveling each linen that resulted in loose coils of hair falling around my back, shoulders and face. When they were all undone, she brushed through them a bit and then folded my golden brown locks all around my shoulders and face, twisting a few pieces here and there.

"You look breathtaking," she said, admiring her work yet again.

I peeked past her to look into my reflection and a small gasp escaped my darkened lips. Thea wasn't wrong. I had never felt so exquisite in my whole life. She had done a fabulous job with the cosmetics and my hair felt soft and luscious and framed my face well.

Even better, I still looked like me, which I liked. A brief thought crossed my mind of what Adaner would think and my stomach flipped over.

"Shall we go then? The festivities are sure to be starting!"

As if on cue with Thea's words, I heard music erupt from somewhere in the kingdom. "What about you? You aren't even dressed?" I said, rising from my velvet throne.

"Golly!" Thea smacked a palm to her forehead and yelled as she ran for her closet, "I'll be two seconds!"

I smiled after her and when she was out of sight I drew my gaze back to the looking glass. I truly had never felt so beautiful in all my life.

I had felt fierce and proud and stoic but never truly pretty.

I turned about the room, realizing I was still barefoot. I shrugged and thought it might be fun to go without shoes. I could hear rummaging sounds coming from Thea's bedroom area but couldn't see her because of the wall that covered that particular part of her room. I stepped over to her bookshelf and briefly marked the ones I wanted to borrow in my mind.

"How do I look?" She appeared and did a little twirl with her arms out. Fitted to her slender body was a deep rose colored gown. The scooped neckline showed off her collarbone, dusted with sparkles and a rose shawl covering her sleeveless arms. The folds of the skirt were a mix of lace with embroidered designs that crept up from the hem.

"Outstanding!"

She gave me a smile that showed all of her white teeth and with her hair flowing down her back, snatched my wrist and yanked me out of her room. "I don't want to be late!"

"I think we already are," I laughed.

CHAPTER

31

This was a celebration I actually *wanted* to be at.

The flow and tempo of music could be heard throughout the entire kingdom. As well as the sound of cheers and laughter. We were certainly not the first ones to arrive. I put all thoughts of Lord Elton Hode's parties behind me as we slowed to a walk, so as not to mess up our appearances as Thea had breathlessly mentioned.

We reached the huge palace doors that were left wide open for the citizens to wander in and out at their leisure. Two guards were posted on either side and they nodded at both of us as we walked by. Nodded and *stared*.

We picked up our gowns gracefully and descended the palace steps that had been freshly waxed and polished. The cold onyx marble shone in the moonlight and hints of deep blue could be seen at certain angles. It sent shivers through my naked feet. Thousands of stars blinked to life above us as if they wanted to see what all the commotion was about, they seemed brighter than they normally were but I didn't have time to stare at them when I heard Thea speaking, urging me along.

"All the villagers and farmers on the outskirts of the kingdom make the journey to the heart of Crescent to attend this holiday. It's the biggest one we have!" Thea's eyes gleamed like that of the stars and her face beamed in the moonlight.

It was so bright out with the sconces ablaze with firelight and the bonfires lining the streets and small glowing lights strung along the cobblestone pathways, that one would assume it was daytime.

"You said the villagers and farmers?" I questioned, remembering the homely village I'd passed on my way to Mount Oblivion. I remembered Thea said she lived in a village that had been destroyed and her parents had been killed.

"Yes. Father and Mother and I all used to make the trek before. . ." Her eyes dimmed slightly but I squeezed her hand.

"Remember, you're keeping their memory alive. They are here with us tonight," I spoke softly and placed a hand over her heart. "They are here with you."

"Heyo! There you are!"

Leave it to Cadeyn to interrupt a sentimental moment, but when I turned to glare at him I watched the way Thea's eyes lit back up and a slight blush stained her cheeks.

She stepped toward Cadeyn and it was the most bashful I'd ever seen her. She wrung her hands together and craned her neck to look up at Cadeyn who was almost two heads taller than her.

"How are you both? Faring well I hope?" Cadeyn barely flicked his gaze towards me and I chuckled.

They were so completely distracted by one another that they didn't even notice when I slipped away. I watched as elven male and females were still unloading their families from the wagons they must have taken to get to their destination. A father reached into the back of one and picked his daughter up under her arms, setting her gently on the ground. She smiled a toothy grin and moved her head every which way as if not sure where to look first.

I continued walking and more than a few times jumped out of the way as children, boys and girls, chased each other across the cobblestones. I heard a mother yell at them to stay clear of the fires and chuckled quietly to myself.

I took in all the sights and sounds and smells. People from everywhere in the Crescent Kingdom, outside and inside the palace grounds mingled together. Old and new friends reuniting with one another.

Rows and rows of tables were set up with silver linen cloths draped over them with too many platters of food to begin to look at. Jars and pitchers full of water, wine, juice and another that had bubbles in it. I thought it looked interesting and gave it a try as I poured some into a small glass.

It tasted like water but with an edge I couldn't quite describe. The bubbles clung to the sides of the cup and made it look like it was sparkling. I coughed as it went down but the more I sipped it the more I began to enjoy it.

The musicians changed to play a more upbeat tune with their fiddles and banjos and cellos and it wafted across the kingdom in a wave of joy. It sounded like roaming hills with the moon shining down and the ocean waves cresting and splashing onto warm sands. It sounded like the laughter of stars and the chatter of the trees.

I closed my eyes and swayed to the sound letting it pour over my body and soul. Before I could stop myself, I joined a group of dancing children. We formed a circle with our joined hands and jumped and kicked and swayed and giggled until my cheeks and lungs hurt. When the tune ended we all clapped and cheered.

I watched the little ones run back to their families or to the tables to snatch a morsel to eat and guzzled my sparkling drink. Dancing was hard work.

My heart thundered, but not just because of the exertion. I had ignored my curiosity and the need to know if he was here long enough. So, while I filled another glass, I allowed my emerald gaze to scan the crowds and even the shadows that the firelight cast in the corners for Adaner.

I thought he'd have been here by now.

I had hoped he would have been waiting for me outside the palace doors but indeed he had not been. My gaze snagged on a few familiar faces that I had seen either in the palace or when the cadre and I had enjoyed ourselves with drink and dance, but I couldn't locate him anywhere.

I sighed and knew it had been foolish. I shouldn't have let my hopes get so high. I hated that I was disappointed because that meant something.

I locked eyes with Thea on the other side of a blazing bonfire, she smiled and waved as sparks floated towards the stars. I stepped away from my sparkling drink and gloomy thoughts and joining her and Cadeyn, gave her a knowing grin while wiggling my eyebrows to which she responded by glaring and swatting at me jokingly.

"This is your first Constellation Eve?" Cadeyn asked, a mug of amber liquid in his clutch.

"That it is."

"You're in for some fun!"

"Isn't this the fun?" I gestured at the crowd of people dancing, the grand array of food and drink and some others who had pulled out marbles and chess on the cobblestones and on top of extra shop chairs and tables.

"Part of it, but not all." He sipped from his mug loudly.

Thea and Cadeyn glanced at one another and giggled. What did they mean *part* of the fun?

When Thea turned her eyes back toward me she glanced behind my shoulder. "Is he not here?"

"I haven't seen him." I shrugged.

"Who?" Cadeyn looked around.

I rolled my eyes but secretly hoped Cadeyn would know. "Where are Tolden and Adaner? Are they too old to join in on the fun?"

Cadeyn shook his head. "I thought they were already here. When I left my shift at the Northwatch tower I assumed they would be too."

Fear kindled inside of me like the sparks rising from the bonfires around us. "And all seemed well?" I wanted to confirm.

"It did." Cadeyn eyed me as if wondering why I'd ask. "Maybe I should check on the other watches. I'll be back, ladies."

So he felt it too. Something was off.

Thea wrapped one of her arms around mine, oblivious to what was going on. Just as Cadeyn disappeared from view I sensed him, that hint of smoky citrus leather filling my nostrils. I casually glanced over one shoulder, then the next.

Through the haze of one of the flames, I caught sight of the dark curls and the figure that I knew to be his. I let go of Thea and without another thought, broke the distance between us. I watched his hazel eyes searching the crowds.

Searching for me, I liked to think.

"Hey, stranger," I tried to say lightly even while I searched every inch of him for signs of injury. "Are you okay?"

Adaner smiled down at me and I watched his hand move as if he wanted to touch me or hug me but he put it back down. "I got caught up in Southwatch." His brows furrowed. "Did I worry you?"

I forced a grin. "That or I thought you were avoiding me." But really I had thought something happened. What with the festivities going on, the villages were emptied and open for the taking if someone dared break the Treaty.

"Can't get rid of me that easily, Ryn." He winked and my heart fluttered.

Thea joined us and we all walked over to one of the refreshment tables. I felt bad Cadeyn left right as Adaner arrived but perhaps he would find Tolden.

My sparkling drink tasted a bit sour going down at the thought of seeing Tolden. It gave me a sinking feeling and made me want to be sick. But I had to act. If not to at least keep them from knowing, but to also protect them from myself.

"We did spot a strange mass moving along the coast and went to investigate. Our guess is it's a merchant ship mooring for the night. We sent a ship out to board and search her just to be safe. With the Territorial Treaty, King Haleth will let some merchants pass if they have the right papers for it," Adaner explained, twirling his mug of ale in his hands.

I nodded. My sixth sense told me there was still something off but deep down I wondered if it was the fact that Tolden was walking down the palace steps, heading towards us at that very moment.

I only had a certain amount of time for a few reactions.

I needed to keep a level head so when we made eye contact I smiled. My insides, however, felt like a volcano had erupted. If I gazed too long or became too quiet or went into one of my panic attacks, they would all question why. Perhaps Thea would mention I had acted similarly when she showed a painting of Tolden and Rayken and it would unravel from there.

I pulled air back into my lungs and pushed it out again, regaining composure.

Tolden joined our group with an annoyed Cadeyn in tow.

"Bloody hell, Adaner we were all worried about you!" Cadeyn slapped Adaner playfully on the back and they conversed together for a bit.

No doubt, speaking of the unknown ship on the waters.

I stepped away to refill my glass once more and opted for the red wine that glinted in the firelight. My hands shook a little as I poured a good amount, the sound of it spilling into my cup drowned out by the music and the cheers of the guests dancing or talking with one another.

I felt Adaner ease next to me and I smiled up at him. He took my beverage from my hand and placed it to his lips, stealing a sip. I glanced at his mouth as he drank.

"You look absolutely radiant, Ryn. I can't take my eyes off of you."

And indeed his eyes took in every inch of me. I could feel a blush rising to my cheeks but truthfully, I was devouring his words and his gaze. Before I became too distracted, I broke our gaze and laughed a little as I watched the citizens, the palace members and even some of the guards enjoying themselves.

"This is truly merry," I observed, scanning the crowds again. "I love how cheerful everyone is."

"It's because of the hope the holiday brings and perhaps a few glasses of wine and full bellies," Adaner laughed.

I smirked at him and we stood side by side watching as Thea dragged Cadeyn into the circle of dancers and musicians on their raised platform.

I turned to face the citrus smelling male before me and asked, "So, what *is* Constellation Eve? I've heard people say the fun is yet to begin and mentioning that there's something else?"

Adaner's eyes twinkled when he turned to look at me. "Just you wait."

I groaned. "Why does *everyone* keep saying that?"

"I wish I could go back to my first Constellation Eve. It was truly the most magical thing I've ever experienced," Adaner spoke softly and I felt it when his hand searched for mine. We intertwined our fingers together and I squeezed him gently.

"Alright, love birds! A redemption dance!" Cadeyn called to us from where he and Thea twirled and swayed.

I cocked an eyebrow. "A redemption dance?"

"Yes, from before where you picked me instead of dear old Adaner here. We all know he wanted you to pick him!"

"Shut up!" Adaner yelled across the expanse and, in Cadeyn's favor, Thea whisked him away to dance in the middle of the crowd.

I put my hands on my hips, feeling the soft fabric of my gown beneath my fingertips and eyed Adaner. "Do enlighten me."

He sheepishly turned to me and ran a hand down the back of his neck. "There's a chance he's telling the truth."

"Just a chance?"

"Not you too!" he growled playfully and before I knew it our glasses were cast aside as I was being pulled towards undulating and twirling bodies amidst fire and starlight.

Adaner's hands wrapped around my hips and I wrapped mine around his neck. I never realized how much taller he was, but now leaning back just to look at him, I sure noticed. He still wore his training leathers from his duties at Southwatch and I could still smell the scent of him; that lovely smoky citrus. I filled my nostrils and gazed up at him through my darkened lashes.

"What are you thinking about?" he spoke, penetrating my thoughts.

We were so close we were almost sharing the same breath. His hazel eyes sparkled and I grinned. "The color of your eyes."

"And do you deem the color worthy?"

I squinted looking at him through the slits of my eyes. "They will do."

"Good. I would hate to have you suffering any time you look into my eyes."

"Oh, I do suffer," I retorted, a mischievous grin on my lips.

He closed his eyes and we came so close our foreheads were almost touching. My hands stayed at the base of his neck and his stayed resting on my hips. When the music changed to a faster tempo with the fiddles and cellos at work to bring a merry tune across the cobblestone pathways, everyone came alive and there was no small amount of movement.

The music flirted with the flames of the bonfires and floated towards the stars overhead. It weaved in and out of the bodies on the grassy cobblestone and made merry with the small string of golden lights draped above us.

Once the music ended, a few couples snuck away holding hands and whispering sweet nothings in one another's ears. But not us, the cadre, Thea and I all dispersed immediately to find food. We filled plates near to spilling over and topped off our mugs of ale and glasses of wine.

We found a quiet spot on the grass, alit by the bright lights and sat to feast and fellowship with each other. We could still hear the music in the background and the chatter of people around us. The palace was in the distance now, seeing as the festivities took place in the very heart of Crescent. Fountains were near us rippling with the trickle of water and some children splashed each other with it until a mother came along and told them otherwise.

"It will begin soon," said Thea, gazing up at the sky.

I followed her gaze and didn't bother asking *what* would begin soon because I knew I would get the same answer as before. The stars seemed to have doubled two fold and there was barely any night peeking through. Just millions of blinking stars covering the expanse of darkness.

I sipped my wine and took a bite of my freshly buttered bread. The spread of food we had laid out before us was grand and oftentimes, we would share what was on our plates with one another. Cadeyn snagged my last piece of bread and winked at me as he shoved the whole thing into his mouth.

"Say, Ryn, where have you been? You've missed a few training sessions," Tolden asked nonchalantly from where he lay on his side.

It sent fear through my veins and I swallowed it down with a bite of bread, trying to think of what to say.

Adaner locked eyes with me, knowing a little more than the rest of them but still not the full truth and said, "She's been busy. . .with me."

It wasn't exactly the rescue I was intending but it worked and distracted them all on a whole other subject. I threw a grateful glance towards him and he nodded in understanding. Even though he didn't know the full extent of what had happened, he knew *something* had. He knew where my mind had been and not only took care of me but. . .perhaps even loved me despite the darkness.

I picked at some blades of grass and wondered if I was right. If my heart told me anything, I'd say I just might be. Maybe he could love me despite what I had done. My heart panged painfully and I tucked those thoughts deep in my heart where they would remain hidden.

"Come on! Let's be the first ones down at the beach!" Thea jumped up, dragging Cadeyn with her and the rest of us quickly followed, leaving our dining spread behind.

I ran alongside them, the ocean breeze trailing through my curled hair and no doubt messing it up. I didn't care though. I was too intent on finding out what was about to happen.

Adaner grabbed my hand sometime when we were all racing to the beaches and it was one of the most wonderful feelings. Hand in hand with him, our feet kicked up sand from the beach with the tide coming in and going out calmly while the luminous stars lit a pathway.

It was magical.

What I didn't realize was that the magic hadn't even begun.

We all took our places in the sand, some laying down while others sat upright but everyone was gazing skyward. Adaner and I laid on our backs, still hand in hand. The sand was cool beneath me and I dug my bare toes into it, my dress spread out everywhere. I opened my mouth to say something but before I could utter a single word, it had begun.

The sky began to move.

At first, only a few stars began to twinkle brighter and began to fly across the sky. They descended fast, catching fire at the last minute and then disappearing into the ocean's horizon, or beyond the peaks of the mountains.

Only a few seconds later, more began to fall. The whole sky was ablaze with the stars shooting across the eventide sky in every direction. It was so bright and it seemed as if they were falling down right on us. The ocean soon reflected the magical scene, glowing bright as the sky alighted in flames and sparkles of the flying stars.

I could not take my eyes away. I could feel the glow of the stars lighting across my face and felt Adaner squeeze my hand as I sat up to watch it, my head tilted back so I could see everything.

I watched a single star from where it began as a ball of light, wiggling free and daring to take the leap that the others were. When it did, it flew fast and smooth, right before it looked like it would hit the water it burst into flames and then disappeared behind the ocean skyline.

I was completely breathless and mesmerized.

"I see why you want to go back to the first time you experienced this," I breathed, barely above a whisper. I felt Adaner sit up next to me but didn't dare take my eyes away from the sky, for fear I would miss something.

"The stars are dying."

I dared a glance away to stare at him. "They're what?"

"The old stars are making room for the new, younger ones. Every year on Constellation Eve, they shed their lives and make their final journey to the Beyond. In their place are younger stars, oftentimes you can tell because they're smaller and less bright. But in time, they will grow and find their light."

Tears smeared my cheeks. It was truly the most beautiful thing I had ever heard of or seen.

Afterwards, when the old stars had finished their journey across the sky and all the fires and streaming lights had faded, in their place blinked smaller, dimmer stars. Just as Adaner had said.

But it was still just as beautiful.

The thought that they now held the legacy of the former stars sprung hope in my heart. I wasn't sure why but it made me feel something.

After a while, Adaner and I were the only ones left on the beach. Thea and Cadeyn had slunk away, waving and smiling at us. I wasn't sure if Tolden had even come down to the beach, but I hadn't really been looking for him either.

"Care for a swim?" Adaner asked into the night.

I smiled and moved my gaze to his. "Tempting."

"Is that a yes?"

I pulled one shoulder up in a sly shrug then began to slowly slip my dress down my arm. I watched Adaner's eyes trail the motion.

"Wouldn't want to drown because my dress was too heavy, now would I?" I smirked.

He flashed me a white toothed grin and began unloading himself of his weapons, first the scabbard over his head then his belt with a second scabbard. He plucked his hidden knives from their hiding places and then tore off his boots. By this time, my dress was laying around my ankles and I stepped out of it, already barefoot.

I watched as he pulled his white shirt off, then his pants went next. And that was as far as both of us dared go. I, in my own underthings and he in his. We laughed at the ridiculousness but took off sprinting towards the water nonetheless.

The cold waves lapped at our feet, then ankles then slammed against our knees as we waded further in. Sea water droplets sprayed everywhere as our arms, legs and hands flew every which way in an attempt to be the first one into the deepest part.

I dove into an oncoming wave and felt the saltwater rush above me and curl over my toes. It was cool and so refreshing. Coming up for air I pushed back my wet hair and looked around for Adaner. I felt something wrap around my legs and screamed in fear, I was dunked under the water, being pulled. I kicked and thrashed but when we came up for air I foolishly realized it was only Adaner.

I slapped the water, spraying him in the face. "Insufferable!" I shouted at him playfully.

"As are you, darling," he retorted, splashing me back. I eyed him warily, my feet brushing the sand below.

"You've got black under your eyes." He reached for me and pulled me close. Taking his thumb he ran it under my eyes where I'm sure the cosmetics Thea used to darken my lashes were smeared.

"Much better," he said, his face close to mine.

"Thank you." I looked up into his eyes and quickly became lost in the golden green of them.

"Always." He pulled me closer until my legs wrapped around his waist. "Are you cold?" he asked.

I shook my head even as a shiver ran up my spine. Our bodies were pressed against one another and his hands were splayed across my back. I was extremely warm.

He nuzzled my jaw with his nose and amidst the calm waves lapping around us, our lips met like the reflection of the stars in the dark ocean meeting to touch the starry sky.

CHAPTER 32

"Hell, this headache hurts." Cadeyn buried his face in his arms and moaned.

The five of us sat, moping around the breakfast table. The entire kingdom seemed to have taken the twilight off. Leftovers were placed on the table before us while we tried to guzzle down water and coffee to stave off the headaches.

Even the fireplace was out cold, the flames having died from not being stoked throughout the night. Cadeyn kept groaning and Tolden muttered something about him stuffing his gab so he would finally shut up. I chuckled at both of them and then winced.

After Adaner and I had returned from swimming in the ocean, drenched through but donning our clothes nonetheless, we came upon the cadre engaging in a drinking match. Adaner soon joined as did Thea and I but we were not so skilled in the art of drinking. Of course Tolden won, he could handle his liquor more than anyone I had seen, or so I'd found out the previous night.

"Am I right in assuming we won't be attending our training lessons?" I asked, biting into my honeyed croissant and popping a blueberry in my mouth.

"Pity's sake, give us a moment, Ryn," cursed Tolden, banging his fist on the table, resulting in all of us cursing at the sound and vibration on the table.

Thea glanced at me rolling her eyes and then rubbed her temples. I nodded my head motioning for us to leave but when we stood, a bell split through the silence, clanging obnoxiously loudly. I watched as the three males instantly sat up, headaches and dizziness be damned, and they waited still as stone, listening to the rhythm of the bells.

When it ended all three leapt up and raced out of the dining hall, Thea and I following at their heels. When I glanced at her questions burning in my eyes, she just shook her head.

She was as clueless as I was.

I didn't dare ask the three males running at full speed, faces a mask of grave concern and determination. Fortunately, we were already in our training leathers and had all our weapons with us, save Thea. I had a gut feeling we were going to need them.

Sprinting through the halls we came to the end and burst through the palace doors. Cadeyn whipped around to Thea and commanded her to stay and to alert the palace that the beach had been infiltrated.

Realization hit at what message the bells had been sending and I filed in behind the cadre. Adaner flicked his gaze back at me.

"Don't even think about it! I can fight!" I yelled at him.

He didn't argue and didn't ask questions. Time was of the essence.

We took a shortcut through a grassy pathway covered with overgrowth and constantly had to duck so we weren't unpleasantly smacked by the branches.

"The other warriors are already down at the beach! Stay alert and stay alive!" shouted Adaner at the front of the line, unsheathing his sword from his back and holding it close to his side.

I did the same, except I snatched my daggers in my hand and flipped them expertly. It had been a long time since I'd fought but the familiarity of it rushed back with the pump of blood in my veins.

I heard the battle before I saw it. The cadre and I briefly glanced at one another as we rushed up the sandy hillside and came to crest the top of the beach, yielding the view below us. Crescent warriors clad in black leather fought nearest us, keeping the enemy at bay. I immediately noticed that the enemy wore fishermen's clothes with rapiers and harpoons as weapons.

Humans. They were men.

Crashing down the hillside and racing onto the sandy shore, we filled the ranks alongside our fellow warriors with the sound of clashing swords and bright light from their ice magic. Save mine, which was the only black ice on this battlefield.

Shouts rang out all around me and I willed myself to focus on the man running at me with chains in one hand and a harpoon in the other. I ducked and swung my dagger across the skin of his knee. He howled in pain and as he went down I stabbed my second dagger into his jugular. Blood gushing out from his vein and splattering my hands, arms, and face with hot liquid stickiness.

Out of my peripheral, I caught more motion and heard the *swoosh* of a harpoon as it sailed through the air towards me. I whirled, narrowly missing it as it stuck itself in the sand behind my shoulder. The second man growled and took off at a run towards me, meaning to take me down by brute force but I bent at the knees and readied myself for him, sending a burst of magic forward to slow him down.

Just as he came close stumbling from the force of my magic, I threw one dagger right in the middle of his forehead. He staggered and reached out as if still trying to grab me. I sliced his hand off and whirled to take the dagger out of his forehead but something caught me beneath my feet. Sky filled my vision right before I slammed into the compact sand.

I gritted my teeth at the force of the fall and immediately located my opponent. He stood above me with his rapier held high but instead of going in for a kill shot, he brought out a pair of handcuffed iron chains.

The hell? Iron chains? Not today, bastard.

He pinned me down with his rapier piercing through my clothes and reached down to put my wrists into the cuffs. I shot my hand straight up, not only breaking his nose but pushing all my magic into his face.

The man hurtled off of me but did not stop there. He glared at me with his one and only good eye left, nose twisted and the other half of his face frozen and bloody. He ran at me, angry and malicious. My eyes snagged on the cuffs still in his hands and I threw a wild toss of magic out but he dodged it.

I inhaled, resorting back to what I knew best, I threw my dagger right into his neck vein. He clutched at it, clawing as he went down, the cuffs falling in the sand next to him.

I held my breath and bolted, snatching the dagger from his neck. Blood coated my hands, face and clothes. I was breathing heavily at such exertion but it was nowhere near over. More men crawled out from longboats and scurried onto the sandy beach, weapons and voices raised.

I briefly scanned the elven lines for the cadre but didn't have time to focus in on any of them when a screaming elven male with one of his arms missing, blood gushing from the wound, came running at me. Before I could do anything remotely helpful, a man clad in brown trousers drenched with blood, pierced a harpoon straight through the elven male's chest.

My stomach churned at the sight and I aimed my dagger at the man who'd just killed one of my own. They both fell to the ground, friend and foe, blood draining from their wounds and staining the sand a deep crimson.

I retrieved my dagger and entered into that familiar killing calm once more. Men fell at my feet with fatal wounds dealt by my hand or magic. I would not leave any of them alive.

But it seemed they had a different plan. Everytime the enemy got close to me, they never went in for the kill and they all had the same rutting iron cuffs.

Sweat trickled down my brow as the unnerving realization hit me as I ducked a rope being thrown my way.

They were trying to take me back.

It surprised me that Elton had the guts to send ships full of men to an elven kingdom. This was an act of war.

A man came running at me with a fishnet and a sword and I was so focused on him I didn't have time to defend myself when the air was stolen from my lungs. I stumbled forward from the hit and fell straight into the fish net that the first man wrapped tightly around me.

Except it wasn't a fish net, it was made of iron and every part that touched me singed me like fire. I let out a scream and extended my magic but instead of it escaping, it shot painful bursts of lightning through me.

I couldn't use my magic in this iron net.

Panic began to settle in and a cold sweat broke out on my temples. My pulse thundered in my head.

No. No. No.

I would not go back.

I kicked and thrashed and lashed out with my daggers, cutting the hands of the men as they tried containing me.

"Bloody hell she is an animal!" one of them cursed.

They stuck a stick through the iron netting so they didn't have to hold me and be plagued by my constant slashing daggers. I instantly began hitting the wood beam with the blade of my dagger to snap it. I kicked at it, dislodging it out of the men's grip which earned me a kick to the ribs and back.

I cried out in pain and fear as they carried me away from the battle, away from anyone who might be able to hear me and towards the ships.

The next thought that came through my head was one that was equally terrifying and comforting. I turned the blade of my dagger to my own throat and began to press the blade into the tender skin—

I was dropped to the ground brutally and suddenly, the iron pressed against my skin, burning me. Out of the corner of my eye, I could see him fighting. Slashing his sword across the throats and into the hearts of the men who were going to take me.

Relief and shame and fear washed over me all at once as he ran over to me. With the sheer strength of his arms he ripped apart the iron netting, freeing me. He hadn't even winced even as the iron burned his palms.

"Ryn?" Adaner's voice was shaky as he picked me up out of the netting to get me away from its cruelty and held me tight to his chest.

The smell of him, the feel of him, the safety in his arms was enough to push past what I'd been feeling just mere moments ago. I shook in his arms and didn't dare speak.

"Look at me, are you alright? Where are you hurt?" He lifted my head to look into my eyes, scanning every inch of me.

I swallowed and looked up into his hazel gaze. "I'm okay."

"Are you sure?" He placed his hands around my face and studied me. "I saw them take you, they tried to hold me back. I've never fought harder in my entire rutting life."

I shook visibly even though it wasn't cold and he held me tight to his chest.

When I was composed enough, we rejoined the battle on the beach. We found that the last few men had been taken hostage and were lined up in a long line of chains. I didn't even bother looking at them. I couldn't bring myself to.

I stood on the beach, Adaner right next to me. My daggers were stained with blood, my clothes soaked through and my hair knotted with it. I absently touched my throat as I stared at the two ships in the water, bobbing up and down. Eventually, the sight became blurry when my vision went out of focus. I blinked rapidly and willed myself to break from the iciness I felt rising deep down.

"How'd they get here?" I finally demanded, turning to face those hazel eyes. His face was splattered with blood and his curls were matted together with gore.

His green-brown eyes trailed the line of captives, down the beach and out onto the water as he inhaled deeply. "I don't know." He focused his gaze on me again. "But I do know that King Haleth will consider this an act of war. Helmfirth has officially broken the Territorial Treaty."

I sucked in air which hurt considering my bruised lungs and ribs. I glanced out to sea once more, a gust of wind blew from the north and tousled my hair. The sails snapped in the wind and the anchors dutifully kept the Helmfirth ships in place. I shuddered painfully at the thought that if it weren't for Adaner, I might very well have been on one of those ships at this very moment.

"I want to be there when they're interrogated," I stated, following the cadre as they began to pick up weapons discarded by the dead. I watched as healers began to unload their medical boxes to attend to the wounded.

"It's not always the prettiest sight," Adaner argued, bending down to feel the pulse of an elven male.

"You should know by now that doesn't bother me."

He looked me up and down and seemed to be processing what to say. I didn't give him time to retort.

"I'm the one who lived there. Maybe they'll add to the information I already know." I bent down to gather weapons and close the eyes of the dead.

"You know something, don't you?" Adaner studied me, watching my reactions and movements. "You're hiding something."

"Just take me to the interrogation room." I ignored his accusations, for they were closer to the truth than I cared to admit.

Out of nowhere, I heard the muffled cries of men and the sound of a sword cutting into flesh. I glanced up just as the Crescent warriors began beheading the Helmfirth men.

My mouth went dry at the brutality of it. Then again, they had broken the Territorial Treaty after all these years. . .this was an act of war.

"You look awful."

I gave Thea a glare but accepted her hug nonetheless.

"I'm so glad you're okay. I felt completely useless," she spoke once more, pulling away.

I winced at the blood I left on her silk blue dress. "You did your job. You informed the palace of the invasion and I'm sure if the tide had turned for the worse you would have been the first one helping the women and children through the escape routes."

Adaner had explained the Crescent Kingdom's escape plan to me on the way back and it was brilliant. Hopefully, it would never have to be used otherwise that would mean the Crescent Kingdom would have been completely compromised and taken over.

"I tried my best." She forced a grin.

"That's all we can do." The truth in my words struck me and I swallowed down the guilt that rose like bile in the back of my throat.

All five of us walked together to the armory where we stripped our outer layer of leathers off and began cleansing our weapons. I sat in one corner and silently and intently worked on my daggers.

My thoughts were consumed with memories of Helmfirth, most were unpleasant. My mind drifted to the memories that had been stolen from me by my father, King of the Crescent Kingdom and then they slowly began to drift to thoughts of my mother.

I seethed and gritted my teeth hard enough to grind. "I think your blades are clean."

I jerked my head up to see that only Adaner and I were left in the armory. I gave my blade a once over and indeed, it was gleaming. I continued cleaning it, knowing it would never be the same after having taken lives—after I had taken lives.

I had been willing to take my own life. I sheathed the blades at my hips and stood almost in a panic.

"Are you sure you're alright? You seem tense, if not a bit angry." Adaner leaned against the wall, inviting me to stay but allowing me to go if I so desired.

I sighed, running my dirty fingers through my blood knotted hair. "I don't know.

I'm trying to piece everything together in my mind."

"Two minds are better than one," he offered.

My heart wanted to go to him but my head told me to keep my distance. To pull away.

I didn't want to pull away. I wanted this. I know I did.

"Let's go to this interrogation first," I said, then seeing his expression added, "I want to let you in, Adaner."

He nodded and those hazel eyes were ever sparkling. "I know you do. I'll be here when you're ready."

I shook my head. "I don't deserve you."

Adaner caught my wrist before I could leave and turned me around. Bending his head so that I had to meet his gaze, he commanded, "*Never* say that again, my love. You do deserve this and so much more."

I bit my lip and nodded as we turned to leave. I repeated his words over and over in my mind, committing them to memory. Desperately wanting to believe him.

And maybe I was starting to.

CHAPTER 33

I felt like the air was being squeezed out of my lungs.

Walking into the dungeon beneath the Crescent Palace brought back more unsavory memories than I cared to admit.

Adaner escorted me with his hand at the small of my back as we descended the onyx steps. It smelled of earth and metal and the air was strikingly cold and dank at the same time. Sconces lined the walls with white flames, which was much appreciated as there were no windows.

At first glance, the prison wasn't grimy. But if I took a closer look, I was sure I would find the stains to prove what might have occurred down there.

The hallway was maybe forty feet long with barred empty cells on either side. At the end of the hall was a single door with light flickering and shadows moving underneath the gap at the bottom.

I ignored the cells, trying not to panic at the memory of living in a cage. My palms began to sweat and I could feel my stomach churning uncomfortably. I felt the awakening of cold darkness deep within me and reminded myself to draw air into my lungs.

Once at the end of the pathway, we stopped outside of the door and as Adaner knocked, he rubbed my back as if to let me know he was there. The door opened from the inside and I instantly assessed the state of the chamber.

My vision was filled with, who I could only assume was, the captain of the ship hanging from chains wrapped around his wrists. He slowly turned with the slight movement the irons allowed him, glaring at us as if it would do any good.

There were only three other people in the room; a male with piercing gray eyes who I knew instantly was the interrogator because the second male held a feathered quill to a scrap of paper.

And the third was my father—if he could be called as such.

I slipped to the back of the room and didn't allow myself to glance towards Haleth. Adaner sidled next to me and the comfort of the cold wall behind me and him standing next to me anchored my thoughts.

The male in charge wore dark gray leathers lined with deep blue trim. His boots were high and seemed to be made of stone. Everything about him spoke of order and obedience. From his neatly cropped black hair, piercing gray eyes and chiseled jaw, he was the picture of unrelenting sternness.

Adaner caught my line of sight and leaned over whispering, "King Haleth's right hand, Baron Valt."

Baron Valt stepped towards the chained man and began rolling his sleeves up. In a deep and gravelly voice he hissed, "Shall we begin?"

The other male began scribbling, only the sound of quill on paper could be heard. I could feel Haleth's gaze on me but refused to meet his stare.

The human looked at Baron with eyes so black he almost looked lifeless. He opened his mouth to reveal rotting teeth and snarled, that only made Baron smile widely.

"It's obvious that Lord Elton of Helmfirth sent you on this errant mission," he said, pulling a knife from the inside of his overcoat and running the tip of it over the man's neck, gentle enough that it wouldn't cut him. A clear threat between life and death.

"So, how about you tell me just *why* the prick of the human realm would do that?" The man kept his eyes on the wall and didn't say a word. A slight nick of the tip of Baron's blade had him gulping audibly and blinking rapidly.

"Afraid to feel the sting are you?" Baron dug in deeper, drawing blood that dripped down his neck to stain his white undershirt. "I'll ask one more time before I cut off a finger. . .*why* did Elton send you to invade Crescent?"

The man whimpered and locked eyes with me. My stomach sank and I knew instantly I shouldn't have come. Because *I* knew why they were here. Hell, they tried to drag me back to the ship in an iron net.

Right as Baron lifted his blade to cut the man's thumb off he exploded, "Her!" He nodded right at me. "We've come for her, the one with the green-gold flecked eyes."

Four pairs of eyes snapped towards me.

I wanted to vomit. How could I ever have thought that I would escape Elton? He was everywhere. He would *always* be searching for me.

"Lord Elton sent you? Not. . .anyone else?" King Haleth asked, his voice low. We all turned to him this time.

"That's right," the man confirmed, visibly shaking.

"And you're sure?" Haleth pressed again.

"Let me out," I choked, pushing past Adaner who's eyes were staring intently at me. He reached to grab me but I swatted his hand away.

"You." Baron's voice boomed across the stone room.

I stopped along the wall and dared a look towards him. My gaze shifted down to the man who was still twisting in his chains but staring at the ground now, as if ashamed. I met the eyes of Haleth, then his right hand man.

"We need to talk." Baron turned to the scribe and ordered, "Get someone to deal with this bastard."

The scribe, wide eyed, nodded, still scribbling without even looking at the parchment.

I left the torture cell, not caring who followed. Had this been Elton's plan? To not only have them infiltrate the Crescent Kingdom but my mind as well? To let me know that I would never escape—never be safe.

"Ryn," Adaner called from behind.

I turned slightly, seeing him, Baron, and Haleth all filing out of the cell. "She needs to be questioned, Adaner," Haleth said.

He spoke as if I wasn't standing right in front of him. *He* had been the one to send me there. This was all his fault. I felt ice crackle and bloom inside of me and I clenched my fists and jaw.

"Don't you dare harm her." Adaner was closer now, glaring directly at Baron.

"Care to join so you can babysit me, then?" Baron dramatically lifted his arm in a sarcastic attempt to be welcoming.

"Don't mind if I do." Adaner fell in step beside me and we took the stone steps back up towards the palace.

I was unsure of where we were going as I followed Baron, Haleth had made his excuses saying he was needed elsewhere and had hurried in the opposite direction. I knew that they would want the truth and nothing but and perhaps it was time I gave it.

I had envisioned it going differently though.

I thought I would have told Adaner while we sat on a balcony, watching the moon disappear behind the horizon. Or sitting along the sandy shores with the sound of the waves in the background.

But no, instead I was brought to a quiet room with a rectangular granite table in the middle and a huge onyx crystal chandelier above it. Leather chairs were placed strategically around the table and there were floor to ceiling mosaic windows around the room as well. I couldn't see out of them, but for a few crystal tiles that gave way to the dark expanse of the sky and the glint of it reflecting in the ocean below.

A council room; high in a tower if the flights of stairs I'd counted were any indication.

"Allow me." Baron pulled out a chair at the head of the table and inclined his head for me to sit.

"I don't get the pleasure of being chained to the ceiling?" I asked, jokingly and the glint in Baron's eyes told me he thought it was humorous.

"I'm afraid that's reserved for our darkest of villains. You don't quite fit that description." Baron inclined his head and took his own seat.

"I'm not too sure," I mumbled under my breath.

After I explained everything they might think differently. I flicked my gaze towards Adaner and my breath caught in my throat at the look in his eyes. I prayed he wouldn't see me any different after he found out the truth.

"If your lover being in this room is going to be distracting, can I ask him to leave?" Baron offered, examining his fingernails across from me.

"Ask your questions." I ignored his previous question and gave him my full attention, dragging air into my lungs. If the Crescent Kingdom was being invaded because of *me*, they deserved to know why.

Baron folded his hands in front of him and leaned forward. "Ryn, why the bloody hell is a ship full of Helmfirth men invading *your* fathers kingdom to try and kidnap you?"

"It's a long story." I shrugged, ignoring the emphasis he had put on his words.

"We've got time." Baron rolled his wrists.

I inhaled, here went nothing. "My magic began to take form early on. Lord Elton started telling me that I was uncommon and I needed to have certain treatments done. He never explained why and I never asked, I was too afraid. At first, my magic was harmless and nothing really came of it but then one day, I almost killed Elton's son. They locked me up soon after, chained to the wall. I spent years like that and every day they would retrieve me and. . .perform these treatments." My throat felt suddenly very dry and my chest constricted against the emotion I was feeling.

"What exactly are these treatments that you speak of?" asked Baron.

I looked down, my entire body trembling. "They were trying to steal my magic." Confessing it tasted sour but relief flooded me at the same time.

"You mean to tell me," Baron leaned forward, a tremor to his tone, eyes squinting, "that they performed the dark forbidden rituals of stealing your magic for years? And you lived?"

I nodded once, glancing at Adaner and the pure fury that was lit in his hazel eyes.

"Well, damn. Elton wasn't wrong when he said you were uncommon." He leaned back in his leather chair and put a fist to his mouth. "Ryn, that takes someone extremely powerful to survive that."

Flashes of conversations in the Glandor Gap flooded my memory, about how the cadre had been shocked at how fast I had healed. About how I had died and my magic had brought me back to life. I turned to look at Adaner and by the look in his hazel eyes, he was thinking the same.

It made sense now why Elton wanted my magic if it was so powerful. It made sense why Queen Cressida had wanted it too.

"There's more," I swallowed.

"Enlighten us." Haleth gestured for me to go on.

"Queen Cressida of the Sol Kingdom is my mother and she wants my magic too."

Baron blew out a breath and cursed colorfully.

"When I got my memories back," I inhaled, the images flashing through my mind, "they showed me what she tried to do to me when I was young. Haleth found out and allegedly sent me away to protect me." I rolled my eyes, having not been protected whatsoever with the horrors I had endured in Helmfirth.

"I'll kill her," Adaner breathed, his first words since we entered the council room.

I inhaled, still feeling shaky but felt a slight weight lifted off of my chest. "When Cressida brought me to the Sol Kingdom she told me that she had been searching for me for a long time and that she had great need of me. Now I know what she meant."

"So, are you telling me that we not only have Helmfirth but the Sol Kingdom to worry about now too?" Baron questioned, staring into my green-gold flecked eyes.

"It appears so. But how would Elton know that I'm here?" I shot back, pulling a leg up and tucking it beneath me. "Do you think Cressida knows that I'm here? And that perhaps they're working together?"

"It's a possibility." Baron nodded, rubbing his chiseled jaw, lost in thought.

I rubbed my temples and shook my head. Uneasiness settled in my gut but I had to force the fear away. There were others who were in danger. "It's not just me. Cressida had people enslaved beneath her palace. They were chained to the ceiling and had markings similar to my own from the torture treatments. When I went back to rescue them, they were gone."

"Hold on, you went *back?* Into the hands of the enemy?" Baron's eyes went wide and his hand was splayed out on the table.

"Adaner, Cadeyn, Tolden and I went back." I shrugged.

"Bring us down with you, thanks," whined Adaner, covering his eyes with his palm.

Baron spoke, tapping the table with his knuckle. "You went into the hands of the enemy when you knew full well that she wanted to steal your powers?"

"Yes. I couldn't just leave those prisoners there."

Baron slouched in his chair and dug his thumbs into his eyes. "So, whilst you were on your suicide mission, what kind of information did you gather?"

"I think she's imprisoning elves and stealing their magic from them, resulting in killing them as well. She must have moved them though because, like I said, they weren't there anymore."

"*Where* is she getting the elves from? We would be hearing about this unless she's stealing them from her own kingdom?" Baron thought out loud.

"*Why* is she stealing their magic? Why does she need it?" Adaner asked.

"That's just the thing. . .we don't know," I replied. "We don't know why Elton *or* Cressida wants my magic. All we know is that Lord Elton is sending people here to invade the borders to get me back. And we know that Cressida has moved the elves she has imprisoned and has allegedly been searching for me since Haleth sent me away." I leaned all the way back in my chair and glanced between the two males.

We all stayed silent for a good amount of time, processing and thinking.

"Is there anything else you want to tell us about Elton that would help us? What did you do while you lived there?" Baron questioned, eyeing me.

My gut tightened and I glanced around the room. "I was his champion in the *Death Pit*." I cleared my throat, it suddenly felt dry. "I killed for sport."

"That is very nasty business, I'm sorry you had to endure that, Ryn." Baron laid a hand on mine and I couldn't bring myself to meet his eyes or Adaner's.

"Whatever you need, I want to help. I know the layout of his manor, his compound, pretty much the whole town of Helmfirth. Whatever information I have, I will give it," I said, slipping my hand from his and glancing at Adaner.

"Thank you for your honesty." Baron stood and glanced between the two of us. "This very well may cause another war, be prepared. Whether

Cressida and Elton are working together or not, having two kingdoms against us will not fare well."

"What can I do to prepare my warriors?" Adaner asked.

"For now just lie low. We will discuss those matters at a different time."

I heard Baron's receding bootsteps and then the sound of the door clicking shut. I didn't know what I was expecting but it was not Adaner moving my chair away from the table and taking my hands into his big, calloused ones and pulling me into his chest. He brushed a hand over my head and I sighed, breathing his scent in and allowing myself to hug him back, I smothered my face against him.

The tears didn't begin right away, rather they were building up, gathering together to let loose the dam.

"Do you want to talk more about it?" Adaner asked, still brushing the back of my head.

I inhaled slowly, shakily. That's when the tears burst forth and spilled down my face. I just shook my head and let years of bitterness come to the surface.

Years of fear, anger, regret and self shaming. Adaner held me through every wave of emotion and stayed. Just like he had on the mountain.

CHAPTER 34

My head rested against the cool mosaic window. I listened to the sound of the raindrops hitting the glass. I was not sure when it began raining but in the quiet council room it was easy to pick up the sounds of the storm wailing outside. Gusts of a heavy gale just off the coast and the *pitter patter* of the rain on the castle ceiling filled the silence.

The council room had grown dark with Eventide and I wrapped my arms around myself trying to avoid the chill that was creeping in through the windows.

"Sometimes I see their faces," I said into the silence, Adaner seated at my side. "The faces of those I've killed. I remember every single one of them." I turned to glance at him and found his hazel eyes already looking down at me.

"It may always be that way," Adaner replied. "But you have to learn to forgive yourself for what you did. That's the only way it will ever truly get better."

"What if I can't?"

"Can't is simply a word to use as an excuse. If I know anything about you, Ryn, it's that you *can* do anything you set your mind to. You can forgive yourself, it will just take time."

"But. . .*I* killed them. I chose to kill so that I could live. Why didn't I just let the first opponent I ever fought cut me down and become a martyr?" I turned my face away and stared at the high ceiling, my chest feeling like it was crippled.

"Instinct. You were protecting yourself."

"While being a chess piece in some sick competition." I rolled my eyes.

"Don't be mad at yourself for your past life. Those are things you couldn't control."

I turned to Adaner. "I want to believe you. I want to understand you. But my heart and mind won't allow myself to even *begin* to process that choosing to kill someone isn't under my control, that it isn't my fault. There's no part of me that can just be okay with what happened."

"But can you understand that maybe you wouldn't have chosen it under other circumstances?"

I shrugged. "Who knows what I would have chosen? That was the hand I was dealt and I took it. Who's to say I would have chosen differently under different circumstances?"

"I think you would have."

"I'm glad I have your vote," I chuckled.

Adaner inhaled and brushed his fingers through his hair. "I'm sorry about all that nastiness with Cressida. She sounds like a real headache."

I sighed and brought my knees up to my chest. "It shocked me when I first got the memory back. I didn't even know what to say or think."

"I remember, you just walked for hours. We had to make you stop so we could make camp for the night. You didn't speak for nights."

"At first, I just replayed the memory over and over in my head. I couldn't believe that my own mother would do such a horrid thing to me." I shuddered and felt the small prick of phantom pain along the scars on my back. "I was so young and yet Haleth just sent me away to keep me safe from her. He didn't seem at all pleased to see me though."

Adaner nodded and leaned his own head against the same window. "I was young when it all happened and was undergoing training at the time, but I remember hearing the rumors that you had been sent away."

It sickened and left me with a cold chill running the length of my spine. All the years I had felt lonely and forgotten and was used and abused, I had had a father but. . .he had sent me away. Seemingly, deeming me unfit to be protected or fought for.

I sighed, rubbing the chill out of my arms. "Sometimes I think Elton or Cressida will come to steal me away in the night."

Adaner turned to me and rested a hand on mine. "I won't let them take you. I will keep you safe."

I could only offer a smile as a reply. What he didn't realize was that they had tried to take me back and I had been willing to kill myself. What frightened me even more was that I would do it again. I would rather die than be taken back to Elton, and if it would have to be by my own hand then so be it.

We left soon after, all of our words having been spoken. The cold seeping through the windows urging us to find someplace warmer. We ate a quick meal in the dining hall before slipping upstairs. When I turned to go down the hallway leading to my own room I felt Adaner tugging my arm.

"What are you doing?" he asked.

"Going to my room," I replied.

He stepped closer. "You don't want to stay with me?"

I sighed. "I don't want to intrude—and before you interrupt me—I think it's good for me to not get used to it."

"Used to what?" He stepped closer.

I shrugged, not sure how to form the words. "I don't want to get used to sleeping in the same bed as you."

"Why?"

"What if I get so used to it and then I won't be able to sleep unless you're there?" I picked at my nails, glancing down.

"In what world will we be separated, Ryn?" Adaner closed his fist over mine and when I looked at him he was smiling ear to ear. Heat colored my cheeks and I looked away. "Let me stay with you," he pleaded.

I glanced back at him, at those hazel eyes and smirking lips. "If it pleases you." I grinned and turned, darting off towards my bedroom door, my heart skipping a few beats.

Night terrors plagued my mind throughout the dark hours, creeping in on me from the shadows and the racing clouds in the black sky. The storm covered what light the moon and stars would have shone through the windows and the rain came down ceaselessly.

It did little to comfort me as flashes of being chased around a table coursed through my mind. I was strapped to that table so my mother could cut into me and steal my magic from my very blood and bones. Blood covered my back and the table that I lay on. My own screams tormented me with the echoes of their memory.

I tossed and turned, trying to get comfortable. Doing anything to rid my mind of the images plaguing me. Adaner stirred at my side and pulled me close to him and just when our breathing became even and I started to drift off, the images would come back.

I shot my eyes open, not wanting to see.

Any time I revealed more truth about my past it always came to haunt me in the dark hours of the night. I sighed and turned on my back. It wouldn't always be this way, I had to believe that.

"Can't sleep?"

My eyes fell on Adaner looking up at me, his hair was a mess, some loose curls sticking to his forehead and his face looked as if he had just woken up.

"Did I wake you? I'm so sorry," I said, turning on my side to face him.

His hand came up to brush my cheek and rested there. "I'm worried about you. You seem restless."

I shrugged, the blanket falling off my shoulder a bit. Adaner's eyes trailed the curve of my shoulder and collarbone and he put the blanket back, tucking it under my chin.

I shrugged again. "This happens often. I'm used to it."

"What can I do?"

His eyes were my undoing. The green and brown mixed together with specks of a color I couldn't quite define. His full soft lips turned up in a smirk or a smile or a caring frown, his chiseled jaw and face. I ran my finger down it and felt the hints of stubble growing.

"Hold me," I whispered. And so he did.

—∞—

Twilight came in bursts of thunder and lightning; the storm still raging outside. The sky was dark blue with hints of violet on the horizon. I dressed in my leathers in the early hours and untangled my hair down my back, the natural wave from the braid I'd slept in showing. I crept towards my door to see if there was a note and sure enough, there was.

Bending down to pick it up I unfolded it and let my eyes scan the words. There was to be a council meeting straight after breakfast and Baron wished for me to be there.

I walked back into the bedroom to find Adaner sitting up, rubbing at his face. At the sight of me, he smiled sleepily.

"They've called us to a council meeting after breakfast," I informed him.

"I assumed as much," he muttered and slipped out of the warm bed, fumbling for his clothes. "How did you sleep?"

I glanced over my shoulder at him, having turned to gaze out the window. That chill since the night before still had yet to leave me. "Fine," I replied.

I didn't look to see what sort of face he was making behind me but I knew him well enough to know it was some sort of scowl. He knew I was lying.

When we left the room, we both wore our training garb, and we walked briskly to the dining hall. It was fairly packed when we got there, everyone seemed to have a mission and bustled about in a frenzy. I spotted our normal group on our side of the room and smiled at Thea. I had not seen her since after the attack.

"Hello you two, haven't seen you both in awhile," Thea commented in a teasing tone.

I rolled my eyes and sat down next to her. "Between the battle on the beach, interrogations and council meetings we've been rather busy."

"I'm sure that's all that keeps you two busy," she laughed and I watched her make eyes at Cadeyn who snickered behind a piece of toast.

"That's enough out of you two," grumbled Adaner.

"Yes, please shut up." Tolden lifted a glass of milk from his end of the table and multiple sets of eyes rolled.

"Will you two be at the council meeting?" I gestured towards Cadeyn and Tolden and they both nodded.

"Pretty much everyone will be there," Cadeyn spoke with a mouthful of bread.

Thea groaned. "Not me."

"It's only for guards of the king and council members, Thea. You know this." Cadeyn eyed her.

She pointed at me. "She's going!"

Adaner and I glanced at one another, wondering how much to say. I trusted her, I just didn't think the breakfast table was the place to mention such things.

I cleared my throat. "I think they have a few questions for me, that's all. Nothing exciting."

Thea slouched in her chair but seemed to understand.

After eating a rather small amount of food and downing a mug of coffee and a glass of juice, a loud bell peeled across the entire dining room and the whole place burst into action. Chairs were pushed back and tables were cleared. I'd never heard the bell before but assumed it was signaling the meeting.

I cleared my dishes away and said farewell to Thea. She looked a bit sad as all four of us left her behind and walked down the hallway but I was too nervous to think too much about it. I wondered why she didn't train with us or become a member of the watch if she wanted to be included so badly?

"You ready?" Adaner walked beside me and his hand brushed my shaking one.

"I don't know what to expect," I replied back. We were following behind a few other elves walking briskly and I watched as they talked amongst themselves.

"Expect nothing, then you won't be caught off guard."

I laughed but him saying that made me all the more nervous. Were they going to talk directly to me? Would I have to share my part in this whole situation again? Hell, would rutting King Haleth be there too?

I slowed, my heart quickening and my hands trembling. My vision warped in a dizzy sensation and I stumbled in the hall.

"You good?" Tolden asked, shouldering past me and glancing back.

I forced myself to nod and continue. When we reached the council room doors, male and female elves were filing in and taking their seats at the long table. My eyes immediately caught the view out of those mosaic windows and I felt a bit calmer even though the storm was still raging outside.

I snagged on the gaze of Baron as he waved me over to him. "I've placed an extra seat near the end of the table, not too many people will notice you down there," he whispered and winked at me.

How he'd known I would be nervous or how hard this would be, I didn't know but I was grateful nonetheless. When I took my seat, I realized Tolden, Adaner and Cadeyn were closer to the king which meant they were further away from me. I felt a slight pang of anxiety but quickly swallowed it down.

I sat next to a jasmine smelling female with the longest black hair I'd ever seen. It pooled around in her seat and some locks even draped across the tiled flooring. She glanced at me and smiled, her lips and nose small.

On my other side sat a rather thin male who's torso was extremely long. I had to look up just to smile into his ice blue eyes, so blue they almost seemed clear. He had auburn hair and an auburn beard.

My heart hammered even harder remembering someone I had known who'd had auburn hair once upon a very long time ago.

"Welcome all," boomed King Haleth's voice, silencing everyone who'd been speaking. "Let the meeting begin. Baron, if you would address the council?"

"Your Majesty." Baron bowed and rose from his seat next to the king.

I briefly caught the gaze of Haleth but he didn't react whatsoever. He didn't blink or smile or frown. I felt small and out of place and desperately needed some air.

"To those who have not been made aware yet, Queen Cressida of the Sol Kingdom is a threat to us. From a trusted source, we have heard disturbing news." Baron briefly looked at me and the slightest upturn of his lip could be seen.

I almost smiled back. He considered me a trusted source? I sat up straighter. I didn't need air so badly anymore.

"It has been brought to our attention that Queen Cressida is harboring elven prisoners in the depths of the Sol Palace and we have reason to believe she is stealing their magic. The reason is not yet known to us." Baron placed his fists on the table and leaned forward. "With the recent attack from Helmfirth and this information about the Sol

Kingdom, we now know that both realms pose a threat to us. What I need to know is, has there been any unusual activity in your certain watchtowers? Have we heard anything from the towns? Outposts? I want to know everything and anything that might seem suspicious."

"Baron, Your Majesty, if I may?" A short, blonde haired male at the other end of the table rose and inclined his head in question.

"Continue," Baron allowed.

"The Northwatch has noticed smoke rising in the distance for a few weeks now. I've sent riders out to investigate and still await word on their return."

Baron nodded his head. "When do you expect them to be returning?"

"Depending on how far they went they should have returned a week ago."

"And that's not at all concerning to you?" Baron raised an eyebrow from his end of the table.

The short blonde male shifted on his feet and glanced around with wandering eyes. "It is possible they went further than originally intended."

"Possible yes, but we need something definitive. I don't want to run off half assed suggestions. Anyone else?"

I glanced around the council table and it seemed as if the female next to me wanted to say something. She fidgeted with her hands and kept unclenching them just to clench them again. It seemed as if she was about to speak when Adaner rose and inclined his head towards the king and his Right Hand.

"Whilst I was on the road a short while ago, I was camped in the forest still in the Crescent border. My comrade and I witnessed a pack of shadow creatures running along the road towards the south, towards Sol. I have mentioned it to King Haleth already but if anyone else has also seen or engaged with said creatures, I'm sure it would be most helpful." His hazel eyes trailed the lines of elves and fell on me for half a second, his eyes twinkling in the chandelier light.

When no one spoke Baron nodded towards Adaner and he took his seat. Baron leaned over and whispered to King Haleth and he nodded ever so slightly.

The Right Hand stood once more and addressed the council. "We have come to recognize that there is a possibility that Queen Cressida and Lord Elton could be in an alliance together—"

"And how exactly did you come to this conclusion?" someone asked in the same row as me, but when I craned my neck to look I couldn't see who it might be.

"From a trusted source, we believe it to be true," Baron replied, his eyes squinting ever so slightly.

I chewed on my fingernail as I watched the events of the conversation unravel. "And who or what exactly is this so-called *trusted* source? Quit speaking in riddles and just tell us, Baron!" the male sitting right next to me bellowed.

I cringed at how his voice echoed throughout the high ceilinged room.

Baron sighed and crossed his arms. "Well, Bronce, the source is sitting to the left of your ass."

Every single pair of eyes in the council room shifted to me. I felt the heat rise to my cheeks and my heart began to beat faster, I swallowed but my throat was extremely dry.

Air. I needed that air now.

"*Her?*" he questioned, eyeing me suspiciously.

I glared back at him and heard the murmurs of whispers spreading across the table. I blocked out the voices muttering my name and that I was the heir and what a shame I was to my name and throne.

I glanced down at my lap, I didn't know this was how people saw me. The female next to me reached her hand down and placed it atop my fingers that were picking at my nails. I glanced at her and she smiled sweetly and softly at me. When she pulled her hand away I noticed she had the same short nails as I did.

"*Silence!*" Baron rose from his seat and every single word got caught in the throats of those speaking.

"The attack on our lands led by the men of Helmfirth was to kidnap Ryn Noireis. As many of you know, Queen Cressida stole Ryn from the human realm and brought her to Sol. We have reason to believe they are working together because they have the same agenda. And if we are terribly in the wrong then at least we thought of all the options instead of ruling the seemingly impossible ones out," he spoke deep and strong and his voice carried across the entire table. "If you have any other words to spew from your forked tongues you can spew them to me in the dungeons."

Collective voices gasped and eyes widened.

"To speak against the heir of the Crescent Kingdom is to speak against me. Test me again and I will not fail to lay down punishment." Baron Valt stood straight as an arrow, his gaze causing all those under it to quake with fear.

I raised one eyebrow and felt a bit smug even whilst what some of the council members had uttered still rang in my mind. Baron Valt had defended me more than my own father ever had. In fact, he just sat at the head of the council table examining his fingernails as if there were some sort of invisible dirt he was trying to remove.

Rutting idiot.

"In conclusion," spoke Baron, glaring once more, "it seems as if our borders are being easily breached so double your watches. We will be sending out a group to investigate the fires in the north and search for our missing riders as well. Is there anything else the council members would like to go over?"

Silence rang out and I briefly glanced at the elven female beside me. She had wanted to say something earlier but never did.

"This council meeting has come to an end then. If there are any other disturbances, send word forthwith."

Once the meeting was adjourned, male and females began dispersing, either talking to one another or leaving instantly in a hurry to carry out their orders. I wanted to stay and say something to Baron but when I couldn't decide what I would say, I followed the longhaired female out the council room doors. Her hair trailed behind her and her heels kicked at it from time to time. How she didn't trip on it was beyond me.

She turned down a hallway and began to descend a spiral staircase. "Excuse me!" I called after her.

She jumped and shifted, turning her shoulders and head. "Ryn," she said with a smile displayed on her small pink lips.

I smiled back. "I'm sorry to sneak up on you, I noticed that you seemed to want to say something in there. . .and you never did?" I cocked my head to the side, inviting her to say her piece now.

She blinked once, her amber eyes seemingly surprised. "You are very observant." She tilted her head. "I'm Mai."

"That's a lovely name."

Mai smiled again. "Hell's Keep would be a good place to keep people that you wouldn't want anyone to know about."

My brows creased together. "Hell's Keep?"

She nodded and then continued on her way down the spiral staircase without saying another word or even looking back. I leaned against the wall and brushed a section of my hair behind my ear.

I glanced back at the empty staircase. She couldn't mean what I thought she meant. Could she?

I pushed off the wall and went in search of the cadre, wasting no time at all.

CHAPTER 35

"We have our orders, Ryn, we have to follow them." Adaner threw a saddle over the side of his copper mare and gave me the honor of glaring at me.

I crossed my arms. "I'm telling you, it meant something! What if the *very* thing we're searching for is in Hell's Keep and that's why she said that?"

"How would she even know?" He walked to the other side of his horse and began strapping travel satchels to the saddle.

I leaned against the stalls wall. "I don't know. But she shared that information for a reason, I have to believe that."

"Ryn," Adaner breathed, closing a clasp and turning to take my hands in his. "Why don't you come with us and see what we find along the way?"

I grinned deviously. "I thought you'd never ask."

"Do you know how to ride?" He let go and patted his mare on the neck, looking at me from the corner of his eye as if deciding whether or not he deemed me worthy to ride a horse.

"Yes, I know how to ride. They have horses in Helmfirth."

"I thought you rode the fish," laughed Cadeyn from the stall adjacent to us. I chucked a handful of hay at the imbecile and he ducked, laughing.

Adaner chuckled and offered me a satchel. "Here, you can pack what you might need for the journey."

"Do we know how long we'll be gone?" I asked, taking it from him.

Adaner glanced at Cadeyn and then at Tolden who'd just walked through the stable doors. "No, we don't."

I nodded, understanding. This wasn't just a quick trip down the river or across the mountains. I left the stables to pack my bag, planning to return as soon as possible.

As I strode through the halls leading to my chambers a sense of excitement filled me. Not only was I thrilled to be joining the cadre, I might actually get some answers about Cressida and the elven prisoners.

"Ryn!" Thea called ahead of me.

I focused my vision on her, replying, "Thea!"

"How did the meeting go? Everyone seems to be in a tizzy!"

I sidled next to her and we walked briskly towards my room. "A lot of us have been sent out. Strange things have been occurring inside the borders and riders have gone missing."

I watched Thea glance down at her feet and her eyes seemed to dim. We reached my room and we both entered. I began to fold an extra pair of underthings and socks and placed them in my satchel.

"Do you think I could go?" she asked, quietly, almost timidly as if she was afraid of the answer. "I know I don't have any training but I can learn. I've seen battles before, I know what to expect. I'm not bad with a bow? I used to practice archery when I was younger."

I stopped moving and looked her in the eyes. "It will be hard. Long hours of travel, no privacy, danger, sleeping on the ground." I tilted my head. "But if you want to come, I'm not stopping you. It might be good for you."

Thea's head shot up and I smiled at her. "Truly?"

"Pack a bag, quick!" I ushered her out the door and as she raced down the hall to her room I called after her, "And pack light for goodness sake!"

Her reply was a simple wave. I chewed on my thumb nail as I turned back into my room, hoping the cadre wouldn't be terribly upset with me. I would make Thea *my* responsibility. They wouldn't have to worry about her.

After a few more minutes of grabbing essentials from the kitchen and meeting up with Thea to grab her a bow and a quiver full of arrows, we left for the stables. Thea hadn't been wrong, the whole palace seemed to be bustling about, even more so than for Constellation Eve.

"You know how to ride a horse right?" I panicked, hoping that her answer was yes.

"I grew up riding them! Father taught me, I used to have this white horse named Lily, she was the prettiest thing," she ranted.

I smiled and chuckled underneath my breath. At least she could ride.

But when we entered the stables with the cadre prepping the last few things on their stallions and mares and all three sets of eyes fell on us and our satchels, all hell broke loose.

"Thea, you *cannot* come. It's going to be dangerous!" Cadeyn argued.

"As if, Ryn's going." Thea rolled her eyes and crossed her arms.

Adaner swallowed whatever he had been about to say as Cadeyn spoke again, "She has been trained since she was young. You haven't."

"I can shoot a bow!"

"Grand," Tolden uttered with a smirk. "She can shoot a bow. She'll save us all!"

"Shut up, Tolden." Adaner stepped in and glanced at Thea, arms crossed.

"She will be my responsibility. None of you will even have to worry about her," I offered, glancing at them with pleading eyes.

"If *anything* happens, it's on *you*, Ryn." Cadeyn stormed away with a glare in his usually joyful eyes.

Thea looked my way and I shrugged, walking towards my black stallion, saddled and ready to go. I clipped my satchel to the saddle and patted the stallion's midnight mane.

"What's your name, friend?" I whispered in his ear.

"That's Bohan. He's one of the most loyal and sturdy steeds we have," Adaner answered, running his hand down Bohan's neck.

I glanced at Adaner's hazel eyes. "Thanks for standing up for Thea back there."

"You better just make sure she stays out of harm's way. I've never seen Cadeyn like that."

"If it really comes down to it, we can send word for scouts to take her back."

There was doubt flickering in his eyes. "I don't think so. King Haleth has sent every available guard and watch member out to find any kind of information they can. We're the group going to the north, but there are others covering every inch of Crescent."

"Why?"

"This reeks of war."

My eyes widened, even though it wasn't news. Helmfirth had infiltrated our border and dared to attack the kingdom. It was an act of war.

"Haleth and Baron are concerned but they're trying to keep it quiet. You should do the same," he warned.

I nodded and a crippling feeling settled itself inside of me. I felt as if everything had plummeted for the Crescent Kingdom since I'd arrived. Their very beaches were stormed and attacked by men from Helmfirth who had crossed over our borders unchecked and unseen and sought to fight and kill just to take me back.

And for what? What did *I* have that they so desperately desired? My rutting magic? If that's all they really wanted, they could bloody have it.

I sighed and watched Cadeyn give Thea a hand as she mounted her horse, if not a bit awkwardly due to the quiver across her back. Oddly enough she rode a white mare and I already knew she was renaming it Lily. She glanced at me and smiled, those violet eyes of hers glowing.

I just prayed we'd all be safe. Danger was out there and there was no running from it when we rode straight for it, seeking it with every fiber of our being.

When all five of us were settled in our stirrups and made sure we had packed food and weapons aplenty, we set out. As I led Bohan down the sandy hillside, I could see the other cadres riding upon their steeds, leaving amidst the moonlight all in different directions.

Truly, every inch of Crescent was about to be covered. I briefly wondered if I should have thanked Baron for calling the meeting or for him keeping my secrets. I glanced back at the palace, it was a bit too late for that now. I had rushed out of the meeting so quickly to run after Mai and I wasn't even sure what I would have said to him, except a measly *thank you*.

It seemed like a waste of time and effort. But now I was beginning to wonder if I had been wrong; who knew when I'd get the chance again?

"Keep your wits about you," Tolden called back from the front of the line. "I don't want to bury any of you."

And so began the trek with that lovely bit of comfort.

Our journey started out considerably well, but once Thea lost her sense of excitement and began complaining about her stomach growling or her back hurting from riding Lily, I began to lose my patience.

The girl wouldn't shut up.

I caught the males glancing at each other more than once up ahead. Gradually, they urged their horses to go a little faster and soon they were out of earshot of the precious whining and groaning Thea.

"Do your feet hurt? Mine do, I don't think I'm used to these kinds of boots. I usually just wear my heels but these. . .ugh." Thea leaned down in her saddle to try and massage her calves.

Back in Crescent, I had asked a seamstress for a pair of training leathers for Thea and she had had the perfect pair for her set aside. I glanced around the room and noticed lots of material for more clothes. Almost as if the seamstress had begun sewing more, possibly due to the new threats about the coming war.

Thea screamed, jolting me from my thoughts and my hand went for the dagger at my hip. The males up front whipped around and Cadeyn began galloping back.

"Get it off Get it off! Get it off!" she screamed.

"What is it, Thea?" I brought my horse close enough and grabbed her hand which was swiping at her face and hair.

"A spider web!"

Cadeyn and I made eye contact and his glare simmered. I pursed my lips together to hold in a curse.

"Thea, it's gone," I mumbled.

"I can still feel it." She shook her hair out of the ponytail it had been in and rubbed her fingers all through it. "Disgusting."

I clicked my tongue and urged Bohan to keep walking, leaving Thea with Cadeyn for a moment.

"Do I want to know what that was about?" Adaner asked when he saw the look on my face.

"It was a *spider web*," I laughed, eyebrows raised and lips tight.

"You were the one who wanted to bring her," Tolden accused, pointing a finger at me. that?"

"She asked! Besides, she's lonely." I turned to glance back at her. "Neither Tolden or Adaner said anything and soon Cadeyn and Thea caught up and I fell back in line with her. And on and on Thea talked about her traumatic experience with the arachnids web and all the bugs. She whined how it was strange all the insects were migrating towards her and not us. She groaned that she was the only one who felt sore and dizzy and thirsty and hungry.

Even though guilt plagued me, I was beginning to regret my decision in encouraging her to come. I thought she would have at least had experience with the great outdoors but clearly she had not. I bit my tongue of the curses that threatened to spill out and I stilled my impatience.

Let her talk, she would wear herself out soon.

Adaner called from the front, "We're nearing one of the towns, let's cut through the fields!"

I veered the reins to direct Bohan into the fields and heard Thea's horse following. We were miles away from the ocean and a forest now loomed to our left. It wasn't as deep or thick as the one that Adaner and Cadeyn had first found and trapped me in, it was even a lighter color foliage.

As we trailed behind one another through the grassy knoll, I looked up at the sky. The stars were growing brighter and soon the moon would be rising, signaling the deeper darkness of the night when we should be sleeping.

All thoughts of making camp vanished when we crested the knoll and laid eyes upon the sight below. Mouths agape and eyes wide we all stared down at the town—or what was left of it.

Whole houses, shops, barns, inns; every single building was charred and black from the fire. No structures were left standing. The whole town had burned. Not a single wisp of smoke rose from the ashes which made me think this fire had happened a good few weeks ago. Only charred bits and flakes left behind to leave the memory of a place that had once been.

"They weren't lying when they said there was smoke in the distance." Tolden clicked his tongue and rode down the hill towards what was left of the town.

"Why didn't they mention something sooner?" I asked. "This looks like it was *weeks* ago."

"They probably assumed it was some sort of controlled burn, maybe only when they kept seeing it did they start to realize something might be wrong." Adaner glanced back at me and kicked his horse lightly, urging it forward.

I followed suit as did Thea and Cadeyn. Trotting down the hill, I directed Bohan to skim the outline of a building. The others were still mounted on their horses, gazing across the expanse of the town and wandering off.

I glanced back at the rubble watching something glint in the starlight. I dismounted, holding onto the reins so my horse wouldn't wander off. Kneeling, I swept my hand over a pile of ashes and my fingers brushed something cold and round. I picked it up and pulled a chain out of the dirt. It had an emerald in the center with silver metal encasing it.

It was stained and covered in soot and blood but for some reason it called to me. It felt familiar but foreign. I rubbed my fingers against it and squinted at it.

"Ryn!" called Adaner, I glanced up and he was motioning for me to join them.

I stuffed the necklace in my pocket and got back up on Bohan, riding over to where they were. We searched the grounds of the town and found no remains of any bodies or anything else. There was *nothing* except for the ashes and charred pieces of the town that had once been.

There would be no hope of finding bodies amongst the ashes, for they would not be distinguished from the other ashes covering the entire village. . .or they never burned.

"Cressida did this," I seethed, clutching the necklace in my pocket.

"How do you know?" Adaner questioned, walking away from a pile of rubble.

"I can feel it. Where else do you think she's been getting elves for whatever scheme she's playing at?" I gestured around us. "She's *burning* entire villages and stealing the elves, I'm willing to bet that's where the missing riders are as well."

"Ryn has a point," agreed Tolden from where he stood, holding his tan horse's reins.

It was sad, but I thought that must have been the first time he had ever agreed with me. Thea just glanced around with a disgusted look on her face and Cadeyn nodded his head, presumably deep in thought.

"We need to keep moving. See if any other towns or outposts have been left like this. If this has been going on for weeks, unchecked and unchallenged then who knows how many elves she's taken." I turned to mount my horse, intent on what I set my mind to. I would search the entire kingdom if I had to.

"We don't know if it's *her*."

I turned slightly and glared at Adaner. "I think we do. Why are you having such a hard time believing that it could be her?"

He glared at me and walked off. I watched him mount his horse and cantor away. When I glanced at the others they seemed to have the same opinion as me. So why the hell was Adaner acting like this?

I sighed and mounted my own horse and rode after him. He galloped all the way back up the grassy hill and across the fielded plain, towards the green forest. Once on the outskirts of the trees, he halted and angled his head slightly towards me. He had known I would follow him.

"What's wrong with you?" I questioned, guiding Bohan so I was facing him.

"Ryn, don't." Adaner closed his eyes and his brows were knit together. "Don't plague me with your questions right now."

His words stung a bit and I glanced down. "Help me to understand."

His eyes flicked up at this and he pinched the bridge of his nose. "I know that you were locked away during the last war," he took a deep breath, "but it was really hard on all of us. I lost both my parents."

My heart softened towards him. He hadn't been doubting me or wanting to argue, he had just been holding onto hope—something I wasn't very good at.

"I'm sorry, Adaner, I didn't realize." I looked away from him and towards the bright starry sky overhead. I heard his horses' hooves crunch on the grass and then felt his hand over mine.

"I have to hold onto the good, dare to believe that there might be some hope and light left in this world even when everything that surrounds us is dark." He inhaled deeply. "This reeks of war, but for just one more night I'd like to believe that it doesn't."

"And I can grant you that," I replied, trying to smile. Whether I had been locked up or not, I had been through hell and back. It was harder for me to hold onto the light.

He leaned into me and brushed his lips over mine gently. "Thank you." He smiled against my lips and just before he was going to kiss me again his copper mare snickered and stepped a few paces forward.

"Thank you *so* much, Reyna," Adaner spewed sarcastically. "That was bound to be a good kiss."

I laughed and steered my steed away and we raced back to where the others were still waiting.

"Did you kiss and make up?" snickered Tolden, his forever scowl still plastered across his face.

"Actually, we did," I spat back at him and Thea blushed, elbowing Cadeyn in the ribs.

"Next time, remind me to bring a female along." Tolden visibly shuddered and rolled his eyes.

"It's not too late for you to return, the paths are just that way." I pointed back where we came from and stuck my tongue out at him which earned a pebble being thrown at my face, which I expertly dodged.

We camped that night along the forest rim, away from the road and away from any travelers or unknown shadow creatures. I squatted near the fire, poking it and restocking it as the flames grew.

I chewed my bottom lip, pondering. Wanting desperately to figure out what was happening and why. I watched Cadeyn and Thea prepare a supper for all of us and noticed how sweet he was to her. Any time she asked for help, he did so without any hesitation. The way they looked at each other was heartwarming. I flicked my eyes over to where Adaner was feeding our horses.

His muscled back and shoulders flexed as he held their sacks of grain, bending down with them and setting it on the ground so they would continue eating.

I wondered if Adaner and I looked at one another like that, or if I even looked at him the way Thea looked at Cadeyn. Did I deserve his attraction or attention? I felt myself tearing at my nails and abruptly stopped, I hated that I instantly went to that when I felt any bit of distress.

I also hated that I was even considering anything remotely romantic when such darkness plagued the realms.

"What's for supper? Beans and bread?" Tolden cursed lazily from where he lay against a log, tossing bits of grass into the flames.

"If you had any sense to help, maybe you would know," quipped Thea. Everyone whipped their heads towards her and gaped.

"Didn't know the wee one had sass." Tolden sat up.

Thea rolled her eyes but giggled, she couldn't stay sarcastic for long. But it did get Tolden to sit up and help stir the beans in the pot over the fire.

"Don't let them burn!" teased Cadeyn.

"Shut up." Tolden rolled his eyes.

I shook my head and leaned back, the fire was stoked enough. I watched Adaner walk towards our group, wiping his hands on his leathers, his muscled thighs rippling. I blushed and looked away.

"Supper is ready, come and get it!" Thea hollered even though we were all standing within earshot. Cadeyn cringed but we all gathered and held out our oakwood bowls and spoons.

With steaming beans, cut links of sausage and a thick slice of bread piled onto my plate, I sat on the log that we'd rolled next to the fire earlier. Adaner sat next to me with the others adjacent.

"This isn't half bad," I offered, biting into the bread.

"Yeah, the beans are stirred to perfection," mocked Adaner. Tolden looked at him incredulously.

"Yeah, I heard your whole conversation," Adaner laughed.

"Cheers to you, Thea.

You got lazy Tolden to get off his ass and do something."

"Oi!" Tolden spat.

Thea grinned and her eyes shone, the stars matching their violet brilliance.

Once we were done eating, I took the dining ware and walking into the forest a few steps, I instantly heard the sounds of a river. I thought I'd heard it rippling earlier too.

"Thought you could sneak off?"

I turned slightly, hands full of the dishes and smirked at Adaner. Reaching the river bank I set the dishes down on a rock and dipped the first one in, scrubbing it and rinsing it with my hands. Adaner walked behind me, brushing my waist with his hand as he leaned over and grabbed the other dishes.

We washed the bowls and spoons in companionable silence, the moon and starlight reflecting and shimmering in the water. Once the dishes were set back on the rock to dry, Adaner leaned on the bank and I took the necklace out of my pocket.

"What's that?" he asked, glancing at it.

I looked back at him. "I found it in the wreckage, I wanted to save it. To remember whomever it belongs to." Once I had dipped it in the water and used some of the sand from the bank to scrub the crusted blood off of it, it glinted and sparkled in the light.

"Want me to put it on?"

I nodded and handed the emerald necklace to him. I pulled my hair up and he placed it over my head and then clasped it around my neck. I felt the cold chain and jewel settle on the soft skin of my throat and chest. I dropped my hair and had the intention of turning once more but I felt Adaner's hand on my waist holding me in place. His calloused hand brushed my hair out of the way and I felt his soft lips place a kiss on my shoulder bone.

Chills raced from the spot where his warm lips were in a trail down to my toes. His hand traveled further up my back and cupped the back of my neck, turning my face towards him as he kissed me.

"Let's finish what Reyna interrupted."

"Please do," I whispered against his lips.

CHAPTER

36

On the back of the blustery winds whipping around us, was the scent of smoke.

We had been smelling it for the past three nights now. Each time we made camp to rest and feed ourselves and horses, we awoke to a thick layer of smog covering the earth around us. And with the ocean further away, the land became dustier and the foliage thicker.

We had passed two other villages and an outpost that had been completely ravaged and burned to the ground. No signs of bones or bodies left. We were nights behind whatever force was doing this, the ashes they left in their wake still cooling.

Cantering in a line down the roadway we were trying to make headway. We had to catch up. The smoke that kept smothering us when we rested was still miles out but if we kept riding and made no stops, we had a chance.

I glanced over my shoulder for a split second to make sure Thea was keeping up and, to my overall surprise, she was. Through the wisps of hair whipping back and forth in the wind and the force of riding, I could see her, crouched close to Lily's neck and gripping the harnesses tightly.

Facing forward again, I leaned close and whispered in Bohan's ear, "Ride fast my friend." As if he truly understood me, he lunged forward and at a speed I hadn't felt before, we flew across the dusty road.

We raced up the dirt path, smoke growing thicker in the air, rocks and sticks shooting out from under Bohan's hooves, dust billowing in clouds behind us. But when I squinted through the dust of the cadre in front of me, I knew something was wrong. Adaner and Tolden had drawn their swords and were charging down the hill but Cadeyn whipped his horse around and came crashing down the hill I was racing up.

"They're here! Weapons drawn!" he yelled at me as he flew past.

My head whipped around following what he was doing as he grabbed Lily's reins from Thea's hands and urged her to follow him into the thicket of the trees. Clearly she was not prepared for whatever was on the other side of the hill.

Not wasting a moment more, I kicked Bohan's flanks. With my sword drawn from my back, I held it close to me as we made it to the top of the dusty hill.

Below were the most terrifying creatures I'd ever seen; the shadow creatures. They had snarling, saliva dripping faces that crinkled up in howls and screams as they scurried towards us on all fours. They almost looked human, the ones walking on two legs, but there was nothing else human about them. They were dressed in dark garb or fur or whatever the hell it was. Their eyes black slits, staring and sucking the life out of me.

"Watch out!"

I dodged the claws being slashed towards my head and swiped my sword across the neck of the creature, blood squirting over my hands and arms. Bohan rode through and trampled over the ones in our path while I leaned over each side, cutting them down.

Dark shadows crowded my peripheral vision and my dark steed reared up braying in pain. I whipped my head around to find the creatures, clawing into his flanks trying to crawl up to get to me. I kicked one in the jaw, hearing its neck snap from the force and shot dark ice through the head of the other.

Yet still, a different one clawed its way up the saddle as Bohan reared and kicked his front legs. The creature jumped before I could react, my magic flaring, and clawed through my pant leathers and tore into the skin of my thigh. I screamed and lost my hold on the reins.

I felt myself falling. . .falling backwards. I crashed to the ground with a thud and rolled so as to escape Bohan's steel hooves. My vision was blurry with blood and dirt and they were stinging. But the feeling of the creature's claws still digging into my leg was enough for me to open them and palm the dark creature over and over with my magic.

When he finally gave up and stilled in death's grasp, his claws were still stuck in my skin. I held in my sobs as I peeled them out one claw by miserable claw. Blood gushed out with each one and the puncture wounds were deeper than I'd thought.

I glanced around and realized the only thing to keep them from bleeding out was to force my fingers inside them. . .so that's what I did. Letting out a gasp of pain, I leaned forward and applied pressure. Glancing up and squinting through my stinging eyes, I watched Bohan circle and limp back towards me. A shadow figure leapt at him with its claws raised and the horse trampled him under his hooves as if the creature were a blade of grass.

The horse nuzzled my shoulder and I raised the hand that wasn't putting pressure on my leg. "I'm alright, that just bloody hurt." I brushed through his mane.

I eventually gathered the strength to stand and limp onto Bohan's back. He knelt as much as he could for me even with his injured hind legs. Glancing around, the shadow creatures were either fleeing into the forest with Cadeyn and Tolden at their heels or facing the wrath of Adaner's blade and wielding magic.

I surveyed my surroundings, hoping to find elven prisoners huddling behind the boulders or tucked into the hillside crevices but there was nothing and no one. I sighed in frustration and led my dark steed to circle back around.

"Are you well?" Adaner asked, wiping his blood stained blade in the grass.

"Well enough," I replied, still clutching my injured leg.

When he got closer he saw the blood seeping through my fingers and leathers. "What is with you and injuring your legs?"

"Oh, you know, it's so some handsome male can carry me around everywhere," I laughed but if I was being honest, my leg hurt like hell.

"Here." Adaner reached up and did indeed carry me away from the blood stains of battle and onto a dry patch of grass. It was cool beneath me and I focused on that while Adaner straightened my leg out. "You might need to take your pants off."

I smirked at him. "Good excuse, you just want to get me undressed."

"Ryn, now's not the time for jokes. You look really pale." All the humor had left Adaner's eyes.

I tried again, "In this moonlight? Of course I do."

"*Ryn.*"

"Fine," I gritted out and started to unfasten the top of my pants. The movement stung but not like it did when my leathers were peeled away from the puncture wounds, some of the fabric being left behind.

I let Adaner take over and gritted my teeth. It was an oozing, bloody mess but I could tell my body was already beginning to heal around it. Adaner carefully picked the bits of the leather out of the wounds and then took a flask of water and poured it over. I inhaled through my teeth and tilted my head backwards. Once all that was done, Adaner took a salve from his horse's saddle and dabbed it on.

"Your body will heal the rest. We will just want to make sure it doesn't get infected."

I nodded.

Adaner helped me stand and then helped me adjust my pants. His hand brushed over my hips as he pulled them up and gooseflesh broke out over my skin. He acted as if he hadn't noticed, even though I could tell he had.

"Ah, I see you two have been busy while we chased the rest of those nasty bastards," crooned Cadeyn as he, Tolden and Thea all returned.

"As if," Adaner argued, turning to face them, one arm supporting me. "Ryn was injured."

"I'm sure it'll heal within the hour," Tolden remarked, winking.

"It already has." I nodded towards him.

"Oh, to have magic like that," sighed Thea.

"Don't all elves have magic?" I questioned, glancing between them.

Adaner nodded his head. "Most yes, there are the rare ones who are extremely powerful, usually from descendants of royalty. And then there are the others; elves who don't have magic are usually from a line where the blood magic died long before even their grandparents' generation."

I nodded my head in understanding.

"We followed the rest of the shadow creatures into the forest to see where they would go but I think they caught on and began scattering," explained Cadeyn, wiping his blade in the grass and sheathing it. "I see you both took care of the rest here."

"These are strange times," spoke Tolden. "Not only do we have Helmfirth men invading the shores of Crescent, but we've had shadow creatures lurking in our lands for months now?"

"It's like the war never ended. . .it just fell beyond watchful eyes," Cadeyn remarked, looking off into the distant smoky horizon.

My heart stammered at their conversation. What if what we discovered was truly worse than we could have imagined. What if it actually was war?

"The smoke is still at least a night's ride, we need to decide if we're riding now or making camp." Adaner replaced the flask and salve back into his satchel, his hair was ruffled and there was blood covering almost every inch of him.

I glanced at the others, waiting for them to decide but they looked to me. Wondering why, I shifted on my feet, then I remembered my injured leg.

"If the smoke is still ahead then why was there this group of creatures left behind? Do you think they were backtracking or stragglers perhaps?" Cadeyn glanced around at the bloody mess of a battle field a few yards away.

"Unless it was a distraction," thought Adaner. "Because she knows we're out looking for information."

"How could she?" I threw back.

"Scouts. Spies." Adaner crossed his arms.

My heart thudded against my ribcage and I felt sick. A thought pricked my mind but I tucked it away.

"Her? As in Queen Cressida?" Thea chimed in, hanging close to Cadeyn's side.

"Seems awfully likely." Cadeyn nodded his head.

I took Bohan's reins, the prick of a thought turning into an idea that was risky but might prove to be worth it.

"We should ride to Hell's Keep," I proposed, biting my lip. "We can keep scouting out for smoke and following the trails and scents of it just to be intercepted by shadow creatures that may be Cressida thwarting us and leading us astray...*or* we can ride to the keep."

Four sets of eyes stared at me and a few mouths gaped open. I shrugged and reminded them about Mại in the stairwell again.

"There's something in *here*," I tapped my heart, "that's telling me we need to go. Even if we just look at it. There's something there." I looked at each member of the cadre, staring deep into their eyes, willing them to agree. Otherwise I was certain I would go it alone.

"You're crazy, you know that?" Cadeyn pointed at me and shook his head.

I laughed. "But do you trust me?"

"I do," Tolden said, tilting his head slightly to the side.

"I do!" Thea bounced and ran to retrieve her horse from the thicket.

I turned to Adaner, a sly smile hiding behind my lips.

In a low but certain voice he said, "I do."

I smiled. "To Hell's Keep we go then."

"But first, we make camp. We need to be well rested and prepared for anything. Hell's Keep isn't an easy trek. It might take more than a month to get there." Adaner glanced up at the sky as he spoke as if it would show him the answers he sought.

We guided our horses away from the battle skirmish and followed the sound of trickling water. Making camp uphill from the stream and a few yards away so as to give each of us privacy while we washed in the river.

The feeling and stench of blood coated me as Thea and I walked to the river together. I remembered my change of underclothing in my pack and brought it, planning to wash the dirty garments I now wore.

Reaching the bank we stripped bare and dove into the running river, there was an area a bit downstream that was calmer and deeper than the rest and we swam towards it. The water was a deep blue with the privacy of trees and boulders surrounding the bank.

Crescent forests were always so dense and beautiful. I could barely see patches of sky above as I tilted my head back, dipping my hair into the cold water and pouring it over my face. It did little to calm my nerves or to help the quaking of my heart.

"I hid in the forest," Thea blurted out.

I lifted my head, brushing my hair away from my face and turned to look at her, collarbone deep and staring at her own reflection, her blonde hair sticking to her creased forehead.

"Cadeyn made me hide while you all fought."

"He did it to keep you safe, Thea. It was all very unexpected."

She shrugged. "Still. I hate being so useless. I don't even know why I bothered to come."

"Because," I said, swimming towards her, "you wanted to help your friends. You wanted to do something for your kingdom rather than just stay in the comforts of the palace. That's brave. That takes courage and a strong will."

She blinked and her gaze flickered towards mine before it lowered again, but I saw the hint of a smile and gleam of pride in her eyes.

"You're stronger than you think, Thea. No, you might not have all the fighting talents or techniques that we do but that doesn't mean that you are not capable or able to learn or to do something else as equally important."

"Will you teach me?" She glanced up again. "I don't want them to laugh at me."

"Who cares what they think? You have to do things for yourself, Thea."

"You don't care what Adaner thinks of you?"

My heart stammered and I felt heat rise to my cheeks, but not from fondness or embarrassment. It was shame that colored my face now. I turned around and faked a smile.

"Of course I do, but I still have to live for myself in spite of the attraction we have for one another." I hoped she would leave it at that because I didn't want her asking any more questions. I deeply cared what Adaner thought of me—what they all thought about me. Which is why I would never tell them about my darkest secret.

"Fine. But in the next fight, can I at least shoot a couple arrows?"

"We need to test your aim first and then decide. I will not have you in the midst of danger if you can't defend yourself."

"Deal!"

When we finished bathing and dressed, we walked barefoot back to the camp the three males had set up. Dropping our things off, Thea grabbed her bow and quiver of arrows and we walked a few paces so she could practice.

"Do you see that knob on that oak tree?" I pointed beyond her shoulder and she squinted.

"I think so."

"Aim for that."

"I can barely see it!" she whined, throwing her hands up.

I crossed my arms and raised my eyebrows. "You wanted to practice, so practice."

She sighed and squared her shoulders, pulling the bow string back not *nearly* far enough.

"Hold up," I interrupted her and walked forward. "First of all, stand shoulder width apart."

She adjusted her stance. "Like this?"

I nodded approvingly. "Now, when you pull the string back, find your anchor point. It has to be further than what you're pulling back to. Try your chin, nose, ear, jaw. Anything in that area and make sure your elbow is straight and in line with the rest of your body, not flailing out like a chicken wing."

Thea chuckled and did everything I commanded.

"Much better. Now, begin again."

She aimed and fired and missed a few times. But each time she got closer and closer to her target. I noticed she was extremely consistent in where she fired which was a good talent to have. When she finally hit the target, she hollered in victory and leapt up and down.

"Remember how that felt." I tapped her chest above her heart. "Keep that victory and practice with it even when you fail. Remember the feeling of victory, familiarize yourself with it."

"I will!"

And so, while I helped prepare something to eat Thea continued aiming and shooting. Sometimes she would fail and miss again but I noticed how she squared her shoulders and kept going until she got it again. Cadeyn walked over to where she was and watched her. They shared smiles and laughter and he cheered her on.

"That was kind of you," Adaner admitted from where he was, squatting by the fire.

"Didn't think I had a kind bone in my body did you?" I teased, throwing a twig at him.

He laughed and threw it back. "I'm glad she came along. It was rough at first but it's good to be all together." His eyes dimmed as he looked into the flames of the fire. "It's good to see them together and to see joy and hope on their faces."

I looked over my shoulder at Thea and Cadeyn and smiled, wishing I could feel the way they looked on the inside.

"I'll look back on this when we're in the midst of war again," his voice trailed off and I could tell his mind had pulled him into some horrible memory from the past.

"You really do hate war, don't you?" I sat back and picked at twigs, tossing them into the flames, watching the sparks fly.

"I don't know anyone who loves it."

"The men in Helmfirth relished it. It was almost like if there wasn't some sort of killing going on, they went crazy. I would hear the guards talking about it when I was in my cell."

Adaner nodded and laid on his side, his elbow propping him up, he looked skyward and spoke, "War to me is black skies with no stars, green fields that once held flowers turned to ash and covered in the blood of your friends. It's crippling fear in any set of eyes you gaze into, its orphaned children and childless parents. Its death and despair and chilling, sleepless nights."

I watched Adaner as his body tensed and his eyes lost their glow as he spoke about the war.

"Then again," he continued, shifting, "war does its finest to bring out the best and the worst of us. Families taking in children that aren't theirs. People opening up their homes to those who've lost theirs. Sharing what they have when they can. Kingdoms opening up palace doors for shelter. Warriors standing together as one force, bringing hope to the hopeless; a small beacon of light in the darkest of nights. It brings kingdoms together and makes us stronger."

"The stars still shine even during the darkest of night," I said, quietly, glancing up at the sky.

Nothing else needed to be said and I noticed the others had gathered around to listen as well. We all glanced at one another and exchanged nods of agreement and acknowledgement. I got the feeling we were all tucking that bit of golden truth away for a darker time.

—⚬—

It took us weeks, close to a month, to get to Hell's Keep.

I hadn't realized how far it was and that it was actually outside of the Crescent Borders in Middle Guard. It was a land that wasn't exactly a realm and didn't have an official ruler except the Prison Lord, Azazel.

The worst kinds of lawbreakers were sent there and the only way they ever left was in a wooden coffin tossed from the balconies of the highest towers to the depths of the black sea below.

The cadre and I rode like Queen Cressida herself was on our heels. The wind whipped past us, tangling our hair and bringing tears to our eyes. Dust swirled around us and then the rain came and cooled us off, calming the dusty roads.

I galloped ahead with Adaner leading the way to Hell's Keep. Not much was said on the journey there, we took a few breaks now and again to water and feed ourselves and the horses. But truthfully, it seemed like we were all hell bent on getting there and finding out whatever there was to find.

There was neither day nor night in this place. It just felt bleak and gray and grew darker the closer we got. I glanced up at the sky, the gray-black clouds looming right above us. Lightning cracked across the black expanse and thunder boomed in the distance. There were no stars here.

"We're close," announced Adaner, hunched low near his horse's mane as if he were afraid someone might see us.

We rode into a dark forest that wasn't near as green or beautiful as the ones in Crescent. These trees were gnarled and charred, their branches reaching for the sky as if in a cry for help. It didn't smell sweet or have the sound of birds chirping. It was dead silent as if the forest itself was decayed.

There was certainly *nothing* living here.

"I've heard Hell's Keep has towers with the eyes of eagles. We're going to have to leave the horses hidden and go on foot from here,"

Tolden spoke quietly but it felt like his voice was drowned out in the silence anyway.

We dismounted and tied our horses loosely to the blackened trees behind a steep dirt hill. If there was any scent or sign of danger they would be able to escape. Hopefully it didn't come to that.

It turned out the hill wasn't actually made of dirt. It was made of coal or black ash, the more we crawled and climbed I noticed it covered my hands and legs and arms. Soon, every inch of me was covered in this black soot.

Getting closer to the top, I crouched lower, my stomach and chest grazing the ground as I crawled on my elbows and knees, pulling and pushing myself across the dry ground.

"Keep hidden, stay low," whispered someone from the back.

I couldn't tell whose voice it was. This place had a strange way of making everything that was once familiar, sound and seem different. I shivered and before I peered over the rim of the hill the sounds of this place hit me first.

Waves crashing against stone and the rumble of thunder and something else shaking the ground. The faint sound of chains and I swore, screams. When I peeked over the lip of the hill I took it all in.

It was a stone fortress with the longest bridge I'd ever seen. It loomed over black waters circling the entirety of the structured prison. There were no windows and right at the top, two towers spiraled into the dark sky where clouds gathered and spewed rain down. Sure enough, there were ledges extending over the tumultuous sea to throw their dead prisoners from.

I shivered. What a vile place.

I wondered if the people sent here truly deserved this kind of punishment. I wondered if the things *I* had done gave me a well deserving cell in this prison.

Another sound drew my attention away and I caught movement in the corner.

I watched as a line of people chained to one another, dirty and bleeding stumbled into the entrance, the portcullis raised to let them in. Guards covered every spare inch.

The prisoners' clothes were ripped and their appearances mangled. I could practically sense their fear from where I hid. Sensing something else, I glanced at the others and knew they felt it too.

Those prisoners were of elven blood.

I had to *do* something. I hated just lying low and watching them. It reminded me of Sol and how I hadn't been able to help. That same sickening feeling plagued me now.

"Ryn," warned Adaner, seemingly sensing my tension.

We stared at another and in his eyes I knew what he was trying to tell me. I growled and turned back to examine the outskirts of Hell's Keep.

Taking one last look, making sure I had all the information I needed, we crawled back down the hill and fled on our steeds as fast as they could carry us.

CHAPTER 37

We rode with the wind thrashing at our backs.

My hair was matted and stuck to my forehead and cheeks and stung at my eyes, but it didn't matter. Nothing mattered except for getting back to the Crescent Palace as fast as possible to inform King Haleth what we'd seen. To gather an army and march on Hell's Keep and rescue our elven kin.

That's what drove us, with little to no rest. Even our exhausted steeds seemed to feel the urgency and raced on with strength.

When the tower spires of Crescent Palace finally came into view an audible sound of relief escaped my lungs. I practically fell forward into the sweaty neck of Bohan.

"We made it," I whispered to myself and to my trusty steed, both of us breathless and spent.

We flew across the sandy beaches and raced up the sandy hills, towards the grass filled path that led to the gates of Crescent. We signaled to the guards at the gate and in reciprocation, they opened the obsidian gates for us. We cantered in, the sounds of our horses hooves crisp and clear on the cobblestone.

I nodded gratefully towards the guards and they put arms over chests and inclined heads in respect to all of us. The very first thing we did was lead our worn out and sweat coated steeds to the stables where we gave them to the stable hands to brush, wash, feed and water them.

Then began the run to the palace. We weaved in between cobblestone and brick buildings with glowing golden lights strung above. My feet ached and practically dragged on the ground but I kept going. Not a moment could be lost.

I vaguely heard the sound of running water babbling over pebbles and spilling into the town below and realized how thirsty I was. My tongue stuck to the roof of my mouth, utterly parched. I scrubbed at my eyes, fighting sleepiness as I stumbled up the steps to the palace, thighs aching from the hard ride here.

But the second my foot hit the obsidian marble at the top something felt wrong. In an instant, I was alert, sensing the danger. I stopped mid step and felt Adaner almost run into me.

"What is it?" he asked, leaning over my shoulder.

I held a hand for him to be quiet and cocked my head to the side. The palace doors scraped open with a creaking sound and guards filed out, followed by Baron Valt, striding right towards me.

Instinct kicked in and my hand flew to the daggers at my hips, shifting my feet into a fighting stance.

"Ryn Noireis, King Haleth has ordered you to be brought forthwith to the throne room upon your return," Baron's voice boomed, hands clasped behind his back as the guards approached me.

"Why?" I didn't budge even as they reached out for me. "Don't *touch* me."

"You are to come willingly and silently or force will be used against you, by His Majesty's order."

Baron didn't look like he was enjoying this, just doing his job. There was no gleam in his eye, the same gleam I saw when he interrogated people.

Everything in me told me to run, that nothing good could come of this.

My heart was hammering and my stomach clenched in anxiety. But even as I looked over my shoulder at my friends. . .at Adaner. I knew I couldn't run. I knew I had to face this—whatever it was.

But I was terrified. Thoughts racing through my mind to plague me with fear and worry. Had they found out?

Nevertheless, I allowed them to escort me to the throne room—what other choice did I have? But I hissed at them when they tried to escort me by taking hold of my elbow. "I know how to walk." I rolled my eyes and sauntered into the palace, allowing my hips to sway back and forth with a confidence that I didn't even slightly feel.

I was filthy. I was thirsty. My hair and face were wind blown and I had been wearing the same pair of clothes for nearly two months. That alone was enough to warrant annoyance, but there was something else deeper down that I could feel.

Baron pushed the throne room doors open and walked down the black obsidian floor towards King Haleth who sat rigid on his throne. It looked as if he had more gray hairs than before and his expression was aware but seemed weary.

Green-gold flecked eyes caught my own and then he lowered his head to speak with Baron. I was directed to the middle of the room while a few guards guided my friends to the back. I made eye contact with Adaner over my shoulder, my pulse beating through my throat.

Baron straightened and cleared his throat addressing me, "King Haleth has received a letter from Lord Elton Hode of Helmfirth."

My heart stopped.

I tried to swallow but my throat wouldn't move.

"Lord Elton has written to King Haleth accusing you of being a traitor to the Crescent Crown and Kingdom," Baron continued. "You will be tried at this hour, do you have any questions?"

My vision seemed to spin and I felt nauseous and dizzy. A few choice words came to mind when I thought of Elton but I couldn't get my tongue to move or even think clearly. All I could see were those ocean blue eyes that had dimmed with death as I snapped his neck.

"Ryn? Anything to say?"

Baron's voice was far away and I blinked, my vision refocused. I brought a shaking hand to my temple. "W-what am I being tried for exactly?"

"The murder of a Crescent Blood." I was going to be sick.

I needed to leave right now. I somehow had to get out of this room and out of this palace and realm and had to run far, far away.

I glanced back at the double doors just as they clicked shut. Sweat started to roll in little beads down my temple and spine, trickling down in an agonizing plea of panic.

They would find out the truth one way or another. Either by me running like the guilty person I was or by me telling them. I couldn't bring myself to glance over where Adaner, Cadeyn, Thea and Tolden stood.

Tolden.

He was going to find out just who exactly killed his brother. There would be no way for me to keep it hidden in the darkest, deepest parts of my heart anymore. Breathing suddenly became unnatural and I swayed on my feet.

They had trusted me.

"Why exactly do I have to do this?" I stammered, meeting Baron's eyes once more.

"Protocol." Baron eyed me. "You forget what my job is here."

He *knew* that I had fought in the *Death Pit*. I had told him I killed for sport. He most likely had already deemed the contents in the letter true. He might have even been the one to push Haleth to call for this trial.

"Damn the protocol," I cursed under my breath. Damn Elton Hode.

"If it isn't true you have nothing to worry about," announced Haleth cooly, seemingly unphased.

But I did have everything to be worried about. Because I was a murderer.

Self defense or not, in my heart I knew I should have let him kill me.

My whole body shook and I couldn't hear anything even as I watched Baron's mouth move. I didn't dare turn around to look at the cadre. I couldn't bear to see their expressions because if I turned around now, I knew Adaner would see the truth hiding in my eyes. I wanted to put this off as long as I could.

"Ryn, please answer the question."

Baron's voice snapped me out of my trance and my hearing came rushing back. I was breathing heavily, sweating and I thought I might actually vomit all over the throne room floor.

"Could you—uhm, could you repeat the question?" I asked, voice hoarse as I wiped my forehead.

Baron glanced at Haleth, then swept his glaring gaze at my cadre. "Have you ever killed a Crescent Blood?"

I cleared my throat and tried to swallow but couldn't. In fact, I couldn't even breathe.

They would all realize that I had been keeping this from them. Adaner would know this was what I was never ready to talk about. Thea would realize why I'd acted so strange when she showed me the portrait of Tolden and his brother. Tolden and Cadeyn would never tease or joke with me again, they would hate me, realizing who they had put their trust in.

I clutched at my throat as a sob ripped out of it in the form of my confession, "Yes. Yes, I have." My heart thundered in my chest, my throat, my eyes, my head.

Ocean eyes plagued my mind. "Who did you kill, Ryn?"

The truth danced at the tip of my tongue and seemed to scorch me. I squeezed my eyes shut. I promised myself I would never share this dark secret and yet I was about to.

I wrapped my arms around my waist, tears spilling down my cheeks. My knees buckled and they gave out as I fell to the throne room floor, certain I was going to pass out from the nausea. I covered my face in my hands and wept.

No. No. NO!!

"*Who* was it, Ryn?" Baron demanded.

I couldn't stop it, fire and ice and bitterness and regret bubbled up and poured out as the burning confession came out. "Tolden's brother."

I hated myself.

I blocked out all sound and sight by tunneling deep down inside myself, to the place that was numb. I so desperately wanted to feel nothing but all I felt was the shame and disgust that coursed through my veins.

I sensed a struggle behind me and it distracted me from escaping into that place I knew all too well. I turned around just in time to watch two guards pushing someone away from me and restraining him.

Tolden.

In my mind I tried telling them to let him go and to let him at me. He deserved it. *I* deserved it.

"Get her *out* of here!" Tolden screamed, his voice so hoarse and strained it physically hurt me.

The guards still restrained him. I made the mistake of looking towards the others and I think my heart actually broke. I could only see the back of Adaner as he ushered Cadeyn and Thea out of the throne room. I could see the rise and fall of Thea's back and hear her audible sobs echoing off the throne room walls. Cadeyn had an arm wrapped around her and when he glanced over his shoulder at me, my soul shattered.

I had hurt them all deeply.

"*Leave*, before I take your own weapons and *run* you through with them!" Tolden was still screaming at me, spittle flying from his mouth, tears building in his ocean eyes.

"Stand down, Tolden!" King Haleth bellowed and stood from his throne. "Baron?"

"Your Majesty," Baron tilted his head and turned to me. "Ryn, when you killed Rayken, Tolden's brother, was it in self defense?"

"Of course it wasn't, she's a murderer!" screamed Tolden, behind me.

I wrung my hands, tears still streaming down. All I could do was stare at Tolden, at those ocean eyes. "Yes, it was in self defense. But you should know that I was fighting in the *Death Pit*, which is a house of sport and pleasure."

"Were you forced into these games or did you participate of your own accord?" Baron's voice seemed so distant now.

I shrugged. "I was forced."

"Liar!" Tolden hissed at me and cursed my name.

"*Silence*, Tolden," Baron commanded. "You are still addressing the princess of the Crescent Kingdom. Your future Queen."

"There's no part of me that will *ever* acknowledge her as such!" Tolden spat at my feet.

And I deserved it all.

Every harsh word and shattered part of him that was thrown at my feet. I deserved every bit of it which is why I still stood there, welcoming it.

Tolden scoffed and tried to take a few steps toward me, struggling against the guards. In my peripheral I could see Adaner's hand flash towards his sword hanging across his back. But I turned to meet Tolden as he broke free of the guards and got right in my face.

"I hate you!" he spat in my face. "I hate that you've *known* that you killed him and you acted like our friend. And you dain to assume we'd ever welcome you as a rutting queen when you've killed one of our own!"

I never wanted this! I never meant for this to happen! I wanted to say, but I didn't.

I stayed silent and took each of his insults.

"It would have been far better for the rest of us if you had been the one killed!"

His words stung as if he'd struck my heart with a blade. I watched as Baron nodded to the guards, silently ordering for him to be taken away. They did, even as he still shouted curses at me.

I sensed Adaner behind me and with a gaze that felt final, we looked at one another. Hazel eyes staring into green-gold flecked ones. There were so many things I wanted to say. So many words to try and explain what had happened. But my tongue was dry and stuck to the roof of my mouth.

Several emotions lodged themselves in my throat and deep in my chest. But I swallowed them down and told myself I had to endure.

That is what I was taught to do after all.

With a rigid spine and dry eyes I turned back to Haleth and Baron. "What is to be the outcome of my trial?" I asked.

Baron stood beside me and we both looked into the eyes of the king.

"Elton was not wrong in saying that you had killed a Crescent Blood but I believe there should be an understanding for the situation, no matter how gruesome." Haleth just stared at me, cold and unfeeling—not that it was any different than how he normally looked at me.

I almost wished he had banished me. I almost wished he had found me guilty so that I might pay the price and have to leave. . .but the truth had been told. My dark secret had been found out, and they found me blameless of any crimes.

It didn't really help ease the nausea or the drumming of my beating heart. My friends, if I could still call them that when I had betrayed them so, had reacted exactly how I'd feared. I wrung my hands as I watched Baron, Haleth, and Adaner leave the throne room, leaving me alone without another glance over their shoulders.

I sat against the wall long past twilight and into the eventide, my head in my hands. As hard as I tried, my mind kept slipping into the past and I watched myself snap Rayken's neck over and over. Hearing the words Tolden had spat at me for hours until it was so ingrained in my mind that it's all I could see or hear.

I tapped my head against the wall trying to *feel* something. Everything had gone numb. All but my heart which felt as if it had been ripped in half a thousand times. The hurt in all of their eyes and in Tolden's voice was what made my heart beat with such pain.

It was in moments like this, that I truly realized how much they had meant to me—how much they *still* meant to me.

Light flooded the dark, empty throne room as a door silently opened. My eyes flew to the opening, wondering and hoping it would be one of them. Alas, my face fell when a long haired female slipped in.

"I thought you might still be here." Her voice was crisp and quiet as it echoed across the throne room.

I didn't say anything as she glided silently over the onyx marble floors. Her hair whispered behind her at her heels and her hands were clasped in front of her.

Mai.

"Might I sit with you for a while?"

I nodded, inclining my head in a poor attempt at welcoming her. She scooped her hair over her shoulder and sat gracefully, folding her legs beneath her.

"It's not as intimidating to be in this room when one sits on the floor," Mai spoke.

A small scoff escaped my lips. "Indeed."

"You are angry."

I flicked my gaze to her. "Yes, very much so."

"Why?"

"Why?" I asked, voice hitting the walls and ceiling and bouncing back. "Because I betrayed my friends."

"So you're angry with yourself?"

What was she getting at? Of course I was angry at myself.

"That's a dangerous kind of anger, you know." Mai leaned back against the wall and gazed up at the high ceiling. "Sometimes, it's easier for us to forgive others far quicker than it is to forgive ourselves."

We sat in silence for a time before I asked, "How did you know the prisoners were being kept in Hell's Keep?"

She looked over at me, a gleam in her eye but said nothing.

"It could not just have been a lucky guess." I shook my head, that was impossible.

"Let's just say someone once betrayed my trust too and I wanted revenge."

Something flashed in her brown eyes. "But how did you know?"

Mai smiled, her perfectly white teeth glinting in the small light from the doorway. "Sometimes you just do."

I shook my head. She reminded me of someone. With her long dark hair, brown eyes and perfectly white teeth. "Fine, keep your secrets." My heart pounded as I glanced at her again. I couldn't see her ears and for some reason, I desperately wanted to know if they were pointed.

"What are you going to do about it?"

"About what?" I grumbled, casting my accusations aside.

"The prisoners."

We looked at each other then. They were still being held captive, no matter what had happened in this throne room tonight, they still needed help.

Mai got up shortly after and left me in the throne room alone. Minutes went by before I, too, got up from my place on the floor and left the Crescent Palace.

CHAPTER 38

I didn't get far.

I had crept through the palace, feeling like a burglar in a home that I didn't belong in. Sneaking into the seamstresses work area that Thea and I had found her leathers in, I stole another set. The one I had seen before leaving two months ago. It was finished and seemed to beckon me to take it. I bathed and changed in my room, braiding my hair down my back as I gathered my things.

This time for good.

Bohan was still exhausted when I went to the stables to fetch him but I promised we wouldn't go far before resting again. I grabbed satchels of hay and apples and tied them onto the saddle along with my own bags of food and water skins.

And then I left.

Back down the grass paths and sandy beaches that I had just seen when my comrades and I were returning home with news of the elven prisoners and to seek aid from King Haleth.

Home.

This had never truly been a home to me, but I had thought that it could have been.

I barely glanced behind me at the dark palace. I knew things would never be the same. I knew I had betrayed and hurt them all. But the truth had come out. In some ways, I felt lighter that the darkness had finally seeped out of my heart but now it seemed as if it strangled the ones I held dear to my heart.

That realization didn't curb the nausea in my stomach or make right what I had done. Nothing could ever make it right and yet there was one last thing I was going to do to atone.

I relaxed against a gnarled oak log, just a few miles away from the palace. My legs stretched out, an apple in one hand and a flask of water in the other. To any I would look like a common traveler enjoying a meal and a break.

The truth?

I wasn't enjoying anything. I was exhausted, worn to the bone that every second bite I took I nodded off into a restless sleep. Bohan rested not far off, both of us using what precious little time we had.

The few minutes of sleep that came, however, were plagued with visions of Tolden's ocean blue eyes and of Rayken's, knowing his name made it all the worse. In the visions the throne room surrounded me all over again and every time I turned to see the hurt and disappointment in Adaner's eyes, it startled me awake.

Tears would be streaming down my face and I'd wipe them away, the pang in my heart never truly leaving.

The weeks leading up to the end of my journey, I spent a lot of time thinking. Bohan and I rested quite a bit, stopping when I needed to save my energy for what was to come. Oftentimes, it was near a river where we would cool off and bathe. I never really felt relaxed or fully rested because I was constantly tunneling into my magic, but I knew my physical body needed it.

As I lay back in the water, floating with my arms outstretched and staring at the green leaves above, I thought about how so often in the past I'd wanted to end my own life. I hated who I was, the person that Elton had made me to be. I thought of how much pain my physical and mental body had been through but how none of it mattered now. I would go through it all again to find my cadre.

They all had taught me how to live and to find joy in the living, even when they could be such pricks. Adaner showed me what it was to love and to be loved and my heart truly burned for him.

I smiled even as tears sprung to my eyes.

I would go through whatever pain this world had to offer *for* them. For my friends.

So, it was no small matter when I sent Bohan off into the forest, whispering my goodbye to him as I turned to climb the black soot hill overlooking Hell's Keep.

I would do what I had to to get my fellow kin out of this stone prison, even if it meant giving myself up to Cressida or Elton or whoever would make the trade for them, but not without a fight.

The wind whipped through my hair as I descended the hill. The scouts would spot me any second now and I wasn't exactly sure what would come after that but I didn't stop. Even as rain began to pour, drenching me through to the bone, making the curls of my hair stick to my face and neck. The emerald necklace I wore bounced against my chest, beneath my shirt. A shiver trailed the raindrops sliding down my spine as a bell peeled from the prison and dozens of guards began appearing on the ramparts and balconies, eyes trained on me.

I sauntered forward with confidence, my hips swaying back and forth, my hair whipping in all different angles. I moved my fingers feeling the electricity of my magic growing. Black frost formed at my fingertips as I watched dozens of guards line up on the rims of the towers, bows and arrows directed on me.

This was just another day in the *Death Pit.*

They, however, did not shoot. It was as if they waited to see what I would do or didn't want to be the first to attack. Odd.

I stood my ground on the black sooted earth, wind and rain howling around me, the dark clouds above flashing and thundering. It was then in the distance, just beyond the stone fortress I saw white sails flapping wildly in the wind.

Ships?

I flicked my gaze back to the keep's guards as they angled their bows and arrows above and behind me. Not at me.

My heart began hammering in my chest. Did I dare to hope?

I slowly turned, first my head shifted to look over my shoulder and then my entire body followed almost in shock as through the thick, wet rain drops my eyes focused on an army coming down the hillside.

Their colors were all black. . .leather black and at the head of the army that didn't stop pouring down the whole length of the hill, was Adaner.

Salty tears mixed with rain on my face and I didn't dare take a step forward for fear it was a dream.

"Ryn," he called out, dismounting his horse and striding towards me.

I didn't believe it. Didn't dare to.

But when Adaner took my face into his strong, calloused hands and I smelled the leather, citrus scent of him and he pulled me into a hug. . .I knew it was real.

"I-I'm so sorry, Adaner," I choked out through sobs.

"I couldn't let you go." He pulled me close and rested his head on mine.

We were both breathing heavily and then he pulled away to wipe the hair out of my face and whisper, our lips almost touching, "I forgive you."

I closed my eyes and rested my forehead on his. Relief crashed over me like the rainstorm around us.

"I love you," he whispered and kissed me deeply.

"I love you," I said against his warm, soft lips.

He smiled and laughed, his hazel eyes glowing bright. "How?" I stammered. "How did you know I'd be here?"

"How could I not, Ryn? I know you." He kissed my forehead and then pulled me toward him. "Now, come on, we can't just stand here kissing while we have a battle to fight!"

He pulled me back into the ranks where our own elven kin had bows and arrows trained on the guards of Hell's Keep. We took shelter behind their shield barrier they had up and I met the eyes of Cadeyn.

He nodded at me, his own form of understanding, words would be shared later on.

I didn't realize I was searching for him until I found those ocean eyes. My heart stopped beating and I held my breath. Tolden looked away but it didn't surprise me.

It had been a month since I had seen all of them. In truth, I thought I would never see them again.

But it was not the end, not yet anyway.

I recognized Baron Valt instantly and we all formed a group as he shared the battle plan which was the same plan the cadre and I had formed on our way back from Hell's Keep the first time.

Baron drew in the black dirt with the end of his scabbard. "The ships are already ready and we are their distraction. We are going to storm the gate and cross the bridge with our shields protecting us from above and on the sides. This fortress was not made to be well equipped to defend from the outside."

He glanced up through the rain. "It's once we're *in*, that's the hard part. This place is a literal hell and is made to never be escaped so we will have to keep our wits about us, eh?"

"Thank you," I said while everyone was standing around. "I wish I could say more." I felt awkward and undeserving of their loyalty.

They had traveled *all* this way. Adaner had known exactly where I'd be and came to offer all of Crescent's aid.

"There will be more time later." Baron nodded at me, smiling.

I nodded, turning towards the prison once more. I looked back at the Crescent army that had begun raising their voices as one, weapons in the air.

"For our kin!" they shouted all in unison.

And then we surged forward, as one army standing together, racing for the gates of Hell's Keep.

CHAPTER

39

All of Crescent thundered down the hill.

Amongst the swirling and roiling clouds above and the black dirt beneath our feet, we raced for the bridge.

Hell's Keep fired their arrows only for them to bounce off of our protective shields. Angry shouts came from ahead as they fought amongst themselves calling out orders and changing tactics.

Good. Let them stay scattered.

We reached the bridge and filed onto it, two warriors abreast as we snuck in a hidden weapon through our shielded entourage. A handful of elven warriors carried the breaker through the tunnel we made with our bodies. When we reached the gate, we spread apart giving them room to angle themselves to run at the door, banging into it with the ram.

Again and again they stepped back and then ran forward, each time smashing the wood of the gate. The whole fortress was made of stone, yet for some reason they decided to have a wooden gate.

Fortunate for us.

One more hit and we crashed through the gate, the wood splintering and splaying. We were ready for whatever the keep had to offer and our arrows went flying into the chests and necks of our enemy blocking the entrance.

We raced in as one and overtook the soldiers at the gate with ease. My daggers slashed across necks and stabbed into chests and under ribs, piercing hearts, spewing blood everywhere.

But I did not stop. And neither did they.

The interior of Hell's Keep was much like the outside, all stone. It was dark and cold and the sounds of the battle raging on echoed off the walls. I caught glimpses of my surroundings even as I fought the enemy.

A stab to the liver.

I glanced at the stairs. A spin and parry.

I noticed more guards streaming down the stone staircase.

I ducked a sword slash and narrowly missed my head being lopped off.

When I ducked and rolled, I noticed with horror that there were iron cages hanging above us. There were skeletons in some, but in others the still rotting flesh of humans.

Blood sprayed from my enemies neck as I dragged my dagger across it.

My stomach clenched in nausea as I realized there was dried blood all over the walls, the floors, the high ceiling, dripping from the cages.

Tearing my eyes away from the horrific sight, I focused on the battle at hand. Arrows from friend and foe whizzed past me. Thuds of bodies crashing and the cries of the dying echoed in the entryway.

I watched as Adaner used his long sword and hacked through the enemy. He spun and parried and thrust his sword through the underside of his opponents armor. I watched as a guard eyed Adaner and raced at him with a raised mace.

Eyes wide, I flipped my dagger to where the blade was between my thumb and forefinger and with skilled practice and aim, I threw it. It hit my mark, the eye of the guard who'd been about to run Adaner through. Adaner turned just in time to finish him off.

We glanced at one another for the briefest moment.

Diving back into the battle, I slipped into that killing calm once more. An arrow streamed straight towards me and without time to duck and roll I held my hand up and willed dark ice to come forth. It flowed through my veins and into my palm, streaming forward.

It blew the arrow up but also took out a chunk of the Keep's wall. I didn't have my magic under as much of my control as I wished and in a close space like this, I could easily hurt one of my own.

Ahead of me, I noticed there were multiple sets of stone steps leading further up into the shadows of the fortress and others leading down.

My gut told me to go down so I signaled to my cadre. The rest of the army were easily taking over this entire floor and would soon move further into the keep.

I stormed down the stairs even as I watched Baron lead the others to take the upper half of Hell's Keep, leaving no surprise attacks for us to be caught unaware.

Taking the steps down, we fought the few guards racing up to meet us, pushing them over the sides of the stairs down to the dark depths. I glanced over the edge but could barely even see it was so dark. I saw a glint of something, almost like a reflection of water, but didn't have time to investigate further.

We came upon a leveled platform, not quite a level of flooring but merely a space that separated the staircase. There were two doors adjacent to us. Bursting in, I tossed my dagger into the eye of a man hovering above his victim strapped to a table. I felt the pulse of the man on the table and realized with remorse that he was already dead, with the way his body was cut up into ribbons it did not surprise me.

Gagging, I exited the room, ignoring the stares I received from my cadre. I glanced at Tolden and he avoided eye contact with me. I felt myself going numb, my magic crackling like ice. There was no time to make things right in this moment but after this was all over—if Tolden was willing to listen—I would apologize.

I would make it right.

A leather, citrus presence neared me and I heard Adaner say, "We need to keep moving. Who knows how many more guards they have."

So we continued descending and I shook off those ocean eyes that I knew were burning into my back.

Right about now, the ships full of elven warriors would be taking care of the towers and the guards in them who would have been caught by surprise because the ground battle would have pulled their attention away from the sea.

Something pricked at my spine and a shiver ran down it. Silence rained down on us from above. The others must have finished off the guards and would be joining us soon.

Nearing the bottom of the long staircase, a coldness crept over us from the yawning darkness. Dim sconces lined the damp stone walls, revealing long hallways with iron cells barring our view from inside.

It smelled of mold and death and waste. Someone gagged at the back of the group and I didn't blame them. This place reeked.

"Search every door and cell," I ordered. "They must be here somewhere!"

But everything was barred and locked shut. It was a prison after all and this must be where they kept most of their occupants. Moans and shouts came from all directions when the prisoners realized someone was outside.

But we were not here to rescue them. For all I knew, they deserved this. I shivered.

Shaking off my thoughts, I tightened my grip on my daggers and began to stomp around on the ground, trying to find some sort of hidden room or basement—anything, damn it!

My booted foot met with a clunking sound when I stomped over a moldy grate. Cutting away the mold with my dagger I wiped the rest away. Below was gushing water.

Could it be possible?

"The place is empty!" Baron cursed, coming into view through the dark hallway. A few elven warriors trailing behind him and guarding their backs. "We went all the way up to the bloody towers—everyone is gone. No bodies, nothing!"

"It's a trap," said someone in the back and others murmured their agreement.

I rose from where I was squatting near the gate and wiped the muck on my thighs. "What do you mean?"

Baron walked towards me through the crowd staring at us. "I mean, there's no enemy to fight. They disappeared."

I shook my head. "That can't be."

"I have half of the regiment searching every single room and door. So far, nothing. It could be a ruse they have planned if ever the keep was under attack."

"Why not just fight?" I was growing frustrated and starting to feel foolish. What if this had been a mistake?

"They might not have the manpower. Or. . .it's their way of confusing us into a corner and then attacking. I told you, this place is not easy to get out of or to figure out."

"Let them hide. Let's find our elven kin and get the hell out of here." But fears crept into my mind. What if they had never been here? What if I led an attack on Hell's Keep for no damn reason? I brushed back the hair that had fallen out of my braid, my eyes kept drawing me back to the sewer grate.

"What about the sewers?" I suggested.

"What about them? It's a load of foul smelling waste." Baron glanced around at the elven warriors.

"We haven't searched them. You said you had half your regiment searching this place inside out, well how about I take the other half and go down there?" I gestured to the mold infested grate.

Baron nodded, massaging his jaw. "It would be a swell place to hide those you didn't want found."

I turned to my kin. "I won't make you go down there with me. Even if no one follows, I'm still going. Make your choice, there will be no judgment."

Baron grabbed my shoulder. "Be careful, Ryn."

A smile flickered across my lips. "Concerned, are you?"

"Go! Find them." He gave me a slight squeeze on my shoulder and it was the closest thing to a hug I think I would ever get from him.

I wedged my knife into the crevices of the grate and wiggled it loose, cutting through centuries of grime. Once it was loose, I used my knife to pry it open.

"You first, Princess." Adaner wiggled his eyebrows at me.

Without another moment's hesitation, I jumped through the hole, splashing into the foul water below.

I closed my mouth and eyes and plugged my nose. The current was strong and pulled me along. I allowed it to move me further into the tunnel until I grabbed onto the rocky ledge and pulled myself up.

I watched as Adaner appeared and then three others who had followed me from the beginning all jumped, followed by Cadeyn. I didn't look twice for Tolden. The three other warriors were Berken, Royl and Travyn. With a nod of acknowledgment, we began to walk along the ledge in the direction that the current was flowing.

At the head of the group, I crouched low so I wouldn't hit my head on the chipped brick above me. We were about to take the corner when I heard another splash. Flicking my gaze back, I watched as Tolden emerged, spitting, holding his weapons high.

My heart stammered. It was enough.

Enough for me that he followed even though I knew it wasn't for me. It was for his fellow Crescent Bloods. To save those that he still could.

"Do you see that in the corner?" Adaner pointed beyond my shoulder and I followed his line of sight.

I squinted and just beyond was a round circle high on the ceiling. It had designs in it and had a lever jutting out of the stone. I jumped into the sewage, allowing it to flow towards the design. I heard the others following suit.

Grasping the ledge with my nails and fingers I yanked myself out of the water, droplets spraying everywhere.

"What is it?" I asked, looking up at it.

"The only way to find out is to pull it." Adaner shrugged, sidling past me to get closer. Tolden pulled himself up next to Adaner, brushing back his hair from his eyes.

"Do you think it's a secret passageway?" Royl eagerly suggested, standing next to Cadeyn leaning over his shoulder to see.

"So obvious though? It's in plain sight." Travyn argued, shaking his dark head and leaning in.

"We're in the sewers, nothing is in plain sight when no one is ever down here." Cadeyn gestured around us and he did have a point.

"Fair." Berken shrugged next to me.

"Shall I pull it then?" Adaner asked, hands wrapped around, waiting for the vote.

"I say, yes. We came down here to search," Royl offered.

Everyone piped in their agreement but when Adaner yanked it, the air rushed out of my lungs as the whole wall shifted and the ledge we stood upon gave way to a dark hole gaping up at us.

I screamed as I fell, plummeting down and down. The others who had been standing on the ledge fell with me, some of us tangling into each other, hitting against the hard, mildew rock encircling us.

I could sense the opening below before I saw it and heard the sound of water. But I wasn't ready when I hit the water and had the air punched out of my lungs. The water that surrounded me was deep and cold and the more I sank, the darker it got.

I lost all sense of where the surface was as I flung my limbs around trying to swim. My ears became muffled and popped and my lungs burned.

I needed air desperately.

Something hit me in the back of the head and sent me spiraling in the tumult of the ripples. Everything was already black but now I could see spots dancing in the corners of my eyes.

I felt pressure in my head and eyes and ears as my arm was practically yanked out of the socket. Water rushed past me just as my lungs gave up and it poured through my nostrils and open throat, burning as it went.

But then, the sweetness of damp air surrounded me and I was gagging and coughing up the water that had just been shoving itself down my throat. Spitting and wiping at my eyes, I turned in the arms of the one who'd saved me.

"Adaner," I choked. "I-I couldn't find my way up."

"Don't worry, I got you now. I got you." He kept one hand firmly wrapped around my waist as the other treaded water.

"What the hell was that?" Travyn yelled, coughing from across the cavern.

And that's when I realized where we were and began examining my surroundings for the first time, water still dripping from my lashes.

A low cavern ceiling spread out above us with algae glowing and reflecting, casting the only light we could see by. The water was dark and deep and around us there was only a damp wall of rock, no ledges or land.

We were stranded in the middle of a cavern with seemingly no way out. I could feel Adaner's heart beating fast and my own soon matched his rhythm. We were trapped.

Untangling myself from Adaner's grip I swam towards the edge of the wall that was closest. My hands felt along it for any sort of groove or dent that could lead to an escape.

"Start searching for a way out!" My voice bounced off the walls and everyone started swimming and moving in a desperate attempt to find something—anything.

But even as I covered the entire length of the wall near me, I didn't find even a sliver of a crack. Exasperated sighs came from all over the underwater cavern. I looked around at my comrades and noted that only Cadeyn and Royl were missing.

A shudder shifted through the cave, making the water quiver around us and eliciting a gasp from everyone keeping afloat.

"Cannons," said Adaner matter of factly.

I half blinked, brows creasing. "Was that part of the plan?"

He looked up at the algae covered ceiling as another tremor passed through the cavern. "We ordered them to fire only if it was a last resort."

My heart sank.

A splash sounded behind me, probably someone trying to find a way out lower in the water. Why bother? It was too deep anyway.

I pushed air from my lungs, anxiety rushing through me as I treaded water, keeping myself afloat in this damn cavern while above, hell knew what was happening. I rested my head against the cavern wall and allowed the coolness to seep into me. The emerald necklace I wore thumped against my chest, matching the rhythm of my heart beat. I closed my eyes to try to think only to hear splashing sounds a second later.

I opened my eyes to watch Tolden emerging from the water, flipping back his hair and swimming toward us.

"Adaner, I found something! Right below the surface, there's a wooden contraption." He was breathing heavily and water dripped from his black hair. He never once looked at me but I didn't blame him.

Adaner followed him and they both dove into the depths of darkness. I idly swam closer, waiting for them to resurface. When they did there was hope gleaming in their eyes.

Adaner faced me. "It looks like a wheel that might open a way out of here!"

Our eyes glowed in the algae lighting and we both turned back to Tolden as he began to speak.

"Listen up!" he shouted, gathering everyone's attention. "There's some sort of wheeled system down here. I'm going to turn it and see if it unlocks a door in the cavern. If it does, chances are the water will be pushed forcefully out and you might be taken with it. If that's the case, let it. It is most likely a system built to leak the sewage out."

Excitement and fear pulsed through me. When Tolden dove once more, a few seconds passed and then the water began to shift. A rumbling sound that wasn't the cannons above began to echo through the cavern and, in the corner behind me, the wall began to shift and move upwards.

Shouts of exclamation rang out as hope was rekindled. We began to swim towards it, the water already swirling us towards the exit. Berken and Tarvyn were the closest to it and it seemed as if the current was stronger where they were as it swirled and pulled them. Just as they were about to reach it before the wall was even out of the surface of the water, it went tumbling down and thudded to a halt.

I whipped around and watched Tolden surface, gasping for air. "Is it working?" he asked.

"Yes!" Adaner swam back to his friend. "We'll take turns. You turn the wheel for as long as you can hold your breath and then I will meet you and keep turning it so that we can open it all the way and the current will rush us out."

He nodded and so began our plan. Tolden signaled to Berken and Travyn who would be the first two out, they put their fists over their chests and inclined their head to him, Tolden reciprocating the movement.

The rumbling started again and the wall began to move again. I watched as the two males were pulled under the water from the force and said a silent prayer, hoping it led to an exit and not another blocked or flooded area.

When Adaner swam down to take his turn it was just me and Tolden swimming on the surface, the current slowly growing stronger and pulling us away from the wooden wheel.

It was silent and strange and when I glanced at him he was glaring at me. I wanted to say something but my tongue and throat wouldn't work, suddenly going very dry.

When the wall was all the way up the current was so strong there was nothing we could do but spiral towards it. I kept glancing back at where Adaner was beneath the surface.

Come on. Swim up.

The wall rose up and up, water dripping from the bottom of it. The yawning black abyss gaping towards us, impossible to see through.

Suddenly, the wall began to plummet down and with a loud thud it hit the water, sending a wave pushing both Tolden and I back. Spitting out water and wiping at my eyes I could make out Adaner swimming towards us.

That wall had fallen fast. Too fast.

Fear began to crawl its way into my heart as realization hit all three of us at the same time.

Someone was going to have to stay behind.

There was no way that any of us would be able to turn the wheel all the way to where the wall reached the ceiling and then be able to let go and swim fast enough to get out.

A lump formed in the back of my throat as I realized what I had to do. For the Crescent Kingdom. The only thing left to give for my friends. . .for Rayken.

This was what I *had* to do.

"No." Adaner shook his head when he saw the look in my eyes. "Don't even *think* about it, Ryn." Adaner's throat moved as he swallowed. "You have to live. No chance in hell."

Tears brimmed in my eyes. "None of that matters! Let me do this."

"I said no! I'm staying." Adaner swam back towards the wheel.

I swam after him, grabbing his shoulder. He whipped around with a look I had never seen in his eyes.

Those hazel eyes once filled with bright sparkles and sarcasm and love now were filled with fear and stubbornness and something else that I couldn't decipher. He shook his head, turning away from me.

"I can't," he choked out. "I can't lose you, Ryn."

"It's not your choice to make." I pressed a cold hand to his cheek, a tear sliding down it. "Let me do this. I owe it to everyone."

His eyes told me so much more than his mouth ever could. In the green-brown reflection of his soul I knew he was telling me that it wasn't true. That I should go on living. That I didn't owe them anything and that the kingdom needed me. But the cadre needed me more.

I would not fail them.

"Would you two stop with all this disgust?"

Adaner and I both turned towards Tolden who was treading water near us, making a gagging sound and rolling his eyes.

"Get your sorry asses out of the way."

Brows furrowed, Adaner and I exchanged confused looks. "You two aren't stupid, now move," he pressed further.

"Tolden, no," Adaner said the words very carefully, looking at his brother, not of blood but close enough.

Tolden nodded. "I'll do it."

I stared at him, so willing to give his life when he could easily encourage Adaner to let me be the one to stay behind.

"Tolden, I owe it to you. . ." my voice caught in my throat, coming out raspy. "I owe it to Rayken to do this. Let me be the one. I'm not afraid."

It was the first time he looked at me, *really* looked into my eyes. Meeting that ocean gaze was not easy but I did not waiver.

"I know you're not afraid, Ryn. Hell, we all know you aren't afraid of anything. And don't think this changes anything between us because I am still extremely angry with you. But I won't be the one to tear you away from Adaner. You're the love of his life and I've never seen him happier. You better not break his damn heart."

Tears were streaming down my face and Adaner's. I didn't know what to say, I didn't deserve this. I deserved to pay for what I'd done. To die for all of them. Yet here was the one who had done no wrong, offering himself up instead.

"But I can use my magic," I protested. "You both have taught me well." The two males shook their heads.

"It's a good idea," Tolden began, "but you need all your strength to defeat Cressida."

Adaner remained silent beside me, treading water.

"Let me at least try." Tears began to slip down my cheeks.

"Let me go to be with my brother. My time has come." A smile came over Tolden's face and he looked so at peace.

"I don't know how," I whispered, my voice breaking. "How can I let you do this knowing what I've done?" I placed a hand over my thumping heart, feeling as if it were going to tear out of my chest.

"It is a gift. Accept it." He swam closer and threw his arms around Adaner in an embrace that would be their last.

I wiped at my tears and bit my lip. I didn't understand the kindness, the forgiveness of such hateful things that I had done.

It is a gift.

I inhaled a shaky breath as Tolden spoke something to Adaner and they pressed their foreheads together.

"In this life or the next, brother." Tolden patted him on the back. "Make me proud."

When he turned to me, I didn't know what to do. But when he embraced me for the very first *and* last time I shook with sobs.

"I'm so sorry, Tolden."

He pulled away from me and looked directly into my eyes, placing a hand on my shoulder. "I am still angry at you, I think I always will be, but you have my forgiveness. The hard part is going to be forgiving yourself. I've made peace with it, now you need to as well."

I nodded, looking away as tears fell.

"Now go. Save them, Ryn." Tolden's blue eyes bore into my evergreen ones. "Save them," he said again and there was such a deepness to his words that I knew I would do anything for the kingdom, for our people.

"I will," I promised.

And with a final ocean gaze he looked at us, taking us in. Then he put his fist over his chest, bowing.

We mirrored him, tears falling and our hearts breaking.

Then he was gone, black soaking wet hair, ocean blue eyes, his stubbornness and stoicness and bravery of heart. . .all of him was gone.

Never to be seen again.

CHAPTER 40

Water churned around us.

Growing stronger as Tolden turned the wheel, opening the wall and allowing us an escape.

I couldn't see through my tears but blindly swam, knowing the tug of the water was soon to pull us under and through to the otherside.

To freedom. To life.

I held my breath just as the water pulled me under, leaving the damp cavern and Tolden behind.

Swirling in the water, holding the air in my lungs I could feel the sobs wanting to overtake me. I could feel the pain wanting to break me but I also knew I needed to focus. Needed to realize there would be a time for grieving but now was not it. We had to find the prisoners and the rest of the regiment and get out.

Surfacing and gulping down musky air, the water churned and churned, leading me where the current flowed. I glanced around for Adaner and saw he was swimming towards me, using the current to catch up.

His eyes were red rimmed but when he caught up to me he caught me up in his arms and hugged me tightly. I wrapped my arms around his neck and buried my face in his wet hair. We didn't say anything, there was nothing that *could* be said.

As the water spun us around and curved around a bend he kissed me. A kiss that was neither final nor the beginning of anything; it was simply a kiss of assurance. To make sure this was real.

We let go of each other and looked ahead as light began to reflect in the water. It was an opening. As we got closer and the opening widened I squinted through the brightness. I could see the ocean's horizon, the waves crashing and the storm still raging. On the sides of the opening were ledges of rock.

"We need to grab hold and get out of the water before it pulls us out to sea!" I pointed at the rock and Adaner nodded, if not a bit hazily.

Two figures stood on the ledge; Berken and Travyn leaning down to help us out. I reached up and let one of them pull me out, the other aiding Adaner. Pushing back my sopping wet hair from my face, I blinked the water out of my eyes and turned to thank either Travyn or Berken, but my breath caught in my throat as a scream tried to escape my lungs.

I ducked the blow the man tried to swing at me and heard Adaner grunt as he was punched in the gut.

It had not been our fellow kin afterall. They were Hell's Keep guards.

I reached for my dagger at my thigh but my hand slipped from the wetness and the guard got my arm wrapped around my back and twisted it up painfully. I cried out in pain and watched as Adaner tried to gain his footing on the slippery rocks while the other guard pummeled him over and over again.

"You're coming with us. We've been waiting for you," the guard holding me hostage hissed in my ear.

I yanked and smacked my head back at him but he only ducked and laughed, pulling his own knife to rest at my throat.

"She'll be wantin' to speak with you."

She? Rutting hell.

I struggled to maneuver and turned my eyes to look as they chained Adaner's wrists together. Then doing the same to my own, my magic dimmed considerably.

"Move!" the one holding my bonds hissed and pushed me forward.

He kept pushing me out of the cave and onto a small sandy pathway. The rain pelted at us from above and when my eyes scanned the seas they widened in horror at the sight of our ship burning in the sea. It was split in half and sinking fast.

I could feel Adaner staring at it too. Had it all been for naught?

We were led up stone steps back up to the fortress of the keep. There was a tower at the back covered behind protective rock that hadn't been destroyed. When I was pushed up the last step and onto the platform, the last person I expected to see was Marcus Hode.

My mouth gaped open as I was shoved to the side and held there with Adaner next to me.

Weak, sniveling, cruel Marcus? How the hell. . .

My thoughts trailed away as out of the shadows of a wooden doorway stepped Queen Cressida herself. She was clad in gold and ivory, not even a scratch or splotch of dirt or blood on her. Her eyes, flashing brown, fell upon me and a cruel smile splayed across her lips.

I curled my lip in a snarl at her and struggled against my bonds, the ice that had once crackled in my veins thawing due to the iron clasps.

Cressida walked up to Marcus and patted him on the cheek. "Thank you, dearest. You've been most helpful. I'll need your help in a little while no doubt."

Marcus bowed, not making eye contact with me and fell behind Cressida, watching her like a dog watches its master.

"So good of you to join us today, Ryn and. . .Ryn's friend." Her arms were opened wide. She almost looked welcoming if she weren't the snake that I knew her to be.

I cursed and spat at her slippered feet.

"Come now, that's not very polite. I liked who you were in Sol much better." She glared at Adaner and Berken and Tarvyn who were crouched in the corner, chained together. "Before you met *this* lot of buffoons."

"You mean you liked me better when I didn't know the truth!" I hissed.

"Since you *are* here, might as well inform you," she mused, ignoring my comment and clasping her hands together. "Your entire regiment is waiting just below for you." She motioned for the guard to walk me over to the stone ledge.

I peered over it and sure enough, the entire Crescent army filled my sight. All of them on their knees with hands on their heads. I spotted Baron and Cadeyn and Royl. Baron glanced up at me with an apology flashing in his gaze.

My heart broke for the hundredth time today.

"As you can see, I have my army with an arrow aimed at each of your dear friends. Any sudden movements, I give the signal and they're *all* dead." She giggled as if we were two friends having high tea on a rainy day.

"What do you want?" I seethed at her.

"Funny that you ask, actually." She tapped her chin with her well manicured finger. "I want you."

"Why?"

It wasn't really a question I needed answered. I knew why she wanted me. She wanted my magic. I was stalling, trying to figure out a plan to get out of here with everyone in one piece.

"Your life in trade for there's." Cressida gestured at me and then pointed at the others on the beach below and on the balcony.

"No!" Adaner shouted, the guards struggling to keep him there. "Ryn, no!"

My heart thundered and I glanced at Adaner. He had already lost one of his dearest friends this day. His gaze told me we could find a way out together but I was starting to realize that that just wasn't true.

There was only one thing left to do.

I stood straighter and faced the Queen of Sol. "If I agree to go with you, you will let every Crescent Blood here, the prisoners you've been gathering and stealing *and* the entire regiment go free unharmed and unfollowed. Is that understood?"

"Very clearly. I shall not harm the hair on their heads."

"Nor will your guards or Marcus or anyone from Hell's Keep?"

I could hear Adaner shouting at me, "Ryn, what are you *doing*? Don't do this!"

"It is as you say." Cressida smiled but it wasn't at all a joyous or even a pretty smile.

I swallowed and looked into those hazel eyes. I could see his heart breaking, *feeling* it breaking as if it were my own. And it might as well have been. Because mine, though already shattered and torn to bits, was splintering anew with a different kind of pain.

It is a gift. Save them.

I had made a promise and I would not break it.

"*Ryn,*" Adaner cautioned, he could see the choice already forming.

"Deal," I breathed the damn words.

"NO!! *RYN!!*" Adaner screamed my name and my heart shattered with it.

"Shut up, you. She made her choice!" hissed Cressida, glaring at him.

"Take me, instead!" Adaner was struggling hard against the guards.

Cressida's crisp laugh filled the damp air. "You stupid boy. I don't want you, though you are tempting." Her eyes grazed over him and it sickened me.

"Let me at least say goodbye." I glared at my sorry excuse of a mother and she flicked her wrist and turned away.

"As you wish."

"Ryn. . ." The pain in Adaner's voice and face was unbearable.

I took his face in my bound hands and stared into his hazel eyes, memorizing them.

"She'll kill you," he whispered, choking up and pulling me as close as he could with our tied up wrists.

"No," I whispered back, tracing the lines of his face. "It'll be much worse."

His body shook with the sobs he was trying to hide and I bit my lip, trying to hide my own.

"I can't let you do this." He shook his head, pulling away, red rimmed eyes swelling.

"I *will* come back to you, I can promise you that, in this life or the next." I cupped his jaw with my hand. "You have to let me go. This is a gift, remember?"

"I'll never see you again."

"Yes you will," I breathed. "In some far, peaceful place where there is no more pain, you will see me again."

He choked on his sobs and tears streamed down his face. I tilted his jaw up and kissed him deeply. Breathing in the leather and citrus smell of him that reminded me of home and the ocean and starry skies.

"I love you, Adaner."

His green-brown eyes fell on mine and he kissed me this time, cupping my face in his hands. "And I love you, Ryn. Damn it, but I do."

We dared a laugh and held onto each other tightly. One last time.

There wasn't enough time left in this world to say goodbye or to hold onto each other. We would always need more time. So when rough hands grabbed my shoulders, tearing me away from our embrace, I reached out desperately and felt the skin of Adaner's calloused hands.

Slipping. . .grabbing. . .gone.

Everything became a muffled blur after that. I felt nothing except the gnawing emptiness that had returned once again inside of me. But this time, hope came with it.

Hope for my friends, hope for the prisoners and the life they had been given. Just like the life Tolden had granted me.

Epilogue

Darkness surrounded me.

Not the kind of darkness that one welcomes in the Crescent Kingdom or at night so that secrets might be told or plans to sneak off to the beach under the stars might be made.

It was the kind of darkness that crept into one's soul. In this darkness of the soul, I had lost all sense of time.

It didn't matter though, I had grown accustomed to it when I was chained to the high ceiling, body laid bare for my magic to be stolen. Exactly like that vision I'd had so long ago in the underground library of the Crescent Kingdom.

Pain and numbness was all I knew. It was like a vicious cycle.

But this time, I welcomed the numbness because it was different. This time it came like the light that would shine through the small skylight above the dungeon I never left. For an hour each day, the sun would shine through. It's rays warming me and filling the room with light.

It was in these moments that the darkness was kept at bay by a ray of light inside of me. It glowed bright at times reminding me of my friends. Reminding me of Tolden's sacrifice, of their forgiveness and of Adaner's love. It reminded me of why I had done this on the days the pain was so great it blurred the lines of my memory.

And no matter how dark, no matter how evil and how painful, I knew I could endure not because I *had* to but because I *chose* to.

For them.

Because even amidst the darkest of night, the stars still shone.

Author's Note

It is wild that I am even writing this page. This book has been 6 years in the making and it is finally done. Not only that, but it's published, which is a dream come true for me!

First, I want to say thank you to Jesus, because without him none of this would have even been possible. Even when I was frustrated, wanting to quit on this writing adventure many times, He gave me the strength to continue writing it and constantly inspired me. Without Him, there would be no story. There would be no forgiveness.

Thank you to my loving husband, Luke, truly one of my biggest supporters in all of my dreams. We have him to thank for the title and I couldn't be happier with it. Thank you for staying up late with me to brainstorm my wild ideas, helping me with names, places, and opinions. You're the best, mate.

Here's to my younger sister, Liberty, for never failing in helping me when I needed it. A good chunk of what you just read is also thanks to her and her lovely ideas that she inspired me with when I wasn't feeling confident with the story. When I am at a crossroads of which way to go, she is the one that I call and she never fails. Thank you, Bee.

Thank you to my older sister, Faith, who I have been writing with since day one. You are always excited to hear what new idea I'm brainstorming. Having your support means the world to me. Thank you for always having the best writing playlists to listen to! They were a lifesaver.

Thank you to my brothers, Kaleb and Jaxon, no I didn't kill all the characters like you said I should. But I know you guys are proud of me and that is one of the best feelings. Thank you both for supporting my dreams and cheering me on.

Finally, thank you to my mom. She is the one I have to thank for instilling a love of books in me. She is the one I have to thank for inspiring me to always forgive. Without her, I don't think this story would exist. So, thank you, Mom.

And thank you to all who have made it to this page! Even if just *one* person is inspired by this book, it will have done its job. I'm excited to continue embarking on this adventure with you all.

Milton Keynes UK
Ingram Content Group UK Ltd.
UKHW030946261124
451585UK00001B/183